T0246516

THE YEAR'S
BEST FANTASY
VOLUME ONE

THE YEAR'S
BEST FANTASY

VOLUME ONE

EDITED BY
PAULA GURAN

Other Anthologies Edited by Paula Guran

Beyond the Woods: Fairy Tales Retold
The Year's Best Dark Fantasy & Horror: 2016
The Year's Best Science Fiction & Fantasy Novellas: 2016
The Mammoth Book of the Mummy
Swords Against Darkness
Ex Libris: Stories of Librarians, Libraries & Lore
New York Fantastic: Fantasy Stories from the City That Never Sleeps
The Year's Best Dark Fantasy & Horror: 2017
The Year's Best Dark Fantasy & Horror: 2018
Mythic Journeys: Retold Myths and Legends
The Year's Best Dark Fantasy & Horror: 2019
The Year's Best Dark Fantasy & Horror, Volume One
Far Out: Recent Queer Fantasy & Science Fiction
The Year's Best Dark Fantasy & Horror, Volume Two

Published 2022 by Pyr®

The Year's Best Fantasy: Volume 1. Copyright © 2022 by Paula Guran. All rights reserved. No part of this publication may be reproduced, stored in a retrieval system, or transmitted in any form or by any means, digital, electronic, mechanical, photocopying, recording, or otherwise, or conveyed via the Internet or a website without prior written permission of the publisher, except in the case of brief quotations embodied in critical articles and reviews.

Cover image © Shutterstock
Cover design by Jennifer Do
Cover design © Start Science Fiction

Inquiries should be addressed to

Start Science Fiction
221 River Street, 9th Floor
Hoboken, New Jersey 07030
PHONE: 212-431-5455
WWW.PYRSF.COM

10 9 8 7 6 5 4 3 2 1
ISBN 978-1-64506-048-2 (paperback)
ISBN 978-1-64506-050-5 (ebook)

Printed in the United States of America

For Lin Carter, Arthur W. Saha,
David G. Hartwell, Kathryn Cramer,
and other giants upon whose shoulders
I gratefully stand.

CONTENTS

INTRODUCTION: MIRRORS

PAULA GURAN

"Fantasy—and all fiction is fantasy of one kind or another—is a mirror. A distorting mirror, to be sure, and a concealing mirror, set at forty-five degrees to reality, but it's a mirror nonetheless, which we can use to tell ourselves things we might not otherwise see."

—NEIL GAIMAN, "AN INTRODUCTION," *SMOKE AND MIRRORS: SHORT FICTIONS AND ILLUSIONS*

Welcome to the inaugural volume of a new series: The Year's Best Fantasy!

Whether this anthology provides any insight into the state of short fantasy (as published in the English language) in 2021 is debatable. I really don't intend it to be such. My aim is simply to provide the reader with an anthology of good fantasy stories all of which were published in the previous calendar year.

If I have a definition of fantasy—and I can't say that I do—it is quite broad, but I think you will find all these stories fall into that category.

Obviously, not *all* the best fantasy from 2021 is included here. There's a lot of great fantasy being written these days. Some of its authors seldom (if ever) write in the short form. (Some wonderfully talented authors simply write much better novels than they do short stories.) There are also fabulous fantasy novellas being published but the length thereof precludes inclusion here.

Even limiting our "best" to short works doesn't mean these twenty-three works are *all* of the best of that length that appeared in 2021. Decisions had to be made. I hope I made good ones. Nor can I (or anyone) find and read every single fantasy story published. I'm sure I missed some that should have been included.

As I've pointed out before in other introductions to other books, anthologies with titles including phrases like *Year's Best, Best of, Best (fill in the blank)* are what they are. When compiling such a volume, I do not feel any editor can completely and absolutely fulfill the inference of the title. Fiction is not a race to be won. There are no absolutes with which to measure it. Every person who edits a "best" anthology exerts tremendous effort in a genuine attempt to offer a book worthy of its grandiose moniker. Choices are made with sincere intention, but personal taste is involved, and—like it or not—compromises must be made. We all hope you, the readers, find satisfaction in our selections.

I sought out stories in magazines (both print and digital), single author collections, and anthologies. I encourage you to read publications like these regularly. Of course, not every venue worth reading wound up with a story (or stories) selected. Still, a look at the "Acknowledgments" section at the back of this book will at least give you the start of a checklist for good sources of short fantasy fiction.

If you know of me at all, it may well be as the editor of The Year's Best Dark Fantasy and Horror series that's been published annually since 2010. Its twelfth volume (even though it is titled *The Year's Best Dark Fantasy and Horror, Volume Three*)—covering, as this book does, the calendar year of 2021—will be published by Pyr in November. So it's fair for anyone to wonder where I might think "fantasy" ends and "dark fantasy" begins or vice versa. There are certainly stories in this anthology that could fit into its darker companion. And any of those darker fantasies are still fantasy and could have a place herein. In general, however, I saved the darkest stories for *The Year's Best Dark Fantasy and Horror.*

* * *

Even if you are a regular and voracious reader of fantasy, my guess is that at least a few of the twenty-four authors included here will be new to you. Make note of their names. I think they are all worth looking for now and in the coming years.

The twenty-three stories selected for this volume are, just like fantasy itself, not only diverse, but diverse in many ways. I don't think any can be called "epic"—limited length alone partially negates that type of fantasy—but some at least have that flavor. There are fairy tales and fables and myth-based stories. Stories set in worlds quite like our own, others in worlds quite unlike this one. Not that the stories are confined to "traditional" fantasy. Anything can happen in fantasy and just about anything happens in these stories. What they have in common is that they take the reader from the ordinary into the extraordinary and the make the impossible seem quite possible.

The authors have found inspiration in several Asian and African cultures as well as variations on Western tradition. There are different styles of writing. Some tales are lighthearted; others more serious in tone. The longest is almost seventeen thousand words in length; the shortest is less than one thousand.

One final note: This is my *fiftieth* anthology—all but one of which has been published in the last sixteen years. It has been a privilege and an honor to edit them and other books.

Last year, for the first time since 1999, I took a full-time job outside of publishing. Not only is the job unrelated to publishing, the work is performed in an office outside my home—also something I haven't done in a couple of decades. I thought, at first, I would start to be able to, eventually, give up editing and such. To the contrary, in the past eight months—despite the challenges—I've realized more than ever how much I enjoy doing this. I hope I will be able to keep doing it.

National Hot Tea Day 2022
Paula Guran

UNSEELIE BROTHERS, LTD.

FRAN WILDE

THE CONTRACT

A week before the Season began, as Mrs. Vanessa Saunders held brunch court at the Empire Hotel, a photo appeared on her phone: a large oak door beneath a pale green sign with silver lettering. *Impossible*, she thought, flipping the infernal device over before Mrs. Lilian Talbott and Mrs. Caroline Rankenfall, her Fête Noire Charity Ball co-chairs, could glimpse it.

But then their screens lit up too.

"The Atelier!" Lilian murmured. "Impossible!" She shifted in her seat, aware the others were watching her. "I just need to run to the ladies' room." Her chair screeched backwards, until Vanessa locked the other woman in her gaze, and held her there.

"Unseelie Brothers," Caroline said, oblivious to the battle of wills. "My mother used to talk about their gowns. Didn't you have one, Vanessa? I remember the Post called it—"

Vanessa Saunders' eyelid twitched. "The Gown of Flowers. Wouldn't part with it for the world." She signaled the waiter. "Too bad they're too late for the Season. Only a fool would try to cancel a Dior or Balenciaga order now, especially on a Saturday. My Merielle has had dresses for months."

"Oh absolutely, us too," Lilian Talbott said, trying to rise with both grace and speed.

Around them, other phones lit up with the same excitement. The designer who promised the most beautiful gowns, usually delivered them, then disappeared, was back, and seeking a select few who would gain entrance, but only if they could find the shop. The Empire's rooftop restaurant swelled with the news that Unseelie Brothers Ltd. had been spotted near Lexington and 78th and then vanished. Women began to gather their purses.

Chin up, with a casual glance at her watch, Vanessa rose from her chair. "There's always quite a cost associated with these things. We'll meet again next week. Dear Lilian, can you manage the check?"

Trapped, Lilian nodded, chewing her lip as tables emptied, her fork tumbling noisily to the floor. She watched helplessly as Vanessa led the charge to pull children out of Saturday classes and locate the mythical atelier before anyone else.

from The Social Season, plate 6. *The Dress of Mists – Worn by Miss Eurydice Louise, née Mumford Von Hiefenlagger, future Duchess of Ladenspiel, to the Women's Junior League Winter Ball in 1879. Photo by Jeremy Avedon (possible ancestor of Richard Avedon). This event was notable for several reasons, including the young man who went missing (a rumor) and the number of proposals for that evening. Designer: Beauregard Von Unseelie.*

from The Social Season, plate 22. *The Suit of Swords – Worn by Prince Reza IV of Persia to the Historical Museum Ball and Gala (before it was replaced by the Artisan's Fête, and other titles) in 1956. Photo courtesy of the former Ambassador to _____. A shining entrée into the rather staid men's fashions of the time (white tie, tails), the suit was made to be seen. The event was notable for the number of duels (two) it produced, as well as two couples who were never heard from again (confirmed, assumed elopements). Designer: David d'Unseelie.*

* * *

Sera Sebastian was too uninterested, and too poor, to worry about the Season. "We have new designs due next week, Rie. And our senior projects. We need to think about graduating. *Focus*," she reminded her best friend and cousin, Merielle.

Rie, having recently endured months of fittings at her mother's insistence, groaned and stared over her shoulder at the bulky coat she'd drawn atop a Fashion Institute-approved croquis. "I think I hate fashion." She held a bolt of sky blue fabric as Sera draped a mannequin in color.

"I think this will work," Sera murmured around a mouthful of pins as she arranged fabric and fondly ignored her cousin.

"You're the one with the talent. I wish I could have worn your gown—" Rie began, as an elevator outside their studio dinged, and Sera chewed her lip. *Focus. Yes.*

The afternoon sun slanted perfectly through the windows across the beginnings of Sera's latest design as Mrs. Saunders navigated a forest of dress forms, stools, and workbenches. When she was close enough to touch her daughter's elbow, she shot a look at Sera that forbade protest. "Merielle. You must come," she urged. "Unseelie Brothers—the shop that made my gown—has returned! You must find it before anyone else."

"Mother, I have plenty of dresses and Sera needs—" Rie began.

"Sera understands, and will help us, won't you, sweetheart?" Mrs. Saunders nodded at Sera, who was already folding her work away, unwilling to fight with her aunt. Rie's mother paid for Sera's art classes. She'd threatened more than once to stop if Sera crossed her too much.

Sera's pulse pounded in her ears. Angry, yes. And curious. She'd heard so many stories about this shop. She and Rie had both seen its creations, including their mothers' gowns in photographs and discussed in fashion classes. She'd even gotten close enough to almost touch one, once, in Mrs. Saunders' walk-in closet, as she and Rie were having an after-school snack while Rie's nanny dozed. "Are you certain?" She hesitated.

"You'll go!" her aunt said, with the same insistence as she'd used when Sera's jam-sticky fingers had nearly touched those amazing chiffon flowers that seemed almost alive. The dress hung in its own display frame in the closet, lit from above and below, looking as perfect as it must have a decade before, when Mrs. Saunders wore it and a pair of elbow-length calfskin gloves to the Winter Charity Ball. The Gown of Flowers had little competition that year, eclipsed only by Sera's mother's own dress, The Butterfly Gown. Which, that dress having disappeared long ago, Sera couldn't touch at all, so she'd wanted to hold the next best thing. There had been a lot of shouting, back then, an abrupt yank away, and a stern talk with Sera's father. No one crossed Mrs. Saunders. Or her closet.

Now, Rie closed her sketchbook tightly on the croquis. She put her colored pencils in their case. Sera gazed at the draped cloth she'd just begun to imagine as movement and light in human form, and did the same, feeling resigned. She took one small risk, hoping to free herself from this latest task. "Don't you want to hunt for the shop yourself, Aunt Vanessa?"

At Sera's question, the older woman paled. "They might not allow me back inside." She said it quickly, and Sera wondered if she'd misheard, because a moment later, her aunt pulled herself up to her full height and chuckled, "How silly. I'm a paying customer in good standing. We'll be fine. You'll locate the shop and you'll call me. I'll stop at the bank, as they expect cash from those who can afford their fees. Go!"

She herded the two young women out of studio. Once on the street, Rie glanced occasionally at the image of the door on her phone, while Sera kept her eyes peeled. After only a few blocks, they caught sight of the Talbott twins, weaving their way down Madison Avenue. A cab ride later, they spotted Odelle Rankenfall and her friend Elizabeth Dorchester in the West Village, peering into alleys and checking the map on their phones. They weren't the only ones on the hunt. Silently, Sera wished them well.

The girls turned left at 68th, near a shuttered chocolate shop, and veered almost too close to their favorite second-hand store. "No, not today." Sera pulled Rie away from the window, knowing she would be in trouble, not Rie, if they didn't at least put on a good show of finding the store. They took the subway to 35th, and walked the garment district until their feet ached, without finding the green sign. The sun was sinking into the fangs of the towers when Sera muttered, "Oh, dammit."

Because there it was. Just as Mrs. Saunders had, over numerous dinners and brunches, described how she'd come by her own spectacular gown for her debut Season. How she'd captured the heart of her very own prince that night—in the form of Mr. Saunders, and in no small part because of her perfect gown. She left out details, of course. Including important ones concerning Sera's mother.

Sera and Rie stood before the broad oak doors, wound with metal vines for hinges, set beside a narrowly arched, darkened window. Sera remembered those details and shivered. It was all a little bit strange, the way the story changed each time her aunt told it, and to whom: how she and her sister Serena spent all they had on their gowns—The Butterfly Gown and The Gown of Flowers—or that they'd gotten them last minute, at discount, or that they had been surprised with them by a well-off relative—and then how *well* they'd done at the ball, how *lucky* Mr. Saunders and Mr. Sebastian had been.

Whatever the story, Sera was quite certain that moments before the shop had not been on 38th street, crammed between an established jeweler and a new shoe store. But there it was, green sign swinging above the window and blank, headless mannequins, peering out at the street. Beyond the muslin models stretched velvet darkness (pricked by a few tiny lights, Sera thought, but couldn't be sure).

"It's closed," Rie sighed, similarly relieved. The green sign swung in the wind as she texted her mother the news. Her fingers had barely left the screen when the phone rang. Even Sera could hear her aunt's joy over the speaker, demanding the address.

"Don't DO anything until I get there. Don't touch anything! And absolutely do not let it leave!"

The young women stared at each other, unsure of how to accomplish either order, much less both.

A couple pushed past them on the sidewalk, eyes on one another. A woman with a double stroller gave them a wide berth, plowing towards some distant goal. Sera's stomach growled and she thought impatiently of her design project. Due in two weeks, and still just a bolt of fabric.

She wanted to get back to the studio, now that she'd done what Rie's mother had wanted. Still, she felt a moment of pride. Despite not having the right pedigree for the Season, she'd found the shop that everyone who did was searching for.

Her mother had worn one of these gowns, yes. But her mother was long gone, wasn't she. And the gown with her, only a few months after Sera was born. When asked, Aunt Vanessa would purse her lips and shake her head, as if implying Sera herself might have had something to do with that. *She fled. Such disgrace, such a flighty girl. Not suited for this world.*

To avoid her aunt's reprobation, Sera resolved early not to be curious about the shop, or the Season, though sometimes she couldn't help it.

The sign, the name—Unseelie Brothers—made Sera wonder who was behind the doors. What magic could they work, what could she learn, given the opportunity?

These gowns had brought everyone in her life together: her aunt and Mr. Saunders. Her mother and her father. But not quite in the same ways. Sam Sebastian had been working the event, not attending, when Serena and Vanessa had appeared at the ball. Serena had become Sera's father's muse that very night. And despite everyone's cautions, they'd married even more quickly, at the courthouse. Sera, born seven months after that, was, according to her aunt's taut words, a perfect scandal.

But now that Sera had found the store, perhaps her aunt would let up a little on the reprobation. *Maybe*, Sera thought, *I'll get a peek inside, before getting the heck out of here.* But the window was too dark. The door, very much locked.

At least the shop was staying put.

Rie slumped against an oak panel, scrolling her phone. "I don't want to do the Season, not without you, Sera. I hate the balls. And the stodgy people. I refuse to try on any more gowns. Your dress would have been so much better."

Sera, having less than no choice in that matter, kept quiet. She'd offered to design a gown for her cousin months ago. Rie had said a delighted yes. Then Mrs. Saunders found out, and then everyone pretended as if *that* had never happened.

Twenty minutes passed before a yellow cab screeched to a stop beside them. Rie's mother emerged, ensconced in a green Versace cape and pale gloves, gold and gems glittering among the layers, her makeup perfectly retouched to make her seem even more intimidating. How she'd had time to freshen up and go to the bank, both, baffled Sera.

Mrs. Saunders beamed at her daughter, paid the driver, and, once she'd pulled the rest of her cloak from the cab, stared at the door in disbelief, edged with something like fear. Sera had never seen her aunt look afraid.

"It looks just the same." Mrs. Saunders reached a gloved hand towards the door. Quickly, she recoiled and shook her fingers as if the handle had stung her. "What now, what now. I need a pen." She looked left and right, then dug in her handbag, as the Talbott twins rounded the corner at a run.

"Mum!" Rie said, more due to the energy of the hunt and the fact that she found the twins awful and pushy than out of any desire to gain entrance to a closed shop.

Sera offered Mrs. Saunders a plastic sharpie marker—Call 1-800-ArtSupply—and her aunt scribbled a note on the glove, signed her name with a flourish and stuffed it through the door's mail slot.

They waited, feeling ridiculous, as the Talbott twins edged closer, texting.

No one seemed more surprised than Mrs. Saunders when the lights came on inside the atelier immediately. And no one was more shocked than Sera, when she glimpsed her own long-gone mother's face in the shadows of the shop.

"Aunt Vanessa—look," Sera whispered, before the doors swung open, then began to shut again.

"Quickly." Mrs. Saunders pushed them over the threshold. The doors slammed closed right in front of the Talbott twins, their chiseled GQ smiles tumbling into glares at the window.

"We've done it!" Mrs. Saunders clapped her hands—one gloved, one ungloved—together. She peered into the darkness. "Hello?"

Sera heard the rustle of wings.

She realized she could not move. None of them were able to step beyond the row of mannequins, any further into the shop. Mrs. Saunders tried, calling out in dismay. Rie was too entranced by the sparkling ceiling to notice.

Did I really see my mother? Sera started to doubt. The face had been young—her age, not sun-spotted like her aunt's. *Probably just my own reflection.*

Then a gust of wind battered them, smelling like it came from deep within the earth.

"Welcome!" A tall young man in a quilted jacket and chiffon skirt beamed at the trio, the curve of his lips a mere tolerance, though his eyes sparkled. His hair was a deep purple and his fingers, when he clasped Sera's hand, were long and pale. "What have we here?" He moved on to Rie, staring deep into her green eyes. "Ahhh, the Season must be upon us. And this is New York, am I right?"

As if there were any question. As if Rie's mother wasn't already messaging her co-chairs to let them know she'd gained entrance first. When the young man approached her, Sera and Rie were stunned to see Mrs. Saunders dip the deepest curtsey possible to him. "Sir. I paid for a gown from your shop, long ago. I wish another for my daughter. Whatever the cost."

A smile broke across the man's still face. "Vanessa. How nice to see you again. Please call me Beau. And gowns for both young ladies?"

"Both?" Sera's aunt blinked, confused. Then she said, "No. For my Merielle. The other's not mine."

Sera took a long survey of the shop's black-and-white walls, blinking once or twice. But she stayed quiet. She'd be able to leave her aunt's presence soon, having done her duty. She wondered if she might return and look around the shop again later.

As if he could read her thoughts, the atelier's owner smiled even more sharply. "Then perhaps she is ours," he said, under his breath. He turned back to Rie, not looking anywhere but her eyes. "You will do nicely."

Rie bristled, and Sera did as well. But Mrs. Saunders caught each girl by an arm, her fingers sharp on their sleeves, freezing them both. "Merielle will be delighted, sir."

* * *

At the slightest twitch of the young man's hand, the three of them moved forward, beyond the row of mannequins. Before them, a broad, velvet-curtained clearing took up the center of the shop, its circumference sparkling with mirrors. Several soft benches, patterned in vines, invited, but Sera didn't dare sit down.

Shop attendants' shadows played around the edges of things. One, Sera noticed, had a mouth that glittered with pins.

Beyond the mirrors, Sera saw once more her mother's face, as young as she'd been in the only photograph Sera's father had kept. As still as that photograph, in fact. Sera was disappointed to discover more life-sized images displayed around the showroom. Girls and boys, all Rie's and Sera's ages, captured in black and white along the walls. Sera's mother among them. Not real, then. Nor her dress of butterflies.

Rie whispered again, but this time her voice had a tinge of awe. "Loooook." She pulled Sera towards a sparkling strapless gown, slit up the side, a glittering beaded confection gracing the sheerest fabric Sera had ever seen. She read the label. "The Ice Queen."

"Absolutely not," Rie's mother steered them back to pictures of thousand-button silks and gently draped sleeves in the shop catalogue. Sera tried not to get caught wrinkling her nose. The designs didn't seem groundbreaking at all. They looked a bit fussy, most of them, except The Ice Queen. That one practically danced by itself.

"Mother." Now Rie was not whispering.

"We will conspire for something very special," Beau gestured at someone beyond the mirrors. Moments later, a dress was laid across his arms like a child. Behind him, two assistants carried shoes and necklaces. Mrs. Saunders looked at them hungrily.

"We thought the young lady might be interested in something more." With a flourish, a muslin dress hung between the mirrors and Rie's eyes went wide as a projector illuminated it with a design: a flock of white birds circling the waist and bust.

"Oh," she whispered, entranced.

"The Murmuration," Beau intoned.

"Perhaps," Mrs. Saunders said.

Sera, momentarily freed as her cousin became lost in the attention, texted her father where they were. *Would you like to have dinner?* It would be good to see him. She settled in to wait for Mrs. Saunders to release her completely, occasionally murmuring, "That's lovely," before turning back to her phone, waiting on his reply. Her stomach growled.

"We are sorry, miss, no phones allowed in the store, you understand." A soft voice, right at Sera's ear.

Sera startled. For one moment, the shopgirl with the mouthful of pins seemed to bristle—cheeks, shoulders, nose, lips—outlined in sharp metal. Then the light shifted, and the girl gazed pale-eyed at Sera, a jewel-pierced eyebrow raised.

"I apologize." Sera stuffed her phone in her pocket. She picked at the smooth cushion and watched her best friend emerge from the dressing room once more and parade the mirrors in a different muslin, with pale flames lapping the hemline. "The Bonfire."

"I think not," Mrs. Saunders said, tersely.

This is going to be a long evening. Sera felt the trap close over her, locking her away from her project. Sera's unofficial role for as long as she could remember had been acting as a mirror for Rie: encouragement or discouragement, or both. Rie had refused all invitations to the Season's charity balls, until Mrs. Saunders declared that Sera would be allowed to watch from the galleries. "Maybe she'll pick up some ideas for her own shop someday. If you agree to go."

How Sera disliked being used in this way. But Vanessa was her mother's sister. Her father had said they needed to be patient with her demands. Her mother's disappearance had been a terrible loss, for all of them. "It makes her try to control everything," he'd explained, drying Sera's tears after the incident with the dress. "So that nothing more can disappear."

Now Mrs. Saunders looked as watchful as a hunter, at Beau, as if the atelier might evaporate at any moment. At the door, as if the Talbotts might burst in. At anything but the photographs on the walls.

"Do not worry, Madame Vanessa. As long as you are here and our fees are paid, no one else may enter," Beau said, reading her mind. "As a valued client, in good standing, your happiness, and your daughter's, are our sole focus."

Mrs. Saunders nodded, relieved. She sat heavily on Sera's couch, the bulk of her cloak nearly pushing Sera off the edge. Sera rose and drifted towards the rejected gowns to study how they were made. Her fingers grazed the glowing beads of The Ice Queen and its neighbors. The delicate fabric—what did the shop favor? Charmeuse? Velvet? Crepe? Not quite any of those. And the way even the muslin mock-ups were constructed! She could barely see the seams.

By the time she turned back to her cousin, Rie had rejected "Nature Conquers," which looked like living vines wrapping her from neck to feet. Mrs. Saunders had waved away "Ad Astra" as being far too bright. And no one was interested in "The Warrior," which, to Sera's touch, was not made of fabric at all, but the lightest and smallest of chain mail.

Sera's stomach growled. *Dinner. Necessary. Soon*, she texted quickly to Rie, trying to not get caught. She saw her father had answered—*How dare she take you there?* Then Mrs. Saunders' own phone was an angry bee in her handbag. Mrs. Saunders ignored the noise, her eyes on the atelier.

Come home, Sera's father texted again. *I'll make pizza.*

At a glare from Mrs. Saunders, Sera put her phone away.

A necklace dangled from a nearby hanger, sharp, like Sera's hunger. She unclasped it and lifted the links towards her neck, hesitating with the clasp.

Long fingers covered her own. "Let me do this for you," the shop owner said. His voice was soft. "The connection has a trick to it."

When he'd finished, Sera looked in the mirror and jumped a little. Her mother's photograph, behind her, appeared in the mirror as well. Serena. Her gown had been made of butterflies. In the photograph, they'd seemed about to fly away.

Standing in front of this image, Sera touched the necklace that wrapped her throat in thorns. She loved it immediately.

"It suits you," the shopgirl whispered.

"You must have it," the owner agreed.

"I could never," Sera replied firmly, though her fingers drifted the cool metal. The way it felt against her skin? As if she was prepared for battle, as if even the worst of her was better than the best of so many others? Oh she wanted it. "I can't imagine what it costs."

She began to take it off, but her fingers could not find the clasp.

"It likes you," the shopgirl whispered, through her mouth filled with pins. "We are looking for afternoon help, if you would like to trade. Only until the Season begins."

A week's time. Impossible. She had classes.

"I have nowhere to wear it," Sera protested, but she knew she was already going to say yes. A job, in fashion.

"But Sera? Our classes!" Rie's voice from the fitting room, came in quiet, jealous protest. As if her mother would allow her to do such a thing.

Sera nodded once, fast, before they could take the offer back.

The shopgirl winked, a smile spreading wider than Sera thought possible. "I'm Dora. I'm the newest here . . . or was!" She disappeared, then returned holding a contract still warm from the printer. "All you have to do is sign."

Sera liked that feeling, of being included, not just dragged along. But then she hesitated. "I haven't—I need to ask my dad." He would want to know. He wouldn't like it.

She gestured to take off the necklace and Dora shook her head. "Enjoy it—we know you'll be back!" It was a gesture of trust that made Sera want to say yes right there, but she resisted.

Meantime, Rie and her mother had agreed upon a gown—The Murmuration, with some adjustments.

"It is a good, safe, dress," Mrs. Saunders smiled. "Not too much. But sure to make a *lasting* impression."

Rie sighed, The Ice Queen Gown, and, Sera realized, her own designs, almost entirely forgotten. "I think it's the best one."

"There will be one more fitting," the owner boomed. "And when is the event?"

When Mrs. Saunders named the date, Beau's eyebrows rose nearly to his hairline. "That soon."

There was a long, dark pause. Rie turned to her mother, eyes welling with want. She'd shifted to certainty, in love with an impossible gown, in love with the idea of appearing before everyone who mattered, in that gown. So much for everything she'd said about Sera's work. About the Season itself.

Sera crumbled her fist as if she could squash the designs she'd drawn for Rie, in secret. Her other hand went to her neck, where the necklace was. She would say yes, no matter what her father thought.

Rie's mother looked nervously between Rie's expression and the smile Beau aimed at her, possibly remembering her own ball. "We will, of course, pay for the expedience," Mrs. Saunders said. "I will need time to gather the funds."

"Then we will see you again, at this time next week." The young man held out his arms as if he would embrace them all.

When the doors swung wide again, it was as if no time had passed outside. The Talbott twins were waiting with their mother. Both boys peered inside the shop excitedly as Mrs. Saunders swept Rie and Sera past the bare mannequins, and then out the door, very pleased with herself. "Good luck, Lilian!" she called, magnanimously, before hailing a cab.

THE FITTING

"A job? No."

"Dad, please. If I can do it, then I'll have something amazing on my resume—imagine if you'd gotten a solo show at the Whitney, while still at the institute—please." Sera hated begging, but she'd never seen him so resolute. It was true that everyone at the atelier had seemed a little sharp-edged, but they knew so many things about fashion that she didn't. "It's real-world experience." She didn't mention the necklace, which she'd hidden with a carefully draped scarf.

"You're nineteen. If I try to stop you, that will only make things worse." He barely turned from the charcoal sketch he was working on, a whirl of butterflies, white on a thick, gray sheet of paper. His hand shook.

She let the tears build up at the back of her eyes. She wanted his approval. The silence became unbreathable.

Finally, he filled it. "Your aunt should know better. That shop is unpredictable. What if it disappears again? With you in it?" His entire posture said, *No.* "Or without paying you? They've done it before—left people high and dry for orders, for years, and then suddenly they're back, gowns delivered to the children of those who ordered them, and a bill to match. It's appalling. Sera, be reasonable."

He sounded so much angrier than made sense.

"You don't understand. You don't care about fashion." He was an artist—why didn't he understand? She knew he paid the bills with marketing work. Their apartment in Queens could have fit inside one of the Saunders' walk-in closets in their Brooklyn Heights high-rise. Sera loved him, but she wanted something more.

"I've seen too much of it up close," he agreed. "Your mother would know what to do."

He never mentioned Sera's mother, unless he was truly sad. He glanced at the photo he kept on his bedside table, in an iron frame: the same image, Sera realized, from the shop.

Sera flinched. She didn't want to make him sad. "I'm sorry, Dad. It's okay. I can get another internship this summer through the college."

And she did mean it. She had no real need for that necklace. She meant it right until he wrapped his arms around her, saying, "You're so much like her. A mirror image." Then, before she could tell him about the photograph, he turned back to his painting.

Sera ran her fingers across her scarf, feeling the thorns beneath. The face behind her in the mirror could have been her own, today. She had to return. Sera pulled the employment contract from her bag.

He heard the paper rustle, but never turned around, knowing he couldn't stop her. "Remember, Sera, just because someone hires you doesn't mean they can make you do anything they want. Or that you owe them."

Sera's art supply pen hovered above the contract. "I'll remember." She signed her name and tucked it in her bag, ready to learn everything Unseelie Brothers, Ltd. could teach her, for the Season, at least.

from The Social Season, plate 76. *The Butterfly Gown, worn by a Serena (née)_____(unknown) Sebastian to the Spring Charity Gala of*

1998. She attended with her sister Vanessa (née) _____ (unknown) Saunders, and soon after married one of the event's busboys. Saunders herself married the scion of the Saunders soap fortune. The event was notable in that several young women and men were discovered the following morning, on the roof, wearing bacchanalian-styled greenery and nothing more, by hotel staff at The Pierre. Photo by Mrs. Vanessa Saunders. Designers: Dora Unseelie and Beau Unseelie, Sr.

Sera didn't see much of the inside of the Fashion Institute studio after that. On Monday, she attended class, then rushed through midtown, trying to find the shop. She arrived late, having found Unseelie Brothers, Ltd. wedged awkwardly between the Museum of Modern Art and a high-end residence next door.

"I'm sorry, I thought you'd planned to be in the East Village today," she wheezed.

Dora patted her hand. "We'd thought so too, but the light is much better here." She wrote a number on Sera's palm. "This is the emergency line, do not share it with anyone. If you cannot find us, call."

Sera memorized it, and then helped Dora carry bolts of shining fabric to the locked doors of the back room. The front door chimed before Dora could open the locks. "New customers," Beau sang out, and the shop transformed before Sera's eyes, the shadows growing thicker, the lights higher. She thought she heard birdsong.

Odelle Rankenfall stood beside the bare mannequins, tapping her foot. Her mother held her coat. When Dora and Sera approached them, Odelle grew outraged. "Where is the atelier himself? Now that we've found the place, I don't want to take my fitting with a *shopgirl*." She looked straight past Sera, as if she wasn't there.

"My regrets, I was detained," Beau said as he appeared. He ushered them back, snapped his fingers, and Sera gasped as Odelle's dresses appeared on the mannequins.

"Circus stunt," Odelle murmured to her mother. "How gauche."

"You would rather wear your other gowns, madame?" Beau said, his smile taut as ever.

"Of course not," Odelle said. "I'll have the best, just like Merielle and the twins. Let's see it."

She changed into a muslin and, as Dora was helping her into new shoes, gave the shopgirl the slightest kick. Sera bristled. So did Dora, her hands pricking Odelle.

"Mother, tell them to stop torturing me."

Sera fumed, but Dora pulled her aside. "Our delight is to help each customer find their ideal. We will help her. They will pay. And we will move on."

Behind them, beyond the locked doors of the back room, sewing machines whirred—Sera realized that was the birdsong sound—and the cutting room scissors went snick snick. Sera's blood kept time with it all. "Fine. But she's horrid."

When Dora smiled, her teeth seemed honed to sharp pins by the lights. "We like horrid, sometimes." The shopgirl showed Sera how to drape the mångata fabric Odelle had ordered just so, and how to avoid the girl's sharp heel. The fabric sat perfectly. When Odelle turned in the mirror, the gown they call "The Water's Edge" gleamed like a full moon on the ocean.

Sera had never felt so proud as when Beau nodded approvingly in her direction. She noticed the tendril of water seeping from the gown and stooped to clean it up.

"Let it be," Dora said, her customer-service smile almost beatific. "Let her get used to it. Who knows, she may drown in that dress come next week."

"You are terrifying," Sera whispered.

Dora smiled then, for real. "We are, a little, aren't we?" And she clasped Sera's hand.

Sera beamed. "We are."

By midweek, Sera skipped a class. Just the one. All right, two. She'd be back next week, she swore. Besides, inside the busy atelier, with the lights glittering, she'd begun drawing new designs. So many more than she had in her classes. Her fingers danced over the pages of her sketchbook, arraying the croquis in impossible gowns.

Other shops were furious, she'd heard. But they could never find Unseelie Brothers to complain. Designers from around the city took to social media to shout their grievances. Which made the atelier even more desirable. And the shop even busier.

Now and then, Sera passed the workroom door, and pressed her ear against it. The sewing machines never ceased. When the fabric for The Murmuration arrived, she hoped to see the seamstresses and designers at work. But the bolt was so heavy, and swirled so magnificently, the delivery men lost their grip on it and Sera and Dora had to spend several minutes luring the gown-to-be down from the eaves. Dora's hair tumbled from her bun as they ran to find the birdseed they kept for emergencies. Once the fabric was contained and had been locked behind the thick doors to the back room, Dora caught Sera trying to peer through the lock, and pulled her gently away.

"Have you lost something?"

Someone, Sera wanted to say, but didn't. She didn't want Dora to think poorly of her as well.

In the silence, Dora lifted the sketchbook from Sera's hand and, without asking, turned the pages.

"These are so good, Sera. You have a talent. Sir, come look," Dora exclaimed. "You do beautiful work!"

Beau approached and pointed out a few things Sera could adjust on a shoulder, at a hem, as Dora looked on.

Sera, despite herself, glowed at the praise. The idea that these designers thought her work was good enough to comment on astounded her. She ran a finger along a table littered with sequins and seed pearls. She touched her necklace as Dora, still flipping through the sketchbook, found Sera's favorite design. "Oooooh."

"It's just all right," Sera demurred.

"It's magnificent," Dora said.

Beau disagreed. "Let me see." He held out an imperious hand and studied the gown. Then he winked at her. "I knew you were one of us. Let's make a mock-up of this one. We will call it The Gown of Thorns."

Sera's heart pounded. "I don't even know what fabric to use." She reached for the sketchbook. She'd been looking forward to drifting the fabric store aisles. Selecting findings. Figuring out transitions from design, to fabric, to form, on her own.

But Dora's smile worked at her until she grinned too. The shop could certainly show her how to add drama to the gown. It might make the ideal senior project. "Okay."

"We have just the fabric!" Dora leapt up and ran to the sewing room door. Her enthusiasm rippled the room in light. Sera was, she realized, blissfully happy surrounded by that light. Dora disappeared into the sewing room and left the door ajar. Sera followed. Inside, the machines—old Singers, new 3-D printers, and everything in between— waited, surrounded by fireflies and shadows. "Let's get to work. We'll be a fantastic team." Dora pulled out a seat for each of them and began showing Sera how the atelier worked its magic on fabric and metal.

Before she knew it, Beau was at the door, announcing customers. Rie, arrived for her fitting. The fireflies disappeared.

"But that is days from now," Sera protested. She looked for her dress, but it was gone. Her stomach rumbled. She was starving.

"Time is a bit strange back here," Dora smiled with sharp teeth. She pulled Sera back through the door and shut it tight.

From the doorway, Rie waved at Sera. "I've missed you! You haven't answered my texts!"

Sera looked around the shop, confused. Outside, she could clearly see Madison Avenue. When had the shop moved? Her father's worries swept over her and disappeared again in the face of more pressing concerns: her aunt. Sera and Dora had been so busy working on Sera's designs, had anyone finished Merielle's gown? What would Aunt Vanessa say?

When Rie walked past the bare mannequins that afternoon, the muslin shapes glittered; and suddenly three gowns dazzled, draped over their headless forms. A lightning dress. The dress made of swallows in murmuration. And, impossibly, Sera's new design. The Gown of Thorns.

Sera couldn't take her eyes off of it. It was perfect. Her hand went to her throat, where the necklace rested. Yes. She would turn the gown in for her final project. It would be glorious.

Mrs. Saunders waited, her foot tapping on the sofa. She cleared her throat until Dora and Sera brought down The Murmuration Gown. Getting Rie into the gown took extra care—the birds' tiny beaks were sharp.

But once she saw her reflection in the mirror, Rie shook her head. "It's not right." Her eyes went back to the mannequins.

"What do you mean? It's everything we've asked for, Merielle." Mrs. Saunders glared at the room for a moment, before settling her gaze on Sera as the safest person to blame.

Beau's smile never faded. "Of course, young lady. We can fit you for something else." He raised an eyebrow at Mrs. Saunders, who sighed and finally nodded. "Do you see anything you like?"

"That one," Rie's fingers pointed towards the dress of thorns. Sera's dress. Sera fought to stay quiet. She didn't want Rie to have it. That was hers.

But the customer, it is said, is always right.

Sera watched Rie try on her gown. It fit perfectly. The gown that had, Sera thought, been just a sketch not long ago. And then it had been real. And now it was gone. She felt empty inside.

Sera's aunt beamed at Beau. "What a marvelous design. I do hope you were paying attention when it was made, Sera."

Beau said nothing, and neither did Sera. Her cousin left the store with Sera's gown in her arms, barely waving at Sera. "I'll see you before the ball!" Then her mother tucked her into a cab.

"That was quite profitable!" Beau said. "You have a grand future here, young lady. If you want it."

Sera's fingers went to the necklace, even as her eyes drifted to her mother's photograph. She remembered her father's words. "My contract ends with the ball," she murmured, not wanting to get caught up in the shop. She missed the studio and designing dresses the old-fashioned way.

Dora pouted. "Please reconsider. It has been so inspiring having another designer—not just a shopgirl! —here." She looked at Beau, as if daring him to speak. "We want to keep you."

"We will renegotiate," Beau said. The machines in the back room grew louder. *We like your work*, the machines said to Sera. *You should design more. Drop your classes. Stay with us. We have much to teach you.* "Perhaps you would like to hear from your mother?"

"How?" Sera whispered.

And Beau showed her a notice of sale, just listed on a couture consignment site: *Original Unseelie Bros, Ltd. Butterfly Gown, worn once. Contact Mrs. Vanessa Saunders for listing price.*

from The Social Season, *plate 112. The Escort's Silver Cloak—a bespoke item for Mr. James Elandin III, created as a gift for Mr. Michael Bland-heim III, who escorted Mr. Elandin's sister to the Cloisters and Wood-lands Ball of 2012. This ball, while highly successful, did not repeat, as only two attendees can vouch for, or remember it occurring at all. Photograph by the Museum of Modern Art, for its collection. Design by D.B. Von Siolagh.*

Sera pounded on her aunt's apartment door until her hand throbbed. When Rie opened it, shocked, saying "Sera, what in the world?" Sera pushed past her cousin, until she found her aunt in her dressing room.

"Where is it? Did you sell it?" Her voice sounded ragged, like she was a child again.

"You've been working too hard," her aunt said. "You should quit that old shop. Go back to classes."

"They've made me quite an offer," Sera replied. She held up her new contract.

Mrs. Saunders paled. "Rie," she called. "Leave us." When Rie obliged and the dressing room door closed, she reached out and took her niece's hand. "You cannot sign this, Sera. There's no end to it."

"Did you sell my mother's gown? To pay for Rie's?"

"No," her aunt finally said. "I took the ad down. I couldn't bear to part with it, after all. It's valuable, Sera. But your mother's memory? Worth so much more." She turned to the closet and lifted The Gown of Flowers away from its display frame. Behind it, a panel, when pressed, slid open. In the shadows, a butterfly wing fluttered. Then another.

"That's not yours," Sera sputtered. She reached out to touch the delicate wings. "What else are you hiding?"

Vanessa Saunders shook her head sadly. "Never accept a contract without knowing your own worth. Your mother gave up everything for this dress, for time with your father. I shouldn't have kept it from you." She stepped aside and let Sera take the dress down from its hooks.

The fabric felt so light, and it rustled.

"Occasionally, there are incidents with the dresses. But you will find her there, what's left of her," Beau had said, from the doorway of Unseelie Brothers. "You can free her if you like." He'd handed Sera a seam ripper, and she'd tucked it into her bag.

With her aunt hovering at her side, Sera looked at the gown closely, and realized that these were real, pale white, butterflies. Their wings had words written on them. The creatures had been living on the dress, in her aunt's closet, the whole time.

She bit back her anger and began to separate the seams. One white butterfly flew free, then another. As the threads broke beneath the seam ripper, butterflies landed on Sera's shoulders, and in her hair, whispering. Soft wings brushed her temples.

"Sera, stop!"

But Sera wasn't listening to her aunt any longer. Instead, she heard her mother's voice, telling her the real story. How Serena and her sister Vanessa had worked their way out of the sewing room at the Atelier. How Vanessa had stolen them dresses and snuck them into the ball. And how, despite everything, they had both fallen for mortals. One who could pay for a gown like this, and one who could not. Sam Sebastian probably never understood there was such a price.

Sera's fingers shook, and a few butterflies began to crumble into dust. Those that didn't flew wider circles around the room. They swooped over Vanessa, who sat down hard on the bed and stared, unable to speak.

Sera knew now: her mother had been a dressmaker. More than that. An Unseelie. A member of the family. Like Dora and Beau. And now she was leaving Sera. Through tears, Sera went to her aunt's window and opened it.

"No!" Aunt Vanessa found her voice, but the butterflies were already streaming out into the city. Sera clutched the remaining fabric of the dress to her chest and watched them go.

"I thought I could free her," she cried.

"You did," Aunt Vanessa said. Her eyes looked haunted. "That dress took more than she could give. Even as she was welcoming you into the world, she knew this. Serena hid what was left of herself in that gown, as a message to us. To you."

Sera stared at her. "And you kept it from me."

"Sera, you must understand. The dresses, they sometimes . . . do things to the dancers. Good things, often, and well worth it. And some not so good things. The Atelier weaves its fingers into everything during the Season, and everyone comes out changed. If they come out. We were hoping to get away from that. We paid for it."

"Perhaps she will drown in her own dress," Dora had said, days ago, about Odelle. She'd meant it.

Sera shuddered. Rie's dress—Sera's design—was made of thorns. "How could you risk Rie like this?" *What was worth that?*

"A future of happiness? A lifetime of successes? Those things are worth a price that we few can afford to pay," Vanessa said.

"But not everyone can." Sera knelt on the floor of her aunt's dressing room, studying the remains of her mother's gown. By morning, she was covered in pale butterfly dust and tiny threads, and the dress was gone. But Sera felt her mother's energy coursing through her. She would not go to the ball. She would not disappear. And neither would Rie.

"Rie!" Sera called for her cousin, as her aunt quietly left the room. Before the sun was fully up, Sera had adjusted The Gown of Thorns to her particular specifications.

"I don't understand what you did, but this is much more comfortable now, thank you!" Rie embraced her. Sera found the clasp for her necklace, undid it, and placed the matching jewelry around her cousin's neck.

When Rie left the room, Sera spread the new contract Beau had pressed upon her out on the carpet. She took out her cheap plastic pen, and went to work on the pages, writing in new terms. For each design of hers they sold, Sera would gain interest in the shop itself. The same for Dora, for believing in her. No more shopgirls, they.

When Sera returned to the atelier, she signed the contract with a flourish. One small white butterfly fluttered in her dark hair. She didn't brush it away.

Beau, unsettled by the butterfly, only glanced at the additions. He signed with a shaking hand, and went back to the workroom.

Then Sera posted the store's emergency number to social media.

By the day of the ball, she'd made twenty designs of her own, sold them all, and Beau was so ecstatic, he set even more stars in the Atelier ceiling.

The Murmuration gown—made of tiny white starlings, that swirl just beyond the viewer's gaze. Worn by Mrs. Mimi, née Mumford Price, 2022, at the Stolen Hearts Hospital Winter Ball. The event is notable in that several dozen attendees were treated at the hospital after a spate of food poisoning that left them all semi-catatonic, and without memory of the evening. Design by Dora Unseelie.

THE BALL

Seamstresses do not often go to balls. Instead, Sera and Dora watched, exhausted and triumphant, from the floor of the showroom at the center of Unseelie Brothers, Ltd. as their gowns made the Season's first gala magical. They sipped champagne while the shop's mirrors showed them revelers entering, curtseying, and beginning to circle the ballroom at The Empire Hotel, in complicated patterns that moved ever faster. When the orchestra picked up the tempo, the dancers became a blur, and the gowns transformed.

The Lighting Gown shocked a dancer's escort. The ocean-and-moon gown seemed to grow heavier on Odelle until she had to sit down. She was found drenched in the restrooms, but alive, much later. Dora's sharp laughter echoed in the empty store.

Sera watched her aunt, beaming, as Rie danced with her escorts. Sera's gown swirled protectively around her cousin. The tiny stitches Sera had put in among the thorns turned to blossoms, and Rie didn't suffer a single scratch, nor did her aunt. Sera understood now, her aunt's fear, her sorrow and guilt. And she wanted none of it for Rie.

Fireflies wove through the store as Sera and Dora watched more Unseelie gowns transport their wearers. Beau joined them, humming along with the orchestra. "My favorite time of all," he said. "Look how beautiful they are. And they know it. No matter the cost. Meanwhile, look how powerful we've grown with so many new clients." Across the ballroom, dancers fell in love with each other, and with their own reflections. They became what they were wearing, for a moment. If they were lucky. Or forever, if they were not.

But not Rie. Sera had made sure her cousin was safe.

For others, there was a cost. The Talbott boys grew tails and hooves to go with their custom tuxedos. (They woke up the next day with pounding headaches and began trading stocks like the world was on fire.)

As the music ended, the Unseelie court beyond the sewing room doors laughed itself to sleep: the machines finally quiet, the scissors at rest. Sera's aunt crossed the ballroom, and stepped through a mirror, into the shop. She wore The Gown of Flowers. "I have come to pay what I owe to my niece." She curtsied deep, before Beau, Dora, and Sera.

Sera helped her down from the mirror. "You could have told me," she said. "You could have let me see her."

"I was terrified," her aunt said. "I'm not any longer."

A white butterfly circled the darkness above the Atelier, among the fireflies. Sera smiled.

"Perhaps we are all a little terrifying," Sera agreed. "Thank you for bringing me home. Tell my father I'll see him soon." She sent Aunt Vanessa back to the Fête Noire, her gown shimmering around her until it bloomed again, with black flowers this time. The next day, Mrs. Vanessa Saunders' transformational gown made page six, and Lillian Talbott was beside herself with jealousy. Sales at the shop increased again.

A week later, Rie returned to class, music in her ears, and a sharp determination to graduate in her mind. Sera submitted The Gown of Thorns as her senior project, and soon after, they walked commencement together, with their families, mortal and not, watching proudly.

And a few days after that, when Beau tried to move the shop, he found that he could not.

"It won't budge without our permission," Sera said.

"We've sold enough gowns to take a majority interest," Dora added. "From now on, we're a team."

Her laughter echoed around the room, startling The Murmuration off its mannequin. They managed to capture it before its buyer arrived for her fitting that afternoon.

from The Social Season, plate 123. *The Gown of Thorns, worn by Ms. Merielle Saunders, twice so far. First at the Fête Noir Charity Ball in 2022; then at the Defenders' Ball for Workers' Justice in 2023. No incidents have been reported at any of these balls or events. Designer: Sera Sebastian Unseelie, Unseelie Family, Ltd.*

SMALL MONSTERS

E. LILY YU

T he small monster, whelped, slipped out of its caul and onto the pebbly floor of the den.

Its emerald scales flexed. Its soft tail swept the earth. The small monster stretched out its new limbs, shuddering. It smelled raw white roots and mud and dried ichor.

The den was an egg-shaped void under a hill. A roof of rocks and matted roots hid the small soft monster and its parent from the moon's white gaze.

The small monster unstuck each gluey eye and saw the ruby scales of its parent, whose side heaved with long and labored breaths. The birthing of monsters is hungry work, a labor of a week or more. And as the small monster looked upon the world, still damp from birth, its parent lowered its great golden beak and bit off a tender limb.

Humming with relief and satisfaction, the parent shifted its gleaming bulk to the rear of the den and settled down to sleep.

The small monster bled, and bled, and wailed.

Like gecko tails and starfish arms, the small monster's lost limb scabbed, healed, and regrew. Its parent left the den and returned with bloodied lumps of deer, bear, rabbit, and hawk. Over time, the small monster sprouted two rows of serried teeth; six hard, ridged horns; and stubby claws.

Occasionally the gold-beaked monster did not return to the den for days, finally dragging in a much-mauled haunch of deer.

Sometimes it returned without anything at all.

Those mornings, when the small monster felt its parent's footfalls through the packed earth, it fled cowering to the steep curved back of the den, though that was of course no hiding place at all. And by noon the small monster would be diminished by a leg or a tail or a bite from its side, too wise and afraid now, as its parent slept, to make a sound.

Though beak, fang, and claw speak more directly, monsters have their own harsh and sibilant language. Now and then the parent spoke, either to itself or in challenge to another monster whose shadow crossed the mouth of the den, and syllable by hiss, the small monster learned.

One morning, after they had devoured the remnants of a mountain lion, the small monster spoke.

Why do you eat me? it said.

Its parent lolled onto one side, spines bristling. Gobbets of meat warmed its belly and weighed it down, and it felt pleasant toward the world and its whelp. **Because I am hungry.**

But why not eat—the small monster took a breath—**your own leg?**

Silly. I am your parent. I birthed you. You are mine.

But it hurts.

It grows back.

And neither said a word more.

In time the parent waxed gibbous like the moon, growing too ponderous to hunt. It tore off and ate all four of the small monster's limbs over the course of a week, writhing and hissing as it did so, without the slightest sign of enjoyment.

At the end of the week, another, smaller monster was expelled in a pool of foul-smelling birth fluid, and the den rang with three cries of pain, snappishness, and distress.

After that, the small monster learned the trick of being farthest from the den's entrance when their parent returned unfed. It was not as helpless as the smallest monster, and so on most occasions, apart from ill-timed naps, the matter was decided in the small monster's favor.

The snapping, crunching, and sobbing were terrible to hear. The small monster quickly learned not to listen.

While its parent hunted, the small monster played. In the evenings, starlight washed the opening of the den. The small monster rushed up to the brink of a world that smelled like wilderness and pine forest, from which the small and smallest monsters were both forbidden, then backed away.

When can I go out? the small monster had asked.

Never, came the reply. **You will remain here always. With me.**

While it was not brave enough to disobey, the small monster was clever enough to consider one claw within the den a perfect observance of the law.

Now a damp wind blew over the small monster, smelling of blackberries and yellow-pored boletes. Night birds hooted and sawed in the trees. Deep in the den, the smallest monster whimpered in its sleep.

Something slunk, lithe and stealthy, through the red-berried brush. It sounded larger than the foxes the small monster had seen, less twitchy than the rabbits the foxes hunted. The unseen thing paced back and forth, whuffing, and the small monster went as still as stone.

It was too late. A step, a spring, and then three slitted yellow eyes looked down upon the small monster.

Where the gold-beaked monster was clad in ruby scales, this monster was all tawny, wiry fur.

Poor thing, it said. **Who ate your leg?**

For the small monster had been unlucky not long ago, though the stump had scabbed.

Parent, said the small monster. **But it grows back.**

I remember being small, the tawny thing said. **Every month the tearing teeth.**

Every *week*, the small monster said.

If you came with me, the tawny thing said, **I would not bite you more than once a month. And only if I had to.**

This sounded like heaven to the small monster. It quivered its horns and clattered its scales. Then it paused.

I can't run as fast as you, it said. **With only three legs.**

No matter, the tawny thing said, lowering its head. It mouthed the small monster like a cat with a kitten. Then it tensed its muscles and bounded into the forest.

Its great paws struck the earth with such force that the small monster's teeth clicked against each other. Trees rushed past them, dark and blurred.

By the time they stopped, the stars had dimmed and sunk into dawn. The forest was gone, and the world smelled new. They were a long way from the den beneath the hill where the smallest monster waited alone.

The tawny thing had scented something; its three yellow eyes grew black and wide. It dropped the small monster and hove into the wheat-fields shivering around them, the long stalks pale under the rosy sky.

From the far side of the field came a stifled shout.

A few minutes later, the wheat parted, and the tawny thing dragged out the body of a man. His throat was open, wet, and red. His old, patched clothes ripped easily.

They ate, the steam from the man's entrails wreathing them. The small monster gnawed on knuckles and spat out the little finger bones. The tawny thing crunched the femurs for their marrow. They licked themselves clean of the sweet blood, then went on.

Around them, plains billowed and shook loose their folds of gold. The tawny thing and the small monster did not converse. Their pace was leisurely at first, while the small monster hopped and hobbled on three legs. The tawny thing often carried it. After its fourth leg budded and regrew, though the limb was soft and tender for a time, the small monster kept up as well as it could.

The tawny thing was swift and lethal, and for a long time, as the moon filled and emptied and filled, the small monster kept all its limbs, and ate well. It learned to catch crickets while the tawny thing hunted.

Then one too many deer slipped the tawny thing's jaws. It did not particularly matter why. An old injury in one whip-muscled leg might have flared, or perhaps the canniness of all living beings in autumn had pricked the velvet ears of the deer. Whatever the reason, balked of its prey, the tawny thing bridled and gnashed its teeth. It returned to where the small monster was pouncing at insects.

When the small monster felt the earth shudder, it leapt up to flee, but too slowly.

A moment later, it was lying in its own green ichor, keening.

The tawny thing said, astonished, **You are *delicious*.**

The small monster moaned.

Bones cracked. Emerald scales dropped like leaves. The tawny thing swallowed what had been the small monster's foreleg, snuffled, and curled up to sleep.

You can still walk on three legs, the tawny thing said, yawning. Two of its yellow eyes shut. The third watched the small monster.

From then on, the tawny thing ate of the small monster regularly, finding itself partial to the taste. For fairness—even the small monster admitted this—it took care to leave the small monster with three legs to walk on, though not always a fine and lashing tail.

Bit by bite, though, even that changed.

The tawny thing hunted less frequently. More and more, its three eyes settled upon the small monster, who shrank from the hunger glowing there. Before long the eating was more than monthly.

There was nothing the small monster could do about it besides weeping and raging as the tawny thing slept. With two legs, it could go no distance at all.

No good, said a razor bird in the tree above them. It lashed its three barbed tails and craned its neck. **Better to eat you all at once. Less moaning. Less waste.**

Is that what you'll do? the small monster said, baring its teeth through its tears.

Only if you want, the razor bird said.

No, thank you, the small monster said.

Or, if you like, I could carry you away. For one of your legs and your talkative tongue. For you are heavy, the way is long, and my wings will tire.

You'll take me to your nest, to feed your own small monsters.

The razor bird laughed a red, raspy laugh. **A good idea! If I had them, I would. But I mean a fair bargain.**

Where would you take me?

There is a hollow tree in a distant wood where no monsters go, wormy with beetle grubs and wet with rain. I will leave you there. For a leg and a tongue.

They're yours, the small monster said, resigned.

Faster than thought, the razor bird stooped from the tree, and its claws closed on the small monster. The tawny thing slept mumbling on, even as the small monster's stumps spotted its pelt with ichor.

Have to do something about *that,* the razor bird said. It spread its wings wider than any eagle's, wide enough to blot out the moon.

They flew north until they reached a glacier-fed lake. There, the razor bird dropped the small monster in. Several times it snatched up and dropped the small monster, until the small monster was half drowned but no longer bleeding.

There, said the razor bird. **Let's see them track you now.**

Mountains passed beneath them, then rivers and woods. Stars glistened icily above them. A two-tailed comet shone in the sky.

But the small monster was too cold to notice, hanging mute and miserable from the razor bird's claws.

The wild flight ended with an angled descent through the canopy of an old beech wood. They landed upon a bare white snag.

There, the razor bird said, its crimson eyes bright. **Now open your mouth.**

Payment was settled with merciful swiftness. When that was finished, the razor bird lowered the small monster into the snag's hollow heart, which was barely big enough for its remaining limbs. The wood had gone spongy with insects and rot.

Mind you, the razor bird said, **I am what I am. I know where you are. If I hatch chicks, I'll look where I stashed you. Don't hide here too long.**

It flicked its three tails and soared away.

The snag was far from comfortable. When it rained, the monster licked at the trickles that ran down the wood and drank from the puddle that formed at its feet. For food, it had watery white wriggling grubs.

On a day it remembered ever after with pleasure, it caught and ate an incautious squirrel. On that diet more fit for woodpeckers, the small monster's lost limbs returned with painful slowness. Its plump sides slumped, and its glossy scales dulled. But there were no severing teeth or beaks in the snag, apart from its own.

Bud by bone, claws and tail and all, the small monster grew into itself again.

When all its pieces were present, the small monster clambered out of the snag and fell snout-first into the grass.

When it had warmed itself in the sun awhile, motionless as moss, it caught a vole by surprise and devoured it, as well as the beetle the vole had been nibbling on. Then the razor bird's parting words came to mind. The small monster shuddered and headed in the direction of the snag's shadow. It snapped at grasshoppers as it went.

Now and then the small monster crouched behind a tree as something larger snorted and shuffled in the brush. Once, it froze under a whorl of ferns as the three-tailed shadow of a bird passed over. The small monster liked its legs and tail, and it wanted no more of monstrous bargains.

As it scrambled and slid down a slope of scree, the small monster chanced upon a gashed and broken thing. Deep gouges in its side showed the white of bone. Its pointed snout lolled in a pool of gore.

One scratched silver eye opened.

Please, the rat-nosed thing said. **Come closer.**

The small monster sat back on its haunches and sized up the battered bulk of the thing. Among the feathery grasses at the bottom of the slope, it caught a speckled frog, which it brought back and dropped near—but not too near—the creature's snout.

The rat-nosed thing licked up the frog and swallowed it, then shut its eyes. Its breathing was shallow.

In the meadows around them, the small monster searched for slithering, skittering creatures, garter snakes and earthworms, thrush eggs and wrens, to feed both itself and the broken monster.

Time trickled past, and the wounds on the rat-nosed thing scabbed. Its scarred eyes followed the small monster.

One day, as the small monster left a lizard by its snout, the rat-nosed thing lunged.

Why? the small monster cried, scrabbling backward, bleeding.

The rat-nosed thing made wet, happy noises. **Better than worms and slugs and grubs.**

Flinching with pain, the small monster fled. Behind it, claws scraped stone as the rat-nosed thing stood. It snuffed the ground and chuckled like boulders breaking. At this, the small monster turned and saw that its own dribbling ichor had painted a path.

Down that path, snout to earth, the rat-nosed thing hunted.

The small monster lashed its tail. Though the wound in its side was a white-hot knife, it scaled the nearest fir and crept out upon a bough. And as the rat-nosed thing came sniffling beneath, the small monster let go and fell.

Its claws clamped onto its pursuer's skull. And as the rat-nosed thing swung its head and shrilled, the small monster bit out one silver eye and slit the jelly of the other. Then it leapt down and tore at the taut, thin skin where the rat-nosed thing's wounds had barely healed. The small monster scratched until the tender flesh parted and showed again the stark white bones. It bit and squirmed into the rat-nosed thing, crawling inside the warm, plush cage of its ribs.

The small monster ate what it found there: bitter, bilious, savory, sweet.

When it had swallowed most of the rat-nosed thing, enough to push apart the ribs and emerge, there was a new sharpness to its face and a silver tinge to its scales.

It kicked a scatter of gravel over the raw red bones and prowled on, wary but unafraid.

A strange scent blew across the small monster's way, one it had never smelled before, and it turned and went into the wind. Days and nights it chased the scent, through forest and scrub, over salt marsh and fen, until the small monster stood at the edge of the sea.

Brown waves roared like dragons along the shore. The small monster lowered its head to drink and found that the water was bitter, and burned.

I see, the small monster said. **This is the end of the world.**

It crouched in the surf and stared at the sharp straight limit of the sea.

After a while, it noticed a little clawed creature beside it, no bigger than one of the small monster's teeth. Its tiny claws worked upon a shard of sea glass.

What are you doing? the small monster said.

Adding to you, the clawed creature said. **Not that you aren't already excellent. But anyone can be improved.**

Several flowery tufts sprouted from the creature's shell. Every now and then the creature tickled one of them and applied an invisibly slight secretion to the sea glass it was pressing against the small monster's scale.

At length it rested, sighing in satisfaction.

Ah, it said. **Art!**

Sorry?

Do forgive me. What I should ask is: Do you like what I've done?

The small monster studied the addition to its side.

You disapprove. I can remove it! the clawed creature said. It reached for the shard.

Don't.

Then will you let me add more?

If that's what you want, the small monster said.

The tide whisked in, rolling a fat seal onto the shore. The small monster took a few neat bites, then offered some to the laboring creature.

In a minute—in a minute—

By the time the tide whispered out, the small monster had been adorned with six chips of sea glass, blue and brown.

Now I have earned my supper, the clawed creature declared, extending its pincers to receive a morsel of seal. It ate with sounds of satisfaction. Every so often, it passed a crumb to the tufts on its back, which grasped hungrily at the flecks of food.

What are they? the small monster asked.

Anemones, the clawed creature said. **Some of the sea's more stinging critics. They keep me honest. And they produce a good glue.**

A seagull stooped at the seal carcass. The small monster broke its neck with a blow.

Wish I could do that, the clawed creature said.

Eat, the small monster said. **You'll be big enough, one day.**

When the small monster was thirsty, it went inland for water. When it was hungry, it dove for fish and seals. But most of the time it sat still and watched, puzzled, as the clawed creature embellished its scales.

Gradually, the small monster's gleaming green mail was encased in glass, agate, and mother-of-pearl.

Beautiful, the clawed creature said. Sunlight glowed in the small monster's new shell. **Exquisite. Exceptional. If I do say so myself.**

The anemones waved their fronds in lazy assent.

Are you done? the small monster said.

For a moment. Beauty must be appreciated. And then!

It's not over?

Never. Life is growth; art must follow. Why, I myself have shed two shells since I started this work! But for the present, I shall scuttle along the beach and search for my next stroke of inspiration.

The small monster did not understand much of what its companion said. Nevertheless, it escorted the clawed creature on its muttering constitutionals, waiting as a striped pebble or shapely stick held it rapt. Any seagull that swooped, thinking it had found an inattentive meal, died in a spray of bloody feathers. The clawed creature hardly noticed.

Sometimes it crept up the small monster's flank, perched upon a horn, and confessed its doubts.

What if it never comes, the next idea? What then? What if my great works lie behind me?

The small monster made reassuring noises, but did not know what else to do, for its life had been biting and bleeding, not art.

One night, the wind rose. The air prickled and itched. Lightning cracked the violet sky. In one sheeting flash, the small monster thought it saw a forest upon the sea.

I have it! the clawed creature shouted into the small monster's ear. **Quick, swim!**

The small monster plunged into the ocean. Though towering waves spun and flung them about, once they dove deep, the water gentled. Soon they reached the broad black hull of the ship, whose masts had looked like trees from the shore.

Wait, the clawed creature said, clinging to the small monster.

They did not wait long. A wave tossed the ship and smashed it down. Clean as a walnut, the hull split into halves. Small bodies tumbled out of it, as well as timbers and chests and drowning sheep. Here and there a broken chest poured a glittering of gold.

That, the clawed creature said. **I want that.**

The small monster surfaced, gasped, and dove again. It caught four coins in its claws and one in its teeth, marked where the rest sank into darkness, and swam back to shore.

Rain lanced down as the small monster hauled itself out of the water.

I hope they're worth it, the small monster said.

They will be, the clawed creature said. **You'll see.**

They huddled together under a dripping pine until the storm blew itself to shreds. A sickly dawn shone in the sky.

Pieces of the ship started drifting ashore, as did a fine banquet of brined sailor and sheep.

I suppose you want more of those round objects, the small monster said.

The clawed creature said, **If you don't mind.**

Day after day, by dint of much swimming, the small monster amassed a heap of gold.

What now? the small monster said.

Now, I work.

Though each golden coin was as large as its body, and so heavy it asked the small monster to hold them in place, the clawed creature labored without rest or food. Every so often, the small monster tried to coax it into eating.

The art is all! the clawed creature said, wrestling with its piece of gold.

Over the small monster's shell of glass and nacre, which had split and been mended as the small monster grew, the clawed creature affixed escudo and pistole. Sunlight danced on their faces and shook bright sequins across the sand.

There, the clawed creature said. **Magnificent. You're a treasure. Worth your weight in gold.**

Stretching, the small monster heard its golden scales clink.

Let them bite me now, it said.

Eh? Pass the fish.

After day or two of dazzlement, in which the small monster flung sunlight every which way, briefly blinding a number of birds, it covered itself in seaweed at the clawed creature's insistence, until not a glint of its golden armor could be seen.

More prudent that way, the clawed creature said.

The small monster ate, grew, fetched whatever shell or skull the clawed creature desired, and watched the ebb and flow of the tide. Despite gusts, gales, storms, and heaving waves, that stretch of seashore was the most peaceful place the small monster had known.

It mentioned as much to the clawed creature.

Nothing lasts, the clawed creature said, as it placed stones in a pleasing pattern on the sand. **Neither good nor bad. But one must always enjoy the good.**

That peace ended abruptly on a clear afternoon.

The wind was crisp and blowing off the sea. The sigh of the waves curling in and out hid for a time the sounds of approach. The clawed creature was carving a sand dollar into layers of lace, and the small monster, admiring, did not hear. Only when sand trickled in rivulets down the dune above them did the small monster lift its eyes and see.

Another monster crouched at the top of the dune. It also boasted a crown of horns, though its sides were stippled with ruby spots.

Uh-oh, the clawed creature said. **Excuse me.**

It tucked itself into its shell. The next wave that foamed in carried it off.

What do you want? the small monster asked.

You.

Do I know you? the small monster said. Then it shook itself from horns to tail in surprise, for it recognized the other monster.

As well as your own blood, the smallest monster said. I've tracked you through mountains and forests and fields. And now I shall eat you.

Why?

You owe me. The smallest monster dug its red, red claws into the soft white side of the dune.

Then it sprang.

The small monster turned sideways, and its sibling crashed into its seaweed-draped mail. Claws clacked on gold; a fang shattered. The smallest monster rolled and rose, snarling.

If you're hungry, the small monster said, these waters have squid and dogfish in them.

I'm not here for *fish,* its sibling said.

The small monster met the next charge with one glass-and-gold shoulder.

No.

Again its sibling found footing and lunged. Again the small monster knocked it aside.

The smallest monster howled. Lie down and let me tear your throat out!

No.

Let me bite you and drink your ichor!

No.

While they fought, shreds of kelp fell from the small monster, until it shone with uncovered gold. The smallest monster champed its needle teeth and struck, but it did no harm. As it reared to strike again, the small monster bowled its sibling onto its back.

The smallest monster writhed upon the sand. I've given up so much for you!

I'm sorry, the small monster said. Go away.

You think you're so *special,* its sibling said. But I know you!

The smallest monster splayed its horns, spat, and padded off. Its tail scribbled arabesques in the sand.

The small monster watched the smallest monster go, until it was too far to see.

After some time, it felt a slight itching on the side of its neck. This was the clawed creature, climbing to the small monster's horns. From that perch, it surveyed the aftermath.

You've lost some coins, the clawed creature said. **I'll fix them. Hold still.**

The small monster waited for it to cement the loosened coins back into place. Then, setting the clawed creature on its back, the small monster waded into deeper water and swam in the opposite direction from its sibling.

For hours it swam, long after the sky reddened and darkened, until a rising tide carried them ashore. The small monster rested its chin on the cold wet sand.

This should be far enough, the clawed creature said. **Sleep. I'll pinch if I hear anything.**

The small monster slept, dreaming of pursuit, and kicked the sand and the clawed creature in its sleep. Its tail flicked and twitched at the cry of a seal.

When it awoke, to screeching seabirds, it was hardly rested.

What is peace, after all, the clawed creature said, **if not a moment of repose. A breath between storms. Most importantly, an opportunity for art.**

The small monster sharpened its claws on a spar.

The clawed creature added, as an afterthought, **I've heard that bad news comes in threes.**

It was a strange, uncertain time. The small monster swam farther south every night, staying nowhere for long. Here and there it startled a family of seals, a cormorant drying its wings against the wind, or a solitary sea lion sunning itself. The small monster ate them carefully, digging up the bloody sand and giving the bones to the sea.

Unlike the small monster, the clawed creature evinced no anxiousness, though it acquired another two anemones. Five times now, the clawed creature had exchanged its home for sequentially larger shells. Each time, it cajoled its critics into relocating as well.

What do they say? the small monster asked. **About your art?**

Sometimes they say: Good enough.

Other times?

You're a hack who couldn't draw a straight line with a sea pen and swordfish.

Which one? the small monster said, eyeing the tufts on its shell. I'll eat it for you.

The anemones waved their stinging petals in threat.

Sometimes they're helpful. They'll say: It's crooked. Left corner's low.

Where did you find them?

Tidepools are full of them. These days, everyone's a critic. The clawed creature sighed. Hard to find ones with discernment, though. No one values an arts curriculum.

Have you gone far into the sea?

The clawed creature waved vaguely. A bit. Maybe. They're discussing the merits of formal education . . .

Are there sea monsters?

The clawed creature did not respond, lost in reverie, or else an absorbing conversation. The small monster waited for a polite interval, then huffed its seal-smelling breath over the flowery shell. Indignant, the anemones snapped shut.

Ah, sea monsters. Deep down, yes. Deeper than you'll ever go, where the water presses with the weight of a mountain. I met vast and insatiable appetites there. Hungry lights in the dark. A bristling of teeth. I should have been a pair of ragged claws . . .

The small monster said, You were not afraid of me.

The clawed creature patted the small monster.

I was inspired. I saw a canvas for my art!

So they will not hunt me from the sea.

Never, the clawed creature said. They live in the deepest waters.

Then I will watch the woods, the small monster said.

Since the day the smallest monster had found them, one particular battle seemed inevitable. When at last a familiar form emerged from the trees, the small monster felt the tightness in its chest unspool, loop after loop unwinding into something loose and useful.

You should leave, it told the clawed creature. **To be safe.**

I won't go far, the clawed creature said.

That's what you think.

As delicately as it could, the small monster picked up the clawed creature in its teeth, then hurled it seaward.

At the dappled edge of the woods, where the sand began, the small monster's gold-beaked parent set its talons, frilled, and roared.

The small monster sat at the shifting verge of the sea, with an infinitude of unknown monsters at its back and one it knew well in front of it. The small monster took a breath of salt air. Then it roared in reply, and the waves roared with it.

You are _mine_, the gold-beaked monster said.

I am not.

Who fed you meat while you mewled? Who carved up lions and brought down falcons for you?

Who fed on me when the hunt went ill?

The parent's scale-sheathed shoulders trembled and chimed. It had grown lean and rangy in the small monster's absence. **Who birthed you? Who gave you life and breath?**

You, the small monster said. **Then you took.**

I've come for what belongs to me.

I am nobody's.

I was kind to you!

The gold-beaked monster loped across the sand.

Once more, the small monster turned to take the blow. Its parent's talons skidded over gold.

Tricks, it hissed. **You forget. I shelled turtles and sucked out the flesh for you.**

With its second blow, it sent a king's ransom flying.

With the third, it broke glass and scale and skin.

The small monster hunched down. It smelled ichor and roots and damp earth again.

Why?

I bore you to feed me when I am old.

The hooked beak dug into the small monster's side, ripping and swallowing. The small monster shrieked, as it had shrieked before, when it was helpless and wriggling in the den under the hill.

But the sound of its shriek was different now, deeper and louder than the sounds a small thing might make.

For the small monster was no longer small.

It felt its strength and cunning then, its size and power and cruelty. It whirled upon the gold-beaked monster.

No. I will not. Never again.

Talons flashing, the gold-beaked monster flew at the no-longer-small monster and was promptly tossed on its crown of horns. Foam and ichor flecked the parent's red sides as it rose.

They clashed, the wet sand churning beneath them, and the no-longer-small monster threw its parent a second time.

You're nothing, the gold-beaked monster said. **What good is your life? Give me it. It's mine.**

They circled each other on the tidal zone. The no-longer-small monster watched the sand sink under its parent's feet, and saw how each step began with a slight stumble. And when the gold-beaked monster struck, swift as an eel, it was hooked and flipped. The no-longer-small monster fell upon the gold-beaked monster, gouging and goring. It tasted its parent's ichor and flesh.

Then the no-longer-small monster stepped back.

As the gold-beaked monster righted itself, ribboned skin trailing in the tide, ichor dropping like green rain, it keened and cringed.

It'll grow back, the no-longer-small monster said. **Now leave.**

The gold-beaked monster retreated, limping. When it reached the woods, it glared hunger and hatred over its shoulder. Then it was gone.

Fog rolled in like a dream, snagging in the bristled tops of the trees, smudging distance and detail.

The clawed creature said from the once-small monster's head: **Family can be difficult.**

Says someone who started as plankton.

Hey! My worst critics live upstairs.

The air was wet and white, and the monster's laughter stirred up eddies in it. They made a brave and merry island in the thick nothingness.

Then they heard the sound of some tremendous thing breaching and collapsing back into the sea.

O, wonder, the clawed creature said to itself.

Again came the fathomless, unfathomable sound.

The fog was too dense to see what moved in the dark and swirling waters offshore.

They listened in silence to the great thing leaping: a rush of water, a crash. Then there was a leap without end. They strained to hear the missing sound.

Out of the wisping fog swam a vastness. Its wings undulated in an invisible current. Its mouth, broad enough to swallow the once-small monster, sucked thirstily at the empty air. It steered itself in an arc with a whip of a tail.

As it drifted overhead, two large black eyes looked down, full of ancient indifference.

A very long time later—or so it seemed to the once-small monster, who had held its breath—they heard the distant boom of the vast winged thing returning to the sea.

Sea monster? the once-small monster said.

Sea monster, the clawed creature said, clasping its own claws.

The world is stranger than I thought.

It always is.

By the time the third trouble came sniffing about, the once-small monster was prepared. The clawed creature had layered it with glass and nacre, then with gold, and finally with bones plucked from a great fish that had washed up dead. The bones curved up the small monster's sides and made a double row of spines.

In those three layers of armor, the once-small monster cut an extraordinary figure. The wolfish, tawny thing that slunk between the trees did not recognize its quarry. It snapped its jaws, perplexed.

Then the sea wind brought the scent of the once-small monster to the woods. The tawny thing, whose hide was now peppered with gray, threw back its head and bayed in greeting.

Old friend, the tawny thing said. It's been too long.

You have terrible taste in friends, the clawed creature said. It slipped from the once-small monster's shoulder into the sea.

This shore is mine, the once-small monster said. You may not hunt here.

For as long as this shore is yours, I'll not hunt here, the tawny thing agreed.

Are you passing through?

Following a trail, the tawny thing said, laughing softly, as if it had told a great joke. Three trails, in fact. All running and jumbled together.

Why do you laugh?

Because if the three had lived peaceably, in this place of plumpest bears and deer—if they offered battle with three sets of claws, beak, and teeth—I'd never have won.

Its purple tongue danced. There were green stains and spatters on the tawny fur.

Contrariwise, the tawny thing said, even a bear could bring down a wounded and brokenhearted beast. For me, the matter was simpler still.

You let me live, the once-small monster said. When I was small.

Small and obedient. I think you are neither now.

So you've come here to fight.

I came here to *finish*, the tawny thing said. To eat a monster and its children whole, beak, bones, tendons, talons—it staggers the mind. Fat as pigeons, I'll be. I'll dig a den to overwinter, and in the spring I'll whelp my own pups.

Am I the last?

You'd find their bones in the woods, if you looked. If I let you. But I won't.

The tawny thing danced before the once-small monster. Its eyes were fixed on the once-small monster's throat.

Run, it said. Let me chase you, catch you, and drag you down.

The once-small monster neither answered nor ran.

Stubborn, every one of you, the tawny thing sighed.

It seized one of the once-small monster's whalebones and shook it until the bone cracked from its carapace. The tawny thing cast it onto the sand.

Hissing, the once-small monster slashed at the tawny thing's ankles and came away with clumps of hair.

Better, the tawny thing said, breaking off another whalebone. **I remember when you had no fight at all. You'd lie in the dirt and cry. Poor little fool.**

Something like thunder rumbled in the once-small monster's chest. It met the tawny thing midleap. Then each fell away.

A gash in the tawny thing's neck beaded red and purulent gold.

The tawny thing purred approval. Then it launched itself again at the once-small monster. The two of them tumbled over and over, grappling. Gold coins scattered across the sand, followed by globs of sea glass and shell. Neat and quick as a gull cracking the valves of a clam, the tawny thing had the once-small monster stripped of its armor, panting and pinned under the heavy paws.

Laughing, its three eyes never looking away, the tawny thing bent its head and gnawed the once-small monster's leg. Clear to the bone its teeth tore and its tongue licked.

As delicious as I recall.

A wave swept in, salting the wound. The once-small monster bellowed and belled. As the sand beneath them liquified, the once-small monster kicked itself free. It stumbled backward into the water, falling, crawling, until each incoming swell broke over its head.

The tawny thing paddled after.

Don't go farther, it said. **Dragging your body ashore will be—well, a drag.**

Though it gasped and gagged with agony, the once-small monster swam on.

When the tawny thing neared, its countenance skull-like under wet fur—when not one of its deadly paws touched bottom—the once-small monster sucked in a breath, clamped its teeth into the tawny thing's neck, and sank.

The tawny thing sank with it.

A silver howl shook out of the tawny thing's mouth. It thrashed in the green water, slicing the small monster open. Everywhere it touched, it carved grievous wounds.

At long last, its limbs slackened.

The once-small monster released it. Its three eyes empty, its terrible jaws agape, the tawny thing drifted down to the seabed. Quick, ravenous shapes swam after it.

Afterward, the once-small monster could not recall how it reached the shore, whether the waves left it broken among driftwood and kelp, or whether it swam with three legs through the obliterating pain.

When the once-small monster opened its eyes, some time later, the clawed thing was scuttling back and forth on the sand. It waved a gold escudo like a shield. One after another, seagulls dove at the once-small monster, but their beaks pinged off of the interposed coin.

Graverobbers! the clawed creature shouted. **Vandals! Philistines! Desecrators of art! Vulgar, disrespectful fowl!**

The once-small monster stirred, groaning, and the seagulls screamed disappointment and fled.

About time, the clawed creature said. **I wasn't sure . . . . You present quite the conservation challenge.**

It'll grow back, the once-small monster said, its voice fainter than the echo in a shell.

If you say so.

For a long time, the once-small monster knew pain in all its colors and conjurings. First it was forked and lancing like lightning. Later it was brown and fogged.

Though the once-small monster was hardly a stranger to pain, this time it had a comforter. And so this pain was not as unbearable as the pain in the den, though it nevertheless was grim and obscene and lasted for an eternity.

Little by little, what had been lost turned soft and silver and regrew.

Eventually, the tawny thing washed ashore. Fish had dined on its eyes and the sea-rotted pulp of its body, and flies clustered and buzzed around the corpse.

The once-small monster retreated to the berried woods to escape the flies and the gaseous reek.

Gulls thronged upon the corpse in a noisy white shroud, tearing and shrieking. They dispersed, shrieking louder, as a three-tailed shadow swept across the sand. From a safe distance, they scolded the interloper, who sat and stripped the carcass clean.

The razor bird paused in the middle of its gorging. Its red gaze found the once-small monster where it rested on moss among the cinnamon ferns.

I think you've learned, the razor bird said.

What did I learn? the once-small monster said.

To be difficult to swallow.

Nothing was left on the bones when the razor bird finished. It cocked its eye at the once-small monster.

You were lucky. I was hungry.

You came looking for me.

And now I am fed. The razor bird shook its feathers, which rasped as they settled into place. Be spiny and sharp, if you can't be quick.

And it flew off.

The seasons changed, and changed again. The once-small monster, with the clawed creature's assistance, grew spiny, sharp, hard, and beautiful.

The clawed creature grew larger and older than any of its kind had a right to be, or so it informed the once-small monster. Defended from marauding gulls, it had increased in size and shell until its present house, dredged from the bottom of the sea, was approximately the size of the once-small monster's head. And one morning, as the clawed creature sorted agates, the once-small monster saw it clearly, in all its jointed and studded detail.

You're monstrous, like me, the once-small monster said, surprised.

Nonsense, the clawed creature said. You're like me.

The once-small monster snorted. I've made nothing.

A life is not nothing.

I've been bitten to the bone and hounded to the edge of the world. I've been dinner. I've been breakfast. An artist, never.

None of us can change what has happened to us, the clawed

creature said. **But if we are lucky, we live. If we are lucky, we do not lose more than we can afford. Much regrows. Claws, tail, teeth, even the vaporous stuff the poets call soul. And bitter experience provides material for art. Ask a shipwreck. Ask an oyster.**

Even so . . .

Tell me, the clawed creature said. **What do you want to create?**

The once-small monster thought. It thought while the tide washed in and out, while the sun rose and set, while barnacles stuck out their pointed tongues and whispered in the absence of the tide.

At last the once-small monster said: **An island. With moss, trees, and small, scuttling things. With crevices and caves for the scuttling things.**

Then you shall create an island, the clawed creature said.

Despite having neither instruction nor prior knowledge, the once-small monster conceived of a plan. It wrested boulders from forest soil and sand and pushed them out to sea with the tide. Stone by stone it worked, slow and purposeful. Soon it had piled up enough rocks underwater that the current could no longer shift them singly away.

Between the boulders, the clawed creature sowed a garden of kelp, bladderwrack, barnacles, and mussels, until the hollow places were filled, and the rocks were knitted and cemented together.

The labor was long and strenuous, and also curiously satisfying.

Years passed before the stony stack was high enough that the highest wave did not douse its flattish top. The once-small monster rested on the stack's summit for a night and a day, watching the stars in their silver parade, then the clouds in their brightening and flaming. It felt the weariness of work well done.

The next morning, the once-small monster began to carry soil by the mouthful to the top of the stack. The clawed thing ferried pinecones, nuts, and dandelion clocks across the water on the monster's horns.

They did not stop when the first seeds put forth their plumules, but continued to lengthen, enlarge, and fortify the stack. In the course of their work, the once-small monster collected three heaps of bleached, bare, monstrous bones from the woods and shore and laid them in stones and roots and soil.

Fish of a thousand colors hid in the seaweed that waved at the base of the stack. Their glittering schools parted as the monster swam by.

One evening, as the two of them sat on the seashore, the clawed creature said: **What work shall we do tomorrow?**

The once-small monster gazed on their rich and cakelike sea stack. The soft green tips of a fifth year's growth were just visible at the tops of the spindly trees.

It is done, the once-small monster said.

Was it worthwhile?

Yes.

Will you rest?

One day and one night, the once-small monster said.

Then what will you do?

See how the waves break like flocked birds against our stack. Look at the water-light that flickers on the underside of the stones. I shall build another island, the once-small monster said. **And another. Until we have made a quietness between the wilds and the deep.**

Let me help, the clawed creature said, as the not-small, not-a-monster knew it would.

I could not do it otherwise.

L'ESPRIT DE L'ESCALIER

CATHERYNNE M. VALENTE

FIRST STEP

Orpheus puts a plate of eggs down in front of her.

The eggs are perfect; after everything, he finally got it just right. Oozing, lightly salted yolks the color of marigolds, whites spreading into golden-brown lace. The plate is perfect: his mother's pattern, a geometric Mediterranean blue key design on bone-white porcelain. The coffee is perfect, the juice is perfect, the toast is perfect, the album he put on the record player to provide a pleasant breakfast soundtrack is perfect. Café au lait with a shower of nutmeg. Tangerine with a dash of bitters. Nearly burnt but not quite.

Strangeways, Here We Come.

Eurydice always loved The Smiths. Melancholy things made her smile. Balloons and cartoons and songs in any of the major keys put her out of sorts. When they first met, she slept exclusively in a disintegrating black shirt from the 1984 European tour. He thought that was so fucking cool. Back when he had the capacity to think anything was cool.

She's wearing it now. Nothing else. Dark fluid pools in patches on the undersides of her thighs, draining slowly down to her heels.

Her long black hair hangs down limp over Morrissey's perpetually pained face. The top of her smooth grey breast shows through a tear so artfully placed you'd think they ripped it to specs in the factory. Sunlight from the kitchen windows creeps in and sits guiltily at her feet like a neglected cat.

Orpheus never once managed a breakfast this good when she was alive. If he's honest with himself, it wouldn't even have occurred to him to try.

"Darling," he says softly, as he says every morning. "You have to eat."

But she doesn't, not really. They both know that. She lifts one heavy, purplish hand and drops it, settling on the only thing she does need: a peeling, dishwasher-tormented limited-edition 1981 Princess Leia glass filled with microwaved lamb's blood. Forty-five seconds on high.

Orpheus winces. She retracts her hand. She is very sorry. She will drink it later, congealed and lukewarm, alone.

Eurydice picks up a slender and very clean fork. The problem has never been that she doesn't want to get better. Her short fingernails have black dirt under them. No matter how she scrubs and scrubs in the sink, no matter what kind of soap she buys. Orpheus hears the water running at 3:00 a.m. every night. The trickling, sucking song through the pipes. The negative space next to him in the bed, still cold from her body. But it doesn't matter. On Sundays he paints her nails for her, so she doesn't have to see it. But today is Saturday. The polish has chipped and flaked. The constant crescent moons of old earth show through.

She slices through an egg and lets the yolk run like yellow blood. Severs a corner of toast and dredges it in the warm, sunny liquid, so full of life, full enough to nourish a couple of cells all the way through to a downy little baby birdie with sweet black eyes. If only things had gone another way.

Eurydice hesitates before putting it between her lips. Knowing what will happen. Knowing it will hurt them both, but mainly her. Like everything else.

She shoves it in quickly. Attempts a smile. And, just this once, the smile does come when it is called. There she is, as she always was, framed by tall paneled windows and vintage posters from his oldest shows:

Open Mic Friday at the Clotho Cafe, $5 Cover!

Singing Rock Music Festival, July 21st, Acheron, NY.

Live at the Apollo.

And for a moment, there she is, all cheekbones and eyelashes and history, grinning so wide for him that her pale, sharp teeth glisten in the rippling cherry blossom shadows.

Then, her jaw pops out of its socket with a loud *thook* and sags, hanging at an appalling, useless angle. She presses up against her chin, fighting to keep it in, but the fight isn't fair and could never be. Eurydice locks eyes with Orpheus. No tears, though she really is so sorry for what was always about to happen. But her ducts were cauterized by the sad, soft event horizon between, well. *There* and *Here*.

Orpheus longs for her tears, real and hot and sweet and salted as caramel, and he hates himself for his longing. He hates her for it, too.

A river of black, wet earth and pebbles and moss and tiny blind helpless worms erupts out of Eurydice's smile, splattering so hard onto his mother's perfect plate that it cracks down the middle, and dirt pools out across the table and the worms nose mutely at the crusts of the almost-burnt toast.

He clenches his teeth as he clears the dishes. Eurydice stares up at him, her eyes swimming with apologies.

"It's fine," he says, curt and flat. "It's fine."

Somewhere between the table and the counter, the tangerine juice stops being tangerine juice. It thickens, swirls into silvery-gold ambrosia, releases a scent of honeycomb, new bread, and old books.

Orpheus dumps it in the sink.

SECOND STEP

Marriage isn't what he thought it would be.

She didn't even thank him for making her breakfast. He doesn't want that to annoy him the way it does, but he can't shake it. She owes him. She owes him so much.

Orpheus remembers the days when he was so full of her nothing else would fit. And then when she was gone, and he dreamed of her so vividly he woke with her scent pouring from his skin. When nothing was innocent. Every chair just an inch to the left or right of where he'd left it the night before. Every book opened to a different page than the one he'd marked. Every lost key or wallet or watch not misplaced but *taken*. Every flicker of every light bulb was her, couldn't be anything but her, his wife, calling out to him, begging him to hear her, pleading through the impassible doorway of her own final breath.

He was so young then, young, stupid in love, unaware that there were certain things he simply could not have. Limitation was for other people. All he'd ever needed to do was sing and the world opened itself up to him like a jewelry box—and she was there when it did, the little pale dancer on the velvet of his ease, spinning inexorably round and round on one agonizingly perfect, frozen foot. If the world declined to open for others, that did not concern him.

When she is back, he dreamt then, *when I have her back, I will be happy again. She will be whole and laughing and warm as August rain and she will look at me every day just the way she did when we first met, as though nothing bad ever happened. Her eyes will be the same shade of green. The span of her wrist will fit between my thumb and forefinger. We'll go to the movies every night. I won't even want other girls. We'll drink ourselves into a spiral of infinite brunches. She will put her hand on the small of my back when we are photographed just the way she used to. Her smile will be full of new songs. When I touch her again, time will run backward and gravity will flee and pain will be a story we tell at parties, a fond joke whose punchline we can never get quite right. Everything will go back the way it was.*

She won't remember anything. Like in the soaps. She will be so grateful and so relieved, and she won't remember any of it. Not dying. And not . . . the rest. I will bear the weight of our past for both of us. I am strong enough for that.

When Orpheus wakes in the night, she is never beside him. She stands at the window, looking out into the chestnuts and the crabapples. The moon blows right through her. He can see mold flowering along her spine. Where she touches the curtains, it spreads, unfurling as luxurious as ivy.

THIRD STEP

They have a little house on a busy street in a desirable school district. Chestnut and crabapple trees frame a chic midcentury modern bungalow in a neighborhood where poor but brilliant artists lived twenty years ago. Orpheus has other properties, more convenient to the city, more architecturally stimulating, more impressive for entertaining. But she's only comfortable here.

Whatever *comfortable* has come to mean for either of them.

He bought it from a day trader who lost both legs in some kind of vague childhood equestrian incident, a year or so after the second album hit like a gold brick dropped from the heavens and money became an abstract painting, untethered to concrete expressions, a defiance of realism, meaning whatever Orpheus wanted it to mean. It still had all the custom railings, ramps, lifts, and clever little automated mobility features installed and up to code. The previous owner joked that it was haunted.

It is. And it is not.

Eurydice doesn't handle stairs well.

After breakfast, she makes her way to the second floor studio, gripping the silver safety rail with desperate tension. Her ashen feet squeak and drag on each step as she pulls herself up hand over hand. Orpheus watches her from the foot of the staircase. Her lovely legs beneath her nightshirt, the hardened, bloodless muscles of her calves, the curls of her hair brushing the backs of her thighs like dozens of question marks hanging in space, so much longer than before.

Hair keeps growing after you die. He remembers reading that somewhere. In a green room. On a plane. It doesn't matter. He used to watch her bound up to the bedroom, a kind of joy-stuffed reverse Christmas morning, reveling in the shine of it, of them, waiting to catch a playful peek before chasing up to catch her, two steps at a time.

Orpheus hears her fingernails crunch on the stainless steel. She hauls herself up another stair. She pulls too hard; flesh sticks against metal. The skin rips right off her palms, leaving a trail of black, coagulated sludge. Eurydice doesn't notice. She doesn't feel it. She doesn't feel anything. Her grey, marbled flesh rejects material reality wholesale. Those circuits just don't connect anymore.

"Baby . . . ?" Orpheus calls out softly.

Eurydice's head whips around. Her eyes are not the same shade of oaken green. They are black, silvered with cataracts. But they still burn. She stares down at him. He stares up at her. They have been here before. Another staircase. Another hall. Without a handrail, without plausibly candid family photographs at pleasant intervals, without Tiffany glass sconces dripping peacock mood lighting onto their path.

Eurydice turns around to see Orpheus behind her on the stairway. Blue-violet fungus uncurls along her jawline. Silver moss bristles along the stairs like new carpet wherever she's walked. Her pupils swallow him whole. She hears his voice and pivots toward it, instinctively, a reflex outside thought or ego.

"See?" she says in a shredded, raw, sopping voice. "It's not hard."

FOURTH STEP

They get a lot of visitors.

If Orpheus and Eurydice were a rising It Couple before, always ready with an open door and a seasonally appropriate plate of canapes and an incisive opinion on the events of the day, now they are the number one five-star-rated tourist destination for their particular and peculiar social circle. The commute doesn't seem to bother anybody. Friends, colleagues, family, fans, people they haven't heard from in years suddenly tapping on the windows, peering into the back garden, offering to help around the house, pick up groceries, medications, her favorite shampoo, his brand of whiskey. Anything at all, poor dears, just know we're here for you both in your time of need.

Rubberneckers, Eurydice calls them all.

At least they bring presents.

And they ask questions. Orpheus used to get asked questions all the time. *What are your influences? What was it like growing up with a famous mother? When's the next album coming out?* Sure, they were always the same questions, over and over, at a million pressers, in a thousand TV studios, but he had charming, humble, yet flirtatious answers for each one, and the interviewers always laughed.

Now it was only one question, still repeated, but with no good answer: *How is your wife?*

Ascalaphus brings organic fruit baskets.

Hecate brings three-scoop ice cream cones.

Rhadamanthus keeps showing up with DVD box sets even though Orpheus has told him about streaming a hundred times.

Minos brings puzzles from the Great Paintings of History series. Adult coloring books. Something to occupy her mind, keep her sharp.

Charon is forever trying to talk Orpheus into going jet skiing with him on a lake upstate. *Come on, man, it's not like you were a homebody before. Do something for yourself. She's not going anywhere.*

Even the rivers come, though never all at the same time. Sopping wet, clothes clinging to their skin. Acheron with an asphodel blossom in his lapel; Phlegethon smoking constantly; Cocytus in jeans, her huge bone-pale headphones keeping the lamentations piping in; Styx, runway thin, bespoke black silk from top to bottom, always asking for change; and Lethe, her wet hair dyed blue, her long lashes inviting the universe to drown itself in her.

They never say anything about the mushrooms growing in the

fireplace, on the windowsills, crowding spotted and striped between the books on the shelves.

And they bring booze. Not the cheap stuff, either.

FIFTH STEP

What does she do all day?

Mostly, Eurydice practices fine motor control.

It was all explained to him at the time, though Orpheus didn't want to hear it then. She has to stay active. Mentally and physically. She has to keep moving. Rigor mortis sets in again so fast. And she forgets. Not just how to move her fingers, but what fingers are and why moving is a good and desirable goal.

Orpheus remembers Persephone in a power suit, standing with one strappy red heel in the shallows of the Styx and one on land, in both worlds and neither, a bridge in girl form. So terrifyingly organized. The brutal corporate efficiency of death. Handing him stacks of neatly indexed and collated instructional materials with bold graphics and a four-color print job. *Don't look at me like that. This is all new territory for us, too. None of our orientation paperwork was designed to handle it. I was up all summer. Now, turn to page six. We can put her back in there no problem, but a corpse is a corpse, of course, of course. Sorry, that was insensitive of me. Office humor. I'm not usually so . . . for-ward-facing with the clients. It's just that bodies aren't really our market focus. I'd recommend putting her on blood thinners, just to keep every-thing . . . liquid. And the blood, every day at mealtimes. Or she'll forget who she is. That's just standard. It's the same down here. Goes with the territory.* She pointed a ballpoint pen at a huge black stone drinking fountain on the beach. A long line of dead faces waited their turn to drink. He shuddered, watching blood bubble out of the spigot and into the basin. *Sheep's blood is fine. Pig is closer to human, though. Unless you can get human! No? You're right, bad suggestion. Are you listening?*

But Orpheus hadn't been listening. He'd been looking at her. Seeing her face again, her lips, the birthmark on her throat. Everything just as it was. Seeing them on picnics, reading to each other, taking cooking classes, standing in line at airports. Seeing her sitting cross-legged in the studio listening to his new songs, her adoring eyes reflecting his brilliance back at him. Seeing their kids. He didn't hear a word.

So now Eurydice does the newspaper crossword, to keep the neurons firing.

She cleans the house, always in the same pattern, starting with the downstairs bathroom and working her way outward in a mandala of bleach and orange oil.

She text banks for local political candidates.

She plays online baccarat and mines cryptocurrency.

She runs a couple of miles a night, hood drawn up, headphones in. It tenderizes the meat. Orpheus has tried to tell her it isn't safe for her to be out alone. She laughed in his face.

She works in the garden, weeding out the mint and asphodel that constantly threaten to take over everything. Asphodel isn't native, it isn't in season, this is the wrong kind of soil altogether, but nevertheless, the white, red-veined blossoms stretch like hands toward the house.

She spins and dyes yarn to sell at the farmers market on Saturdays. She writes out the names of the colorways on little grey cards and ties them to the skeins with scraps of ribbon. *Die Like Nobody's Watching. Live, Laugh, Languish. Whatever Doesn't Kill You Is a Tremendous Disappointment. Thanks, I'm Cured. L'Espirit d'Escalier.*

It took Eurydice a year to be able to write again. And when she did, though her lettering came elegant and careful, it wasn't *hers*. It wasn't anyone else's, either. It was just new.

But no matter what she writes on the cards, whatever color she pours into her big glass dyeing bowls, the skeins all come out the same shade of black, and no one buys them.

On Thursdays they have couples' counseling. They hunch together on the couch so they can both be seen in the little black eye of the webcam. Orpheus talks and talks. *I just want you to be happy. Why can't you be happy? After everything I've done for you. You're so fucking cold.*

Eurydice never says much. *I'm sorry. I'm sorry.*

The therapist gives them worksheets about Love Languages. Eurydice fills them out. Orpheus does not. So she answers for him.

His says: *Physical Touch.*

Hers says: *The Soul-Consuming Fires of the River Phlegethon.*

Once, Orpheus came home to find the crossword left out by the fire-place, every square filled in with the same tidy, alien letters.

Fuck you. I hate it here. Fuck you. I hate it here.

He tossed it into the grate and flipped the switch. The pilot lights along the fake log popped to life and devoured the puzzle, the mush-rooms, the deepening, ripening mold.

SIXTH STEP

Orpheus's mother comes whenever her book tours bend their way. She can never stay long. Calliope is a household name; the arts are the family business. She never stops working. She writes sprawling doorstoppers about war and romance that lounge effortlessly atop the bestseller lists. She doesn't knock.

Calliope breezes in, all sensible heels and comfortable beach dresses, reading glasses hanging on a strand of pearls around her neck, a faint forgetful hyphen of lipstick on her teeth, a full color spectrum of pens stuck behind her ears and in her hair. She sets up a battle station in the dining room: stock to sign, contracts to go over, laptop, tablet, phone, a headset like a crown of laurels into which she dictates her next project while she bakes and cleans and runs the soundboard for her son in the basement recording studio. She brings a bag of thick, hideous hand-knit sweaters for Eurydice, who is always, always cold, even with the furnace playing at top volume. She raised Orpheus alone, a single mother in an era when that was an impossible ask, bouncing him from auntie to auntie whenever she had to hit the circuit. He adores her. She smells sharp and warm and welcoming, like a used bookstore.

And she takes over bath time.

It has to be done every night. Otherwise the mold gets ahead of them. It flowers deep in her joints, thick enough to pop her shoulder out of the socket or a tooth out of her gums. Once, in the early days, he stayed up working and forgot her bath. Eurydice didn't complain. She never complains. He woke up and found her on the front porch holding their newspaper. The rot had colonized her eye sockets in the night. Eurydice stared at the headlines through a sheen of black mold tipped in blue spores, spanning the bridge of her nose like a starlet's sunglasses.

"There was an earthquake," she'd said quietly, without looking up. "In Thessaly."

Somehow Calliope always knows to visit when Orpheus doesn't think he can bear to lift Eurydice into the tub one more time. It's not safe to let her do it herself. Her heart no longer has the capacity to keep everything churning along thump by thump, so a stubbed toe or a bruised elbow is a potentially catastrophic hydraulic leak. But Calliope doesn't mind. She has enough energy for everyone. She lifts her daughter-in-law naked into the clawfoot tub and pours in bleach like bubble bath. She scrubs the little fractal spirals of mildew from Eurydice's livid back, her hair, under her arms. The water is warm, but it doesn't matter. She doesn't feel it.

Calliope sings to the beautiful corpse of Eurydice as she washes away the evidence of her nature. She sings like a cake rising, a dove's egg hatching, a memory of goodness. The anthurium on the bathroom sink stretches its crimson heart leaves toward the song. So does the clay in the tiled floor. One by one, the black hexagons crack and buckle, straining to get closer to her. Even the tiny threads of fungus on the nape of Eurydice's neck prickle like hair, erect and aware, moronically yearning without understanding toward the profound thing Calliope is.

She squeezes the sponge out against her daughter-in-law's mottled shoulder. Water trickles backward down along her spine and forward over her sternum, and somewhere between the two, before it splashes down into the bath, it forgets to keep being water. It thickens, turns pale gold. The ribbon of bleach twists into honey. A sudden smell of apples and asphodel exhales from the tub: sharp, autumnal, crisp red skins and crisp white wind. Eurydice sobs in recognition, an ugly, stitch-popping sound. She cups her hands and lifts them to her chapped lips.

But the cider-mead of Elysium does not want her. It shrinks back, the bath begins to swirl down the pipe the wrong way round, and where her mouth catches some meager slick of the stuff, it catches a cold blue flame. The faint fire spreads, burning off the alcohol, licking at her knees. Eurydice wails in horror and hunger, trying in vain to stop up the drain with her feet and suck the wine from her fingers at the same time.

Calliope strokes her wet, sweet-scented hair and nods tenderly.

"I know, my love. Marriage is so hard."

SEVENTH STEP

Orpheus and Eurydice met at a party thrown by his agent. A hundred thousand years ago. Yesterday. A blur of balconies and city lights and swaying earrings. A fizzing, popping, positively carbonated evening. Discontent was simply not on the guest list.

"Darling boy," his agent had crooned, guiding Orpheus by the shoulders around a river current of oyster puffs and mini souffles and out-of-season vegetables cut to look like birds of paradise. "Everyone is just dying to meet you." Hermes hit his stride in sneakers so white and new they glowed like angelic wings, discussing cheeks and kissing percentages, managing the room as no one else could.

And finally there she was, drifting between little clutches of conversation. Spangles and crystals the color of olive leaves shimmered down her body like rain, a thin fringe that danced every time she laughed. She wore her hair up in a complicated twist with a jeweled comb, and when Orpheus remembers this, when he dreams of it, he sees them all at the same time, overlaid like double-exposed film: the dress and the comb and the twist and the long, limp, greasy hair as it is now, strands stuck in the milky fluid of her dead eye.

"Have you met Eurydice?" Hermes' voice trips down the halls of that other life, that correct life, the life he'd been promised. "You absolutely must, she's a treasure."

And she'd turned away from some studio exec pestering her and offered him her gorgeous hand tipped in gold polish. A faint blackbird of a bruise rising already on her forearm. Hearing her voice for the first time is like hearing a song you just know is going to hit hard.

"Well, aren't you something?"

And what were you doing at that party? their therapist asks later, so much later. Eurydice shrugs and stares at her knees. Cypress trees cast shadows like black arrows on her face. They never planted cypress. But thick green spearheads crowd the windows on all sides now.

She doesn't remember, Orpheus sighs.

I'm asking her. Active listening, Orpheus. You'll get your turn. So what was happening in your life that night? Were you in college? Working? Promoting your own music?

She was never in the industry, Orpheus says. It was one of the things I found so refreshing about her, considering her father and all.

Eurydice picks at the scabs between her fingers. Finally, she rasps: *I . . . I used to sing.*

No, you didn't.

Okay, she surrenders quickly, as she always does. *I didn't.* They used to fight till the rafters came down and make up on the ruins. Orpheus usually won, but he enjoyed the battle. Now he gets his way so easily.

You never told me.

Okay.

You could have come into the studio with me. Put down a backup track.

I didn't ever sing. I can't sing.

Eurydice, do you want to talk about the man who grabbed your arm?

No.

A small bubble of trapped gases slowly inflates her cheek.

But he *was* something. And so was she. He was famous. She was beautiful. What else did anyone need? They were young and it was easy. Orpheus saw himself as he knew he could be reflected back at him in that heated, shimmering stare. He wanted it. He wanted that ease forever. He wanted himself as she saw him.

Just because he went home with a maenad that night and had to be reminded of her name when they met again a month later doesn't make it any less love at first sight.

Orpheus has repeatedly explained that to their therapist.

EIGHTH STEP

Orpheus knows they're here before he even gets to the foot of the stairs. A guitar case leans casually against the wall next to the guest bathroom, perfectly centered in a spotlight of morning sunshine. It's not one of his. This warhorse is more stickers than leather by now, held together by memory alone.

Orpheus sighs heavily.

Eurydice's father and his dirtbag friends don't call ahead. They don't bake, they don't help with chores, they don't come bearing takeout, and they definitely don't do baths. They just turn up. Once or twice a year. Orpheus rounds the bannister today to find the boys all smoking around his living room, feet up on the coffee table, a random girl asleep on the piano bench, empties stacked into green-and-brown hecatombs on every surface. He recognizes the labels.

Orpheus and Calliope are merely famous. The old man is a legend. Seminal. Iconic. No one comes close to his influence, his sheer ubiquitousness. He *is* music.

He lounges in the big swayback armchair, a man mostly his haircut, perpetually stuck halfway between Robert Plant and David Cassidy, a catwalk in the form of a man, leather jacket, leather pants, massive paparazzi-proof hangover shades, a big golden sun stamped on his black T-shirt, herpes sore like a kiss below his lip. A face that invented magazines, a voice that filled them to the brim. He laughs wolfishly at something or other one of his strung-out friends said and puts out his cigarette on a sunbeam as though it were solid stone.

"There he is!" Apollo brays. "Big O! We were just talking about you, weren't we, boys? And where's my beautiful baby girl this morning?"

"She'll be up soon," Orpheus mumbles.

Apollo pats his ribs for more smokes. "Call her down. Lazy cow-eyed lump." He finds one and jams it unlit between his teeth. "I'm up every morning at the crack of dawn, you know. No excuses. Sleep is for the dead, kiddo!" He catches himself and grins sheepishly, a grin so pretty even Orpheus finds himself trying, once again, to like the man. "Whoops. Awkward. Don't want to offend. You know how sensitive the youth are these days. Can't say anything anymore. Oof. I'll want a drink. You want a drink, mate? Probably need a drink before she . . . ah . . . before *that*." He digs in his pockets for a light. "How's things, anyway? Everything back to normal?" Apollo's eyes glitter suggestively. "Back in the saddle, so to speak?"

Orpheus stares. He coughs out a hollow laugh.

One of the old gang leans forward from the depths of the plush grey couch. He winces; his stomach's wrapped in sterile pads and medical gauze signed by the whole band like a cast. Prometheus flicks a lighter for Apollo's wobbly cig.

"Yer a life saver, thanks," the legend mumbles.

Dionysus heads for the kitchen. Orpheus tries to tell him they barely keep anything in the house, but he opens the fridge with a *Hey, hey, hey* straight out of afternoon reruns. Row after row of wines so old they could draw a pension. The crisper drawers packed with Harp lager— the old man doesn't do wine. His sister favors Blue Moon, but they haven't seen her since the wedding.

It's always like this. Prometheus and Dionysus and Pan, hiding his horns under a fedora, along with whatever nymphs they were shacking up with that week. Ransacking the house, talking about themselves and the old days until you wanted to rivet their mouths shut.

Apollo throws back a beer in one long swallow and gestures for another as they wait for the dead to rise. "When are you going to start touring again, son?" He taps out his ash onto the sleeping girl. She's gorgeous, but they always are. The grey flakes drift down to land on her necklace, a chain of silver laurel leaves looping around her perfect, warm, and living neck. Orpheus stares. He can see her pulse faintly beneath her skin. He'd almost forgotten people's bodies did that. She smells like a river, a forest. Alive.

"Don't want to wait too long between albums. I should know. Can't go radio silent just because the going gets a bit uphill, eh? Gotta get back out there."

"I couldn't stay cooped up like this." Dionysus shudders as he upends a bottle into his gullet. "This house gives me the creeps. And I think you've got a serious mold problem." He wrinkles his nose at the ceiling. A delicate charcoal filigree mars the drywall. Orpheus doesn't have to look. He knows. He'll call someone. Tomorrow. Soon.

Orpheus grimaces. Pan glances up from his endless scrolling through whatever hookup app he's on this time. *Swipe, swipe, swipe.* "You can always open for us. The fans would lose their minds." *Swipe.* He lowers his voice. "You can't stay cooped up like this, poor thing. It's not healthy. Life goes on, yeah? There's only supposed to be five stages of grief. What are you on, stage twenty? Does she even . . . does she even know you're here?"

"Of course she does," Orpheus snaps defensively. But she steps out behind him as soon as his voice hits the air.

Eurydice's face glows with health. Her lips shine ripe and red. Her cheeks blush. Her hair shines. Bare, tanned legs delicate as knives beneath a loose skirt and the oversized mustard-colored sweater Calliope knit for her, a friendly cartoon snake on the front and *gnoqi seauton, y'all!* sewn on with black thread in a circle around its winning smile and forked tongue. Orpheus's chest throbs. It is her, it is her, as she always was, as the sun made her, as he dreamed of her over and over until it wore a groove in his brain. She clasps her hands to her chest like a little girl. Moves her shoulders up and down slightly so it looks like she might really be breathing. But she isn't. Of course she isn't. It's all a show, all for *him.*

Apollo looks nauseated. His throat works to keep the bile down. He looks his daughter up and down, his dancing warm eyes gone distant, flat, glassy. The words he doesn't say hang in the air between them. *I thought you would be different this time, but I guess not.*

She forgot to do her hands. Her father can't help but goggle at them, fish-colored, embroidered with black veins. She ran out of foundation, couldn't find her gloves. Prometheus goes to open a window—there isn't enough Red Door in the world to fix the smell, rich and putrid and earthen.

"Why don't you play us something?" Dionysus suggests.

None of them can take it, they're so fucking fragile. Orpheus hates them. He hates her. He hates how hopeful she gets. Every goddamn time, and for what? They're so empty, they need something pouring into them all the time just to escape knowing it, into their mouths, their eyes, their ears. Music is just the sound of time blowing across the lip of their nothingness.

Eurydice never puts on the makeup for him. She'll take off the glossy, thick wig as soon as they go. The contacts, the fake lashes, all of it. A pile of girl on the floor.

"Yeah, come on, give us a little song," Apollo agrees eagerly. Anything, anything to avoid having to be here and now. "You must be getting brilliant material out of this whole mess. Deep, experiential stuff. Raw, authentic, blah blah blah, the whole aesthetic. I'm here for it. Front row center. Can't wait to hear your new sound. Hey, you can even play my ax if you want." He signals for Prometheus to go get it from the hall. The titan hops to it like an eager spaniel. "Would you like that?"

Orpheus doesn't want to do it. He knows what will happen. So does she. But Eurydice's blown-out pupils bore into him from behind green contacts. She can take it. She doesn't mind. Anything, if it'll make Dad happy.

Apollo puts his guitar into Orpheus's hands. What is he supposed to do, then? It is an instrument made of forever. It is the beginning and end of song. Eurydice fixes her silvered eyes on her father. She puts her cold, heavy hand on his knee and the great man flinches. He fucking *flinches*.

But Orpheus's fingers do not move on the strings. He doesn't want her to know. He doesn't want her to hear. *I haven't done anything wrong*, he tells himself. But nothing in him answers back. So he begins to play a slow, lilting version of an old Smiths song. For her, for them. "Pretty Girls Make Graves." A good joke or a bad one. Who cares? Just let it be over. The voice that moved rocks and trees to life and even the fish to dance fills up a living room with wallpaper twenty years past chic. The girl on the piano bench opens her startlingly green eyes.

He's not even through the first verse when he sees it. Eurydice trembling, vibrating, barely able to hold still. She's shut her eyes. Her jaw clenches so hard they can all hear teeth cracking. But she does not, cannot cry.

Her fingertip blossoms with blood. Real, living blood. Just under the skin. It goes pink and brown, the nail a little round moon, warm, soft. The rest of her hands remain skeletal, ashen, mouldering. But her fingertip wakes to the sound of his music, like the rocks, like the trees, like the fish of the stream and the sea.

Finally, she cannot bear it. She cannot be a good girl any longer. She howls in pain. She claws at the living tissue. Her eyes roll back to find some path away from anguish. She drags her hands down her face, smearing away the careful makeup, the meticulous lip. Chunks of flesh come away. Orpheus stops; the color ebbs away. The nail blackens again, little lightning bolts of mold snaking back up out of the cuticle.

Her family scatters like raindrops.

Orpheus and Eurydice sit alone in an empty room.

The carpet has turned into long silver grass. A wind from somewhere far off shakes tiny seeds into the air.

NINTH STEP

Orpheus has tried to touch her a thousand times. She has never said no. She has never covered up or cried or told him she needed time. She'll let him do anything he wants.

But he doesn't. Not often. Not anymore.

Once she slid into bed with him and the touch of her flesh shocked him almost into the ceiling. She was as warm as the earth in July, hot, even, the air around her oily and rippling. Orpheus wept with relief. He kissed her over and over, drinking her up and in, so grateful, so stupidly grateful and urgent and needy. She was back and she was his and it would all be fine now, it would all go back to the way it was and when he sang to her she would dance again, she would dance and drink her juice and eat her eggs and maybe they would get a cat. A big fat orange tabby and they'd name it something pretentious and literary nobody else would understand. *I knew you were there*, he whispered into her hair. *I didn't doubt it for a moment. You're always there.*

Only afterward, when he was brushing his teeth, did he notice her slick silver hair dryer left plugged in by the sink. He felt the barrel. She'd run it so long the metal was still almost too hot to bear.

So when Orpheus starts sleeping with the maenad from his agent's party again, he tells himself it's not his fault. It's not her fault, either. It's not even *about* her. He tried. He really tried this time.

Let me hear the new song, the maenad says, and rolls over toward him, tangled in sheets like possibilities, everything about her so alive she glows. Her apartment is so clean. No grass or mushrooms or fine purple mold in the ceiling roses. She runs her rosy, licorice-scented fingers through his hair.

And when Orpheus sings, it doesn't hurt her, not even a little. *I love you*, the maenad breathes as she climbs on top of him. *You're amazing. You deserve so much more than this.*

TENTH STEP

Every night at nine-thirty sharp, Eurydice opens her lavender plastic birth control compact and presses down on the little blister pack with the day of the week printed over it.

In those moments, Orpheus always wants to ask her what she's thinking, why she bothers, what's the point. But he never does.

A pomegranate seed pops out. She closes her eyes when she swallows it.

Orpheus goes to the coffee shop down the road most mornings. He gets a latte for himself and one for Eurydice, then drinks them both on a park bench between here and the house. Cinnamon on top. No sugar. He likes all the sugar himself, but that's what she used to drink. So that's what he drinks now forever.

He tells the cute young barista behind the counter his name. She has a nose piercing and huge brown eyes like a Disney deer. She spells his name wrong on the cup.

"No," he says with his most charming half-cocked grin. "Like the singer."

"Who?" the girl says innocently. "What singer has a weird name like that?"

Orpheus puts the coffees down on his bench. He squints in the sunshine. Watches some kids fight over the tire swing. Pulls out his phone and jabs at the keyboard with his thumb.

Are you around? I need you. I want you.

She texts back right away. Quick as life.

When he gets home that night, he has to step over the green-black river that churns through the foyer, separating the land of the living room from the land of his wife.

ELEVENTH STEP

It's afternoon and there are crabapple blossoms all over the front walk like snow and a smart knock at the back door.

Orpheus feels a rush of excitement prickle in his chest. He knows the face on the other side of the glass. His friend. Maybe his only real friend. The only one who gets him completely, who understands what he's had to go through, who can make it an hour without saying something that makes Orpheus want to punch them in the mouth or beg them to take him away from this place forever.

"Hey, fuckbrains," Sisyphus says fondly as Orpheus turns the bolt and lets him into the kitchen, sporting three days of stubble, ripped jeans, steel-toed boots, and a faded black T-shirt that reads *Rock 'n' Roll Forever* in white letters with lightning-bolt tips.

And a dog. Three dogs, actually. German shepherd puppies, maybe four or five months old, all gangly teenage limbs and ears that don't know how to stand up straight yet.

"Hey, crackhead," Orpheus answers. "They give you a day pass?"

The pups sniff at Orpheus. They gag and growl, showing tiny bright teeth. They look past him as one, curious, black-nosed, alert. Past him toward the brand-new river of ash slowly flowing up the hallways.

The ash weeps audibly.

Eurydice hovers behind her husband in another of Calliope's grotesque sweaters. This one with a doofy purple horse and *menin aiede qea*. Three canine heads tilt toward her at precisely the same time. One dog. Three bodies. They move like a stutter.

Sisyphus sinks into the breakfast nook, a heap of handsome limbs. He rolls a milky gray marble over the tops of his tattooed fingers, back and forth, back and forth. His left hand says *prde*. His right says fall. He nods at the dogs and mumbles:

"Well, I had an idea."

Eurydice holds out her blood-purple fingers to the puppies. They advance slowly, uncertainly, huffing her ashen, green-veined hand. Then they fall all over her, snapping the leash, their movements identical, licking her face, wagging great shaggy tails they haven't grown into yet, howling in recognition and joy. Eurydice beams, grave dirt showing between her teeth, caking her gums.

"I thought, you know . . ." Sisyphus says sheepishly, holding one of the leftover cans of Harp between his threadbare denim knees and cracking it with one hand while the other rolls his marble knuckle to knuckle to knuckle. "Emotional support dog. Worth a try."

"You thought *that* would make a good emotional support animal for my wife," Orpheus deadpans as the three hounds loll in Eurydice's lap, their furry bellies as white as death.

Sisyphus gestures with the beer. "Hey, Cerberus is a good boy! He's had loads of training. Sit, stand up, shake a paw, do not chew souls, do not let the living cross into the realm of the dead, the whole package. And nothing spooks him." His voice softens. "He wanted to come. He misses her. They got to be quite good friends, you know. Nobody pays much attention to the old fella once they're settled in. But not our girl. She brought him snacks."

"The fuck does he eat?" Orpheus asks.

"Kindness," Eurydice growls. Cerberus licks her nose and whimpers in furry ecstasy. "Don't we all," she says into his downy ear.

Sisyphus rolls his stone back and forth. "She took him for two walks a day, every day, and not short ones, either. All down the new riverfront walks, along the Lethe and the Phlegethon and the Acheron."

He glances toward the sobbing hallway, but Sisyphus is far too polite to say anything. "She let him stop and sniff whenever he wanted. The shops and galleries started leaving out bowls of water for him."

"I never heard about any of this. What shops?"

Sisyphus lifts an eyebrow. "Didn't you have a look around while you were down there, man? See the sights while you were in town?"

"I was a little busy."

"Who is that busy? It's hell. You weren't even curious?"

Eurydice laughs hoarsely. It is not a kind laugh, and Orpheus doesn't like it at all. She would never have embarrassed him like that in the old days.

"Well, yeah, shops. Saltwater taffy and glass bowls and shit. Revitalization. It's Persephone's whole thing. You do *not* want to let that woman get bored. The saltwater still comes from the rivers, though, so it'll make you forget or be invincible or relive every lamentation of your life just the same. It's just . . . nicer now. Oh, and her yarn. All the shops carried it. They couldn't get enough. She called each lot the funniest things, had us all in stitches. Even Clotho had a standing order. So soft! And the *best* colors. I made this shirt out of it. Do you like it?"

"Whose yarn?" Orpheus asks in confusion.

"Who do you think?" Sisyphus laughs.

Eurydice heads out the side door without a word. The dogs walk primly on their leash, heeling perfectly and staring up at her in abject adoration.

"Be honest, man," Sisyphus says, leaning forward. "How's it going?"

Orpheus's eyes burn and his chest crushes in on itself. "It's like I don't even know her anymore."

"Well, I mean, yeah." Sisyphus chuckles.

"What does that mean?"

"Look, I love you, you know that. But did you ever really know her in the first place?"

"What kind of bullshit is that? She's my wife. How can you even ask me that, after everything I did to get her back? Just to be with her again? Of *course* I knew her. Know her," he corrects himself.

"You didn't know she had a dog."

"What happened down there . . . it isn't important, don't you get that? It was a horrible dream. A bad trip. I don't want to know about it. Neither does she. That's all behind us now."

Sisyphus shrugs. "Okay, what's her mom's name?"

Orpheus blinks. "It . . . I don't know, it never came up. But that's not fair, it's not like I don't know her family. Her dad's around all the time. He's never mentioned her, either."

Sisyphus sighs, gets up, and helps himself to the vintage Star Wars glasses in the cabinet. He picks Lando. "Where'd she go to college? What was her major? She have any siblings?" The dead man looks around awkwardly for a moment before Orpheus snatches the glass out of his hand.

"I'll do it," he snaps. He gets a blood bag out of the fridge and sticks it in the microwave for forty-five. They stand on the ceramic floor while the machine hums toward its inevitable beep. Deep green mold crawls through the cracks between tiles under their feet toward the river in the hallway.

"A little bleach will probably take care of that," Sisyphus says quietly.

"Yeah," Orpheus mumbles, pouring the blood out for his friend. "You'd think."

"I don't mean to pry—"

Orpheus laughs in his face.

"But did you ever ask her?"

"Ask her what?"

"If she wanted to come back."

"Why the hell would I ask her? Nobody wants to be dead. I did the right thing. For us. For her. You were there. It was heroic. I was selfless. I was strong."

"Were you? Or could you just . . . not accept that something pretty was taken from you? Did you know her? Or was she hot and rich and uncomplicated?"

"Fuck you," Orpheus whispers.

"Okay, okay. Calm down. I'm not accusing you of anything. I'm just asking questions."

They sit in ugly silence, letting the sunlight through the dusty, spore-spackled windows say the things they cannot.

"How's the new album coming?" Sisyphus asks finally.

Orpheus grabs the rough cut out of his bag, sliding the disc across the table. A fine mist of silvery pollen puffs up in its wake.

Upstairs, asphodel flowers explode out of their bed, a detonation of white-and-red petals like blood and skin. They spread and spread, tumbling onto the floor, nosing the curtains, suckling the wallpaper.

Sisyphus rolls his stone across his knuckles, patiently, endlessly. With his other hand, he touches the disc and knows every song in a moment.

"Wow," Sisyphus whispers. "Oh, wow."

TWELFTH STEP

Orpheus decides to leave on a Wednesday. Not markedly different from any other Wednesday. She can have the house, he doesn't care. He stops giving her the lamb's blood in the morning. *It'll make it easier*, he tells himself. *She'll forget. She won't suffer. I'm not hurting her. Not really. I'm doing what's best for both of us.* Fuck the house, fuck the cars, fuck his outstanding record contract. None of it matters. If he doesn't come back, that's just fine. But he doesn't know how to start. Where to go. What to take. This isn't his gig. It isn't anyone's gig.

Orpheus asks his mother. She tells him the obvious: *the entrance to hell is always in your own house, silly billy.*

The house didn't have a basement when he bought it. It sure does now. A door between the studio and the library that was never there before. A door and a long, long staircase leading down into lightlessness.

Mold has colonized the house. Tiny blue mushrooms on the fireplace. Carpets of pink fuzz climbing the stairs. Black water flowing past the front door. Weeping ash rippling down the hall. A gurgling stream of fire between the kitchen and the dining room. Asphodel everywhere. Ambrosia in every takeout container.

The rivers visit all the time now. They don't even speak to Orpheus anymore. They just go straight to her.

Eurydice doesn't clean anymore. She and Cerberus lie in a pile together and watch the country inside the house grow by candlelight. When Orpheus asked if she felt like pulling her weight on even the most basic level, she turned her head like a stone door and stared in the direction of his studio, panting like a wolf.

Cerberus doesn't let him into her room anymore. If he tries, the three pups growl and drool and their eyes flash green in the dark.

Orpheus sings for his wife. He sings for an audience of two: of death and death's great love. The most important studio boss there is. He sings everything she ever was or could be. He sings every moment of their life together, every kiss and whisper and quiet joke, every intimate space that opened between them like dark flowers, every good day, because they were all good days. He sings her heart out. He sings what will become his comeback anthem, a song no one can get out of their heads, topping the charts for years, used in every film about love and loss and even an anti-depressant commercial. Orpheus strips Eurydice of Eurydice and transforms her into a song so perfect death gives up and life buries him in laurels.

The song of them, that she never hears. He simply never thinks to play it for her. It's his. His best work. Besides, she never asked what he sang to get her back. He'd have shown her, if she'd asked. Probably.

And what he sang for her and only her, what he sang before the great starry unweeping face of death, is sitting on a rough-cut demo in his leather bag as he walks out of his house on a Wednesday years later, in a padded envelope with his agent's address on it.

"Do you still love me?" Orpheus asks her Tuesday night, the night before he leaves her. She sits on the porch with her dogs, putting together a puzzle of *Starry Night*.

Eurydice runs her fingers over the black half-assembled chapels and cypress trees. She hasn't had lamb's blood in two weeks. Sometimes she forgets she is dead and starts screaming when she sees herself in the mirror. But today was a good day. They watched TV together. She watched Cerberus play in the backyard. One of him ate a bee. She laughed.

"I see my love for you as though it hangs in a museum," Eurydice says slowly. "Under glass. Environmentally controlled. It is a part of history. But I am not allowed to touch it. I am not allowed to add anything new to it. I am not even allowed to get close." She puts a golden star into place without looking up. "Why didn't you turn around?" Eurydice whispers.

Orpheus tells the truth. "I knew you were there, baby. I never doubted it for a minute."

Children yell and play in the neighbors' gardens, high-pitched giggles fizzing up into the streetlights. "You didn't know. You assumed I was there. Behind you. Like I'd always been there. Behind you. You couldn't even imagine that I might not do as I was told, that I might not be where you wanted me to be, the moment you wanted it. That was my place, and you assumed I would be in it. What in your life has ever gone any way other than as you wished it?" She glances toward the house, toward the demo still sitting where Sisyphus left it. "And now you have what you want from me. What you always wanted. I am no longer necessary. And yet. I am still here."

Her hand settles down on the leftmost puppy. Cerberus wears three weighted coats, to help with his anxiety. Maybe Orpheus should have gotten her one. He thinks of that now, and dwells on it long enough that there's no easy way back into the conversation, and Orpheus just tells her to shut the lights off before she goes to bed.

Orpheus and Eurydice step blinking into a summer's day. The blue of the sky throbs in their eyes. He takes her into his arms and swings her around. *You're back, you're back, and it'll all be as it was, you'll see. I saved you. I did it. Aren't you happy? Baby? Put your arms around me. Don't you want to?*

Orpheus walks down the porch steps of his house. It is dusk, and he can smell everyone's dinner. He can see all their lights, the illuminated windows of their worlds. Owls are heading out to hunt. Business on the west coast closes in an hour.

Orpheus stops on the stair. For a moment, just a moment, he thinks that perhaps she is there. Asking him not to go. Eurydice as she always was, adoration in human form, the way he remembers her. The way she should have been. Maybe it will all be all right, and this was just the last test, the last barrier between life and death.

His phone buzzes in his pocket. He knows without looking that it's his maenad, warm and rosy and waiting.

Orpheus turns around on the staircase. For old time's sake.

Eurydice stands in the window, watching. Acheron and Phlegethon kiss her cheeks, lay their heads on her shoulders. She smiles with such tenderness, but not for him. She shuts her eyes in their embrace.

Orpheus straightens his shoulders. He turns away. He has places to be. A maenad. A record. He has a life. He has a legend to become. He knows it's all there, just waiting for him.

Behind him, asphodel devours the house whole.

FROST'S BOY

PH LEE

I have heard it on the rumors that when the tale-spinner's guild gathers in their secret places, a full half of them are sworn to never tell the truth, and the other half to never tell a lie, even if it mean their life. Being one of that trade myself, I can tell you that that's more or less the shape of it, and I tell you so that you will know that this tale is true, just as it happened and just as it was told to, for I am one of the ones sworn to the truth.

The name I'm called is Dusty Boots, I come from the valley of Erwhile, and I am in love with a girl that I can never have. The story I tell you now happened right near to us, in a place no more than a walk away, although where exactly I cannot say, for the village where it happened is many years lost to frost and forest and no one alive today quite knows exactly where it stood.

Once upon a time, in that place right near to us, there lived a man and a woman, together as man and wife, though, like most peasants, no one had married them nor given them any word. It was simply that their love for each other was stronger even than their poverty. Not that there are wealthy men in these lands—how could there be wealthy men where winter sleeps an inch below the earth?—but this man and this woman had so few stores that it was only their love for each other that kept them warm through the long dark. And so, of course, the woman became pregnant.

As poor as they were, her pregnancy was merely a cause for more sorrow. How could they possibly keep a child, when they could scarcely keep themselves?

Still, somehow, they managed to scrape by three seasons, and the man was strong and the woman was stronger, and she birthed to him a son, healthy and so beautiful that to look upon him was to love him, and in that moment in both their hearts they knew that they could not give him up for dead. But the heart's will and the world's will are often apart, and as time wore on a year, it was plain that they could not keep the boy. So, in the dark of the night one year after their son was born, the man awoke in the middle of the night and, slipping away from his sleeping wife, he took their only child, that beautiful boy one year old, and stole him out into the forest to do what had to be done.

He had intended to smash his son's head with a rock, to spare him the pain of the cold, but, as he laid the sleeping child down in the nook of a tree, he looked on his beautiful face and could not bring himself to do it. Instead, he kissed his son one last time, held him for a little too long, and left him to die in the hollow of an old tree. He cried as he walked back to his wife, and I am told that his tears froze on the ground where they fell. If you were foolish enough to brave the woods tonight, you might see them still.

I do not know what became of that man, or his wife, or the love between them. Perhaps their circumstances bettered, and they had many more children, although surely none as beautiful as their first. Perhaps they starved to death that very winter. Perhaps that unspoken murder sat between, festering at their love until it turned to hatred, and they never spoke again until they died. I do not know. Every story tells it differently, so how am I to know the truth?

It is better to speak of what I do know of, for I do know what happened to that child as he lay there in the cold and the dark in the hollow of an old tree in the depths of the forest and the winter. It's like this: As he lay there in the snow, sleeping slowly, two ravens came and perched above him.

"Ah," said the first, "another child has been left to die in the dark! See how his eyes are innocent—think how soothing they will be. And his skin is soft—think how luscious it will be. Truly he will make a feast for us! Let's not wait until he's hard and frozen and dead. Damn our oaths to scavenging, let us eat him alive!"

But the second raven merely shook her head. "You can start if you like, my husband," she said, "but look at the child! See how beautiful he is! I cannot bear to harm such beauty. I will not stop you from eating him yourself, but I must look away, or my heart will surely break."

"No, you are right," said the first raven after some consideration, "I cannot bear to harm him, either. Let us go and seek some less perfect carrion, then, wife, for if we do not eat in this long night then surely we shall die."

And, with that, the ravens flew off.

Time passed, as it always does, and the night grew deeper and darker as the young boy slept where his father had abandoned him. In time, two wolves padded up through the snow and stood on either side of the child's hollow.

"Ah," said the first, "another child has been left to die in the dark. See how his cheeks beam so brightly—think of how succulent they will be. See how his heart beats so softly—we will each take one half of it and savor its purity. Truly he will make a feast for us! Let's not wait another moment but leap on him and tear him limb from limb, spilling man's red blood across the snow."

But the second wolf sadly shook her head. "You can start if you like, my husband," she said, "but look at the child! See how beautiful he is! I cannot bear to harm such beauty. I will not stop you from your dinner, but I must run away, for if I even hear a single cry from those lips, my heart will surely break."

"No, you are right," said the first wolf after some consideration, "I cannot bear to harm him, either. Let us go and seek some less perfect prey, then, wife, for if we do not eat in this long night then surely we shall die."

And, with that, the wolves padded off.

Time passed, as it does, and the night grew deeper and darker and colder. Slowly, the frost crept up from its resting place an inch beneath the earth, higher and higher until it covered the roots of the trees, until it covered the edges of the bark, until it crept into the depths of the child's body, chilling him, slowing him, turning his flesh first blue then hard. But, just as the frost was about to claim him entirely, the boy stirred in his sleep and spoke. "Dada . . ." he said, his first word, and the words were so innocent and perfect that even the frost took pause.

"Well," said Frost to itself, "well." It was not used to feelings, and it did not know what to make of them. "It seems I cannot bring myself to kill this boy. See how beautiful he is! No, it is decided. I cannot kill him."

And, with that, Frost made its way off to do its other duties in the long night. But, unused to thoughts, it kept pondering the boy. "What if, in my absence, some other beast or peril were to beset the boy and kill him? What if my long-fingered mother were to find him? Then, surely, all would be lost, that beauty would be broken, just as if I killed him myself. No, there must be some other way."

And Frost thought and thought to itself, thought as it froze through the ponds, thought as it drove through the ramshackle homes and killed those unprepared, thought as it snapped bowls and troughs that had been left in the open. And, in time, it returned to the boy and hung itself around him, staring at his sleeping beauty. "Nothing for it," thought Frost to itself, and shook the boy's shoulder gently until he woke.

"Boy," said Frost, speaking in the oldest manner, so that even as a child one year old he could understand, "you cannot go back home. Your father and your mother have abandoned you to die by my hand.

"And do not think that I would not have done it, boy. I am cold and cruel and have killed a million children left to my devices. It is simply that each winter is longer, each cold more pressing, and each year my work grows greater. I will need a boy to prentice my profession, for soon there will be altogether too much work for me alone. So, boy, what say you? Come and be my apprentice, or stay and die by the thousand perils of the forest."

Even though he was half-asleep and dreaming, the child smiled, and Frost took that as good as a yes, and carried the boy off to his home an inch beneath the earth.

* * *

Years passed, and though Frost's talents were not given to raising children, it brought up the boy as best it could, and taught him the trade just like he'd been Frost's own. Each year, the boy grew up more beautiful, but each year, his heart grew colder, for he knew no warm love from no mother and no father. The only thing he loved was Frost, and the love of Frost does nothing to warm a human heart. Each winter, he helped his adopted father with the work, freezing ponds, breaking branches, waking up the storms that roll from the north to rain down their hail crack-crack against the roofs. And each winter the boy's heart grew colder, until it was as cold as ice, then colder still.

For Frost to have a cold heart, for winter to have cold depths, for the dark to be cold as it lurks behind the sun, that is neither kind nor wicked. But Frost's Boy, he was not like the frost, or the winter, or the dark. He was a man, or at least was a boy, and as a boy his cold heart was wicked to the core, wickeder than any man's has ever been, almost as wicked as his long-fingered grandmother's.

It was because his heart was wicked that his favorite work of all the winter was freezing the hearts of pretty girls. At first, he did it just as his father did, catching them unawares in the early dark, or when their parents had left a chink in their wall against frost's siege. He would sneak in at night, kiss them right on the lips, and watch as the chills took them and their skin turned cold and hard. How he loved to watch them die by his cold! But he would not stay to hear the shrieks and cries of their mothers, as they discovered their cold, dead daughters, for there was much work to do in the winter, and he could not linger long, even for work he loved.

But, as time passed and he came to understand that he was beautiful, he began to freeze girls' hearts with other methods. He would chase after a girl, show her his beauty, hear her confessions of love before he kissed her, froze her heart with his chill, and left her dead where she stood. He would break her heart, and freeze her tears to her face with his breath, touch her breast and freeze her heart with his fingers. He loved to freeze those pretty girls so much that he would venture out in the summer, snuck away from Frost's rest beneath the earth, and catch them in the woods where they went to gather berries and medicines, or even as they played with each other right outside their house.

Once, he found a girl gathering firewood, deeper in the woods than she should have been. He snuck up behind her and breathed his cold breath on her neck, and though she thought it was just the wind from the earth she turned to look and caught his gorgeous eyes. When she looked at him, and saw how beautiful he truly was—how graceful, how manly, and how cold—she gasped, dropped her firewood, and very nearly fainted.

"Do you think I am beautiful?" he asked her, a glint in his eye for he already knew the answer.

The girl, terrified and fascinated and overwhelmed, could not even speak. She simply held her hands to her breast and nodded, staring deep into his eyes. He smiled, and for all the world was twice as beautiful as he had been before. He took a step in towards her, and almost touched her.

"And do you love me?" he asked, with the same cold smile.

Her eyes widened, and tears began to form at the edge of eyes. She still did not speak, but shook her head.

He jumped back, shocked and confused. "What?!" he demanded. "Am I not the most beautiful boy that you have ever seen? How could you not love me?"

The young girl looked down, away from his eyes, and finally found her voice. "It is not that you are not beautiful," she said, "for truly you are gorgeous, and I would have you for my lover if it were not that I know you. My gran told me about you. You are Frost's Boy, who comes for pretty girls to freeze their hearts, and to love you is, in that same instant, to die by your cold kiss." And, with that, she ran as swiftly as she could back towards her father's house, which was snug and proof against the cold.

But, fast as she could run, the boy had learned his speed from Frost and wind. He caught up with her with ease and took her hand in his.

"It isn't like that!" he lied as he looked into her eyes. "I love you! I loved you from the moment I first saw you." And, with that, she was lost. He leaned towards his, kissed her right on the lips, and she froze plain dead.

Another time he came across a girl in a clearing, gathering the last flowers of summer for the festivals, and came up behind her and breathed his cold breath across her neck. She jumped, looked around, saw his face, and fell in love.

"Do you think that I am beautiful?" he asked her, a glint in his eye for he already knew the answer.

The girl smiled, and threw her bundles of flowers up into the air. As petals rained down around them, she said "Yes, you are more beautiful than any of my flowers."

He smiled, and for all the world was twice as beautiful as he had been before. He took a step in towards her, and almost touched her.

"And do you love me?" he asked, with the same cold smile.

"Yes," she said true, "yes, I loved you from before I saw you."

He smiled wider, and stepped in to kiss her, but she held out her arms and kept him at bay. "I do not want you to think," she said, "that I am taken in by your ruse. I know who you are."

He took her hands in his, and asked, "If you know who I am, why do you not flee from the sight of me, for your know that my kiss will freeze your heart."

The girl smiled a mysterious smile. "Yes, you're Frost's Boy, and it's just as my gran told it to me. But I know the rest of your story, and how you have come to be so cold. How you have grown without the warmth of a single loving human heart. I do not fear you."

The boy was startled, but did not lose his grip on her hands. "And why is that?"

"Because I love you," the girl declared, "I love you more than any girl has ever loved any boy ever in the world! I loved you since I first heard your sad story, and with my warm love I will melt your icy heart, 'til your heart is warm and beats from its own emotion."

"Can you save me from Frost?" asked the boy, and truly grinned from hope. He let go her hands, and embraced her, and she embraced him. For hours, they stood like that, but though her love of him was warm and hot, and greater love than any girl has ever had for any boy, the cold in his heart was older than her, older than her grandmother who told her of him, older than the village where she lived, and her love was not endless and thick and hard like the winter that sleeps beneath the earth, and in time her skin hardened, and her heart froze, and she died just like that. He left her in that field, no warmer than he had been before, and laughed with the chill wind at her foolishness.

Yet another time, though, he came across a girl out on a frozen pond, fishing with hook and line for a little food. He blew across the ice behind her, scattering shards, and breathed right across her neck. She turned around, gasped, and nearly dropped her line as she saw his brilliant clear eyes.

"Hello," she said quickly, "I didn't hear you coming."

"Hello," he said in return, and then, "do you think I'm beautiful?"

"Of course I do," said the girl as she pulled in her line, though she did not look at him as she spoke. "It's clearly plain to see that you're the most beautiful boy that has ever walked this earth."

He stepped in towards her and helped her wind the line. "Then do you love me?"

"Of course I do," she said, still looking away from him. "How could I not love a boy as beautiful as you?" But as he leaned in to kiss her, she ducked away.

"No," she said as she held him away, "not yet."

"But why?" he said. "If you love me, why won't you let me kiss you?"

"Well," she said, as she stood and began to walk back across the ice, "surely as you are so beautiful, and surely you are, and surely as I do love you, and surely I do, you are surely the boy I've heard tell of, Frost's Boy, whose kiss is frozen death."

"I won't deny," he said, "but surely you know it's foolish to resist me."

"Just so!" replied the girl. "If I were to run, or try to turn away, then like the first girl you'd catch me and I'd love you just the same as if I'd never run at all. It is no good for me to run away."

"Yes," he said, "it's just like that. But still you put me off. Surely it will come to nothing in the end."

"It's true," she said, "and I know that, though I love you with all my heart, it will not be enough to make up for your impenetrable cold, and like the second girl I will die frozen in your arms."

"Yes," he said, "it's just like that. But still you put me off. Surely it will come to nothing in the end. What can you hope to do?"

"Well," said the girl, "in truth I cannot hope to live, nor do I hope to live, for once I have seen your face I know that I can have no happiness to but kiss you, and to love you, and to have you as my own. I know I will die frozen in your arms, and as far as I am concerned, the sooner it comes the better."

"Then why do you still put me off?" he asked, circling around her and trying to catch her eye.

"It's that I am a good girl," she said, looking away, "raised honest and pure. I will not so much as kiss a boy without my father's word, and so I'll take you back to meet him, and once he has given his word, then you can kiss me, and I will die glad to have had you for that one moment as my own."

The boy laughed and laughed, but still he followed her to her father's little cottage on the edge of the lake. The girl told Frost's Boy to wait outside, then went inside and told her father that a boy had come to eat supper with them and to ask her hand in marriage.

Her father was overjoyed because, truth be told, his daughter was not particularly pretty. That is, pretty to be sure, but their house by the lake was far away from the village square, and she wasn't pretty enough that her fame had reached the other families to bring court for her.

He went to tell his wife and share his joy with her. "Wife," he said, "our daughter has come with the most wonderful news. Finally a boy has come to marry our daughter. Is it not excellent?"

"No, husband," said his wife, who was cleverer than her husband by three times or more, "for that is no ordinary boy outside, but Frost's Boy, who freezes the hearts of girls everywhere, and he has not come to marry our daughter, but to kill her."

Her husband blanched. "Well, I must drive him away with such strength that he never returns."

His wife, who was more clever than her husband by three times or more, shook her head sadly. "No, my husband, it is too late for that. It is plain to see that our girl is already in love with him. See how she stares out the window and sighs at him, her eyes wide with affection, her cheeks flushed with desire, even when she knows that he will be the death of her! No, now is not a time for force, but for wits. We must do exactly as I say, or our daughter will be lost forever."

"Wife," said the husband, "you have always been cleverer that me by three times or more. So if you have a plan, and I'm sure you do, you need only tell me my own part of it, and I shall do it the very best I can, because I love our daughter more even than myself, and if there is a way yet to save her I will stop at nothing until it is."

"Go on, and tell our daughter that she should come to the hearth and cook her wedding feast. Then go outside and find work to occupy the hands of our would-be son-in-law. Have him chop wood for the fire, have him draw water from the deep well, have him do what you would have him do, but do not ask him inside, even for a moment's rest, until every last bit of the meal is prepared."

"I will do as you ask as best I can, my clever wife," her husband said, and with a kiss on her cheek he went off to see Frost's Boy. He was trembling with fear and doubt, but his love of his daughter and his faith in his wife gave him courage, so he went out into the cold.

Now that she was alone with her daughter, the clever woman took her daughter into her arms. "Now, my daughter," she said, "we must cook your wedding feast together, and quickly, for I fear your father will not earn us as much time as we would like. As we cook, you must do everything exactly as I say, or else surely you shall be dead by your love's cold kiss." The girl nodded, crying a little, for although she coveted her love more than her life, it was not that she had no care for her life at all.

"No tears," said her mother, wiping them away, "no tears while we are cooking. Every part of the meal we make, we must think only of the love between us, your love for your father, our love for this home we have made in these dark cold lands where winter sleeps an inch beneath the earth."

As they cooked, and cook they did, the girl's father met his daughter's love outside the house. He was still standing there, beautiful as ever, a thin and impatient smile on his face, still laughing to himself at this girl's strange and novel foolishness.

"Well," said the girl's father, his voice quavering a bit in fear at the strange birth before him, "you seem like enough." He stood at arm's length from the boy, afraid to touch him.

"You know who I am." said the boy. "And you know that I will be the death of your daughter as soon as our lips touch. You know that nothing in this world will keep her from me, now that she has seen my eyes. Why do you persist in foolishness and prolong your grief?"

On hearing the boy's words, the man grew angry, and reared back his fist to hit him. But, before he struck, he remembered his wife's words, and that no strength would save their daughter, and so he stayed his hand, shrugged his shoulders, and said the rest of the words he'd lined up in his head. "Well, before the dinner gets made, there's some work to be done, and if you could help me with the work, it'll go that much faster."

When he heard that, the boy laughed like the wind in the darkness, stretched long across the narrow trees, and if you heard it even now it would chill you to the bone. "Well then," he said to the man, "let's go and see what work you've set for me to do." Then he stepped aside, to follow the man where he might take him.

The man, still shaking a bit, though whether from the cold or from fear or from anger he could not be certain, led the boy behind their little house, to where the wood had been piled high under the back eaves. "Well," said the man, "the first thing we must do is split wood for the cooking fires. If tonight is to be your wedding feast we must burn the fires high, for we must eat until we can eat no more." With that, he lifted up an axe and, handing it to the boy, said "Let's see how you handle yourself with this axe."

The boy smiled his thin smile and did not take the axe. "What need do I have of the tools of man? I am the son of Frost, himself the son of Winter out of Bone. I need no axe to split a tree or two." And, with that, he walked up to where the wood was piled, laid his hand on it, and with a great crack the wood blew itself apart into shards and splinters and boards. The man leapt at the sound, and covered his ears and cursed his deafness while the boy laughed and laughed and laughed until he did not stop.

When the man finally took his hands from his ears, the boy turned to him and spoke. "Well, old man," he said, although in truth the man was not very old at all, and the boy much older, "do you have any other tasks left for me? I am eager for my wedding night."

"Well," said the man as he recovered his hearing and his wits, "well," and could not think of what to say. But then he remembered what his wife had said, that he must keep this boy busy until the wedding feast was made. "Well done, my son-to-be, but there is more work to be done. Next, we must draw water from the deep well, water to toast your happiness, for we are poor folk without a coin for wine."

The boy laughed, and smiled his smile, and followed the man to the well.

The man led the boy to his deep well, a well so deep that even at summer's noon you could not see the bottom of it, that ran with the sound of an underground river and gave water even in the dead of winter. He handed the boy the bucket and rope and said, "Best to start soon, for the drawing will take a while—the well is deep and its water heavy."

The boy simply smiled and did not take the bucket. "What need do I have of the tools of man? I am the son of Frost, and in my father's house beneath the earth my playmates were the waters and the worms. I have no need of a bucket to draw a draught of water." And, with that, he walked up to the well and called into it softly, with the sweet words of his childhood, speaking in the oldest manner that his father used with him, and all of a sudden a great rushing sound came up from the well, and a fountain of water came up from it, and the boy was bathed in cold, clean water from the earth. The man leapt at the sight, and cowered away from the water and swore aloud while the boy played with the water, and laughed and laughed and laughed until he did not stop.

When the waters finally subsided, leaving the boy clean and dry, he turned to the man and spoke. "Well, old man," he said, although in truth the man was not very old at all, and the boy much older, "do you have any other tasks left for me? I am eager for my wedding night."

The man stood there for a moment, agape at the spelling that he had just witnessed. When he recovered his wits, he tried to recall what his wife, who was cleverer than him by three times or more, had told him to do next. But, try as he might, he could not recall it, for in truth she had not said anything more to him. Clever as she was, how could she have anticipated the prodigy of Frost's Boy?

The man hemmed and hawed and stilled and stalled until the boy grew impatient, and his lenient smile turn colder and darker until it was not a smile at all. Finally, he lost his patience entirely. "Out with it, old man!" he shouted. "Or else I shall be back at your house before you breathe again and claim your daughter as my own by force and by guile."

Finally, though more out of desperation than cleverness, the man hit upon another task. "Well done, my son-to-be," he said, "but there is more work to be done before the feast. Next, we must slaughter one of the pigs, for we must have fresh meat for a wedding feast, for the wedding of our only daughter is not a time to spare a single thing, and we must eat until we can eat no more." And, with that, the man led the boy to where they kept their hogs and, pressing a knife into his hand, said, "Take care with the knife, for I've just sharpened it the other day."

The boy scoffed, and threw the knife into the earth. "What need have I of the tools of man? I have labored long winters beside the coldest winds, comrades with the night, and done the work of the gripping hunger in this tall dark and in all that work, the killing is the work that I love the best. I have killed ten thousand in my time, and in my time to come I shall kill ten thousand more. Why should I need a knife to kill a simple pig?" And, with that, he walked over to where the hogs huddled together in the straw and, laying his hand upon the largest one, froze it dead.

When the pig was cold and dead, he turned back to the man and spoke. "Well, old man," he said, although in truth the man was not very old at all, "do you have any other tasks left for me? I am eager for my wedding night." He grinned, for he knew the man would not set another task before him.

But now the man laughed, a single great guffaw from deep in his chest. He smiled right back at the boy and took up the knife from floor and pressed it into the puzzled boy's cold hand. "The slaughter that men do," he explained, "is much more than simply killing. After the killing comes the butchery, and I'd imagine that you've made it ten times harder on yourself with whatever strange works you've done to that poor hog. For it'll be cold and frozen guts that you'll be cleaning."

Now the boy knew he had been tricked, and his eyes flashed with anger. He almost killed the man where he stood, killed him dead with a glance and walked out into the snow never to speak another human word again. But, then his mind thought of the girl that waited for him in the house, the pretty girl that he could kill, and he knew that if he lost this chance, if even one girl was the better of his beauty, it would haunt him for the rest of time. So instead he set to the cold and dirty work of cleaning the pig.

When Frost's Boy was done with his long work, he was covered in blood and the bloody guts of the pig he had frozen and drenched in the strange sweat of his own labor. For while none would say his father's work was easy, such world's work is done just as it is done, as we breathe or as we cry, effortless and smooth without toil nor tire. The work of man, though, is the work of purpose, and such work of doing what's easiest undone was strange to him. So when he was done rooting out the dead pig's guts, he collapsed from the exhaustion. And when the boy finally stood once more, the man offered out his hand and spoke to him for the first time without fear.

"Well, boy, I'll say it was the worst butchering that I'd ever seen, but that wouldn't do it rightmost, so we'd best just leave it all unspoken. But it seems you've got some spirit in your frosty little heart, for when I handed you a knife the second time I'd answer you would have stalked into the long night and never spoke a human word again. You've done it, for better or for ill, and I'll say a second time tonight I see you're like enough, and this second time you'll have the meaning of it, too."

The boy had thought that he would have been too tired for anger, but at the man's words he found it welling up inside of him like blood from fresh cut. He spat into the man's hand and it crackled in air and struck, bruising like a stone. "You ignorant fool!" he screamed at the man. "You ignorant moribund fool! Don't you see what's in front of your eyes? Don't you hear what's spoken to your ears? I have come not to glorify your hold, but to destroy it! When I have your daughter as my bride, I will not love her, I will not hold her, and there will be no posterity for your line. My first kiss is death for her, death for you, death for your house. I am not your hopeful fluttering suitor; I am the son of Frost, and I have done the work of winter for longer than the memory of man. Do not give me your welcomes but guard your house against my frozen heart that brings nothing but its ruin!"

With that, the man stopped laughing. He lifted up the knife from the place the tired boy had dropped it, and began to clean it. "We'd best be back soon," he said at last, without looking up. "Your wedding will be waiting."

While the men had done their work outdoors, the girl and her mother were hard at cooking the wedding feast. When boy and man crossed the door, they found the table piled high with all manner of foods: soup from salmon and red cabbage, stew with dumplings from beets and carrots and onions and old beef, hot breads in all ten types, pies and puddings and stuffings and smells like the boy had never known before in his cold and quiet home an inch beneath the earth. The heat of the hearth and the sense of the smells and the empty hole of his just-passed anger crashed against his frozen heart, and he stumbled a bit as he stepped to the table.

When the girl saw her love stumble she leapt to his side to hold him, but her mother held her back. "Remember what I told you," she said to the girl, although in all the times I've heard this story they've never spoken plainly what that was, "and you must do it just so or your love will only last a night." And, though the girl was eager for even the slightest touch of her love's cold skin, she was a good girl, raised honest and pure, and so she heeded what her mother had told her, and instead of any touch she pulled out a chair, and asked him to sit at the head of the table, closest to the hearth and furthest from the door.

Her mother, meanwhile, greeted her husband, and took from him the frozen pork. As soon as she touched the icy meat, she knew at once what had happened, and she smiled at her husband and praised his heart. "Truly," she said, "I would not have even thought of it myself." He smiled at this, for he knew that his wife was cleverer than him by three times or more, but she went on with barely a pause. "But now is not the time for praises, for we must cook this meat before these courses are finished, or our pretty daughter will yet be lost to us all."

With her love so seated in the place of honor, the girl wanted nothing more than to ignore her mother's warnings, stop her work, and stare at that beautiful boy's face and kiss him until they both should die. But she clung to her obedience, and got from the hearth a boiling pot of soup, made with salmon, red cabbage, and other clever means known to her mother for such circumstances. She served up the soup in a bowl of old wood, so hot that it still churned as she laid it before him, and gave to him a new copper spoon. "Here is the first of our wedding feast," she told him, "made by my own art so you might know my skills, made by my own hands so you might know my love, and both so as you might welcome me as wife. Eat it up now, and tell me what suffices."

The soup smelled of love and red fish in the winter and the fire that raged behind him, but as the boy dipped his spoon to it and brought it succulent to his lips it began to change. For hot as the still boiling soup was, the cold of Frost's love was colder, and by the time he had lifted to the spoon to his mouth the soup had cracked and crackled and frozen solid. Still, he chewed it deliberately, and the girl heard the slow crunch as his teeth ground the ice into snow. "It is not the flavor that I mind," he said after a time, "but it is cooked a bit tough." Nevertheless, he finished the bowl that she had set before him, taking bite after bite all frozen by his cold and tired heart.

No sooner had he finished the bowl than she served up on a cracked clay plate the first five hot breads—made with meats and what spring vegetables remain. "Here is the second of our wedding feast," she told him, "made by my own art so you might know my skills, made by my own hands so you might know my love, and both so as you might welcome me as wife. Eat it up now, and tell me what suffices."

The breads smelled of home and butter and wheat left long in drying, yet even as the boy lifted them up to his lips, the fat on them curled and congealed at the chill of his blood. And as he bit into the hot breads, even the puff of steam held within them froze as ice around his lips, for hot as that steam was, the cold of Frost's love was colder. Still, he chewed and swallowed each of the breads in turn, and the girl heard the crackle of the freezing steam within his mouth. "It is not the flavor that I mind," he said after a time, "but it is cooked a bit dry." Nevertheless, he finished the plate that she had set before him, each bread after bread all ruined by his cold and tired heart.

And so it went from one dish to another, and although there are those that tell the detail of every course I will not worry you with them. In truth, there is not much difference from one bit to the next and I find the whole accounting of no merit at all. So let us simply say that that she set dish after dish before him, exactly in the manner appointed by custom, and he ate and ate and ate all manner of new things that he had never had before, though each was ruined a different way by the cold within his blood, until at last the woman and her husband came out with great slices of the pork that they had roasted, that he had slaughtered by his own beautiful hand.

The mother put great cuts of the meat before him—all flesh and fat and neither bone nor gristle—and spoke as she did so, just as her daughter did and as custom demanded, for clever as she was she could find no better words to say. "Here is the last of your wedding feast," she told him, "that pork was slaughtered out of this home's stock, but by your foreign hand, and if you find it good, then it shall be the last of things and we will call all such matters settled, and ours yours, and yours ours, until nothing shall end it, for the rest of all our days. Eat it up now, and say if it suffices."

The pork sizzled with fat and hot fire, and although he was by now quite stuffed, it was quick and eager that the boy lifted it to his mouth and bit it. The taste was heat and blood and death and all such other works of men in winter, his own labor and this home earth, the warm hearth dug against the cold, and the smooth flavor of fat, and he knew that by his own hand it was done and it was good. And the girl, who all along had had no scrap, no bite for her own (though she did not mind it for her lovesickness), watched as the hot fat ran down his face, not chilling nor cooling nor whitening, but running smooth and clear in its own heat. And she knew at once—for she was a good girl, raised honest and pure, and remembered her mother's word just as it was spoken— and because she was a good girl she knew that the curse on the boy had been broken, that the ice around his heart had melted, and all at once she threw herself on him and embraced him and kissed him with all the strength that her longing would muster.

Her love was true. When she kissed Frost's Boy, in that first of many, his heart had already melted, and he was no longer Frost's Boy at all. She did not freeze nor die at the touch of him, and instead they were just a boy and a girl and loved each other in simple ways accordingly. And though it was spring before they could be given a word for their marriage, from that night on they lived as husband and wife, ordinary except for their beauty and their honesty.

I am told, and it must be true, that they lived happily and together for that and all the rest of their days. I am told that he never raised a hand to her in anger or in fear; I am told that he never had a harsh word for her, and that she never gave him cause for harshness; I am told that he never took their son out into the great drifts of forest snow and shoved his face into it, over and over, laughing all the while, punishing him for not being as beautiful as his father, until the boy stopped shaking and turned blue; I am told that she never found their son holding the frozen body of their cat, even in the high heat of a summer long-day, looking at that animal he loved and crying and then looking up at her and smiling; that he never came back late in the winter's long night, not saying where he'd been, with his skin cold and his breathe icicles, and the neighbor's daughter dead the next morning beneath the ice of the old pond; that he never froze the breath in her mouth even as she slept, just so he could watch and laugh as she struggled and choked and gasped for life; that he never got cold and angry, so angry that he woke her up in the morning with both of their children crying in front of her and asked her which one she loved more, because that's the one he would kill for whatever slight he had imagined; that she never took her children, wrapped in their winter coats even in the summer, to flee in the middle of the short summer night; that the winds and the ravens never saw them, never told him where they were, never drew him to them, seething with an anger so cold it froze the air; that she never wrapped herself with her daughter in every blanket and shuddered her to life; that she never had to do it over and over, every time he was angry, every time one of them had drawn his notice, or his gaze.

I am told that none of those things ever happened, and it must be true because, after all, this is a story. How can stories end but with a "happily ever after"?

THE TALE OF JAJA AND CANTI

TOBI OGUNDIRAN

I: THE END, ALMOST.

Seated on the balcony of the house across the street is a man. He is slumped in his chair and has remained unmoving for several hours. The tattered frays of his agbada spreads about his person like an old sail-cloth, snapping in the wind. His equally tattered hat is positioned on his head such that you cannot see his face. He has maintained this position for nigh on a day (which is much, much longer than you think).

If you think him dead, then you'll be wrong; if you think him alive, well . . .

Look closely.

You may find that the skin of his hand is the texture of old wood, the shriveled grains of a tree long exposed to the elements. You may find that the wrinkles on his face are unmoving, the tight curls of his beard a little too solid, the globes of his eyes a little too elliptical. Don't be alarmed, it is exactly as you think: he is made of wood.

After some five hundred-odd years of roaming the treacherous terrain of the Midworld, his journey has led him here. Now. Sprawled on that balcony as unmoving as a tree.

Waiting.

II: THE YEARS BEFORE, BEFORE.

Jaja's first memory is of a weeping, wizened face.

"Papa?" He stretches to touch his Papa, and a thin wooden hand appears in his line of vision.

"Oh," Papa gasps, tears streaming down his cheeks even as he smiles. "Oh, bless the stars!" As Papa sweeps him off the table into a hug, Jaja sees the hem of a dress vanish as the shop door clatters shut. He glimpses the impression of a woman through the dusty shop windows.

This is the first he sees of the woman who gave him life. His mother.

The act of procreation was a deceptively simple thing: Papa carved him from the finest wood, and the woman he calls mother filled him with life.

"Who is she?" Jaja asks Papa several times in the intervening years. It is from Papa he learns her first name: Moremi.

"Moremi?"

"Yes, my boy," says Papa, filing the wood that will become the hand of a new toy. Jaja wonders vaguely if that is how he was assembled. He *knows* that that is how he was assembled.

"I met her at the edge of town, on my way to the forest to . . ." He gazes shiftily at Jaja. "Life had not been very good to me, you see. Once, I had been wealthy, the most renowned toymaker in all the land, but soon people forgot about me, and the shop became as silent as a tomb, quieter still when my wife died. So, I decided to walk into the forest, walk until I could walk no more.

"It was hard to notice her at first, yes, because her skin was the dark of midnight, but her hair, oh . . . it was like light trapped in locks!" His eyes glaze with the sheen of reminiscence. "There was something about her that made me forget my troubles. She said, 'That is a fine boy you have there, sir.' And that is when I realized I had been cradling you in the pit of my arm. My wife and I, we never could have children, see. So, I made you for her, the child she could never have. When she died, you were the only thing to remind me of her.

"This woman, she knew why I was going into the forest. She knew what I intended to do. So, she took my hand, and led me back here to the shop where she commanded me to fix you up. I gave you new hinges and oiled the rot of your hand. And she watched me night and day as I worked. And when I screwed on your last finger she wept."

"She wept?"

"Yes."

"Why?"

"She must have seen what a beautiful boy you are," says Papa, "Weeping, she took you and cradled you to her breast like a newborn babe, singing a song as old as time. When she placed you on the table, you were . . . you." Papa wipes his eyes. "Moremi, she gave me purpose. She made me want to live again. She gave me you. And she did not even wait for me to thank her."

The years pass and Jaja doesn't age. But he doesn't worry much about it; he knows he's not an ordinary boy.

Still, boys will be boys and in his free time he makes mischief. With friends from down the street he terrorizes the neighborhood with the sweet abandon of childhood.

And he watches his friends go gangly, sprouting like beanstalks from childhood and into youth. And they in turn look at him with fresh eyes, the scales of innocence lifted, as they realize that he is different.

They turn on him. With sticks and stones and hurtful words, he is reminded that he is other.

He weeps.

The shop is his refuge: his endless youth is given to toil; to filing wood and oiling hinges, to air-drying wood just right, to wiping it down with vinegar and scrubbing the uneven surfaces with glasspaper, to oiling with beeswax and lacquering for durability.

Papa does not have much, but he cares for him. Jaja knows what it is to love and be loved. And he loves that old man right until the very end.

Jaja stands long at the fresh mound of Papa's grave, wondering who will love him now that Papa is gone.

That is the moment he decides to find his mother.

That is also the moment he starts to age.

III: THE SEARCH.

Jaja travels the world in search of his mother.

All he has is a description of her and the vague memory of a song. When he tries to sing it to people, all that comes out is a tortured clack, like the rattling of wooden shutters. He walks farther than he's ever walked in his life, and then some. He passes through sentient forests and wades through thrashing waters. And when he can wade no more, he boards a passenger ship whose captain is missing a nose.

It is from him he learns of her second name.

"The Midnight Queen," says the captain when he gives him her description.

"The Midnight Queen?"

"Oh, yah. Das what I call her. She got skin as black as a starless night, hair white as da morning sun." He chews on his pipe, squinting at the frothing waters. "Very beautiful. Me an' my old boys, we got attacked by a kraken. Damn beast tore right through da ship till we were all of us screaming for our mothers. It ate my boys, bless em, an' took a rightful chunk off my face." He taps at the hole in his face. "I was convinced I was dead. Everything went black. Next thing I know I hear singing an' da kraken is dropping me all sweet and nicely on da shore. I saw her then, very briefly. Coulda sworn I was hallucinating. But I no forget her since." Jaja looks in his eyes and thinks he can see something there: kinship. "This be one hundred years ago and I haven't aged a day since."

Jaja feels his age in the creak of his wood and the rust of his hinges. He is startled to learn how much time has passed since he set out on his quest.

The world changes around him as the years pass and he remains the only constant. He feels like the axis around which the wheel of time spins. Still he ages, slowly, painfully.

He has long left the realm of men when he hears the sounds: rhythmic pounding sounds coming from deep in the forest. He enters into a clearing with a modest hut, where he finds a young girl laboring over dinner while her mother snoozes in the corner. The sound Jaja heard is the pounding of her pestle into the mortar as she cooks a steaming meal of pounded yam.

"I am looking for a woman," he says, "you may have seen her."

"Does she have dark skin, with hair of light?"

"Yes!"

"Why, she was here only yesterday," she says, then pauses. "I think. I am never sure about time in these parts."

A flicker of hope warms Jaja's heart. "This woman, what did she do for you?"

"We had eaten our last meal weeks ago, me and my mama, and were waiting for Death to claim us when I heard a voice singing. So, I followed the voice to the glade in the forest where I found the woman. She told me I would always find fresh tubers as long as I lived."

"Do you know where she went?"

She thinks for a moment. "Yes. She took the road. It leads only to one place: Orisun."

Jaja thanks her profusely and heads down the road.

IV: ORISUN.

The city, Orisun, is filled with ethereal threads of light shimmering in the air: iridescent, like sunlight on the skin of a bubble. The single paved street is flanked by strange houses, stretching as far as he can see. As Jaja makes his way down the street, creatures stare at him through the windows. He understands that these creatures are as old as time itself. He sees people too, many of them children, doing unchildlike things. They look at him with old eyes.

He knows that she is close.

Someone seizes him from behind and Jaja turns to see a young boy with cowries for eyes.

"You're lost." It is a simple declaration.

"No," Jaja says, "I am . . . looking for someone. A woman with dark skin and hair of sunlight."

This is when he learns her third and final name: "Canti."

"Canti?"

"The singer. The one who gave you life. That is what we call her. Don't you know never to look for Canti?"

"Why not?"

He looks at Jaja like he is stupid, then *really* looks at him and nods solemnly. "You are already far down this path. What difference does it make? Go to the house at the end of the street. You will see a chair on the balcony. Sit there. Wait."

Jaja wants to thank him but he is already scuttling down the street.

V: JAJA AND CANTI.

Here is Canti, the singer. She was, before the dawn of time and will be long after. She sang the world into existence and will sing it into oblivion.

She knew the moment he decided to search for her. She followed him through whispering forests and thrashing waters to dissuade him. She has watched him sit there for a day (which you now know is much longer than you think), hoping he will go, go far away and never seek her again. Hoping he doesn't set eyes on her a second time.

She opens the door and crosses the street toward him. Jaja sits up at her approach, taking off his hat.

"Mother," he whispers.

Her heart shatters. She has been called many things: Canti, the Midnight Queen, Moremi, Oluwa, but never "mother." It is a word that carries the weight of his pain and yearning. It is a word that drips of undying, unparalleled love. It is a word she's longed to hear ever since she learned to sing.

"You shouldn't have come." Her tears betray the swell in her heart. "Twice you can look upon me."

Jaja rises, the old wood of his body groaning in protest. He reaches out a hand and touches her.

"I am Life, and Death," she says.

Hasn't he known this? Hasn't he suspected from the stiffening of his wood, from the rings that marked his years, and from the rust of his hinges, that he drew closer and closer to Death? But none of that matters because all he wants, all he's ever wanted, is to feel love if only for one last time.

She presses his head to her breast in a gesture to mirror when she sang him to life.

"Tell me you love me, mother."

She would tell of all the ways she loves him, explain the endless facets of that word and what they mean. She would tell of the dying notes of her life-song thrumming in his wood, of how in a moment of weakness she sang her desire into him. She would tell of how quickly she fled so he wouldn't see her, so he would never die. But words are not enough, have never been enough for one like her. So, she gathers him in a hug instead.

"I will sing you a lullaby. *My son.*" The tears that flow down her cheeks are hot.

"Yes," Jaja says. Skin dark as night, hair locks of light, this is the last he sees of the woman who gave him life. "I would like that . . . very much."

The world explodes with her song.

VI: THE END.

Standing on the balcony of the house across the street is a tree. It is a magnificent tree with each limb spreading out regally in the directions of the seven worlds. The leaves are tendrils of light hanging from the limbs like curtains of Dawn itself. The powerful roots are firmly entrenched in the earth of the Midworld. The tree has stood for a long time (which is longer than you think) and will stand for even longer.

Look closely.

Upon closer inspection, you may find carved into the trunk the lines of an ancient face, the delightful crinkles of old eyes, the suggestion of lips upturned in a contented smile.

Don't be alarmed, it is exactly as you think.

THE CLOUD LAKE UNICORN

KAREN RUSSELL

Before I started living on extraordinary time, I used to set my watch by Garbage Thursday. My landlady often jokes that Garbage Thursday is my Sabbath. Garbage Thursday is a secular ceremony of reckoning and forgetting. You hear the same hymn booming across our leafy block each Thursday evening: the trash bins bumping and scraping over asphalt, the rolling harmonies of a neighborhood remembering in unison that this is our weekly chance to liberate our lives of trash. Smells and peels, used neon condoms and yolky eggshells, kombucha six-packs and leopardy bananas—down the driveways they come, our open secrets straining at white Hefty bags. Clink-clink-clink, we rattle together, the Ghosts of Garbage Thursdays Past, Present, and Future.

Via neighborly telepathy, I always reach the curb at the same moment as my friend Anja. She lives in Unit B of the Cloud Lake apartment complex across the street. The name "Cloud Lake" is like a cemetery marker for the acres of water that once flowed here, drinking in the sunshine of the last century; we live in Multnomah County, Oregon, where the names of the dead can be found on condominiums and athletic clubs and doomed whimsical businesses. Anja says she can feel the lake water rippling below the pavement. What I see as early-morning mist, she says, is actually the vaporous ghost of Cloud Lake. Anja vibrates at a special frequency. She emigrated to Portland from Sarajevo, and tells me she was epigenetically altered by her childhood experience of the Bosnian War. She smokes prerolled joints and has a secondary addiction to deep-dish pizza. We have developed a kind of whistling camaraderie on Garbage Thursday, what I imagine to be a gravediggers' rapport, like something out of Shakespeare. "What's good, Mauve!" she waves to me across the street, centaured before her own overflowing bin. "Disposing of the evidence, I see!"

The curb is like the diary where we record our hungers. A diary slated for weekly erasure. The amnesiac's log of "refuse." This used to strike me as a squeamish euphemism, but now I think it's the perfect word, noun and verb, for the toxic mosaic we make in our ad hoc collaboration on Ninth Avenue. Through the upstairs window on Thursday nights, I watch a small, ephemeral mountain range building itself on either side of the street. Everything my neighbors have refused to hold on to that week—our dubious purchases and irreparable mistakes, the husks of daily life. On my pilgrimage to the curb, I've seen an imploding piano gusting sheet music like autumn leaves; an artificial lemon tree; a still-running Roomba vacuum cleaner, flipped onto its back like Gregor Samsa; family-size KFC buckets and like-new KETO LIFE diet books; a Lynchian arrangement of IKEA "Malm" dressers, the Stepford Wives of furniture; ferrous badminton rackets and mossy novelty bongs; a silver cage into which a wild crow had flown, sleekly pillaging some poor ghostbird's uneaten seeds; an unlucky vanity mirror with a lightning crack; a buck-toothed donkey piñata, mysteriously intact; red rubber galoshes, size 14, that made me picture a barefoot giant wandering into the rain; a crushed VHS machine next to a box of time, a stack of unspooling tapes; a live bait cooler from which a dead prawn hung like a pirate earring; a child's Civil War diorama; many desecrated Swiffers; deflated kiddie pools in summer; toothy shards of sleds in winter; confusingly geometric sex toys in every rainbow hue; a flattened pyre of Fisher-Price tricycles. It amazed me, each Thursday, the sheer heft of what we could not digest, the aftermath of our appetites. Anja bent to stack her pizza boxes into a cheese-and-rain-cemented tower, while I arranged my bottles into a calliope in the blue bin. Ruby and indigo and emerald glass, so pretty in the moonlight. Sometimes I wonder if it was these jeweled colors that first drew the unicorn to our street.

Strange prohibitions govern what can be said between two neighbors, even friendly neighbors, on a slab of asphalt in haunted October. Anja claims that she knew I was pregnant before I did. "But I didn't want to say anything, Mauve. You weren't showing yet, and the beginning is so touch-and-go . . ."

The tell was not subtle. Anja watched me collapse in my driveway. Last October, I was dragging the bins to the curb under a jack-o'-lantern moon, enjoying the lullaby of the little wheels, when something twisted sharply inside me. Pain dragged me to my knees. Anja ran across the street to help me up. When I could breathe again, I walked down the hill to the Cloud Lake Pharmacy. I am almost certain this "drugstore" is a mob front. They sell hemorrhoid creams and medicated lollipops and almost nothing else. Once I'd tried to buy Advil and the sheepish clerk suggested that I try the Walgreens on Holgate. But, incredibly, these likely mobsters had a single pregnancy test for sale.

"What's gotten into you, Mauve?" asked Edie that evening. "You seem nutso lately. More than usual, I mean."

Something had, indeed, gotten into me. This new life marked reality so faintly—a watery pink line on a test. I held it up to the light, watching the pale line firm and darken. What a strange way to take the temperature of one's future. It seemed impossible that a life had planted itself inside me without my awareness. I had been moody and queasy, cratered with surprising acne, but these signs seemed far too subtle to herald a baby's arrival. The mildest augurs of a stow-away. I felt the mind-body split acutely that night, studying my thirty-nine-year-old face in my landlady's mirror. The glass stared beyond me to the night sky in the window, where a full October moon bobbed over my shoulder. Trick or treat, I thought.

Next came the cold thrill of betrayal. A positive result meant I had already been pregnant for several weeks. You'd think women would be alerted at the moment of conception, receive an unmistakable sign, like the crystal ball dropping on New Year's Eve in Times Square. We should levitate above the bedsheets; our eyes should change color. Instead, my body had behaved like a surly teenager—cranking her music behind a locked door, bass shaking through the walls, none of the lyrics intelligible. Why hadn't my body trusted me enough to say, "Mauve, we are pregnant"?

A line of poetry drifted back to me then, something I'd memorized in college for a grade and managed to hold on to all this time—"And of ourselves and our origins / In ghostlier demarcations, keener sounds." To figure out the age of my possible baby, I turned to Google. Older generations felt connected to their foremothers by handwritten diaries, the ghostly wheel ruts of the Oregon Trail; I had Autofill. Millions of other women at this same phantasmal threshold, it seemed, had also typed my question into the search engine. Google directed me to a dubious oracle: the Pampers Due Date calculator. I plugged in my dates. The Pampers genie congratulated me: YOUR BABY IS SIX WEEKS OLD! The illustration of the embryo looked like a scowling pencil eraser. I waited to feel whatever you were supposed to at this juncture—something, surely. I realized that I was freezing, chilled to the bone. Perhaps I had been for some time. I went fishing in the hamper and borrowed two of Edie's sweaters, pulling one on top of the other. Out here I struggled to do a load of laundry, and yet somehow in the deep privacy of my body, an embryo had built itself a spine. It was braiding neurons into a brain. Soon it would discard the tiny comma of a tail, which was vestigial and marvelous, tadpoled between two futurelegs. With every heartbeat, I realized, a stranger grew stronger inside me. More human and more animal.

I was afraid to leave the computer screen, afraid to blink, as if I thought that by freezing myself in one location I could bring Time to heel. I would need years, I felt, to prepare for this pregnancy—an event that had already happened. For an hour or more I sat there, sick with vertigo. A belly growl broke the spell. I tossed the pregnancy test in the wastebasket; I'd been holding it midair like a demented conductor. Then I walked downstairs and began to eat. I opened jar after jar with the blank ravening of a bear. I stole and ate Edie's raw wildflower honey, which moved like liquid amber and tasted sweetly green and prehistoric—eating it, you could imagine crunching down on a trilobite. I sprinkled sea salt onto the black honey, picturing my baby's tail. Under my conscious mind, a longing began to spread—a hope I was afraid to speak out loud, even to myself. Was it possible I could be the mother of a child? A violent desire took root—and this time I felt it. I wanted to know my son or my daughter. I wanted to be this baby's mother. Later I'd remember this moment as a second conception, the one I was sober and awake to register, although no less mysterious to me. Alone in the dimming kitchen, I licked the salty honey from the spoon and continued digging, wrenching amber from the jar, waiting for my stabbing hope to dull.

When I finally called the doctor, the receptionist said breezily that they would see me in six weeks for my first ultrasound. The rider to this appointment lifted out of the silence on the line: *if you are still pregnant in six weeks' time.*

My first trimester unfolded inside green parentheses. A long-held breath, where I tried only to think about my baby in italics. *Your baby is seven weeks old today. Eight weeks. Nine weeks.* Your baby is the size of a pomegranate seed, a blueberry, a red grape. Every pregnancy chart I consulted compared the size of a human fetus to fruit. Figs, papayas, rhubarbs. As the weeks advanced, your grocery basket grew heavier: a lime at week eleven, mango at twenty-three, a cantaloupe at thirty-four, until at last there was a triumphant exit from the produce aisle. At week forty, the fruit bowl of metaphor abruptly disappeared, and the analogy sutured itself into a circle, beautifully tautological: your baby is the size of a baby.

Why fruit? In the OB-GYN waiting room with Caro, we debated this. Maybe, I said, the makers of these fetal charts loved fairy tales. Perhaps, like Milton and the Brothers Grimm, they understood the power of a seedling taking root inside a woman.

But my sister had laughed angrily and told me, "Mauve, don't give them too much credit. These charts aren't relics. Someone thinks that mothers are too dumb for the metric system."

For the past four years, I'd lived alone in the basement apartment of a house I shared with Edith Stone, a white woman in her early sixties who had grown up in Walla Walla, a lifelong smoker of Kools cigarettes and warm misanthrope. In our time as roommates I had never once heard her apologize to anyone, for anything, which I viewed as a feat worthy of a trophy. Edie was a kind of Social Olympian that way—she refused to dye her blue-gray hair and had a parroty rasp, and she said yes only when she meant yes, and no the rest of the time. She made enemies everywhere she went, including places where this seemed impossible, like the St. Stephen's Religious Bookstore where she worked. She was as dedicated to her God as to her vices. No nicotine gum for Edie. She lived with a bald-faced integrity I could barely imagine—I had grown up believing it was a woman's job to be the sugar stirring through life's lemonade, and I often said "Yes" when what I really meant was "Go away," or in the more extreme cases, "Please don't kill me."

I asked Edie to be the godmother of my baby.

"No way," she told me. "How much longer do you think I want to stick around here?"

"Do you mean 'here' as in our house? Or 'here' as in life?"

"Both," she said, after a moment's reflection. "But rent is still due on the first."

I didn't see the unicorn until the tenth week of my pregnancy.

One Garbage Thursday in November, facing a curtain of lightly falling snow, I put my boots on and pulled the compost bin through the slush—a quiver of arrows that week, amputated cherry boughs. I'd rescued one of Edie's quartz rosaries from the trash, where it had snaked around the deadest branch. Too cheap to call an arborist, Edie had taken to hanging these discounted rosaries from the ailing foliage.

Now our yard looked like an Uber driver's windshield. She bought them in bulk with her employee's discount from the St. Stephen's Religious Bookstore; she left a lot to God's care, and sometimes I had to step in for God with the pruning shears. At the curb, I stopped to catch my breath and stared up our driveway in time to see a feral creature lifting its pale skull from Anja's garbage. A single antler speared out of the middle of its brow. A deer, I thought at first, squinting through the fog. I had never seen a deer on Ninth Avenue before—certainly not in the dusk light of November, a blue hour when the porch lights switch on but the moon is unrisen and the northern stars are few and aloof.

Was it a snow-covered doe? Could snow cover any creature so completely, from ankles to skull, eyelids to hooves? The antler wasn't an antler after all. It was a horn, long and cetacean, white as the birches that stood sentinel on our leafy block at night.

"Anja?" I called shyly from my side of the street. Her windows were dark. Then I remembered Edie was volunteering at the women's shelter until ten, and so I had no saner pair of eyes to summon to my side as night fell around the Cloud Lake Apartment Complex. As far as I knew, I was the only person to witness this eerie scavenger as she cantered down our block toward the highway, an ancient piece of pineapple pizza dangling from her lips like one of Edie's cigarettes.

I decided not to mention her to anyone. I was afraid that I would chase her back out of time and into eternity if I spoke the word "unicorn" out loud.

Craving salt is a survival mechanism, said the doctor. But in you, it's gone haywire.

Cookies, kiwis, ice cubes, salad, bread, the webbing of my hands— I was salting everything. I bought a spice rack and filled it with garlic salt, turmeric salt, black lava salt, red chili salt, a keg of your good old-fashioned Morton's salt. Food became a vessel for iodine, and if there wasn't a shaker on the table I wasn't interested in eating.

Dr. Barretto told me that I was severely anemic, and that I should remedy this with iron supplementation, not an ocean. "Try cooking on a cast-iron pan," he suggested. Dr. Barretto was a portly Argentine man in his fifties who seemed to feel I was ridiculously old to be having a first baby. He always hit on Caro when she accompanied me, even when we spoke loudly about Caro's girlfriend, Nieves. He scheduled my delivery for July 2, and it astonished me to learn that we could choose my daughter's birthday. Because I would be forty in July—a *geriatric mother*, he kept repeating with increasingly angry emphasis, as if this were a punch line I'd failed to get—he would be performing a Caesarean section.

"Perform" is a disconcerting verb to hear in relation to one's surgery.

It made me think of sad circus seals and belligerent stand-up comedians. Caro teased me about this, the medicine she mixes for me when I'm afraid; her jokes are more potent than anything the gangsters stock at the Cloud Lake Pharmacy. "Catch the June 2 performance—live, for one night only! Standing room only, your C-section!"

When I made it to week twelve, that spectral mile marker when a miscarriage becomes less likely, we had a small party. My sister bought me a Himalayan salt block. I'd never seen one of these things before, although she told me they were bougie fixtures in all her Vancouver friends' backyards. It was a twelve-foot-by-eight-foot slab of salt, crystal pink and twinkling in the night air. Caro held up a candle so that we could see the waves of rosy inlaid mineral. It looked like a mountain sunrise planed into a rectangle, or a doorstop for an archangel.

"Wow, Caro," I said. "Thank you. Where did you buy this thing, the Narnia Gift Shop?"

"You're going to love it, Mauve. Everything you cook on it will have your favorite taste: brine." She handed me a cookbook filled with pictures of raw meats sweltering on the sunburn-pink block. "It's also a present for my niece," said Caro, touching my belly. I'd been crediting so many of my strange appetites to this fetus, including the insatiable need for salt. Did these cravings originate with her, or with me? I no longer knew.

At another office, they did a high-tech new test. A vial of my blood disappeared into a sterile back room and got shaken down for information. "You are having a daughter," said the friendly, bored technician, a middle-aged Black woman with a photograph of twin girls in blue school plaids on her desk, and a yawning conviction about my baby's future reality that I wished I could feel.

One night at the start of my second trimester, alone in our yard, I bent to lick the salt block. I don't know what possessed me. The pink crystals scraped at my tongue. Under my rib cage, the baby began to kick. We developed a rhythm: *lick, kick, lick, kick.*

When I rose from the salt block, the unicorn had reappeared.

It had been hours since dinner, and the block had cooled, its color changed from sandy pink to Martian lake. The plants in the yard were a uniform blue. But the unicorn was lit unsteadily from within, flickering from white to gray, the wattage jumping each time she snorted. I recoiled in an awe that was also revulsion—what was a unicorn doing in our backyard?

"Deer are vermin out here," my boss, Steve, told me when I first moved to Oregon from Florida, eager to live closer to my sister and to work for a real newspaper. My boss was one of Seattle's jaded children—a transplant like me—an ursine white man with a combustible ratio of insecurity to entitlement. He seemed to find it hilarious that I was so enraptured by the sight of a doe and her two fawns. I could see them from our office window, grazing in the alley of daffodils beside the Willamette River. "You grew up with sharks and alligators, and you're creaming yourself over a *deer*?" (Steve's teasing could make even my hairline flush. He made a blow-up doll's face to mimic my stunned expression, fluttering his eyelids. I couldn't recall how I responded that day. Said nothing, probably. Possibly I laughed. I sent up a prayer of thanksgiving to the pantheon of does that Steve was not my baby daughter's father.)

"Girl," he'd chided me. "Put your camera away. Don't you know that miracles are regional? To us, a deer is like a big antlered rat."

Now I wondered if the same was true of unicorns in the west. Could a unicorn be rabid? Were their eyes always this feverish? I stared into her bottomless pupils and I felt dizzy with echoes, filling with some kind of primordial déjà vu; my arms shot out as if I were wheeling over a stairwell. As I crept closer I could see gray scuff marks on her hooves and horn; they made me think, insanely, of bowling shoes. Parts of her were emaciated—her wishbone haunches, her thinning white mane. The unicorn whinnied once, exhaling spume. Her rib cage lifted like a shipwreck at low tide, the long bones curving up with each breath, while her large belly swung heavily below her. It sounds silly to feel sorry for a unicorn, but I did then. Time predates unicorns, just like the rest of us. Eternal beings, it seems, are not exempt from aging. The unicorn kept changing as she walked toward me. Like a hologram, she seemed to flicker between realities. Now she was a scabby trespasser, now an otherworldly traveler. Ordinary, extraordinary, beautiful, ugly, starving to death, and luminously alive. Each time I blinked, her status shifted on me. Even her shadow seemed to change on the grass, elongating and twisting, melting and transforming, molten with light.

"Oh!" I shouted like a *Jeopardy!* contestant, startling us both with my *eureka!* syntax, having recognized her uncanny condition. How had I missed it? "Are you pregnant?" I hadn't guessed that an immortal could get knocked up. I wondered what the gestation time for a unicorn might be: hours, centuries? Now I guessed the reason she'd come bounding out of the mists to nose at Anja's pizza boxes.

Cravings are ephemeral, but also undeniable.

She trained her dish-huge eyes on me and began to steadily blink, like a carpenter aiming a nail gun. If she'd hoped to bolt me to my shadow, it didn't work. I could still move, but I did so slowly, not wanting to scare her off. I took a few steps backward, snapping my fingers to beckon her to me and instantly regretting it—a unicorn is not a lost puppy. And I wanted to earn her trust. I wanted to soothe the concave ache that had driven her out of the ultraviolet and into the range of my senses. This hunger I believed we had in common, me and the unicorn.

Carefully, I negotiated backward through the shining rosemary, around the dented meteor of the BBQ lid, making my way to the salt block. I watched her lower her long face to the illuminated surface, which glowed more intensely by the second, brighter than the porch light, brighter than the cloudy moon. It was her phosphor, I realized. She had suffused the block with her strong light. In my own body, I could feel her blood pressure rising, iodine funneling to her starved cells. Branches were caught in her dirty hair. I wished I had something else to give her: a garland of flowers, a heating pad. I smiled as I watched her purple tongue rowing across the block: "So you're a salt freak too?"

On an ordinary night, our yard is a thoroughfare for tame raccoons and stoned Anja. I had never been visited by a beast before. Her horn had the bioluminescence of marine life, and her tongue seemed almost prehensile. She ran it around the edges of the salt block, snorting with pleasure. Salt and thirst go hand in hand, I thought as I turned on the sprinklers and watched her lap at the whiskers of water. Then she shook a cape of droplets from her mangy, magnificent coat and took off. She went soaring over the hedge, knocking a few more branches off the dying cherry tree as she disappeared into our neighbor Jessa's yard.

I was never a horse girl. I was never even a mule girl. The sound I made to call her back to me was my poor ventriloquy of the child actress in *Black Beauty*. It didn't work. She did not return. Did the unicorn know I was not a virgin? Probably, I thought. Any stranger could tell.

I'd grown up believing that I was infertile, and the hundreds of uncontrolled experiments I'd conducted over many sozzled nights seemed to bear this out. I had hosted boyfriends and girlfriends and bartenders and AA sponsors and wizard-like poets and party acquaintances and true strangers inside my body, and for decades none of these visits had ever resulted in a pregnancy, or even a "scare," as teenaged Caro used to call them. I had gotten a single period at the age of fourteen; our family doctor had discovered that I had a rare hereditary mutation. Everyone had seemed so sad for me, even the guy who cut my mom's hair, even my Aunt Rhea who loved her life as a happily single and childless engineer, and so I'd had to reassure these adults that I was much more excited about being a mutant than being a mother. The diagnosis was a relief to me—a non-fatal answer to the case of my missing menstruation. They'd sent me home with a peacock fantail of glossy brochures, thin legends about married couples overcoming infertility. "Help will be available, Mauve, when you're ready to have a baby," the doctor told me. But that day never came. I had never longed for a child like some of my friends, whose crisp, adult voices went doughy at the sight of baby hands. It was strange to feel this new appetite growing at pace with the fetus inside me. *Fifteen weeks. Sixteen weeks.* At night, I paced my basement bedroom, sweaty and nauseous, flush with the terrible hope. I felt as powerless over the longing to hold my baby as I did over the hunger for salt.

Garbage Thursdays excepted, I would ordinarily never spy on my neighbors. But that night I could not resist peering over the hedge to look for the unicorn. I saw Jessa's Jacuzzi and cheerfully unseasonable Christmas lights, and beside it the two giant raccoons that split their time between our yards. Usually these twin behemoths move in slow, panda-like circles between our properties, carrying greasy Styrofoam shards from the Lucky Devil dumpster in their mouths. Sometimes, I swear, they wave at me. I love their tiny, sleek hands, which make them look like lady assassins. Tonight, however, the raccoons were standing straight up on their hind legs, bristling all over. Had they just seen her, the horned interloper?

They stood shoulder to shoulder, staring forlornly down the empty road like tiny stockbrokers watching the market plummet. "You two look the way I feel," I told the raccoons. It reassured me to know that other animals also felt surprised by a unicorn manifesting on our residential block, and bereft at her disappearance. Under my navel, the baby woke into a somersault—she was most active at night. I loved the sharp surprise of her foot discovering my ribs. This alien metronome inside me.

"Come back anytime," I called softly over the hedge. The sprinklers were arcing water over the grass in liquid scimitars, unlit rainbows in utero. "I'll leave the salt lick out for you."

"Are you worried about people calling your daughter a bastard?" Edie asked me one warm night in the backyard, where the hedge shivered suggestively but kept its secrets. "Jesus, Edie," said my sister, but I laughed to let her know this brusqueness was just Edie's way of stamping a valentine. Her frankness makes me think of a lizard's throat—that bright scarlet bulging out, as irrepressible as life itself.

"No," I said. "Besides, she has the best aunt in the world. And the best . . ."

"No honorifics, Mauve. I can't be a godmother, okay? The houseplants are already too much for me."

At the twenty-week ultrasound, Edie and my sister flanked the bed. They stood there quiet as the Secret Service while the technician murmured, "Good, good, all good. Would you like to see inside her heart? Let's count the chambers together—one, two, three . . ." She clicked a long ellipsis against the roof of her mouth. "Four!"

"Fuck!" said Edie, who never whispers to be polite. Cigarettes have thinned her voice. "Is four too many or too few?"

"Just the right amount of chambers."

We watched the pinprick of light that was the baby's beating heart. It pulsed on the dark screen, the cosmically black screen, and I shut my eyes between blinks and saw our unicorn's horn moving off into the distance.

In mid-March, I harvested six sullen-colored cherries from the sick tree. A week later, I nearly lost the baby. At the ER, the first doctor who examined me was cagey as a carnival psychic. "The pain and bleeding may go away, and you can continue to have a healthy pregnancy and baby. Or things may get worse."

I was discharged and told to take a "wait-and-see" approach—was there another option? I wanted to ask the nurses. Edie prayed for us, Anja sat in silence with me on the basement couch, Caro stayed over and made us dinner on the salt block: the baby stayed inside my body, and after seventy-two hours I began to breathe again. But the fear never left me. After that scalding day and night at the ER, trying to mentally separate the six gloomy cherries and the blood clots in the toilet bowl felt like pulling magnets apart.

Not an omen, said Caro. You read too much into the world, Mauve. You think everything has to mean something. But you're not the addressee on the envelope here, okay? Mostly, the world is talking to itself.

I knew my sister was right, and yet I could not make myself believe her. A part of me felt certain that I had been punished for trying to become a mother—for failing to listen to the world as it whispered and shouted "no."

"Hope can be agonizing," Anja told me one Thursday night, three weeks after I'd been discharged from the ER. "But you have to keep hoping."

I was still pregnant, but Anja was losing her mother to a long battle with ovarian cancer. We stood bracketed by our garbage bins, staring down the hill toward Mount Hood and a wall of advancing rain. I wished the unicorn would come galloping into view to frighten flowers out of the mud, to bring Anja comfort from a world beyond this one.

I combed my memory for something true and consoling. In one deep pocket I found the lint of a half-forgotten poem.

"Hope is the Thing With Feathers . . ."

"Is that the Obama book?"

"Emily Dickinson. Wilin' out with the Capitalization."

I managed to reassemble most of the first stanza for Anja, the only one I still knew by heart

"The Thing." Anja smiled. "God, I used to love that movie as a kid."

We riffed for a while: Hope is a dolphin's fin. Hope is a cherry lip balm. Hope is an unwritten Rihanna song. This week, your hope is the size of a mustard seed, a blackberry, a four-headed dragon.

Hope is a salt lick, I said. Muscle and mineral. Hope is a habit that the living can't quit. Anja was right about the verb and the noun of it. Hoping was nothing to romanticize. It was a necessary, excruciating activity.

I was thinking about the pink slab waiting outside our house in the rain. All the women in history before me who had tried to tempt a unicorn out of a glen. I was remembering the sound of my baby's heartbeat faltering, the lengthening hyphens; we had watched her ultrasound on a large black screen, the ER residents crowding in as if we were the football game. The ice-water voice of the weekend nurse who told me, "Your baby is performing poorly." The sound that wrinkling paper makes under skin, the disposable hospital sheet tearing as I swung my legs wider for another stranger's gloved hands. In the taxonomy of losing, these must be the two fundamental categories: those things we lose and believe we might find again, the sting of grief lightened by the hope of retrieval; and those losses that are final, insoluble, eternal.

April rains covered Portland in a steady mist. I reached Week 28, my third trimester, another spectral mile marker—even if the baby was born prematurely, the odds were now very good that she would live. At 4:00 a.m. when the baby and I were both awake, I prayed a four-word prayer to her pummeling fists, to her head butting at my ribs in the womb's windowless darkness: "Please, come. Please, stay." I had not seen the unicorn for eleven weeks. Not an omen, I told myself in Caro's voice. She is an immortal ungulate. She has a life.

There are events for which I fear I'll never find language. Whole years of my childhood that have lost their magnetism, sending the alphabet clattering to the floor, a pile of symbols that won't stick to the door. Even talking to my sister, I often feel like a clumsy surgeon botching the operation—using the wrong-sized tongs for certain slippery red truths. I must be constantly underestimating and misreading everyone in my life if I can't describe one painful hour to Caro, or even to myself. Every human body must be a library of silent experience. Glaciers go sinking through us before we can utter a word.

But now I know that the unspeakable can also be beautiful. Delicately, deliriously joyful. Secrets can sieve through a heart, fine as stardust.

Here is a secret I am happy to share, even if I can only do so in this galumphing sentence, which is too coarse, too clumsy, too earthbound, too human for what I wish I could evoke: the unicorn came back.

I had no history of miscarriages, I told the first and the kindest of a rotating cast of ER doctors on the night of the blood clots. (I continue to see these in nightmares, dark red and gnarled as tree roots.) Yes, I'd confirmed when the doctor's eyebrows lifted. I was turning forty, and this was my first and only pregnancy. Gravida 1, para 0. He pushed his eyebrows down politely and hid his face behind the clipboard. He was a handsome Black man who looked to be half my age, his shy eyes lassoed in spearmint-green glasses. His hands were as reticent as his voice during my examination, prodding only where necessary, taking great care to avoid causing me additional pain. I told him that I was surprised to be a gravida too; I had grown up believing that for me, pregnancy would be impossible. The nurse who had been tightening the black cuff on my arm, a white woman with veiny hands and beautiful smile lines, paused to stare at the side of my face. "Would you have made different choices, honey, if you'd known you could get pregnant?" she asked me, with the mild, automated curiosity of a waitress inquiring, "Cream or sugar?" I answered honestly. I said: "I don't know." As I've mentioned,

I haven't always been aces at safety. I had a history of "kamikaze pro-miscuity," as my sister calls it. That's a longer story, but suffice it to say that I have no interest in solving the mystery of my baby's paternity—the main suspect has already informed me he wants nothing to do with me, which is really the best possible outcome. I don't want to disparage the possible fathers of my baby, so I'll follow Thumper's mother's sage advice and say nothing at all. My daughter had so many arms waiting to hold her. My sister Caro, whose love is infallible. Anja, hostess of the best CBD pizza parties. Edie, who couldn't fool me into thinking she didn't love me and my baby.

We had the blessing of a unicorn.

And if our unicorn looked a little like a curbside sofa left to moulder in the rain, a FREE sign disintegrating on its soaking cushions? Well, I thought, I'm no spring chicken myself.

At the OB-GYN, they treated me like an audacious cadaver. The twentysomething nurses spoke to me with a tenderness reserved for the terminally infirm. I began to feel so self-conscious about this that I bought a push-up bra and cream blush. "Uh-oh!" said Caro. "What happened here? You look like Mel Gibson in *Braveheart*."

"Thirty-year-old Mel?" I asked hopefully, and she declined to answer. I wondered how the pregnant unicorn felt about her own growth and decay. I'm sure there must be ups and downs on the tram-poline of eternity.

I didn't wash the Himalayan salt block before I cooked on it again. For the first time in my life, friends treated me like a master chef. My sister said, "You seasoned this perfectly!" Even Edie asked for seconds, then thirds. I demurred, shy with pleasure—I credited the salt block. I thought we were tasting her magic, but I knew better than to tell anyone about the visiting unicorn. Everything I grilled on the salt block had a lavender taste now, ineffably fresh and bright as graveyard bouquets. I wondered if we would all live forever.

Sodium chloride, I've since learned, can bring on muscle contrac-tions.

On the night the unicorn returned, we both went into labor. Week

36–four weeks before my scheduled delivery, when my daughter was the size of "a large jicama"—I left the house to take out the trash and found myself drenched and speechless on the damp grass. Nothing I had read or heard about labor could have spoiled the surprise of my water breaking; for a moment I thought I might be dying. The unicorn was watching me silently from the shadow of the cherry tree. She chewed the bark off the sickly trees with the nonchalance of an old pro; I thought she must have given birth many thousands of times before. At one point, she craned her neck over the hedge and dipped her horn into my neighbor's Jacuzzi, purifying it forever. I considered lumbering through the hedge into Jessa's yard, naked and hairy as the Sasquatch, and lowering myself into the bubbling tub. The Portland water birth that nobody wants to see cannonballing into their Thursday evening.

Then the unicorn shouldered through the thin branches to the salt block, and I crawled over to join her, hunched on all fours, gathering my strength between what I realized must be contractions. They seemed to be happening everywhere that night, not only in my body. The black sky curved into an hourglass above us, opening outward in twin parabolas, forcing the constellations earthward; I waited for stars to fall on our heads like grains of sand. A warm, mammalian calm filled me. My breaths synced themselves to the accordion inhalations of the laboring unicorn. Anja's ghost lake under the Portland streets, hidden moons and satellites, pregnant strangers moaning as they parted the glass hospital doors, every laboring animal, bats dreaming under bridge trestles and matronly whales skimming Antarctica—I felt myself expanding and contracting in secret solidarity with so many near and distant bodies. That night I drew as close as I ever have to the wordless domain of the animals. Carnality without estrangement, knowledge without thought.

Dead light came slingshotting across the galaxy; Edie's automated sprinklers turned on, dousing us with chittering water. Whatever was earthquaking down the length of the unicorn's body did not seem to frighten her, which helped me to welcome my own spasms. (She seemed, if not bored by them exactly, casually resigned; I saw with horrified awe that a coltish leg and hoof was now dangling from her lower body.) Between contractions, we bent and licked at the salt in tandem. I wondered if Edie could see us from the upstairs window, if she was sitting at the typewriter, smoking her Kools and questioning her sanity. Knowing Edie, if she was still awake she would most likely be out here on the deck shouting instructions, reminding me that she was not liable for any injuries sustained if I was gored on her property.

As the unicorn shuddered beside me, I wondered for the first time if she'd come to me specifically, despite my slovenly habits and erratic employment and inability to apply cream blush at age forty. Maybe so, I let myself believe. We had a powerful lifewish in common. We had formed and carried the same heavy dread inside our minds. Eternal life is no guarantee, it appeared, of delivering a live baby. Her gray belly swayed, and I saw the unspeakable possibility shining in one inky eye.

I was too shy to stare directly at the unicorn, but I watched her in profile. The huge eye was all pupil, with the thinnest rim of violet around it. Soon I could only see her in flashes. Pain was blanking us out of the canvas. Her dilated eye swallowed me into it. A full moon floated in the center of the vanished iris.

My hospital bag was packed and waiting by the door. Caro had volunteered to drive me to the labor and delivery ward months ago, but I didn't want to bother her until things were further along. And I didn't want to leave now—who could abandon a unicorn? My own contractions were becoming faster and stronger, waves of hot crenellated pressure that pinned me to the ground. I could still sing, which I did. The O of my mouth echoed down, down, down, a wild guttural sound, threading through the tree roots and the ghostly lake. I should call Caro now, I decided, just before my body caved in on itself. Then I understood with a piercing shriek that I would not be having my baby in the hospital.

When I recovered from the final push, the cherry tree had split down the middle, and a new voice came wailing into the world. My daughter was born on a nest of sticky red grass beside a raccoon-masticated Frisbee and the balding rosemary bush, where the pink quartz beads of a rosary glowed like tiny berries. I'd awoken the entire neighborhood, it seemed, with my final scream. Six minutes later, an ambulance came roaring down Ninth Avenue, whisking panic out of the dark firs and the silent bedrooms with its spinning red siren. But the emergency has passed, I wanted to tell them. My daughter is here with us, alive.

What fresher salt lick exists in our universe than a newborn's eyelids? The unicorn leaned over and licked the angry tears from my daughter's blossoming, astonishing, ocean-blue eyes. Then she dissolved from sight a final time. In her place was a warm, bloodwet, tiny mortal. A verifiable miracle. Her fists windmilled everywhere as the paramedics put her onto my chest, her wrinkled face furious and waxy, ashen white as a Pompeii survivor. I was afraid she would vanish as mysteriously as she'd arrived. Diffusing into the void again, like the unicorn. "Please stay," I begged my daughter that night in the garden. So far, she has.

THE WHITE ROAD; OR, HOW A CROW CARRIED DEATH OVER A RIVER

MARIKA BAILEY

Long ago—well before now but not so distant as *then*—there was a crow called Broadfeather who worried she'd never find a name.

Back then, oh baby-love, all of the crows lived on an island so small it barely merited the name. That green upstart rock was split in two by a river that ran in both directions away from its source.

On one side of the river was Life and everything that breathes, bleeds, and breeds. On the other was Death and all Her treasures. Smack dab in the middle of both grew the moko forest where poison and pleasure grew leaf-to-petal close, and the mist was knit together from the last wishes of wistful ghosts. In the canopy of that forest First Crow, the very first of her kind, god and many times great-grandmother to Broadfeather, had made her home.

The many children and grandchildren of First Crow roosted in the jumbie-haunted trees and were plentiful. There was Rumblecaw Crow, who was such a good mimic that she could imitate Old Django Thunder himself, startling the flock out of their roosts and near falling over laughing at her own joke. Stoneweaver Crow was the builder of the clan. Her nests were sturdy and strong, her eggs never falling in even the highest wind. When First Crow decided to expand the royal nest, it was Stoneweaver she called upon to lead the work.

It was the way of First Crow's most ambitious children to throw off the egg-name their clutch-mothers had given them and find a name for themselves. Rumblecaw had once been Brighteye, and Stoneweaver's clutchmates remembered when she was named Strongfoot.

Which brings us back, my dear, to young Broadfeather, who was worrying herself so badly, she'd begun plucking at her mantle. She'd had no adventures, no stories, no special gift to share with the flock. Nothing to bring the First Crow and say, "I demand a name." She was neither very big nor very small. Not very bright or very stupid. She couldn't tell jokes. Couldn't sing. And had never found any treasure worth mentioning. She should be content with the name given to her, but she just couldn't. It worried her. It gnawed at her, and she in turn began to gnaw at her trousers, cawing in worry, until she looked ragged and plucked.

"Child," said her mother who'd run out of patience, "if you're so worried, you have to *do* something about it."

Broadfeather stopped in the middle of pecking her trouser feathers. Well, could she? *Could* she?

With a sigh, her beloved mother opened the broad shadow of her right wing and swept her daughter out of the nest.

"Go and have an adventure and stop hurting my head about it!" she called to Broadfeather, who'd managed to right herself and flap away. Then she gratefully returned to her nap, in the way of all mothers before and after her.

Broadfeather did not know where to go. She had to find an adventure or treasure worthy of a name, since she had no particular talent with which to earn one. Perhaps the sugarcane fens where the blood of the dying fed the snakes who twisted through the rotting fertile muck? Or maybe the groves where guava ripened, holding the names of stars written within them? She couldn't decide. So she simply flew.

Her wings stretched out wide, wide as she was lifted by a warm current of air. The green of the moko forest grew smaller and smaller until she could see the whole of it laid out below her, and beyond it the divided sea.

To the East were the dark waters that had given birth to all of the ancestors, First Crow included. And to the West was the still, white blanket of ocean where the sun went to die every night before being reborn. They covered the whole world and beyond. Broadfeather found herself gliding lower towards the ancestral sea, as if she could scoop up a mouthful of its sparkle to bring home for her own name-prize.

As she came lower to better admire the lapping waves, she saw it. A glimmer of something white. Not the sun's reflection on the caps of the waves, but down, very far down. Something white, and shimmering, and possibly quite wonderful.

It could have been anything. The first bloody cough of a dying star crystallized and fallen to earth. Or a secret, pulled screaming from the mind of a god, shut away in the heart of a pearl. Something special enough to build a name on.

Broadfeather pulled her wings in close for a dive, piercing the air with her body. She broke through that water like a clap of thunder.

Down she went.

Past the waving shoals of *tri tri* fish no bigger than her smallest claw, green-scaled and pearl-eyed. Past the bullying crowds of king-fish, curious and scarlet-crowned. Past the chattering schools of beaked parrot fish. (Seeing them for the first time, Broadfeather assumed they must be distant, scaly cousins, and gave them a polite nod as she zoomed past.)

The little crow held her dark wings even tighter, pulling the last bit of remembered warmth closer to her breast, and spiraled down into the deep.

A name, my name could be there! she whispered to herself.

The water grew dark, then *darker* than dark. If she'd turned her head back she would've seen the circle of the sun shrink and then wink out.

This was a stupid thing to do, thought Broadfeather. It is the same thought that has occurred to many a new adventurer hurtling off the cliff of mortality.

The sea was dark, but it was not empty. As she swam further and further down, there were creatures that Broadfeather was sure had been made either in madness or mistake. Snakes with eyes as big as her head, and curved teeth long as a wing. Light swam out of the darkness to reveal the ponderous monstrosity that wore it as a lure, thick scaled and white-eyed. There were sounds in the darkness that never became sights, for which the young crow was very grateful.

It was some time later that she finally and happily reached the glittering beacon at the bottom of the sea and saw it for what it was: a white road, curving and bending into the long watery distance. It glittered and glowed as brightly as the first diamond ever stolen for a queen's crown. Broadfeather hopped and purred in excitement, bending closer, her beady eyes keen.

The road was made up of finger bones as long as her beak, crystalline, and pregnant with light. It was the most beautiful thing she had ever seen.

A crow is a trickster and a hoarder, but most importantly, a crow is a keeper of memories. What better way to keep memory than in the marrow of bones softly melting against your tongue in remembrance, or the sweet jelly of an eye sliding down a throat? And to compound that, the sparkle! The pulsing luminescent glow from each delicately carved knucklebone and talus. Phalanges lying in opalescent splendor among the carbuncled diamonds of capitates.

What a treasure! What a find! This would be the making of her name.

Delicately she picked up a glowing carpal bone in her beak, and thrice as quickly she spat it back out. The shiny had spoken to her.

Broadfeather hopped and flapped and shivered in distress. Even now as the deep current refracted its light, it spoke in a voice that she could not escape or shake out of her head, try as she might.

"Are you Death?" asked the bone.

Broadfeather huddled, wings up, head cocked. Sparklies were not supposed to talk back. Or have opinions about being picked up. Sparklies—to steal a phrase from her least-favorite clutch-aunt—were definitely supposed to be seen and not heard.

But after some thinking she supposed that encountering offal that talked back was what adventuring was all about.

"I'm a crow, not Death Herself, though my ma has always said we have some distant family connection with that good Queen. But since we're chatting all friendly so, what are you?" Remembering her manners, she added, "If you don't mind me asking, sir, or madam, or them as the case may be?"

"We are souls, and in need of help, young crow who is very lost."

Broadfeather bristled. "I am not lost! I wanted to see what you were and now I have seen and that means I am the very opposite of lost!"

"Our apologies, friend crow who is just where she wants to be. We do not get many visitors here. We are alien to this place and the sluggish languages of the deep dark. We do not have much practice in speaking to any but each other."

"This is a strange place for a soul to be. And an even odder—though beautiful—form for you to take," Broadfeather replied, awkwardly hopping over to the light. The more she looked at it, the more it seemed imbued with personality and life.

"Do you have a name?" she asked. "I am called Broadfeather. Or rather, that is my egg name. I have yet to earn another."

"I had a name once, too. Though that was long ago and far away. It is a sad story," said the bone.

"I would hear it, if you would share it," Broadfeather said, settling down like a mother over an egg.

The bone was silent for a moment, as if considering it, then came to a decision within its crystal shell.

"You are here, feather child, so I may as well tell you my sad tale.

"I was born in a country I do not remember the name of. I no longer know the names of my mothers and fathers. Or my sisters. There was a man I loved, but his name is gone too. All of the names that have made up my life have been stolen, First Crow's child. And if there were any justice in this world of shame and death, it would not be me at the bottom of the ocean. It would not be we bones piled one atop the other like so much dust and sand. If there were justice, I would have my name and my death.

"But there is none.

"I went for a walk, Broadfeather Crow. That is how I came to this end. *That* is what I dared.

"One morning in that home I will never see or name again, I rose from my bed and went to the beach. There were shells on a particular strand of sand, colored like dawn's tears. And I wanted them for a necklace. My eldest sister was heavy with child and it would be a gift.

"And I liked to walk alone. I liked quiet.

"But that morning, oh night-born, I did not find peace or shells. I found men with guns. Or they found me. Hunters of men and sellers of people. Filth! Corruption!

"Should I tell you that I screamed? Would it matter that I fought?

"I was taken all the same. Beaten and bound with cold metal.

"And when they dragged me to their ship, covered more in blood and chain than in cloth, they threw me in its belly. A pit darker and more fouled than any hell and filled with others like me, brutalized and in chains.

"That, I—we!—might have survived. A body imprisoned does not necessarily mean a body destroyed. But these men, ashen as doves and smiling like hungry ghosts, did not stop at stealing my body.

"No, child. They brought me up from the pit where my fellows and I slowly died of rot and hunger and brought me before their wizard. We had something else that he found valuable, beside our bodies for sale. At first I couldn't look at him straight on. He shone. Even under the sun, he shone like the reflection of the sun off the sea. It was the light of what he stole. He wore it over his shoulders like a blanket, a thief unashamed of his crime. His face was white as salt, his mouth a dark red gash like an open wound, and his eyes were no color at all.

"There is power in names, as you know. You, young crow in search of another name, you must understand that! Our true names are what bind us to Creation, the delicate shell that protects our souls on the journey from Life to Death and declare our existence whole.

"So much power in that, if you can strip it from a soul. The power of self. The power of memory.

"When that grey-eyed magician stole my name, plucking it from my chest as I screamed, he smiled. It gleamed silver and green in the sun and sparkled as he opened his mouth and swallowed it.

"I threw myself from that ship and let the water have me. Dying and deathless, until my body wore away and there was nothing left of me but a fractured soul captured in a bone.

"Look into the distance child. Into the water dark and deep. These lights you see are the souls of those who were stolen, who jumped from the ships because they could not bear to carry the weightlessness of what had been taken from them."

The bone darkened as if in remembrance of sorrow.

Broadfeather was not sure what to do. So she moved close to the bone and laid one wing gently over it, as she would do for any weeping cousin.

There are some things that remain the same for all children of blood and breath. Comfort is one of them. Bird and lost soul sat in the deep dark of the ocean floor and mourned together.

After some time, Broadfeather spoke. There was a grain of an idea tossing through her mind.

"Lady Death can't take you without a name, is that so, friend?"

The crystal's light pulsed once and dimmed. "Yes, that's so. We are unmoored from Creation."

Broadfeather hopped up and began to pace, a habit she'd aggressively stolen from First Crow.

"But there's got to be more than one way to get a name." She cocked her head in thought. "I am here in pursuit of a new name. There are those who pull their names out of the alphabet sea of the oracles. What if we could give you all new names?" Broadfeather stared excitedly at the soul. She saw them differently now. They were another person, like she was, and grievously wounded.

"I . . . don't know," they replied. It had been long and lonely in the deep dark of the sea, and hard to hope in that lightless silence. But *oh, to be free*! To rise from limbo, no longer a stone revenant, beyond the curse of what had been done to her! To them all.

"What would you do for us, young friend?" the soul asked. She listened as Broadfeather outlined her plan, then shared it amongst the other souls that marked the long white road at the bottom of the sea. The road of the lost.

Bone to bone, the story passed, each deciding if they would put their fate into the not-very-large beak of one not-quite-grown crow. And soul to soul, they replied back: "Yes!"

Long ago, before there was any land at all, First Crow stole the sun. Now, we don't need to get into the nitty gritty of why she did that. In her youth First Crow would have stolen Father God's underpants just to keep limber. The point is, she did it. Broadfeather reasoned, with every cell of her remarkable crow brain, that if you could steal something *from* the sky, you'd be just as able to steal something *to* the sky.

She turned to the first little soul, the only one she'd spoken to, and asked, "Friend, would you mind if I picked you up with my beak?"

"Sounds more fun than living at the bottom of the ocean!" answered the bone, who was picked up as gently as the crow could manage.

Broadfeather could not give warning while clutching her passenger in her beak, and when she crouched down and sprang back up, the little bone made a tiny squeak. But that was soon drowned out by the sound of tiny osseous laughter, as the crow rocketed them up through the forever night of the sea floor, and up through the water to the sun.

Up they flew, past the many-toothed guardians of the deep cold. Past the waving forests of kelp and the million-rich schools that bejeweled their haunted roots. Up towards the round flame of the sun, sparkling brighter and bigger with each passing moment, until they broke the surface of the sea, and Broadfeather heard a sound from the glowing soul in her mouth that could have been a sigh or cry.

Up they continued. The air felt good on Broadfeather's wings, and the sun's warmth was a blessing. If her young bird life had a purpose, Broadfeather would have said it was this flight, this moment of rising faster than any she'd ever experienced, up past the sapphire sea and through the lapis-lined sky. The world below shrank into smudges of color, and still the young crow did not feel her strength flag or her breath give way. She could fly forever, up past the last swirling clouds, until they reached the sticky blackness of the Roof of Creation where the stars lived. Gently, Broadfeather released her passenger, placing it gently into the glossy black of the sky. The bone slipped into its new home with a glowing sigh of release.

"Is this good, friend?" the young crow asked.

"This is more than I could have asked for, friend Broadfeather. This is a gift," said the bone. It glowed rose and gold, like the goddess of sunrise on her wedding morning.

Before they could say more, the crow turned back towards the earth in a swirl of feather and speed, flying away so quickly she looked like a smudge against the painting of the distant earth below.

Broadfeather felt as if her blood had been replaced with fire and her breath with starshine. She flew back to the waiting sea within the space of a blink, and in another she was at the bottom of the sea, another stone safely caught in her beak, ready for its journey to the sky.

Over and over she flew between one dark to the next, the black of deep sea to the midnight of deep sky. One hundred times. One thousand times. One million. Until the white road at the bottom of the sea, the long line of lost and name-robbed souls, now lived in a swirl of glory across the blue and black of the universe. Shining pink and purple, silver and gold, as beautiful and bright as any star born of dust and nebula.

Only as she placed the very last bone, the wrist stone that had once belonged to someone very small and very, very young, did she pause. Drifting along the currents of space, Broadfeather returned to the first stone, they who'd first spoken to her at the bottom of the sea and asked her help as the goddess had predicted.

"Friend! Friend! You are all freed. Is it good?" She asked.

"Good? Baby crow, this is the greatest good. This is a blessing."

Broadfeather, being a crow of darkest feather, could not blush. Instead, she cartwheeled in joy. Caterwauled the crow song of happiness.

"A good thing! A blessing!" she cried.

"Friend, you have a new home now, with the stars and the distant worlds on the dust roads. When the children of the gods look up at you and your fellows, they will make heroes of your bones. Archers, lions, and dancing princesses. You will have names once again!"

Broadfeather burbled and danced in joy at her great trick, her grand theft of souls from a stealer of names. Oh what a day! Oh what a time!

The bones, now infant stars, shone bright and sparkling for the young bird in thanks, spelling out their joy as she twirled and laughed her way back to the moko forest, her family, and First Crow.

She returned to a nest in full uproar. Her mother, who she'd last seen ungently nudging her out into an adventure, was flying in circles around the royal nest. With every revolution she dropped rotting fruit and curses upon the head of the clan. First Crow huddled under her wings, her red eyes glowing malevolently from the darkness therein.

"You and your stupid special names," yelled Hopfoot. "Putting ideas in fledgling's heads, as if they aren't *all* special!"

Splat! went a semi-fermented guava. *Squish*! went the rotten egg that followed it onto the royal nest.

"My daughter is gone and it's all your stupid fault! With your stories and legends!"

Broadfeather saw her mother turn her rear to the royal house and aim a liquid fart in its direction.

"You don't stop that right now, Hopfoot, I swear on my mother's underbelly, in your next life you'll be a cricket!" cawed the crow matriarch. "The names are gifts!" First Crow dodged a falling mango with the agility of a crow hundreds of years younger and flew up behind her attacker. "Your chick was grown, and you pushed her out the nest your own fool self just like your mama did to you!" Hopfoot yelped as First Crow snapped a tailfeather in a flash.

"Besides," said the elder. "The chick's back home, and laughing behind you."

Broadfeather's mother went slack-beaked at the sight of her baby, quickly enveloping her in a tight black-winged hug.

"My *baby*! How *dare* you go out on an adventure!"

She tried to answer around her mother's feathers, but there was no air.

"I *know* I told you to! But that's not the point! You've been gone for days! Do you know how much I worried? I had all your clutch-mates searching the forest for you."

"And bothering *me*!" added First Crow. "As if *I*, an embodiment of Mother Dark, have time to be nagged by anxious mothers."

Broadfeather felt her mother yell over her shoulder, "You're our first, it's your *job* to care!"

She struggled out from under her mother's wings and her anxious grooming. "Mama, it's okay! I had an adventure. I met lost souls! I have a story for the whole clan."

At that, First Crow seemed to grow bigger. Her eyes shone like garnets and her beak was wickedly sharp, glossy obsidian. She narrowed in on Broadfeather, her huge wings unfolding behind her like the train of a storm cloud's wedding dress.

"*Enough. All of you.*" Gone was the genial grumbling voice she usually used on her children. This was the voice of midnight and command. The voice that called down feather and claw for retribution and remembrance.

"Young Broadfeather will stay and tell me her story."

The prodigal crow shivered under her elder's gaze.

"The rest of you go back to what you were doing. Yes, even you, Hopfoot. Your child will be safe with me. GO."

Broadfeather received a small nip of beak and a strong hug from her mother, but then she was all alone with the first of her kind. The mother of her people. She remembered the feeling of warmth from her friends in the sky and the sound of the goddess' voice in the deep of the sea, and pulled her shoulders up straighter.

She had a story. Her voice as steady as she could make it, Broadfeather told First Crow all she'd seen on her journey.

At the end of her tale, First Crow's eyes were narrowed in thought. She sent the young crow back to her family, assured that she would receive her new name as soon as First found a suitable one.

It was good. Getting what she'd dreamed of for her whole life was *great.* Broadfeather didn't have a new name yet but she found that she didn't mind the wait. Even without it, she felt . . . different. Changed. Her world had gotten so much bigger. A name could wait. Her heart knew who she was. Those she'd helped knew who she was.

Being home felt restful, after such a grand adventure spanning the bottom of the sea and top of the sky. Broadfeather realized that what was coming was a special kind of joy. She relished resuming her nightly spot sleeping between her closest clutch-mates, falling asleep to the sound of White Eye's snore, and Cherry's happy dream chirps.

But, you see, Broadfeather still worried.

At first she didn't even know that what she felt was worry. What, you thought she went home, put her heart away and forgot? Crows never forget!

Broadfeather thought and thought and thought some more. She went and cuddled under the massive wing of First Crow to see if she could think bigger thoughts there. First Crow wrapped a sail-like wing over her and tucked the smaller bird in with a sigh.

Broadfeather thought about stealing.

Stealing, she thought, *was a crow's right.* Why did the theft of the bones' names make her so angry? *She* had stolen fruit a thousand times. First Crow had stolen diamond puzzles, cinnabar anklets made of a fire god's blood, and even the sun. Her mind twirled her worry over and over again, you could practically hear it turning.

The eldest in question opened one beady eye, its kaleidoscope colors glinting in the dark. She watched her many-grand-daughter's restless form proudly before speaking.

"Those were all *things,* baby-love."

It hit Broadfeather then, with the strength of the first lightning bolt to ever bridge the sky and the earth, that people were not *things*.

It was a truth so obvious that she felt silly for not thinking about it before. But so many things are like that. Feelings deep inside oneself that eventually condense and sharpen into brilliant diamonds of understanding.

You can't steal people, she thought. And right behind that, *Someone has to set this right.*

It was not enough that the souls of the white road had been given to the sky as stars. Those who'd stolen people, and stolen their lives and names from Death, had to be stopped.

"Exactly," said First Crow.

* * *

Some while later, Broadfeather gathered her least obnoxious clutch-mates and cousins and told them her plan. As soon as the sun began its shrouded descent into the sea, they left the crow nests and crossed the moko forest into the lands of Death. The leaves of the trees slowly shaded from deepest green on the side of life to become paler and paler as they approached that land beyond.

When the whispering leaves were whiter than the newest of eggs, the crows knew they had crossed over. They flew wingtip to wingtip, as closely as possible. When the sun slipped all the way down into night, white skeletal forms came to join their flight. The skeletons of crow ancestors, white crystal feathers over bone, having heeded the call of First Crow to come guide "the youth-dem" safely through Death.

Underneath them, the misty land that would be the destination of all born in Life sparkled like diamonds. Every color of white and every color held beneath white colored this land. Its people, linen-shrouded and cloud-cauled, looked up to stare at the delegation of crows flying towards the seat of their Queen.

Death Herself lived in a palace in the caldera of a cold and quiet volcano. She watched from a high tower of crystal and bone, past the moko forest and the white seas of her domain all the way to the other side of the world. Her view went all the way to the distant bower of her beloved, Life. On the coldest and darkest of nights, you can see the ancient and arcane signals she sends across the sea.

Most of them roughly translate to, "I miss you."

"I love you."

When the crows, live and dead, arrived in the tower room of Queen Death she was waiting for them.

The largest of the dead crows bowed and approached his monarch. She nodded and raised one hand for him to rest upon, smoothing the razor sharp crystal feathers on his back affectionately with the other.

"Silverleaf, old friend," she said to him. "You have brought me very interesting visitors."

Her voice was the sound of galaxies colliding, or the taste of rum distilled from a black hole's laughter. Broadfeather could not decide which.

She ruffled her feathers up to seem as big and proud as possible and addressed the immortal who would gather her when her First no longer could.

"Lady Death, you have been robbed," said the little crow.

"There are new stars in the sky, child of my cousin. A river of them, too many to have been birthed all at once in these orderly times of rules and gravity. And you, feather-baby, smell like old magic and my own far-flung sisters. Tell me your story, child."

So Broadfeather did, just as with First Crow. But she added one thing.

"It is *wrong*, my Lady, to steal people! It is wrong to take their names and rob them and you of the respite all living creatures earn. To remove them from the wheel of creation is an . . . a . . . a . . ."

"An abomination," answered First Crow from a shadowed window.

Death narrowed her eyes. "How did *you* get in here?"

"I tricked my way in. That's what I *do*." First Crow rolled her blood-drop eyes in laughter.

"And you sent your children here . . ."

"To say that we must go to war."

"First things like us cannot go to war. That has been decided by those older even than we," snapped Death peevishly. She'd never quite forgiven First Crow for stealing a favorite pair of her earrings at their cousin's wedding.

"You have an army, cousin. Enough to bring fear to any wizard who dares to steal from you."

"True, but conditions must be met for my shadows to cross into life. Conditions that we do not have," she sighed. A sad mist rose from the frost-tiled floor.

Broadfeather tried to bat it away from her and froze mid-flap when she saw the ruby gleam of First Crow's eyes sidling towards her. It was difficult to hide behind a skeletal ancestor, but she tried.

"The jumbie soldiers of your armies may not cross the river, cousin, but my children have wings, and a duty to bring the high low."

"You would do this?"

First Crow nodded solemnly. "It is right. We must."

Death smiled and reached out a finger to shake the talon First Crow offered.

"We have a deal then," she said gladly. "And a truce between us, cuz."

"Those earrings looked stupid on you anyway. I did you a favor."

Death sucked her teeth and went to gather her soldiers.

Broadfeather and First Crow waited in the pale fields of Death for its Queen to call her soldiers to arms. When Death appeared among the misty reeds, First laid a quelling wing on her descendent, gathering her closer. Shadows froze like mid-winter ponds, and from their jagged darkness the moko jumbie pulled themselves into existence. Their skin was painted white with shifting runes. Each mark defined their contract with Death, binding them for eternity in honorable service. Only the shades of heroes and honorable warriors were offered a space in Death's revenant army. That night they came to her call once again, faces covered in straw reed masks painted blood red, knees and feet on backward to differentiate them from the living.

The jumbee crooned in a haunting wail and the crows rose up towards the sky. The shadows jumped up, latching their darkness to shining feathers, each no heavier than a shadow, but cold enough to burn paths of killing frost. Broadfeather shivered in flight, but let no sound of discomfort touch the air, as she carried a pair of jumbie from both legs. In a contest between the frost-laced grip of undead soldiers and the disapproval of First Crow, she knew the latter was the clear winner. Just a glimpse of the ruby glimmer in her elder's eye was enough to have her straighten her feathers and fly higher.

As she passed over the moko forest, her cousins in formation behind her, an angry hiss rose up from the tress below. Clawed vines and branches rose up to the night to clutch and trap the ghosts and bar their path into Life. Broadfeather's tiny heart quivered. But she remembered her eldest (and those beady eyes) and she thought of her star friends who had lived an eternity in the deep dark sea and knew she had to go on. On a signal from First Crow they wheeled up, higher and higher to the curve of the sky and approving light of nameless stars. Down flew the flock to the painted stone houses of thieving wizards.

In the settlements below the moko forest, in dirt-floored cabins, stolen people rested in the few hours given to them.

The wind howled from the river, spilling a rolling fog down to the sleepers, leaving a trail of crystal frost in its wake. It was the smell of cold that woke the grandmother up. Beneath the shadow of the moko forest, cold was foreign. A disturbance to air and earth that lived in perpetual humid fecundity.

The grandmother opened the creaking shutters at her window with hands gnarled from decades harvesting in the sugar swamps. She peered into the frost-garlanded darkness and saw the shadows of the undead flying through the air. She laughed, deep up from her belly, and waved. Shadowed against the moon, ghosts trailing behind her like a war god's banner, Broadfeather cawed back.

(You've probably never heard a flock of crows laugh while their jumbie riders giggle in anticipation. *Pray you never do.*)

Word went from shack to tiny shack. Grandmothers and aunties, graybeard uncles and rumpled eldest children passing along the news.

The jumbie are coming! Death is coming over the river. The ghosts are risen from the water and whispering in the sugar swamps. Out of bed! Get the babies and get your gran! Up, up to the hills with those who can't fight. This will be the end or the beginning.

The wizard, taker of names, stealer of people, murderer and abomination, slept peacefully in his bed. He did not wrestle with bad dreams or a restless conscience. Angels have passed more troubled nights than he, enslaver of people, did that night as Broadfeather and her cousins spread their black wings and dropped the shadows of death down upon his house. After all, he had a very nice house. There were dozens of rooms, all of which he'd had furnished in the gold and mahogany style of his foreign homeland. It was easy to lay his head down to rest at night when the barracks behind his house was full of men like him with guns and knives, paid well to defend him from anything that might stalk the night. Trading in abominations and genocides, you see, can be quite lucrative. Many of the finest homes in the world are built on the very same foundations.

The shadows of death, however, care nothing for money or men.

They brushed aside the magical webs of protection the wizard constructed around his home. His soldiers and guardians fell one by one into darkly spreading pools of their own blood. Spilt as quietly as a falling dusk and quicker than a fly's blink.

The jumbie, close in on their prey, cried a howl to their Queen. A ripping, tearing of air, the scream of ten thousand souls. In the shacks surrounding the house, the strongest and canniest of those captive rose up with machete and makeshift mace. Answering the call of Death's shadows to battle for their souls and names.

The sound of the night was the sound of body and soul separating forever.

From the height of an ancient mango tree, Broadfeather and First Crow watched, exulting in their work, anticipating the feasting that would follow. (Broadfeather had high hopes of an eyeball or two.)

"You've done good work child," said the elder.

Broadfeather rustled in proud delight. "Thank you great grandmother. You taught me, and I remembered. That is what crows do." *A compliment from the First! This is as good as an eyeball. As good as an eyeball and a tongue!*

"Well, I've thought of a name for you," said First.

"Really? Oh! What is it?" Broadfeather asked giddily. In all the excitement, *she'd forgotten all about her new name!*

First eyed her with a knowing and amused look. "You sure you want me to tell you now? Maybe after the battle?"

"Nope! Now. Now is good!"

First Crow laughed. "We will call you Fisher of Bones, my girl."

The young crow held the new name in her mind, twisting it this way and that, tasting the roundness of it in her mouth. It was *good*. She cawed and jumped and gamboled in happiness.

Oh what a day! Oh what a name! She near shivered in excitement and delight.

"Yes, you have earned it. Even better than finding a treasure, you have done a good and right thing." the ancient replied with affection and satisfaction. "Now, let us eat."

The crows still roost, fight, and fly over the moko forest. Younglings still journey the wide world looking for mischief and adventure, letting the white road in the night sky guide their way. The stars shine on them fondly, in memory of their dear friend who saved them from the dark. And as long as there is memory in our bones, no one can ever steal us again.

THE RED MOTHER

ELIZABETH BEAR

A pall of ash turned my red horse roan as he and I ambled between tuffs of old lava. Basalt fields spread on either side, dotted with burnt-orange or gray-green lichen. Flat flakes of ash drifted past the brim of my hat.

We were crossing a big flow near the Ormsfjoll, and the reek of sulfur in the air left both Magni and me overeager to complete our trip. It couldn't be too much farther to the village. Magni's ears were pricked. His walk tended to rush into a tölt. I knew he had scented or heard other livestock that was still too far away for me to detect.

He knew that where there was livestock, there was fodder. He was thinking of grain and grass and company, and I couldn't blame him. It had been a long ride, and a lone horse is never comfortable. They're meant to be in the company of their own kind.

Some would snipe that this makes my horse the opposite of me.

Fair enough. I felt no need for company. I *did* need supplies, however, and—if it were to be had—information to complete my quest.

My journey was for kin-duty. I had an obligation to find my brother and give him the news that his name was cleared, his honor restored, and his exile ended. To that end, I had spun the threads of his fate by sorcery and was following them.

This was where they led.

* * *

The first sign of my return to civilization was a graveyard. The road passed through it, flanked on both sides by neat cairns. Some were marked with runestones; some stood uncommemorated. The lichen had grown over a few. But lichen grows slowly and most of the graves stood barren, sad heaps of brown-black rock with the sea in the distance behind.

Not long after, I came within sight of the village.

It wasn't a big village, Ormsfjolltharp, and I was in among it almost as soon as I noticed it. Men and women working outdoors turned to watch me as I rode past the two dozen or so houses. Turf houses, some with goats or sheep grazing on roofs that looked more like low hillocks than dwelling-places. I had been corrupted by too much time spent in southern lands where exotic building materials like wood existed. Any trees that grew here would be for boats and bows and axe-hafts, not for houses.

A group of men stood around an open-fronted cattle shed not too far from the well, the baker and the blacksmith. They were doing what folk generally do in such circumstances: passing the time of day and pretending to work a little, in case their wives should check on them.

I fingered the ebony and bone spindle in my coat pocket. The thread on it was wound tight, and I was almost to the end of the roving. I'd followed the thread all the way here, woven my path along Arnulfr's fate-thread. I'd soon need a new thread to follow. It would raise questions for a solitary man to buy carded wool in such a place, however.

I rode Magni to the hitching rail—not too far from the cluster of gossipers, but not too close either. There were five men: one black, one red, one dun, and two as nondescript in color as I had been before my hair and beard went to pewter.

They looked up as I swung down from the saddle. Magni stood placidly except for turning his head to glance over his shoulder, hopeful of a treat. He got a scratch instead and sighed in companionable disappointment when I didn't loosen his girth. You never know when you might need to leave in a hurry.

"I know," I said under my breath. "I'm a grave disappointment to you."

I seemed to be a grave disappointment to the cattle-shed malingerers as well, judging by the scowls they turned on me. I forced my own face into a friendlier expression than I was feeling, stopped a healthy few paces back, and said, "I'm looking for a man called Arnulfr Augusson. Or his wife, Bryngerthr Thorrsdaughter. It's possible they passed this way."

"Be you a kinsman?" the black-haired one asked. His cheeks were suncreased above a thicket of beard.

I nodded. That sharpened their gazes.

One of the nondescript ones asked, "Would that make you the one they call Hacksilver?"

I tipped my head to let the question slide off one side. A weight shifted along the broad brim of my hat, but it was just all the ash piled there. We go viking or we starve; we send our sons off to settle the coasts and rivers of Avalon and the Moonwise Isles; we build our trade towns and send our mercenary bands almost to the heart of the Steppe. And still there aren't so many Northfolk that a man can escape his reputation—or a lawsuit—with ease.

"Some sort of sorcerer, I heard," said the black one.

"Right," said the red. "They say he laid warfetter on a whole castle full of sentries. A double dozen of them, out in Avalon. Across the poisoned sea."

"Little renown to be won in such work," I remarked, conversationally. "Who'd sing a man's name for butchering the blinded and limbbound?"

"Womanish work, spell-weaving," said the black-haired man. "Don't they usually keep camp whores for that?"

He watched me with narrowed eyes.

I made myself sound as if I were not disagreeing. "A curious tale. From whom did you hear it?"

My voice gets a little more precise when I'm being Not Angry. I pulled my hand out of my pocket so I wouldn't finger my spindle, and I didn't place it on the hilt of my knife.

"There's an old Viking up the cinder trail," the red man said. "A Karlson. Supposed to have been a sea-king in his youth. Nobody here calls him naught but Half-Hand."

A chill lifted the hairs on my neck. Behind me, Magni snorted and shifted, making the saddle creak. I knew a man with half a hand once, a man whose father's name was Karl. A Viking, a sea-king, a giver of arm-rings. Yes, he had been those things.

I said, "I never heard of a sorcerer who could lay warfetter on as much as a hand of men all at once. The strain of more would kill the wizard . . . so they say."

The skalds and the seers tell us we ought to love war. And somebody must. There's enough of it.

Maybe Ragnar Karlson, called Half-Hand, called Wound-Rain, was still that man. Men get old—even sea-kings—and I hadn't seen him in ten years or more. So I couldn't be sure. He certainly wasn't a skald, or a seer.

I might have passed for a seer, but as for the man who loves war . . . I didn't think that was me. I was the man who didn't know what else to do with himself if he wasn't fighting a war that he hated.

Farming's harder work and at least as uncertain as raiding. Because the world is not a fair place, farming doesn't win renown. Extorting towns and ransoming priestlings and chieftains, that is where the glory lies.

Magni was less than pleased with me when I dusted the ash off his saddle and climbed back on. He'd hoped our walking was over for the day, and there might be hot mash and cool water before long. But after a longing look and a little drunken swerve toward a paddock across the square populated by a half dozen other horses, he cooperated.

Ragnar's homestead was not too much farther. We crossed another finger of the basalt flow and came down into a second grassy valley. From experience, I knew that turf lay over soil no more than a finger-length deep, comprised of dust, sand, and loess that had collected in this valley that was little more than a crevice between tuffs. Ragnar would have worked himself and his thralls hard to enrich it with dung and fish guts and make it bear the rich green grass that now poked forlornly through drifts of ash.

Cattle would starve this winter if the hay were lost. And if cattle starved, men starved as well.

Viking *was* an easier way to make a living. Until you weakened.

Ragnar's homestead was more than a turf house in the village, and less than a sea-king's hall. I saw its long shape against the hillsides that would have been green with the flush of summer grass. It was built of thatched basalt, not sod and turf, and it seemed to have been built over a stable dug into the slope behind it. The beam over the door was wood, carved with dragon heads on the ends like a ship's prow.

Ragnar was cutting dried turf in the yard. His ropy, scarred back did not suggest that *he* had weakened. I halted Magni well clear of the gate and whistled, then dismounted once he turned. He would have heard the hooves, but it was polite to let a man know you were not a raider.

As I walked up, leading my gelding, Ragnar's eyes flicked from me to Magni and back again. His face went through a couple dozen expressions before settling on incredulity.

"Auga Hacksilver, you old bastard. Making friends already, I imagine?"

I shrugged, and in attempting to brush some ash off Magni's flaxen mane merely ground it in.

Ragnar shook his head at me. "I'd wish I'd known you were coming. I would have laid odds that you'd turn folk against yourself in the first half-day, and I would have cleaned up. I've never met a man like you for going to a new town and finding somebody who's already mad at you there. It's almost as if you make enemies on purpose."

"Some would say that those who spread the tales make the enemies," I answered easily.

"A man's earned fame shall never die," Ragnar replied.

I snorted loudly enough that I could have blamed it on Magni. It's a comforting thing to tell ourselves, that the name lives on. And in my experience, it's nonsense.

He continued, "Speaking of death, what are the odds that you're still breathing?"

I laid my fingers on my throat. "Two to one," I offered. "I'll give you a better spread on it this time tomorrow."

"Isn't there some sort of ill-considered decision-making process regarding other people's spouses you could be engaging in right now?"

"Hey, your wife came to me, Ragnar." I waggled my hand noncommittally. "She wasn't so great that I'd think it would be hard to keep her at home if you put in a little effort, though."

He cursed like a piked bear, and I wondered if I'd overplayed. I've never had the skill of knowing when to walk away from a flyting.

It was safer to take the punch than to look at him. You had to seem like you didn't care. Like you didn't fear.

Nobody ever won a flyting by seeming a coward.

He surprised me, though. He didn't swing. He glowered, and then he said, "What the hell brings you to the ass end of Ormsfjoll?"

"One thing and then another."

Ragnar's lips worked. "Stay in my hall tonight. Turn your horse in with mine. The wife won't thank me if I let you pass without paying your respects."

Does he have a new wife? I wondered.

I did learn a few things from the time I spent with Ragnar. One was that if you're going to fuck a man, and fuck his wife, it's better for domestic harmony if you make sure everybody involved is on board with the plan right from the beginning. Another was that no one ever got anything out of Ragnar Wound-Rain without paying for it—one way or another.

I untacked Magni and sent him off to the herd with a pat. Then I knocked the ash off my hat and followed Ragnar up the steps to the door.

The fire on the long hearth was banked low, to not overwarm the house in summer. The food was rye bread and ewe's butter with stewed fish and onions. Ragnar still had the same wife, Aerndis, and somehow she'd kept everything from tasting of sulfur and ashfall. I was surprised at how warmly she greeted me. Perhaps Ragnar's irritation was not without basis.

I sat at the trestle and washed my hands in the bowl she brought, drank her ale, and bantered with Ragnar while Ragnar's tenant farmers filed in and found their places along the board. There was plenty of food, and Aerndis served me again before the bondi ate. Then she sat at Ragnar's right hand, and a couple of women who might have been wives of the farmers present brought them their bowls and their ale. All three of us were stretching uncomfortably to ease our fullness by the time the tenants were fed and filing back out again for the work of the afternoon.

I watched them go, and watched the women clear the table, and thought that there should have been children about: grown and near-grown sons and daughters. I didn't ask after their absence. It might have been that girls were married into nearby farms. It might have been that sons were away viking, or trading, or a little of both, but in that case you'd expect a young wife or two carding and spinning and tying off leading-strings to keep the babies out of the fire. You'd expect them in silks with silver brooches to hold their gowns up—or even gold, like the ones Aerndis wore—and not like the wives of the bondi with their bronze and pewter.

It might have been that they'd had ill luck conceiving, or ill luck in keeping children alive. But it's hard on a couple my age to run a farm all on their own, even with tenants. Tenants have to be supervised, and thralls have to be driven.

Under most circumstances, Ragnar and Aerndis would have taken on a few oath-sons and oath-daughters, to everyone's benefit. They might have elevated the best of their bondi, or they might have taken in the children of dead companions of the war-band.

Curiosity might seem insolent, and I take care never to seem insolent unless I mean to. It might cause grief, and that's another response I do not seek to provoke unintentionally.

Ragnar had, it seemed, no such bounds on his inquisitiveness. He looked at me rubbing my belly and laughed at me. "So. What are you doing up in the bright country, so far between good meals? Running from a weregild yourself?"

"Might be looking for a place to settle," I said noncommittally. My fingertips automatically reached for the spindle in my pocket. I eased them away again.

He'd taken me in and given me guest right. I knew, based on our history, that that probably meant he wanted something. We hadn't parted on such warm terms that I would expect him to put me out in the ashfall. But . . . farm me out to one of the cottages of his bondi, maybe.

His giving me guest right in his own home meant he couldn't take a physical poke at me. Nor could any of his men.

Perhaps it was unkind of me to provoke him with the threat of my continued presence. But kindness has never been a fault that much afflicted me.

"Can you buy land?" he asked.

I shrugged. Ragnar had to know that I had money unless I'd lost it—and he knew that by preference I diced with fate rather than for silver. My years of viking had been several and my needs while traveling were few. A path for my gelding; a mossy rock to lay my head on.

I could buy land. "It remains to be seen if I want to. It seems you've been spreading a great many rumors about me."

"Your rumors spread themselves."

I refrained from provoking him further. It took an effort when he handed me straight lines like that, however.

"I could just kill you for your money. Your brother being absent, there's no one to pay a weregild to, and it's not as if anyone who knows you would complain."

"If I were fool enough to carry my money with me." The money was in a bank twenty days' ride south, or five by boat if the wind were favorable. "If I filled up my saddlebags with gold, Magni would waddle. And it would be bad for his back. And there would be no room for my food."

Aerndis had always been a quiet one, but clever with it. She gave me a sly look. "As I judge from the crumbs in your beard, there's been little enough room for that as there is."

"Your cooking outshines mine, it's true." Especially when I was cooking up boiled soup-cake thickened with shreds of wind-dried fish.

I found myself reluctant to open the bargaining. When you want something from someone that you can't just take, letting them know it exposes your vulnerability.

Still, I had to try.

And maybe Ragnar would be feeling generous with a full belly and his ale-cup to hand.

I said, "You weren't far wrong when you brought up my brother being missing. The real answer to your question of what I am looking for is, 'Arnulfr.' Did you hear my brother was exiled for manslaughter?"

"Hm." It sounded like agreement, around a mouthful of rye bread. Ragnar had gotten ropy with age rather than thick and I couldn't imagine finding a corner into which to fit another bite of anything, but cutting sod is hard work.

I glanced toward the hearth-stone, as if fascinated by its ornate carved and dyed reliefs. "The line of Arnulfr's fate led me here, and it ends here."

Aerndis refilled my cup while Ragnar wiped ale froth from his beard. "What do you want with him?"

"I found the real killer. He can go home."

Ragnar swallowed, washed it down with ale, and snorted. "Who'd you frame?"

"You wound me."

He said, "In that case, you could have kept your father's farm."

"And what about Arnulfr?"

"Your brother's got his patch of ground by now."

I gestured to his rough hands, the whole one and the one the axe had split. "Farming looks like hard work."

"I've half a hundred head of cattle and seven horses. Sheep and goats. Chickens and geese and a dog. Four bondi look to me for protection. I even managed to keep nearly all of them alive last winter, which wasn't easy." He waved vaguely at the doorway, through which the ashy dooryard was just visible.

So the eruptions had been going on that long. Perhaps that explained the number of new graves along the road. "Not a lot of Vikings this far north."

"It's a long swim to civilization," he agreed. "You really cleared his name?"

I nodded, looking back toward my host, away from the fire.

Ragnar eyed me levelly. His eyes were light, for such a black-haired man. "So, when you say that someone else was to blame. In all seriousness: factually, or conveniently?"

I smiled.

"And if you can find him and tell him, you're delivered of your kin-duty."

"Yes."

The sun had not set, would not brush the horizon for hours yet. Its rays crept through the vents beneath the roof. It lit the underside of the thatch and all the things stored in the rafters sideways, creating a bright and alien relief. The interior walls of the longhouse were plastered white with lime render and lime wash to make the interior bright in daylight, painted with coiling trees and flowers in ochre reds and yellows. I wondered why they hadn't finished a ceiling under the thatch.

Ragnar rattled his fingertips on the trestle. "Why *not* take that land and farm it yourself? It's an easier living down south than up here in the bright country."

"I wasn't lying when I said farming was too much hard work for me." I decided to be generous. "So you don't actually have to worry about me buying the next farm over, and my presence weighing on you the rest of your days."

Ragnar frowned judiciously. "What's news worth to you?"

"Curse you, Half-Hand. This is a kin matter—"

"Sure it is, and so you shouldn't mind running a little errand in return for news of your brother." He smirked. "And his wife."

I weighed it. Ragnar always had known me a little too well. "Your word that you know where he is."

Ragnar shrugged. "I know where he was, and where he was going."

If he'd been lying, I thought, wouldn't he have made a bigger promise? "What's the errand?"

"Let's go outside."

He drained his cup and set it down. I did the same, standing as he stood. I nodded to Aerndis, then put my hat on as I followed him into the yard.

If Bryngertha *had* wanted me, I might have been content with the quiet and backbreaking life of a farmer. Might have made myself contented, anyway. But Bryngertha had wanted Arnulfr, and all Arnulfr had ever wanted in truth was Bryngertha . . . and that quiet and back-breaking life.

Though my brother's experience showed that even the life of a simple landed farmer was not without its risks.

Ragnar leaned on a stone fence and watched his seven horses and my single one brushing the ash aside to graze. I leaned beside him. I waited a long time, watching his expression from the corner of his eye, before I ventured to ask, "About that errand . . ."

"So," Ragnar said by way of answer. "I don't suppose you're still a witch."

His braids were down to his waist now, befitting a chieftain. If you ignored the bald spot they framed, impressive. He hadn't bothered with a hat.

"Eh," I said. "Are you about to claim I ever was one?"

He snorted. "You were a clever shit, anyway. Clever as Lopt and just as likely to get snagged on your own pretensions. How are you at volcanos?"

"I can ride away from them as well as any man. They say you ought to head upwind and keep to the high ground."

He pointed at the thread of smoke that rose through the smoky sky. It was just discernable through fumes and falling ash. I could imagine the outline of a conical hill poking above the horizon if I squinted.

He said, "What about one with a dragon in it?"

"There's no such things as dragons," I said.

"Should be easy to slay, then."

"No," I said, wondering if it was Arnulfr's fate-thread that ran out here in the bright country, or Auga Augusson's. "What kind of natu-ralist would I be if I went and slew every strange beast I ever came upon?"

Aerndis sniggered, which was when I realized she had come out behind us. Woman moved like a cat.

Ragnar glared at her but spoke to me. "So now you're a naturalist?"

"I'm not a dragonslayer."

Aerndis spoke in a tone I recognized as the voice of sweet reason. "If you slay the dragon you stop the eruption, I warrant. He's been digging around in that volcano with his great black claws. There was nary a rumble until he showed up, this time last year. We were lucky to get enough hay in for winter, and then the sickness came and a lot of us got a late start on planting this year. There isn't much left, and people are going to be hungry when the dark comes again, especially with a dragon picking away at the livestock. Folks would be grateful to the man who saved this harvest. Grateful enough to give him a home. And they say dragons hoard gold . . ."

Ragnar glared at her.

"Darling of you to think of my future, sweet Aerndis, and to want to keep me around," I said.

Ragnar glared at me.

"All right," Ragnar said, when the glare was well out of his system. "Well, getting rid of that dragon is the only way you're getting to your brother."

Aerndis suddenly, abruptly, turned and walked away. Too far away to hear us, and then she kept walking. I had seen what her face did before she turned, and a chill lifted my hackles. "What do you mean?"

Ragnar cleared his throat and spat over the rail. "Arnulfr's here."

". . . here."

He tapped the earth underfoot with his toe. "Buried. Dead. His wife too. And my daughter and two sons."

"I don't—"

"They came. And they stayed the winter. And they never left."

Ah, Auga Hacksilver and his famously glib tongue. I was struck as dumb as a stone when the sea washes over it.

"Aerndis understates. There was a great sickness," Ragnar said, taking pity. "It was a hard winter. And the sickness was especially cruel. It fell hardest on the young and those in their prime."

"Oh," I said, because it was what I could think to say. I touched the spindle in my pocket, felt the wisp of roving at the end of the thread.

Ragnar drew a deep breath and shook himself together, turning his bright gaze back to the horses. The horses were calm, and I watched them, too. We stood together for a moment. Then he turned and grinned at me, gap-toothed, as I stared. "And that dragon, Hacksilver. That dragon's man-long fangs drip venom. *Eitr.* So if you want to send your brother home, and his wife, you're going to bring me the gall of that dragon, and you're going to help me get my sons back, and my little girl."

Eitr. There was a word I hadn't heard in a while. A complicated word that could mean *anger,* or it could mean *poison,* or it could mean *gall,* in all the senses of gall—the sort that is spoken, and the sort that burns flesh less metaphorically. But *eitr* was also the source and the font of all life in the world.

Life and death are not so far apart, as it happens, and neither are venom and the truth.

"Have you turned into the cowardly sorcerer they call you, then? You'd leave your brother lying in his grave, and Bryngertha beside him, doomed to the meagre afterlife allotted those who die of pestilence?"

Ragnar was trying to get a rise out of me and coming perilously close to an insult I could not with honor ignore. But guest right stood between us. I crossed my arms the other way on the top course of the fence. A few of the horses, including Magni, decided it was a good time to amble over and see if we had carrots.

"Usually, one doesn't have a lot of options, once a man is in the grave. Anyway, people pay more attention to what a man says than to his deeds, and even more than that to whatever lies others tell about him." I pushed a soft, inquisitive horse nose away from my pocket. "It's all spin. Maybe I can buy him a better afterlife if I write a few songs about him. Why don't you go and get your own dragon venom?"

"Most folk are stupid," Ragnar replied. "And I know the truth behind the stories. At least as far as you're concerned. You've got a better chance of walking into a dragon's lair and back out again than I do. Than any man I've ever met."

"Simple. Kill the dragon, collect its gall. Raise a bunch of people from the dead and save the harvest. That's what you want of me."

"I'll feed you breakfast first."

Despite myself, when I met his gaze, I found myself smiling at the audacity in his smirk. That audacity is why I sailed with him. It's why I did other things with him, too.

"I'd think—"

He rolled his eyes. "Nobody cares what you think. They only care what you do."

I wished Ragnar to Hel in company with my brother. I stared him in the eyes and said, "Your word that everything you've told me is true."

Without looking, he flicked his knife from its sheath and across the back of his hand. A thin line of blood formed, the wound-rain that was his byname. We'd spilled enough in each other's company.

"My word of honor," he said.

I sighed gustily, from the bottom of my lungs. Ash whispered past my forehead, swirling on my breath. I took my hat off and nodded.

"Sure," I said. "I'll need some jars with stoppers. And for you to give me your fattest horse."

"What's wrong with your horse?"

I stroked Magni's neck. He hated having his face touched. "I'm not going to feed *my* horse to a dragon."

Ragnar pursed his lips, making the moustache jut. Then he nodded, reached out, and gave Magni a scratch under his mane. "All right. But if *you* get eaten he belongs to me."

We went back inside, and when Aerndis brought me more ale I caught her attention and said, "I have agreed."

She brought me seed-cake, too.

They gave me a sleeping place on the bench along the wall. Sometime before the brief interlude that passed for sunset, we retired. I slept alone, and better than I had any right to in Ragnar Karlson's house.

The sun was already high in the sky when we awoke, washed, and broke our fast. I followed him outside, still trying to reckon some way to avoid the task he had set me. There wasn't any dragon, I thought—just the living land heaving beneath us. And there was no god I knew to pray to and no spell I knew to weave that could so much as delay the eruption of a geyser, let alone make a volcano stop smoking. We'd all be lucky if it didn't decide to send out a tongue of lava to fill up this grassy valley nestled between its previous flows.

Ragnar grumbled some more, but he brought me the horse.

The dark gelding was fat, all right. He was shaped something like a mangel-wurzel, and his hooves were overgrown, and he limped in the off hind.

"This horse is lame."

"You said fattest, not soundest. And you'd not expect me to give you a sound one, to feed to a dragon."

"It's far to walk." I gestured at the smoking hill on the horizon. "And I can't ride him."

"Why not?" Ragnar cackled like a raven that has spotted an old enemy. "It's not like riding him is going to impede his healing. His name is—"

"Don't tell me his name." I gave the horse a withered piece of carrot. "There's no point in getting attached."

Ragnar didn't have a saddle that fit the gelding, round as he was. And I wasn't going to hop on a strange horse bareback and try to get him to take me, all alone, to the den of some monster—or even to a fiery hole in the ground. So I walked and led him. The basalt hurt my feet through my boots; it seemed to hurt his feet, too, because he minced along like a courtier in heeled shoes. It didn't help that he tripped on his own overlong hooves with every third stride and limped on that bad leg. Watching him try to move was a sad old comedy.

I lured him on with bits of turnip and carrot. He wasn't terribly enthusiastic about the turnip. He grabbed at the carrot, and I knocked on his teeth. "Manners."

I laughed at myself. Was there any point in civilizing this animal?

A sharp bit of basalt stabbed me in the sole as if my bootleather didn't even exist. I stopped, leaned on the gelding's neck, and inspected my foot. No blood, and it hadn't gone through that I could tell.

I turned and glared at the horse. He put his nose in my face and blew carrot-scented breath over me. He had braced himself as if standing on tiptoe, the bad foot cocked off the ground so his weight wasn't resting on it. I ran my hand down the leg. He didn't like me handling it. But there was no swelling, heat, or sign of a fracture. No bulge of a bowed tendon. No sign of a bruise inside the hoof or any of the other thousand things that could go wrong with a horse's foot.

Which meant the injury was probably a strained ligament, which might heal with a few months of rest, or might be with him for the rest of his life. If he were going to have a life beyond the next few hours.

He wasn't badly made, if you didn't mind the hooves and the fat and the fact that he might have been born dark as night but the long summer days had weathered him the same red-black as the crumbling lava underfoot. He was smaller than Magni but built sturdily enough to carry a grown man. The only marking on him was an ash-fall stippling of white hairs on the flat plane of his face, stretching from brow to muzzle but not defined enough to be properly called a blaze.

He had a pretty head with defined cheekbones and a tapered muzzle. Intelligent ears. I had his full attention as I stood back and looked at him.

He nickered at me.

I felt a pang for the basalt-colored horse. There probably wasn't a dragon. But if there was a spirit of the volcano, it would want some kind of sacrifice, and if I couldn't trade with a dragon for *eitr* to bring my brother and his wife back, maybe I could trade with the whatever-it-was to end the eruption and save the harvest. But one lame horse still probably wouldn't be enough to fix anything.

. . . the basalt-colored horse.

I'd been going along for such a while without one that the tickle of an idea surprised me. I heard myself whistle.

The gelding's ears pricked, and he limped a step toward me.

"Don't get your hopes up," I said. "But if you get really lucky, maybe there *will* be a dragon."

He took another step . . . and tripped again. Those feet were a disgrace. Long as a town woman's pattens, and the pony couldn't walk any better in them.

I pulled my hook knife from my boot. He looked at me suspiciously. I let him sniff it. He obviously considered it something of a disappointment.

"Sorry, boy. It's not a weird carrot." He had to be motivated, to get that fat eating lichen and silage and straw chaff and turnips and wind-dried fish all winter. Ragnar probably would have slaughtered him for horsemeat come the frost.

I bent to lift one foot. He leaned away from me, worried. Ragnar had never been much of a farrier, and I remembered that most of his horses were afraid of having their feet handled. He apparently hadn't improved.

With the aid of carrots and some rye bread sweet with birch syrup, I got the hooves trimmed anyway. He was easier about the last one than the first one. He was still lame after, but at least he stopped tripping.

The trim made him even more footsore on the basalt. After watching him mince for fifteen or twenty steps, I sighed in disgust, pulled my hook knife out again, and cut a wide strip and a narrow strip off the edge of my oiled leather cloak. He fussed at me while I tied the crude boots around his ankles, but when he stepped out again he seemed surprised and pleased at the improvement.

I fingered the spindle in my pocket. *Dammit, Hacksilver. Don't you go getting attached to your bait.*

After several more painful hours of walking, the basalt was replaced by a steep slope of cinders. The air stung my lungs and we both grunted and leaned forward, pushing up the slope, cinders crunching. I started to notice the bones. Not complete skeletons, or scattered limbs. But here the skull of an ox; there the pelvis of a horse. Big bones, with scraps of meat cured on them by the hot, lifeless air.

The horse didn't like the smell.

Unease pricked through me, sourceless and unsettling.

I was not, as I mentioned, *really* expecting a dragon. The basalt-colored horse was apparently smarter than me. He stopped halfway up the cindery slope, ears pricked, head craned, neck tense. A steady fellow: he was spooked and snorting, but he stood his ground and inspected the way ahead instead of skittering or trying to bolt.

I stopped also. Strained every sense, as the horse was straining his. The air reeked of brimstone. My eyes teared; wreaths of smoke obscured what vision I retained. But as I held myself still, my bones and the soles of my boots were shaken by a low sound. One that seemed to emanate up from the burnt ground underfoot as much as propagate through the air. It felt like the rumble of a geyser gathering itself to explode.

I pulled the spindle from my pocket and inspected the thread wound around it. Gray, scratchy, thin as wire and as like to cut you. The measure of a kinsman's life.

I'd spun fine to spin long. Long enough for my purpose, maybe.

It would have been better woven into a net—a net to catch the vision and imagination. But even the long summer days were not long enough for that. So I found a rock about the right height, dusted the ash off it to be certain it wasn't a desiccated pelvis, and sat down. A silver coin from my pocket had already been clipped and shaved a fair bit in its travels. I used my hook knife to shave it a bit more, dulling the edge but collecting a pinch of silver dust in a fold of my trousers. Silver like mirrors and silver like tongues.

I put those tools down and picked up the spindle, dipped my finger in the silver, drew a loop across my open hand, and gave the spindle a twirl. It dropped, and I rubbed metal dust into the chain-ply of my brother's life, making the thread into yarn that could be unwound from the spindle without unraveling.

I supposed it didn't matter, really, if the thread unwound itself—assuming Ragnar was telling the truth and Arnulfr and Bryngertha were dead. A poor omen perhaps for Arnulfr's legend, but Arnulfr's legend was the tale of a quiet man quietly damned for a crime by treachery. There are a lot of sagas about lawsuits. There aren't too many about the losers of lawsuits.

Being born again by dragon venom would be the most songworthy thing that had ever happened to him.

Was Ragnar telling the truth? Well, I had known Ragnar to be sly, to misdirect, like any good warlord. I had not known him to betray his word of honor.

Getting eaten by a dragon was a death worth singing. Maybe that would be enough of a legend to gain me admittance into one of the better heavens. Or maybe the End Storm would blow up while I was plying, and I wouldn't have to worry about legends or kinsmen anymore.

Having thought of songs, I sang to myself as I worked. As the ash fell around me. Songs for the goddesses who measured every man's life, and then measured him for his coffin. Songs for the spinners. Warlock songs, seithr songs. Women's songs, but there was no one to hear me except the basalt-colored gelding, and he was in no position to impugn my masculinity.

At last, I was out of silver dust and all the yarn was plied. Gray, scratchy. Smelling faintly of lanolin and lye. I stretched it between my fingers and let it twirl into a skein. If there had been any sunlight beneath the ash plume, I might have detected a subtle sparkle in the twist.

The basalt-colored horse dozed disconsolately at the end of his lead rope. I'd bored him to sleep.

I hoped it wasn't a comment on my singing.

I let him sniff the skein, which he did with curiosity but no apparent concern. That was a relief. Some animals will not abide the smell of sorcery.

I started by braiding his mane, working the fate-cord into it as I went. I wound the line around his chest and shoulders like a girl binding her wooden horse with thread to make a play-harness. He stood for it, remarkably still and even-tempered. I braided traces back on themselves without cutting the line and let them trail, then bound the whole thing off just as I ran to the end of the thread.

The horse craned his neck around to watch me, ears alert, eyes bright and expression dubious. I wished I had a walking stick or a long bone from which to make a whiffletree, but it would only drag on the ground. And probably spook even this horse. So I just draped the traces over his rump and tied them in a little bow.

It was, after all, the symbolism that mattered.

"Well, buddy, I hope this works," I said.

He blew a warm breath over me. We resumed climbing the cone.

The slope leveled as we came close to the top of the volcano. We stopped to drink at a spring that bubbled up from a cluster of stones, clearing some of the ash from our throats. I splashed water on my face. It was lukewarm and fizzed like surf, full of bubbles. It reeked and tasted of brimstone, but at least it wasn't boiling. The horse drank, snorted to clear the fumes from his nostrils, and gave me a look before drinking again as if to say, "Yeah, I've seen worse."

When I lifted my head, I realized we were nearly to the vent. The horse grew increasingly restive as we came up the final slope, and with a couple furlongs to go he planted his feet in their ridiculous leather bags and refused to walk another step.

I chirruped to him and shook the lead. He planted his hind feet, rocked back, and reared. Not a dramatic, sky-pawing rear, but a clear declaration that he was not moving.

It was honestly surprising we'd made it this far. "Good lad," I told him, and turned him around to face downhill. I wound the fragile-seeming traces around a head-sized piece of pumice and tied them off.

Careful not to loop the lead rope around my hand, I stepped up beside the twitching horse and unfastened his halter. I stroked his sweating, ash-gritted shoulder as I slid the straps off his nose. He stood harnessed in sorcery, fate-threads, and kin-duty, leaning against the yarn-spun traces as if against a plow stopped by thick turf.

I stepped away and tossed the halter onto the cinders before turning back uphill. I cupped my hands to my mouth and used a little twist of luck, a scrap of thread wound round my fingers, to shift the wind so that my voice would carry. I took the deepest breath I could, tightened my diaphragm, and bellowed.

"Here, dragon, dragon! Nice fat pony. Lame, too! An easy dinner!"

For a long moment, nothing. The reek of fumes swirling on the breeze I'd conjured up; the steam rising from the cinders. The vast silence of the lifeless mountainside.

Then came a rumble, and a long hard clatter like a bag of armor bits and chopped-up candelabras dragged over stone. The scraping of stone on stone. I levered my neck back, peering through streaming vapors, blinking away the fume-begotten tears.

A great head that only seemed small because it was on a neck as long as a ship's mast poked over the rim of the crater. The head was hammer-shaped, and scaled, and horned, and fanged. I could have called it red or orange in color and not been wrong, but the rough scales seemed translucent, and refracted rainbows in their depths, like the planes of light struck within an opal. Even under the dim overcast of smoke and the haze of fumes, it dazzled.

The owner of the head—and the neck—sniffed deeply. Once, twice. Then it reared back and struck with surprising speed.

I threw myself to the side, cinders bruising my palms. The horse, being nobody's fool, took off. I winced for his bad foot, because I am a soft, womanish fool of a sorcerer. He galloped down the slope with all the alacrity and focus of a horse running Hel-bent away from a dragon, the boulder bouncing behind him in its traces. The glamour that I'd spun and sung and knotted around both horse and stone caught on the weave of threads and mirror-bright silver scrapings and made it seem the whole mountainside was collapsing into a vast horseshoe depression. The basalt-colored horse was just one more boulder bouncing along in the midst of the rest.

I was rather proud of the effect, and the way the sound of hoofbeats was lost in the simulated rumble of the rockslide.

I turned my attention back to the dragon as it pulled back again and took a long, slow sniff. Red nostrils flared darker in the fire-faceted muzzle. The upper lip drew back to move air across the palate and a forked tongue flickered.

Steam hissed from its nostrils. My vision swam with acrid tears. The head swung down again, falling toward me like the hammer it resembled.

If I'd been some hero out of sagas I'd have swung up a sword or had a venomed spear at the ready. I just raised my empty hands as if that could somehow fend off an avalanche.

The blow stopped before it fell, the dragon's enormous head so close that the heat of its hide and breath curled my hair. I smelled the ends scorching.

The dragon spoke, and despite the shape of tongue and mouth it surprised me by uttering words I could understand completely. Its phrasing was archaic, its voice as deep and hollow as caverns.

"I smell a horse," it said. "But much closer, I smell a witch. Hello, little witch. That was a clever thing, for a wisp such as you."

Well, I had been hoping to impress it. And I'd lured it out all right. Now what?

It sniffed again. "Have you come to slay a dragon?"

A bead of saliva gathered along the edge of the dragon's lip. I stepped to the side as it dripped, stretching a long thread behind it. The venom looked like honey glowing in the sun, but when it touched the ground it sizzled on the ash. The spot smoked slightly.

I thought about the jars in my pack and felt as cold as if the blood were draining from my body.

I gulped down the lump in my throat. "I came to bargain with one. You see I carry no spear, no harpoon—"

The rumble of the dragon's words shook my diaphragm. "If you wish gold, I will not give it. If you wish ancient and storied weapons, there is nothing you can give me that I could not take. If you wish to die gloriously and be remembered in song, you should have brought a poet. You reek of sorcery. "

"As long as I don't smell like a snack. "

"Hmmm." It tilted its head to one side. "You smell pickled and stringy."

The wings rustled as it shrugged.

Perhaps it was not strange that the dragon's verbal jousting made me feel as if I had come from the wilderness into a safe and familiar hall. I was comfortable in an argument. The fear and tension drained away and in their place a manic energy buoyed me.

I crouched and held my hand over the smoking *eitr*. I turned my face up to the dragon. I was gray with ash and streaked with tears.

I felt the warmth of the poison and the warmth of the ashes on which it rested as if I held my hand over gentle coals. "I've come to bargain for this."

The great head tilted and drew back. The lambent eyes with their shattered planes of iridescent scarlet and vermilion blinked lazily. "I could give you more of it than you wished for, little witch."

"Your presence here, your awakening of the volcano—they've brought a blight upon the land. Men and women have died of illness and hunger. The cattle will die as well, if the grass is buried under ash and pumice, or they will choke on the poison fumes of the volcano. I have been asked to win your *eitr* to bring back those who have died."

"Cattle die and kinsmen die, little witch. If they cannot live in a place, then they should go."

"Look," I said bluntly, "what can we give you to leave this place and not return?"

"What can you offer me? A fat horse is all very well, but I can fetch my own when I want one. I have . . . commitments that will keep me in this lair."

"For how long?"

"Not long," said the dragon. To my amazement, it placed first one and then the other enormous talon on the rim of the vent. Having done so, it settled its head between them, bringing its eye level down to mine. I could see the great humped shoulders, the leathery folds stretching back from its forelimbs. Like a bat's, they seemed both wing and foot to walk upon. Unlike a bat's, they shimmered with all the colors of flame.

It tilted its head and rippled the taloned fingers as if counting. "Hmm. Perhaps a hundred seasons more."

Well, twenty-five years of active volcano and dragon occupation would certainly put paid to the village—and all life within miles. I rose to my feet and discovered that the air was slightly better up there. Apparently the fumes were heavy.

"Assume for a moment that I can get you whatever you desire," I said. "If you will only leave this place and give me some of your venom."

The dragon curved its sinuous neck like a goose and glanced over its shoulder, back down the length of its body into the vent. I wondered if it were assessing a hoard I could not see. I wondered how anything remained unmelted, down in the hot mouth of the earth.

It turned back. With a sigh, it said, "I have no need of human treasures."

"This obligation you mentioned—is there a way I could help you fulfill it?"

If you have never seen a dragon throw its head back and laugh (and I suppose very few have), it is a sight not easily described. I hastily tugged my hat down as a fine mist of caustic venom descended around me. A few invisible drops smarted on the backs of my hands.

"You are not boring, little witch," the dragon said. It looked this way, and then that. To my amazement, it seemed to be making a show of casualness, of reluctance.

"Hmm," it said. Then: "Do you like riddles, little witch?"

I closed my eyes.

I hated riddles.

"I have played at riddles a time or two."

"Well then." The dragon shifted its weight, settling into the mountainside like a great jarl settling into his broad, bearskin-adorned chair. "Come up a little closer, witch, and choose a stone to sit upon, and we can play at riddles for what you wish. But if you win, you must grant me a boon."

How under the Wolf Sun of my fathers did I keep getting myself into situations like this?

But I was a man on kin-business, blood-bound to do what I could. Damn my brother anyway, for being a simple farmer, for being the victim of a brutal scheme, for dying of a dragon's miasma, for getting me into all of this.

I walked up to the smoking crater as if I had not a fear in the world—certainly without *any* cringing as I came under the shadow of the dragon's wings—and while I was selecting a rock of the correct height for sitting, could not resist a peek over the edge into the vent.

I almost fell in.

I had expected the vent to contain . . .shining masses of gold, perhaps. Seething masses of lava.

Not a careful circle of boulders each as big as a cart, and a claw-raked ground of soft ash within, like a giant's campfire ring. Upon that, dead in the center, lay three enormous mottled eggs like the last remaining embers.

The dragon, it seemed, was not an *it* but a *she*.

"Well," I said. "I see what you mean by 'obligations.'"

Have you ever heard a dragon chortle? I have, and it was in no way rendered less unsettling by the knowledge that this was a female with young. For nothing on the waters and the wide, wide world is fiercer than a mother.

I found a rock, as directed, and as directed I seated myself upon it. I swung the pack with the jars down between my knees and set it gently on the stones.

"So, little witch," said the dragon. "Shall we play?"

"You go first," I said. "Best two out of three?"

The dragon stretched and sighed, settling itself. "I believe it is traditional. As for that boon—"

"As long as it's not my stringy hide."

She sniffed. "I dislike the taste of woad, and I see from your forelimbs that you're pricked all over with the stuff."

I glanced down at the old and faded ropes of tattoos. They were meant to be for protection, to ensure the forbearance of the gods.

First time in my life that the damn things actually worked.

"If you get a boon if I win," I said, "I get a boon if I lose."

"It can't be the same as the stakes," she said cagily.

"What forfeit will you have of me if *you* win?" I pushed my hat back as she thought about it.

"Have you a hoard?" she asked, finally.

I thought of gold and silver and jewels of great store. The wealth of a lifetime spent riding the whale-roads, reaving and trading. The price of my retirement, when I found a place I wanted to retire. All safe in a vault down in Ornyst, where there were bankers and banks.

I thought about kin-duty. I thought about my sister-in-law.

"Not on my person," I said.

"Wager your hoard against my venom, then," the dragon invited.

"Don't you even want to know how much I have?"

She hissed a laugh. "It's enough that it's valuable to you. That's what makes a wager interesting. That, and the story that attaches to it. That someday I may say to my children, yes, this is the gold I won riddling with a sorcerer, while you were yet in the shell."

It was a dragonish way of thinking, and not so alien to anybody who had gone a-viking. I touched my arm-rings, fingering them until I found the one that had been a gift from Ragnar when he was a sea-king and I sailed at his command. When we had been bright and young and too naïve to know any better.

I said, "If you will wager both your venom and your leaving, I will add my adornments to the pot. Those mean more to me than any hoard."

None of it was the richest that I owned, but it was enough—earrings and arm-rings, the brooch that closed my cloak and the clasp that pinned my hair—to lend me dignity. I felt a sentiment for each object. Especially since I had so recently won it all back from a murderer.

At least it wasn't my coat and boots this time.

"Your folk should move on, not me. This land is far more suitable for me than . . ."

There are few things more eloquent than the dismissive flick of a dragon's talon, it turns out.

"That's likely true," I admitted. "But you have to understand that the people of the village have built houses and barns and planted crops. Our lives are short. They won't have time or resources to up stakes and build those houses anew someplace else."

She said, "There are far more suitable places for your sort to live than there are for brooding eggs. I won't be the last to come here, so long as the earth stays hot."

"I can't wager for my folk any more than you can speak for yours." I hoped she wasn't a dragon Queen, or something, who did have the power to bargain for the whole. Anyway, the future wasn't my concern. She was right; this was a stupid place for a settlement.

She huffed at the back of her throat, not hard enough to spray venom—but hard enough to cause a mist of it to curl from her nostrils and ignite into a transparent lash of flame. She tilted her head to regard me, and I got the oddest sense that her interest was more in the bargaining and the company and the game than in who lost or won.

Sitting on eggs must be extremely boring for a creature with wings to span the open skies. I'd only had the broad sails and swift rowers of a dragon-boat to carry me, and although now my joints ached even in good weather and my feet hurt every day, I could not bring myself to settle into a farmstead and raise cows. Though I was no youth to harden my muscles on an oar without injury, I could not see myself raising a hall and draping a big throne-chair with wolf-hides and bear-hides to cushion my ass and seem fierce at the same time. No matter how much the saddle galled my behind.

I might have more in common with this dragon than I did with Ragnar or with my brother.

Damn Arnulfr.

"Done," the dragon said. "I shall begin.

"I am the shrill singer

"Who rides a narrow road.

"With two mouths I kiss hard

"The hot and pliant maidens."

I blushed, because I hadn't been expecting racy double-meanings from a dragon. But I knew the answer to this one, when I thought about it a little. "Hammer," I said. And then, "Smith's hammer. The road and the maidens are the metal to be forged. The mouths are the two ends of the hammer."

The dragon snorted another curl of fire, slightly larger than the last one. How good was the word of a dragon, anyway? Especially when exposed to a little frustration?

Perhaps I should have been surprised that the dragon knew about hammers—but the dragon knew about treasures, and steel for swords and gold for gauds alike must be refined, then hammered pure.

I hoped there were other human things the dragon knew less about. I said,

"I am the black horse.

"On eight legs I bear my rider.

"He holds no rein.

"At the end of the journey it is he who is left in the stall."

I am not sure dragons frown. Their scaled foreheads are not designed for furrowing. But I could not shake the sense that the dragon was frowning at me.

After a little while, she responded calmly, "A coffin and its bearers."

I sighed. "You can't blame me for trying."

The tongue flickered. "Can I not? Here is my next one.

"We are the old women

"*Who walk on the beach*
"*We braid the shells and seaweed*
"*In our white hair.*"

"Damn," I said.

"Do you forfeit?" The dragon leaned forward eagerly. Its talons tensed as if already imagining raking through treasure.

"Not so fast!" I held up a hand and tried to ignore the warmth of the dragon's breath ruffling my hair. Unless that was just the wind off the volcano. *What walks on a beach . . . ? Crabs. Birds.*

"Waves!" I said suddenly, as it came to me. The word burst from my lips before I could second-guess myself. "It's waves!"

"It's waves," the dragon agreed, sounding slightly disappointed.

"My next." Of course, because I was looking at a dragon, I could only think of one riddle.

Hoping she wouldn't be offended, I said,

"*I am a dragon with only one wing.*
"*But of limbs I have a score.*
"*I fly to battle.*
"*I grow more fearful when I shed my scales.*"

"Really?" the dragon said.

I spread my hands. The rock was making my backside ache. I tried not to fidget. It would only make me seem nervous.

Of course, I *was* nervous.

"A long-boat," the dragon said. She yawned before she continued. "The limbs are oars. The scales are the shields hung over the gunwales and retrieved when the men go to fight."

"You've seen that?"

"I've destroyed a few. Sometimes they're full of livestock. Or treasure."

If dragons didn't frown, did they smile? Or had she always been as toothy as she seemed now.

"What do we do if it's a draw?" I asked.

She chuckled. "A sudden-death round? By which I mean, then I eat you."

I couldn't tell if she was joking and I didn't want to ask. It might be better to let myself lose. I could always find more treasure, after all.

Never mind that it would take a desperate Viking indeed to give a berth to a man as old as me, and those were the sorts of raiders who did not come home with their ships wallowing with gold.

"Last one," the dragon said cheerfully. Did they play with their prey, like cats?

"*A stone on the road.*

"*I saw water become bone.*"

How on earth did that happen? It was a metaphor, of course—riddles always were—but what was water a metaphor for? Blood that clots? A stone was hard, and so was a sword . . . brigands? Something that could stop a journey?

No. No, of course not. The water wasn't the metaphor. The *road* was the metaphor. The whale-road, the ship-road. The sea. What was a stone on the sea?

"An iceberg," I said.

"Brave little witch," the dragon remarked. She lifted one talon and waved idly. Her opalescent eyes seemed to enlarge until I felt as if I were falling upward into them.

I'm not sure how long I gaped at her, but I was startled abruptly back into my skin when she said, "Hurry up, then. Let's see this done."

My mind went blank.

My wit ran dry.

I could think of not a single riddle.

No, not true. I could think of a riddle. But it was a children's riddle, and not one worthy of a dragon. I needed something better. Something clever. Something I stood a chance of stumping her with.

She sighed a slow trickle of flame.

Dammit.

I said,

"*Fat and full-bellied*

"*Welcome and warm*

"*I rise with joy*

"*Though my bed is hard.*"

A loaf, of course. A loaf, puffing up and baking on a flat hearth-stone before the fire.

No sooner had the words left my mouth than I thought of half a dozen better ones. The onion riddle with all the dick jokes in it . . . anything. Anything at all would have been better . . .

There was the end of my chance to save my kinfolk. There was the end of my chance to put this obligation to rest—

I was so engaged in flyting myself that I thought I must have missed the dragon's answer. And indeed, when I lifted my eyes again, she was staring at me quizzically.

"I'm sorry," I said. "I didn't hear you."

She snorted rather a lot of fire this time. "I said, I don't know. I don't know the answer."

"What?" I said, foolishly.

"Little witch, tell me the answer."

"Bread," I said. "A loaf of bread. It rises when you cook it on a hot stone."

"Fascinating." The tip of her tail twitched like a hunting cat's. "Fascinating. Is that where bread comes from?"

She sounded genuinely excited.

Dragons, it seemed, knew about death and war. But not so much about baking.

Her wings folded more tightly against her sides. "Well, you've won. That's the end of the riddles, then."

"I have another one for you," I cried, struck by inspiration now when it was too late. "As a gift. No wager."

The dragon definitely had facial expressions, and this one was definitely suspicion. "No wager?"

"None."

"What do you want if you win?"

"Just the joy of winning," I said. "Here.

"Alone I dwell

"In a stone cell

"With a gray roof.

"Though kept captive

"None holds the key.

"I am not soaring above the halls of dawn.

"I do not see the sun rise.

"What creature am I?"

She stared, tongue flickering. Moments passed, and I worried I had misunderstood her—or worse, offended her.

When she burst out, "Me!" she nearly incinerated me with the spray of her venom. "It's *me*! Oh, sorry . . ."

"I'm fine. It's fine." I remained standing, so I could dodge faster if there were more outbursts. And to get away from the eyewatering, sinus-stinging smoke curling from the cinders where the *eitr* had fallen. "Unscathed." I held out my hands to demonstrate.

"Good," she said. "How odd it is that a small, frail, temporary person like yourself should make me feel so clearly seen."

Well, from her point of view, I supposed I was all of those things.

She had been lying along the edge of the vent, just her head and forequarters poking over. Now, with a motion that was half slither and half chinning herself, she crawled up to the rim and stretched out. "Did you bring vessels?"

"Jars," I said, lifting the pack.

"Cheeky," she said.

"What's worse?" I asked. "Preparing too much and not using everything, or needing a thing and not having it to hand?"

"You swore to grant me a boon."

She had me there. "I did."

"I'll give you the *eitr*. You won the wager honorably. And I will leave this place and take with me my two children. We shall make our nest further from human habitations, though I must complain that there are more and more of you with every passing season. If you cover the whole damn landscape and keep breeding even when you encroach on other people's nesting grounds, I don't see how you can complain about a little volcano." She sighed. "And here I am helping resurrect your whelps, who will probably just make more of you."

They weren't my whelps, but I was more concerned with something else she'd said. I snuck a sideways glance over the rim of the vent. Yes, three eggs. "Wait. You and your *two* children?"

"Yes," she said. "That's the boon. Don't worry, I'll leave you plenty of *eitr* for feeding the whelp on. And I will come back every season or so to be certain the whelp is well taken care of and replenish your supplies."

That sounded less like reassurance, and more like a threat.

"You want to raise a brood of your own."

"Not I," I said. "A friend."

"Well, if I save his children, let him care for one of mine. But you, little witch—you must see that the care is good. Yourself."

"Why me?"

"Because," she said. "Because I have tested your word and your mettle. And because I'm giving *you* the foster of my whelp. I have seen what you will do for the bonds of kinship. And because you understood me and gave me a gift, so I know you understand how bound to this boring rock I am."

"But I . . . I don't want to stay here either."

"Once a turning should suffice," she said, relentless. "As I said, it's only another hundred seasons or so. The egg will hatch in . . . twelve more seasons. Make sure your folk know that if they don't take care of my little one, though, I *will* come back and eat them."

I imagined the little whelp—perhaps only as large as the horse—looking up at the giant creature before me with wide, adorable eyes and begging, "Mama, can I eat him?"

"What about the volcano?" I asked. "My people cannot survive it. Doesn't the egg need its heat to incubate?"

"Oh, a lone egg will do well enough if they bury it in dry ground near a hot spring," she said.

"Like baking a loaf of bread," I mused.

"You," she said, "and your baking."

The dragon said she would give me time to return to Ragnar's farmstead before she flew the egg down and delivered it. My backpack sloshed with jars of *eitr* as I walked, the downhill steep and full of rocks that stubbed my toes through my boot leather. I'd be lucky not to lose a nail or two.

I was lucky that was all I seemed to be in danger of losing. Unless

I tripped and fell and broke the jars, in which case the venom within would saturate my clothes, melt my flesh, and then probably catch on fire for good measure.

I walked very carefully and kept my eyes where my feet should be going.

It was a good thing, too, because the glamour I had cast on the little horse was strong enough that it even fooled me until I tripped over one of the spell-spun traces.

I had been singing to myself as I walked, songs more fitting for a warrior this time, and I had not been fingering my spindle. My hands, being free of my pockets, flung out and smacked into the horse's warm flank.

The glamour fell away in the face of concrete evidence, and I could see that the boulder he was dragging had gotten jammed into a crevice and was stuck there.

I slipped off my extremely caustic load and set the pack down carefully before going to unwind the string from around the boulder. Then I had some extra string and a horse that was already wearing a conjureish harness, so it only seemed fair that the horse carry the pack. That was what horses were for, after all, among other things.

I lashed it on over his withers. He was a convenient size, not so tall I had to reach up to tie things across his back. While I worked, I thought about getting back to town and explaining to Ragnar that he could have his children back, and all it would cost him was to spend his dotage babysitting a dragon.

I would get out of town before my brother and his wife woke up, I decided. It would be preferable to watching their teary reunion. Or having to endure either their thanks, or their lack thereof.

I finished my harnessing and patted the horse on the shoulder. He nickered at me under his breath, friendly. Or hoping for carrots.

I draped an arm over his withers. He was a good height for leaning on. I made up my mind that I was taking him with me when I went, in addition to Magni. I would have to find someplace easy for him to recuperate, assuming the leg could—and would—get better. That would mean a winter off the road, which was probably wise for a man my age anyway, even if it griped me.

Anyway, if I left him here, Ragnar would probably eat him. I felt after using him to bait a dragon, I owed him better.

I scratched under his mane. He leaned into me, lip twitching in pleasure.

"Good lad," I said. "I think I'll call you Ormr."

HER GARDEN, THE SIZE OF HER PALM

YUKIMI OGAWA

Somehow I was more relieved than anything when I found out that my father had used up the money my late mother had saved for my college. First pachinko, and then races to make up for the losses, then back to pachinko to make up for more losses. Disappointed, but relieved, I was. My life was a mess, an irreparable one, and it was not my fault. There was nothing I could do to make it okay. My father told me to go find a job right after he complained to me how unfair pachinko was; education was a luxury for a girl, anyway, in his opinion. So I walked out of the house, managed to get to the job center. I was trying so hard to not scream or cry that the whole hour was a blur that I still don't understand. The next thing I knew, I had a job, with a room to sleep in, far, far away from our house, too far for my father to come collect his money for more gambling.

I hadn't even a chance to pack, but really, there was nothing to be packed. They told me to go to the end of town, where there was a tree. They also said I'd have to take a blood test, but no one was around to perform it. Beneath the tree, there was a hole between the earth and some of its roots. This might sound weird, but at that time, it only felt natural, not like an adventure at all, as I climbed under.

It was the first wormhole. The other side of it was a cozy little house with a garden and a grandma waiting for me.

* * *

Grandma wasn't a typical grandma. She had many heads, for starters. When I first knocked on her door, she was halfway through changing heads, holding one in each hand (I now suspect she timed this with my arrival on purpose). If my father had taught me anything, though, it was that giving the exact reaction others wanted from you only made them feel they could manipulate you all they wanted, which would not make life any easier. So I remained silent for a second, before I bowed and said hello. She made me peer into her torso down the severed neck, and I saw a clock inside her rib cage. Then she placed one of the heads and grinned.

Her house, and the garden enclosing it, looked like a snow globe. When we were in orbit around a planet in another space, Grandma's eyes turned into a projector that could reflect a certain area on that planet onto her garden. When that was happening, I could interact with creatures in the area of the said planet. My task mostly was to hunt creatures from other planets in other spaces, vegetables and animals, and everything in between.

I vaguely recalled the job description had said something about helping an old lady with her gardening.

How so very inaccurate, I thought, as I shook my butterfly net as if my dear life depended on it. A net couldn't offer much in the way of protection, of course—especially when the target was shooting some unknown substance from above, among dense foliage. The leaves tried to poke my eyes at every swivel of my arm. And . . . wait, where did it go?

Through the headset in my ear I heard her boom, laughing.

There was then a sucking noise, and I felt the world turn with the gravity shift. I landed hard on the patch of grass in her garden, narrowly avoiding her rose arch; I wasn't even aware I'd gone that high up, blindly chasing my game on her order. After a moment I started coughing, air finally back in my lungs. I was covered in grime. I so wished that would have disappeared, too, along with the strange forest and the expensive insect.

"How come a butterfly spits?" I asked, almost sobbing.

"It's a moth, silly. Make sure you keep samples of the spit," she said, leaning on the windowsill, her voice reaching me directly through the air. Now she looked like an old scholar, or what I imagined a scholar might look like—soft outlines and serious eyes under a somewhat fluffy bob. "Come on, on your feet! I didn't pull you back down here to let you take a break!"

I slowly stood up, my back and calves protesting, and peered in through the window. Grandma's study impossibly had access to every window of the house, and yes, sure enough, I could see the bug comfortably perched on one of the low branches in the north patch at the back. So while I was attacking the foliage in vain, it had escaped to the other side of the house.

I grabbed my net and ran, through the corridor, out of the back door in the kitchen.

Everything was in slow motion as I felt the air shift; oxygen thicker, the scent of mint in the north patch gradually disappearing, giving way to a more suffocating smell, a bit like smoke, of the planet's wild undergrowth. That damned moth soundlessly took off from the branch, slowly made its way toward the farthest bushes, which, in Grandma's garden, marked the end of our little globe.

Beyond that was the unreachable forest.

My foot found wet, grassy soil. I kicked as hard as I could, raising my net, yelling involuntarily.

The moth shrieked angrily, even as the net came down on its head. "Well done," Grandma said. "Now you can have a proper bath." And she chuckled on at me, almost immobilized, entirely covered in the moth's slimy spit.

The bathroom was opposite the kitchen, and the bathtub was a bit small, but for Grandma and me it was more than enough. I went down into the hot water without bothering to get rid of the slime first. The water smelled wonderful, with herbs from her garden and other things she made me smuggle in from other planets. There was a small window near the ceiling, and I closed my eyes for a second and the next moment the sky was reeling with stars.

I could hear Grandma singing. Her humming, and the ticking of her clock, carried us through the wormhole.

Most of the grime finally out of my hair, I went back into the kitchen, where Grandma had somehow managed to pin the fat moth alive onto the top of the wooden table. She now scooped up something out of a glass jar that looked empty to me, then dumped the invisible contents into a sieve held over the bug. Silvery powder fell out of the mesh onto the moth, and after a few spoonfuls, the creature was covered with a shiny layer. She flipped it over and did the same to the other side.

And then it was like a silver statue of a moth lying on her table.

Grandma casually grabbed the thing and tossed it my way. I had to catch it with my shirt—I was never good at catching anything. "Go sell this thing," she said, pointing at the bug. "Make sure you get as much as you can out of that jerk."

No one, not even Grandma, explained anything to me, so this I had to figure out myself: There was this one space where globes like ours gathered from time to time, at the center of which floated an especially large space station, where "that jerk" resided.

I crouched through Grandma's rose arch and found myself at his door.

As usual, just before I could knock, he said, "Come in."

He looked to be made of something similar to Grandma, though I would never feel comfortable calling this man Grandpa. "Sir," I said as I stepped in. "Good day."

The man gestured me toward his table. I placed my bundle there, let him open it.

He regarded the silver bug as if it were a long-lost masterpiece of art. Not touching it, but viewing it from every angle possible. "Did you catch this thing?" he asked me like he could not believe it.

"Yes, sir?"

"Did it not attack you, like, with some goo?"

"It did, sir. Nothing bad followed, though."

He looked at me, a bit like he'd just looked at the silver moth. "How long have you been working for her?"

"Um," suddenly my scalp felt itchy, "for six months, sir."

"Do you miss home?"

Home? "Do you mean Earth, sir?" He nodded.

"No, not really. Should I?"

The man cocked his head, looking amused. "She chose you well."

I couldn't help but frown; we didn't choose each other, we just . . . happened. I said nothing to that.

"Look." His fingers almost brushed the moth, but didn't, just hovered over it. "Maybe you can work for me instead."

Now what? "Sir?"

"You'll find life much easier, better at my place. It's much more spacious to start with, and there's a lot more entertainment ready for you. And you'll make friends here. Her globe is much too small for a young, promising person like you."

My brows started to ache. "I . . . sir, I don't understand."

He gestured for me to wait, and went around a desk near the window, opened a drawer, and then came back with a small wooden box. "Take this," he said. "Of course you need time to think. When you make up your mind, open this box. It will guide you."

I hesitated, but he made me hold the box. Later, as I walked under the rose arch, I hid the box deep in my pocket.

"What do you mean, 'no fire'?" I asked, wondering if these words were audible through the chatters of my teeth.

"How could there be any other meaning there, that's only two words. No fire. On this planet. We need to avoid dust explosion at all costs."

I was in layers and layers of clothes and still shivering, while Grandma with her long, witchy head stood at the kitchen table wearing nothing but a knit dress and a scarf. "I cannot work out there like this," I said. "I need at least the inside of the house to be warm. I might freeze to death, or just catch pneumonia and suffer and die slowly if I'm lucky—or unlucky."

Outside, according to Grandma's windows, a storm like nothing I'd ever seen was apparently trying to topple this little house down. Oddly, there was nothing violent about it—the atmosphere looked as though it was full of tiny rainbow grains, like there were countless suncatchers hanging from the sky, only the crystals were invisible. The grains skittered and bounced around, and then . . . some of them, all of a sudden, left nasty scars in the ground, taking enormous chunks out of it with them. The creatures here looked to be all thread-ish or wiry, sticking out of white, powdery soil like spotted garden eels, and whether they were moving because of the rainbow storm or of their own accord, I would never know for sure. For now, there was no real contact between this garden and the planet somewhere below or above us, but when Grandma properly reflected the outside world onto her garden—

—it was already deathly cold at this window-surveillance stage— what would happen when I actually set foot there?

Grandma snorted, her pupils clicking as she made calculations. "As I said, in this place, all you need is a bagful of air." She blinked twice. "Well, three bagfuls, obviously. Just catch them from the front steps, don't even bother going into the garden."

"What are they, anyway? Those rainbows?"

"Air, as I said. And we don't have pneumonia germs up here, so rest assured."

I growled involuntarily, but then there was nothing I could do but put another hood over my head and pull the string along the edge of it. I grabbed three of the sealant bags from a kitchen cabinet and stomped out of the front door.

And lost my breath immediately. It didn't even feel cold any longer. It was something totally different from any winter I'd ever known. For the first time ever, I missed my subtropical hometown. It hurt. My skin, my nostrils, my lungs, and my tears started to solidify right at the edges of my eyes.

I peeled one bag off the others and opened it wide. Made it sail in the air as far as I could with my short arms. And sealed its mouth. Some of the rainbows apparently tried to escape and made a sound like popping candies against the bag material. I threw the bag into the house through the front door behind me.

Same with another bag. Somewhere in the house, Grandma was ticking. My whole face was starting to turn into a lump of ice.

One more bag to go.

Right in front of me, a black thread emerged out of the white soil. One large particle of rainbow landed on its tip, and the black thread seemed to suck it in.

I coughed, pulling my scarf over my mouth.

Another rainbow grain, much smaller this time. The black thing stretched toward it. Air. I knew that I should probably not inhale it, but to the creatures here it represented a very vital element of life.

When this tiny grain touched the thread's tip, though, it exploded.

The black thread was torn into many thinner threads that fell onto the ground radially, before vanishing into the complete whiteness of the soil. I wanted to scream, but only a muffled sound came out. I hadn't been aware that I had leaned forward to see it better; I lost footing and slipped down the couple steps that divided the house and the soil. I twisted, made myself fall onto my bottom, changing the direction of the momentum to stop sliding. The pain and the cold knocked the breath out of me, but when I looked, I was mostly safe, only one foot immersed in the powdery ground.

Forcing myself to inhale and exhale slowly, I tried to free my foot.

But no, it wouldn't come out as easily as it went in. It was powdery a second ago, but viscous the moment I tried to move in it. The harder I wriggled my foot, the heavier the whiteness seemed to become. It was as though my foot was trapped in a cement pool.

Above me, tens of thousands of millions of the deadly rainbows danced a crazy dance.

Another wiry thing sprang to life right beside my buried foot. One rainbow particle floated down, toward the wiry thing. I shouldn't be inhaling too hard, the current might pull the rainbow to me instead. But every second that passed while I sat there, my breaths got faster, my shoulders heaving.

Somewhere, Grandma was ticking. Grandma. Grandma. Grandma.

I would not beg for help; the thing was, I couldn't. My father had made sure of that. It was not the unfamiliar air that was nailing my mouth shut, stopping me from calling her.

I saw the rainbow burst out of the corner of my eye . . .

Finally, they all vanished. All of them. I was in her garden, my foot dangling over the grassy ground.

I hugged my mug, smelling the honey-ginger herbal tea. I sucked the steam in, and then coughed, and shrieked when a few fragments of rainbow came out of my throat.

"Easy, you little fool." Grandma slapped the rainbow fragments with her palm as though they were tiny bugs and rubbed the stains off her hand over the sink. "Take a few hours' rest and you'll be fine."

"You should have warned me," I said, still shaken. "This is way too dangerous for me to handle."

Grandma, her clock ticking unusually loudly, stood there for a while, her hands on her hips. "Something is wrong," she said after a while. "I don't believe I'd been given the correct information on this place. Or at least not precise. Everything is just too different here." She shook her head. "Something is wrong," she repeated.

"You don't care," I said, not quite listening. "I'm a trivial thing to you. An easily replaceable gear, screw, or something." Somewhere at the back of my head I knew I was being absurd—I didn't ask for her help. Tears and other fluids were streaming down my thawing face. "You don't care."

"You know that is not true—"

"I don't!" I stood, upending my chair in the process. "You should have warned me, and you should have . . ." I shook my head. "I didn't want to stay on Earth, but that doesn't mean I want to die here!"

I ran out of the kitchen. She didn't come after me, of course.

My usual escape was the bathroom. Grandma didn't really need a bathroom, after all. I did have a bedroom of my own, but its door didn't have a lock. Not that I thought any lock would keep her out if she wanted in.

I sniffed, and looked up.

Through the window near the ceiling the stars winked down at me. I sniffed again, wiped the tears, and shifted to sink deeper into the empty tub. Something dug into my hip.

I winced and touched my pocket. The box that the buyer man gave me.

In the dim starlight, some of the gaps between panels seemed to glow when I held it up. As if responding to the stars. I stood, bringing it closer to the window. There was a grain in the wood that was brighter than any of the gaps. I tapped that place.

The box unfurled in my palms, like a puzzle solved, and revealed a large piece of moonstone. The whole thing looked like a wooden lotus flower with a peculiar dew at its center. The stone illuminated in a way that the trickle of starlight from above could not explain. I swallowed.

Even the stone started to unravel . . .

The moonstone liquefied, and light skidded over the ever-shifting surface as it sloshed. The web of lights began to tick like impossibly flexible hands, and my heart skipped to its rhythm.

I shouldn't, I told myself, but even as I did, I was climbing out of the tub. The hands of the clock did the unlocking of the door for me. After a while watching the light, I found myself in the front garden, at the rose arch.

The stars didn't change places much, so I could guess we were still orbiting the same planet. She intended to get that final bagful of air, she intended to make me go again. I shivered at the memory: only a split-second's distraction.

The rose arch was just a rose arch when Grandma was not singing the right song. I couldn't hear her now, but the other side was pitch black, not the small fence of *Rosa banksiae* vine at the end of her garden.

It was so warm on the other side of the arch. It smelled nice, though I couldn't tell the source of the scent. It took some time for me to figure out it was one of the globes attached to the buyer man's station. I'd never had to go through one of these midsize globes—his door was always right in front of me when I got here. I wondered if Grandma had been manipulating things around me with her songs, to keep me from exploring. Because now in front of me was the most interesting, the most intriguing, the weirdest place I'd ever been.

Was it a museum, or a library, perhaps? Warehouse? A shop? I couldn't be sure. At a glance, the place looked like a botanical garden, but by now I had the eye for these things: fruits that pretended to be fire; scaled birds and their feathered fish siblings. Things that were not quite, but somehow different, from their equivalent on Earth, as if seen from odd angles. Things that entities like Grandma collected and sold to that man.

So this was a place we helped to build? Such a beautiful garden—not the kind of beautiful of Grandma's well-tended yet modest place, but something much, much grander. I had no idea just how many beings like Grandma were out there, but a lot of the things displayed here hadn't come from us. Many hands, like ours, like mine, had added a piece of beauty each, amounting to this wonderful thing.

"Whoa." A voice from behind, and I couldn't help but jump. "Such a rare visitor. In such wee hours."

I whirled around, the wooden lotus shivering in my hands. A girl, roughly my age, stood there grinning. I could not rub my eyes, with my palms occupied, so had to blink many times. There was . . . a strange air about her, though not in an unpleasant way. "I'm sorry for invading," I said quietly. "I must be causing trouble."

Her face glowed. "I adjusted my time when yours pinged me, it's completely nothing," she said and nodded to my wooden lotus.

I blinked again, self-consciously stroking the flower with a thumb. "I . . . sorry, I don't understand a lot of things. Where am I?"

Her laugh boomed, not entirely unlike Grandma's. "Master's garden, of course. You are one of the contributors, I presume?"

Contributors. "And you are?"

"I am the assistant gardener. Do you want me to show you around the place?"

I nodded involuntarily, and she closed the distance between us in a way nobody ever did to me: swiftly, no hesitation at all in the move. I had to hold my breath so that she wouldn't smell it.

Her hands hovered over the lotus, and with her face leaned over the clock, she looked up at me just with her eyes. "May I?"

I had no idea what it was about, but nodded again, anyway.

The assistant gardener picked up the ends of the clock hands, which were made of light, and tweaked them this way and that. And then she tapped the very center of the moonstone. The stone shivered, so did then the whole lotus, and when she blew her breath over it, it glided over my hand like a leaf on water, disappeared into my chest.

I gasped.

The gardener girl half-smiled, half-frowned. "Are you okay? Surely it was a lot less safe, holding it outside of you like that."

I touched my chest, felt the hands ticking inside. Did being Grandma feel like this?

Grandma? Who was Grandma? "It's still a bit cold." I ran my hand over the place where the clock entered me.

"How long have you been keeping it out in the air? That is crazy," she said, laughing. To my surprise, I didn't have an answer to that. She gave a quick shrug, and then extended a hand. "Shall we?"

And I took it without hesitation.

Water couldn't run on its own, and I was fascinated by the tiny gears and bearings that somehow pushed the liquid through the place, installed on the streambed and the pond bed. They ticked, shimmering, like pleasantly awkward clockwork. Flower petals wriggled against the current. A bee with oversized wings fluttered down, sprinkling pollens onto the water, and the petals and the clockwork made the powder swirl in elaborate curves that spiraled up into the air after a while to mingle with sunshine.

Everything was beautiful as it should be.

"Right?" the girl said, taking both my hands and making me look her in the face.

I blinked. "Sorry, what did you just say?"

She rolled her eyes. "I said, he is a great man, isn't he?"

"Master? Of course."

Everything was built to his meticulous calculation. The place where the artificial sunlight was generated, the point where the water first trickled out, they were angled perfectly so that everything that needed them would get their share. Not everything thrived on these things, of course, and there were beautifully crafted hideouts for the rippling velvety fungi and the moss like modest constellations. I spotted clockwork in leaves, too—there was no wind, of course, so these leaves sang in their places. Everything here worked the way he designed it to. And yet, something in my chest ached. As if I was feeling guilty of something—something like taking this beauty for granted.

I frowned.

"Are you okay?" asked the gardener girl. "Why are you looking so worried? You have no reason to worry."

A prickle in my chest. The hands of my clock were hitting something inside me, and I had to gasp and gag. "I don't know," I managed to say. "Why do we need this place?"

She shook her head, with a smile—a smile that was so, so dreadfully beautiful that my clock stopped for a second. "She hasn't even taught you that?" Her voice sounded different from a moment ago—even the way the muscles on her face moved seemed changed from a moment ago.

"She?"

"See the sun up there?" He pointed at the top of the heavenly border of the globe. "Everything started when I invented that. I incorporated into it little bits of elements from every sun in every habitable universe. These things that the foot soldiers—like your superior—contribute, they can only survive under the light from that pseudo-sun. And the people in the universes these things come from, they can only survive in the presence of these things; we all need little bits of elements from home, but these elements cannot fit in one globe if they are too different from each other. I made the perfect merge of universes in this globe, and I'm still working to improve it every day, so that the representatives can gather without harming their health."

It sounded totally familiar and entirely new at the same time. "And what do they gather here for?"

"Business, of course." He shrugged slowly, the gesture so unbecoming of her girlish features. "And war, maybe, somewhere along the way. Whatever comes, everything here is arranged the way I like it. I will always win." And his eyes, looking out of the girl's pretty eyes—I could only shudder. "Join me. I am the right side, I always will be. And you'll be well fed, well clothed. You will be treated *right*."

The clock hands hit something in my chest again, harder this time.

My eyes stung. "I see. That is why she doesn't like you."

The master of the garden frowned, using the girl's brows. "What?"

"Grandma." The word came out like a whistle. I tried again: "Grandma, *help*!"

The wooden lotus ripped out of me, and I screamed, more surprised by how the thing was strangled with thorny vines than the pain or the hollow it left in my body. Even the master of the garden yelled, stepping back. The wooden panels of the lotus split, and the moonstone cracked, spitting more vines. Grandma's rose arch grew out of it right between us, though a smaller version.

A very grumpy-looking Grandma, with her oldest face, crawled out of it. "You gave me the wrong coordinates." She adjusted her spectacles as she said to the master, "I should've known better than to trust you."

The gardener girl's face twisted, no longer serene or innocent. "You are invading my perfectly configured soil."

"Your perfect globe, which wouldn't have come together without any of us, huh?" Grandma heaved a sigh, and then looked at me. "You silly thing. Your heart would have turned into one of his machines if I hadn't lodged a thorn there. You would've turned into one of his puppets."

I glared at the master. "You headhunted me because I looked obedient enough to willingly be your puppet?"

"Of course." He laughed, his voice laced with amusement and scorn. "Who would catch that poison-spitting moth without complaints, and then carry it with bare hands even if it was silver-baked?"

I barked, not knowing how to process the many things that went wild in my head. I pulled an ampule out of the small breast pocket of my shirt, cracked it in half, and threw the entire thing into the pond. Immediately, the color of the water turned wrong.

Now he screamed. The gardener girl dropped to the ground right there the moment he was done screaming.

"He's back in his own body," Grandma said. "Come on. Let's get the hell out of here."

The arch was a bit too small for me, so I came out with a lot of scratches and tears on my shirt. When I was fully in her garden Grandma cut most of the roses on the arch. The flowers dropped onto the soil, like that gardener girl had. I shivered and hugged myself. "Your arch is ruined," I said at length.

"Yes." She threw the scissors near the end of the garden. "It was my favorite. But it's not like I can never fix it."

The roses blurred and looked to my eyes like blood of her beloved arch. I tried to say something, but nothing would come out.

Then she chuckled. "Why did you have the moth spit sample hidden in your pocket?"

"I . . ." I coughed. "Um . . ."

"Were you thinking of poisoning me or something?"

I felt my face burn. "No! I mean, I didn't even know what it was, but it tasted awful, so I thought I could maybe use it to spoil your tea—"

Grandma laughed. "He'll need a long time to fix his water. He'll surely fix it in time, but he hates it when he is carried away like that. He'll be mad and will certainly come after us, but only after he's done getting everything perfect again. So for now, we are safe." She sighed, and slowly started walking toward the front door. "He told me he wanted to make a museum of a garden, a safe place for everyone who needed it. Not a war conference room."

"And that is why you help him."

"Helped him. Past tense. I'll never do that again."

I took her arm, helping her walk. "When did you lodge that thorn in my chest?"

Grandma stopped and looked up at me. She was using the versions of herself well, I realized. I could not argue with such a small, frail-looking person. "When you first came here, of course," she said. "Trust me on that. I know you don't trust me and that you are prone to do stupid things. I have installed many fail-safe functions in you. But nothing so that I can control you, the way he does his young workers. Now let's get you a cup of tea."

In the kitchen, I inhaled the steam of the honey-ginger tea and it felt like a million years had passed since I last drank it here, angry and miserable. "Grandma?" I called, to the bent back of the woman.

"Yes?"

"You knew that moth spit was poison all along?"

She grinned—in such a way that her core system was almost visible to me through that deceiving layer of an old lady. "I did. But I also knew you were immune to it. You passed the blood test, after all."

"Oh, Grandma!"

"You survived." She resumed walking, her face turned away. "That is the only thing that matters."

GISLA AND THE THREE FAVORS

KATHLEEN JENNINGS

As Gisla's mother lay dying, she called her daughter to her.

"When you were only a hope and a happiness, Gisla, I begged three favors of three ladies. I have not lived to repay them. This you must do for me, else when I die, Gisla, my soul will fly up out of my body, as all souls do, and it will beat against the windows of heaven, but it will not get in."

Then she breathed out, and did not breathe in again. Just as she had said, her spirit fled to the edge of the sky but could not get through.

So Gisla left her sheep on the hills and went down to the pool where such meetings must happen, and made old magic with blood and milk and iron. Then the three ladies came to her.

One was tall and pale, like a waterfall, save for her feet, which were dark as a deep pool. One was squat and hard as a boulder, rough and patched with hair. The third was sleek and wild-eyed as a seal.

"I am here to repay my mother's debt," said Gisla.

The ladies looked at her and laughed.

"Very well, Gisla. This is what you must do. You must go to the festival of the prince-in-the-hill, which is strung over the first three nights of the year, after the heart of summer when there is no night. And you must bring us the sun and the moon and the stars, which were taken from us."

"This is my only dress," said Gisla, who knew what a festival required, even if she thought little of princes, "and these my only shoes. But my mother's soul flies crying over the sky. I will go."

"Come to the pool again and call to us," said the ladies. "On the first evening after summer."

So Gisla returned to watch her sheep and worked through the long day which is summer, and did not worry how she was to find the sun, the moon or the stars. After all, she first had to get to the festival-under-the-hill, and she did not squander worry lightly. But when the sun sank low, low, low in the sky, she went at last again to the hidden pool and the ladies came to her.

They gave her a gown like the sea, beaded with salt and basalt, and lace like foam for her hair; they put shoes of jet on her feet and brought her a horse slick as kelp.

"Your mother did not beg beauty or wisdom or wealth," they said. "Only wit and grace and luck. May they serve you now."

So Gisla rode up into the greatest of the circling hills as the first true night fell, and reached the door of the prince-in-the-hill. It stood open for revelries on this evening, as it would on each of the three, and then not again for a year.

Gisla walked in.

"By whose bidding are you here?" asked the guardians of the door.

"The sea bade me, the stones directed me and the waterfalls marked my path," said Gisla. And the guardians let her through.

What a crowd there was, of secret people grown visible and daylight folk who did not understand all they saw. But none had a dress like Gisla, made of the sea, and none spoke with such wit.

"Who is her mother?" asked the people who saw her.

"A white bird," answered Gisla.

"What wealth has she?" asked the secret people, who knew how rare a gown she wore.

"All the gold that fills the land between hill and shore," answered Gisla, for as everyone knows most of the secret people cannot long bear the weight of the day.

"What power do you wield?" asked the prince-in-the-hill, whose eyes glowed, and who could not look away.

"I hold the fate of a great nation of gentle folk in my hand," answered Gisla the shepherdess, in all pride and all truth.

The prince-in-the-hill would have kept her for himself, but Gisla had little time for princes and eyes only for the sun, which shone as a gold brooch, tamed and confined, on the shoulder of a troll and she danced only with him.

"Riddle me this," he said, "and you shall have whatever you desire. What teems amid the green, what gleams white on the stiff wave ever standing, what is armored against the water's blade, while on the fire its bed is made?"

A fish, thought Gisla at once, but bit her tongue since wit is nine parts silence. I am dressed in the gown of the sea, she thought. A troll would think I would guess "fish" at once. Then she laughed.

"Good is your riddle, and guessed it is!" she said, "It is a flock. For the hills stand like the waves of the sea, and wool is a good coat, and a sheep is good eating."

She thought quickly in her turn. "What judges and pardons, is treasure and burden, beats its wings in a cage and glides over the sky?" she asked.

But trolls' souls behave quite differently from those of humans, so he could not guess, and Gisla won.

"I should wish for a trifling brooch like yours," she said, and, grumbling, he gave it to her, for those are the rules of riddling games. But Gisla knew he was angry, and so she slipped away before the short night could end, and fled down to the plain as the great sun rose. And trolls, of course, cannot follow then.

The next evening she went again to the hidden pool. She gave the gold brooch to the lady of the waterfall, who tossed it like a ball, and laughed.

Then they dressed her in a gown as stiff and soft as moss and stone, embroidered with flowers and banded with sulphur, with lace of lichen for her hair, and shoes of velvet green as the hills. They set her up on a steed broad shouldered as a boulder, and sent her off to the festival.

Again everyone wondered who she could be, and the prince-in-the-hill, in his coat of ashen grey and molten scarlet, was wondrously flattering and charming. But Gisla knew that she must look for the moon, and soon she found it, on the shoulder of a frail creature as soft and twilight-bright as a moth.

"Let me see you dance," it begged. "You move like the wind over the grass." So Gisla danced. She danced even with the prince-in-the-hill himself, whose hands were hot and whose smile was bright as a burning mountain, and all the grace she had needed as a shepherdess on rough ground stood her in good stead now.

"What boon will you have?" breathed the moth-feathered one, while the dust of its winged gown drifted to the floor.

"What can I ask more humble than the brooch pinned to your shoulder?" said Gisla.

All had heard the promise, so Gisla got the brooch. And again she slipped away swiftly, for she had seen jealousy and anger in the promisor's huge eyes, and did not care to stay. Not even to bid farewell to the prince-in-the-hill.

The next evening, when she brought the moon to the hidden pool, the seal-slick lady took it, smiling. Then the three ladies gave her a last gown, wild and white as falling water, with diamonds of spray in her hair and shoes clear as glass. And the horse she rode was swift and narrow-shouldered as the dark crevasses through which secret waterfalls cascade.

How glad the prince-in-the-hill was to see her. He would have spoken to no other. But although he seemed kind and handsome, witty and constant, she knew she must finish her errand.

At last she found a ring of children, squabbling like terns, their feet and hands clawed and webbed and yellow, about a game of dice and marbles. The coins they gambled with sparked cold and more distant than the moon.

"What have I to lose?" thought Gisla. "Either my luck is good or it isn't." So she left the prince-in-the-hill and knelt to play. She gambled the spray in her hair and the brooches of ice in her gown, the beads on sleeve and hem and the shoes clear as water. But her nerve held, and her luck, and at last the stars fell to her lot, shining like fortune and promises in her hands.

Wit, grace and luck, she thought. Thus her mother's debt was repaid. Then she gathered up her winnings, her ornaments, and her shoes, and turned to go.

"Stay, stranger," said all the folk. "Stay with us. This is the last night of the festival."

"I must leave," said Gisla.

"Stay," begged the prince, grasping her fingers with a hand veined in fire.

"Alas," said Gisla, for she had begun to think more kindly of princes.

Then she ran. The troll chased her, shaking the rocks, and Gisla's glass shoes shattered, but she kept her feet. The great moth swooped at her, shaking dust in her eyes, but Gisla knew her way. And the children darted and snatched at her, with fingers sharp as talons; they screamed in her ears and tore at her white gown, but the fine threads dissolved into mist, and Gisla fled through it, and lost her pursuers.

She ran all the way to the pool where old magic is made, and gave her winnings to the lady of the rocks, who arranged them about herself so they glittered like crystals in the night. Gisla thought them very beautiful, and was glad that her mother's debt had been repaid. But she grieved twice over: that she would not hear even the bird-cry of her mother's soul again, and that she had looked her last at the prince-in-the-hill.

"It is as well," said the ladies. "You aren't of his folk, nor he of yours. Besides, when he finds what you were about he will be furious as burning, for he rules the fire that sleeps in the hill, and what is a prince but temper and title? Best not to show your face there again."

Gisla went back to her sheep and her loneliness. But it would not do. "I have grace and wit and luck," she said. "Gowns and lace and shoes aside, that must count for something."

So she went back up to the door of the prince-in-the-hill. It was closed now, but she called outside, "I have taken your sun, I have taken your moon and your stars. I, Gisla, shepherdess, with no magic but grace, wit and luck have freed the heavens and a soul. What will brighten your long nights, prince-in-the-hill, until summer comes again?"

As the sun dipped below the world, she heard the rage of the prince-in-the-hill, that all the revelry ought to have held at bay another year. It shook the earth and melted the stones. Gisla waited until it was nearly too late, until liquid rock broke the door, and then she fled, trusting to her mother's gift, and the prince like fire after her.

Down from the hills ran Gisla, one last time, bounding across the plain, all the way out across the emerald moss-tussocks and the black stones to the sea. When she reached the water, she took off her shoes and waded through foam and swam through the salty swell to a seal-wet rock. There she balanced and waited as the prince-in-the-hill seared his way to the beach and, without pausing, without thinking, quenched himself in the water.

Gisla could not bear to see him suffer long. She jumped into the waves, burning her hands as she turned his face to the air. Then she dragged him to shore again while day broke and the new-hardened stone sloughed from him, leaving neither prince nor power, but only a man.

So that is the tale of how Gisla repaid the three favors and won the prince-in-the-hill. As for the rest of it: they did not live much longer than any other man or woman, though it is to be hoped they were happier. In time they too died, and if they begged no other favors of the three ladies, I daresay their souls went much where other souls go.

PASSING FAIR AND YOUNG

ROSHANI CHOKSHI

MYTH

They told me it is dangerous to be passing fair and young, but I think they meant it is dangerous to be a woman unclaimed. I was lovely enough to draw attention should I walk alone but not lovely enough to demand constant protection. I was too young to bear children but old enough that a man might try anyway.

My mother noticed the traces of myth on my skin the day I turned fifteen.

I could not see it on myself. But later, when it was too late for me, I would see that smear of iridescence across my son's brow. When I kissed him, I could taste it on my tongue: snow and ghosts and sugar. My first taste of myth was impossible and familiar, like the forgotten flavor of my mother's heartbeat when I slept inside her womb.

But I did not know those things at fifteen. "What will happen to me?" I asked my mother.

My mother touched my face. "You have a choice before you, as I once did."

A choice to do what?" I pressed.

She sighed. We were in her quarters, a place untouched by my father, whom men called the Fisher King. My mother's quarters were warm but scentless. She had no scent. Only after she died did I bother to wonder whether that was part of the bargain she struck when she was presented with her options. That she leave no trace behind, not even the perfume of her skin.

"I do not know how to read such things, but I know someone who does, and I shall summon her on the eve of your eighteenth birthday," she said. "For now, go, go and learn what makes you happy."

I did not appreciate back then the choice my mother was giving me, but I understand it now. How can anyone make a choice when they do not know themselves? I knew myself only a little in those days. I knew I liked solitude and the quiet wonder of the gardens, where the alchemy of roots and sunshine pulled forth roses from the winter thaw. I liked that I could be part of something greater than myself, though I did not know that was what it was back then.

I liked the company of girls my age, where we would huddle in the darkened corners of a banquet and spy on lovers' trysting or wonder at what it might be like to be a woman who inspired ballads both terrible and beautiful.

I liked laughter. I liked, truthfully, to notice but not be noticed.

I did not like the weight of others' eyes. It made my skin feel too tight, even then.

As I left my mother's room, I paused at the doorway. My mother had her back turned to me, gazing out the stone window which looked out over the castle gardens.

"Mother, what was your choice?"

For a moment, I saw my mother as she must have appeared in her youth. Long limbed like me, with skin the color of a fawn's rich pelt, for my mother came from a land of spice and sand. There were crescents around her mouth and furrows between her eyes. Her face held the shadow of long-faded poetry.

"They told me I could know a love like no other. They told me I could live forever on the lips of bards and minstrels. They told me my bones would become a ballad and my blood would turn to the golden ichor that belongs to immortal gods," she said. "But they told me it would be violent and brief." She took a deep breath, trailing her brown fingers down her neck as though feeling for the pulse of that life not lived. "Then they told me I could choose, instead, a life in exile, cast far from my father's home. They told me I could become forgotten and nameless but that I would have a chance at contentment and, though it would not shake the earth, a different kind of love." At this, she smiled warmly at me, and I felt guilt at her warmth. I have often wondered if she resented me and if only love for me kept too much bitterness at bay. If I am being honest, I felt jealous, too, of the man or woman who would have been her great, immortal love, for I wished to be enough and knew that I was not.

"I feel, sometimes, the phantom ache of another life," she said. "Sometimes I dream of orchards and the taste of pomegranates, though I have not eaten one in years. Sometimes I dream in a language I have not spoken in decades. But that is nothing but the ghosts of choices made, and I would rather keep the company of those ghosts than others."

I knew this meant she loved me, and I was pleased.

"Now go," said my mother from her perch by the window. "Go and be lighthearted."

I left her then, flying down the stairs as though I could outrun whatever terrible choices would soon catch hold of me. I ran into the sunshine, and I put all thought of myths and resentment from my mind until I was eighteen. I caught her watching me in the garden from her bedroom window, but she never said a thing, and each time I caught her, she would move discreetly into the shadows.

It did not occur to me until years later, when I had my own child and watched him from my room, that this was an act of love. I did not want him to feel trapped by my watchful gaze.

I wanted him to feel free, even though he was tangled up in the sticky, silken threads of legends long before I pushed him into this world.

Here was my gift to my son and my mother's gift to me: to watch from afar and not disturb, to cast light out into the darkness and hope my child's ear would lift to it like a hungry seedling craving the bright afternoon.

I am still not sure what my mother wished for me to know. Or whether she simply wanted me to know she was there.

MAIDEN

When I was eighteen, the woman whom men called Morgan le Fay came to read my myth marks.

My mother had made a pretense of a pilgrimage to pull me away from my father's court. It was the first time I had left Corbenic, and I was entranced by the sight of my home dwindling through the curtains of our carriage. I watched my father's castle, saw the turret that tipped curiously toward the sea, the silver seagrass that sounded like chiming bells. Though I could not see it, I knew my garden was there, too.

And as it grew smaller and smaller, I saw the entirety of my life shrink to the size of something I might fit in my pocket. "Terrifying, isn't it?" asked my mother beside me. "For something so important to us to turn out so . . . small." She moved from the window, settling into her cushions.

I said nothing as I looked away from Corbenic. I did not agree with my mother. I did not find it terrifying at all, but comforting. The world was vast enough; I did not wish to compete with it. If I could keep this small corner of joy unnoticed and out of sight . . . then perhaps I might just be happy. In a castle choked with weeds and ivy, I was told to strip off my clothes and step into a bath. The bathtub was unlike anything I'd ever seen. Its clawed feet were carved from bone, and the shape reminded me of a half-bloomed rose with petals of finely beaten gold. The water was so hot that a tremor ran up my spine, and my hands shook on the lip of the tub. "You must bear it, Elaine," said my mother.

I had never had cause to doubt my mother before, and so I followed her advice.

There are many days where I wonder what would have happened had I simply said . . . no.

No, I shall not bear this.

No, I will not carry the shadow of your unlived lives or stillborn dreams.

But I did not know there was such an option then. I knew only that I had to choose, and then Morgan le Fay appeared at the lip of the golden tub.

"Elaine," said Morgan, nodding to my mother. "I have come to read you, child."

I know now that it does not matter, but it seemed important at the time that she should be beautiful. As if whatever terrible pronouncements might be made about my life could be bettered by a pair of full, dark lips.

There are many kinds of beauty in the world, but I liked Morgan's best. She was beautiful in the way of smoldering fires and spurts of roaring thunder when the sky has visibly begun to clear. It was a fading beauty, made all the more lovely for its scarcity, where every drop lost becomes nectar for a poet's imagination.

I was not beautiful.

I was only ever passing fair and young. But for most men, that seemed to be enough.

Had the water in the bath not been so hot perhaps I might've felt a stroke of envy, but all I could see was my reddening skin and my brown hair sticking to it.

Morgan swiped her hand across my wrist, rubbing her fingers together. She looked at me and smiled.

"Well," she said, "I suspect the choice here will be quite easy."

"What is it?" I gasped.

"I see myth markings of a life full of movement, Elaine," said Morgan. Her eyes clouded over. "You will not find rest in any world, but you will be great. You will have powers that rival my own. You will conquer kings and steal their sons' hearts. You will be remembered by all, celebrated and feared in equal measure. You shall move through the world with such speed that even your shadow will struggle to keep pace with you—"

"What's the other choice?"

My mother winced at my poor manners, but the bath was so hot, and I did not want to bear the pain anymore.

Morgan shrugged.

"You shall sleep in the arms of greatness. You shall bear greatness.

But you will never be great," said Morgan dismissively. "The world will look you over, and you shall be naught but a footnote in the legends of others."

Steam plumed up from the water.

I tried to get out of the bath. I could not think for the heat, the pain.

Morgan pushed me farther into the water. I screamed then, noticing too late the bubbles that popped across the water's surface. Scalding liquid splashed up my thighs, spat against my breasts. I saw black crimping the edges of my vision.

"You must make your choice now, child, while the water is hot and the myth is malleable."

I looked at my skin, and I saw it then. The sheen of legends on my flesh, glyphs made of colored light. I thought I glimpsed a life unlived in their gloss—there, a lover's hand drifting over my belly; now the weight of a helmet tucked under my arm and a sword bouncing against my hip; then a gnawing restlessness to move and move and keep moving; now the damp velvet petals of the first rose pushing through frosted earth. I knew that earth. It was home.

I remembered the sight of Corbenic Castle from the roads. My whole life something so small I might pocket it. My whole world worthy of no notice but no less worthy to me.

Everything was so loud.

I never liked such loudness.

It always rattled me, threatening to shake me loose from my skin.

"Choose greatness, my love," sobbed my mother. "Do not be afraid as I was."

I thought I heard the sound of horse hooves just outside the castle.

The bath scalded me.

"Your mother is right," said Morgan. "It can be a path of loneliness, but that is the cost of such glory. Do not be afraid."

I was not afraid of greatness. But I was afraid of loneliness.

I had seen my father surrounded by courtiers, drenched in the power of the Grail cup locked away in our kingdom. And yet for all that power and might, he was alone. Yes, his name passed from mouth to mouth, and even I had heard the tales people told of the legendary Fisher King, but I had never heard him talk about himself. Perhaps he didn't see the point. He belonged to everyone but himself. The myth of him had drained away his human blood, filled his veins with gold, and perfumed his every breath with omens.

That was not me.

I am not a girl sculpted from fire like Morgan. I did not and do not need to feast on wonder to feel sated. I had seen the sharp talons of myth, and I did not want to be ripped beneath them.

I started to speak. "I choose—"

I tasted blood at the back of my throat. The patterns of myth swirled across my skin. My ribs spread apart, as if making room for vastness.

"I choose to be looked over by the world," I said, repeating Morgan's prediction back to her.

To myself, in private, I made a different vow.

I choose to belong to myself.

No sooner had the words left my lips did the golden tub spit me out.

I sprawled slick as a newborn across the tiles while my mother sobbed behind me. Steam curled off my reddened skin. The bottoms of my feet looked like ribbons. I ached all over as my body cooled in the night air.

Through the windows, the sound of horse hooves grew louder.

A man's voice rumbled through the abandoned castle, and my skin prickled.

"Who is that?" I asked. "Who is coming?"

Morgan looked at me, her lip curled in disgust. "The consequence of your choice."

My mother hauled me to my feet. I dripped water to the ground, shivering. No one offered me a cloth, and though the heat had gone, a different fire kindled within me. I was no fool. I could trace their disappointment as though it were a shadow on the wall. It angered me. It was my choice, was it not? Why should they judge me when only I had to live with it?

"I will grant you one last mercy, child," said Morgan. "I can take away the memory of the choice you made. You would not be the first. Arthur's queen chose to forget that she ever made a choice."

"What choice did she make?" I asked, curious in spite of my fury.

Morgan looked at me closely. Too closely. When she smiled, I saw that her teeth were white as milk. And yet there was nothing soft or flowing about her.

"Guinevere chose power even though it came at the price of extraordinary guilt. She chose power and immortality over anonymity."

"And did she choose correctly?" I asked.

"A story that ends poorly is still a story."

That was not an answer, but it no longer mattered.

The sound of hooves grew louder. I could see the appeal of Morgan's offering. Perhaps the day would come when I would regret the choice I had made, and then I would return to this hour over and over again, dreaming of the life I had not lived. I could see how my mother had fared beneath the whispers of her own ghost selves. I did not want to be like her. But if I was going to belong to myself, then surely that meant never closing the eyes of my soul. Not even to spare myself.

"No," I said. "I shall remember."

"Then let me take that mercy," said my mother, with an embarrassed glance in my direction. "For I fear that I cannot love her as I used to if I know what she has done. Let me imagine that I never once saw myth marks on my daughter."

"It is done," said Morgan, looking to the window. "Careful now . . . . He is coming and we all have a part to play."

MOTHER

Morgan said I would sleep in the arms of greatness.

I knew the moment you touched me that you were who she meant when she spoke of greatness. But the first time I saw you, you were, forgive me, rather uninspiring and thoroughly human. Years later you found this thoroughly amusing, but I must confess that I was rather disappointed.

The legends can never seem to agree on what you look like—whether you were tall and solemn, with quartz-gray eyes and a sheaf of thick, wheat-gold hair beneath your helmet, or whether you were of average height with a peculiar fae glint in your green eyes that turned heads, with close-cropped, dark hair the color of soot.

So I shall set the tale straight, though no one has ever asked me and my answer likely will not be remembered.

You were handsome in an unimaginative way. You were taller than most men, but not noticeably so. You had broad shoulders and a scar on your left forearm from when a dog bit you. You had eyes the color of rain on a tree trunk, fair hair that looked as if someone had unraveled a candle's flame, and a slightly crooked nose from slipping down the staircase even though you told everyone it was from a nasty tumble from a wild stallion.

I liked that you told me the truth.

I liked knowing how to separate you from the story of you.

I liked knowing you as you wished you might be instead of as Sir Lancelot du Lac, a name foisted upon you by your adoptive mother, whose own title was just as mysterious. Lady of the Lake. Was it a lake? Or a pond just outside her house? You never told me, my love, but you insisted with all the solemnity of a hurt child that it was magic.

I do not know what magic Morgan wrought that night. All I remember was that for one moment I was outside the boiling bath and the next moment I was thrown back into its steaming waters, my face held down by my mother's and Morgan's hands.

You would not recognize that the other woman, hooded and screaming, was my mother. The official story released by my father's kingdom was that I had been taken on the road by witches and kept in an enchanted bath from which you rescued me. Later, Morgan would meet me in my father's castle and throw me a conspiratorial wink.

My mother did not remember anything about a choice or how I failed her.

She was content by reports of your own greatness.

More than that, she was determined that I would bear your child, who was destined for greatness.

She kept staring at you throughout the feast my father threw. I noticed that you did not drink any of your wine. Perhaps you noticed her gazes and suspected her of enchanting your cup. Good on you. I always did think you saw the world too plainly. I knew that the moment I met you. When Morgan and my mother orchestrated my rescue—though I wonder if it can be called that in light of what I know now—you did not blush at my nakedness. I think that was what I first noticed about you: you never looked away from me.

That first night was supposed to be our last. It was supposed to be the only intersection of our lives, and because I did not know you, I had made peace with the state of things. This was the choice writ upon my skin; I might as well get on with it.

That night my mother bade me go to your chambers. She told me to offer you a drink and that if I should do so, you would mistake me for *her.*

Guinevere.

Everyone knew she favored you above all Arthur's knights.

Everyone suspected your devotion to Arthur's queen was far more than it should be.

But back then, she was only a name to me, as inconspicuous as a shadow in the dark.

I came into your rooms at midnight, bearing only a stub of a candle and a cup. I did not bother to knock.

You were not in bed and had not removed the brocade garments that my father had loaned to you for the feast. You were broad shoul-dered and handsome, but the clothes shrouded you, and I almost laughed. Behind you stood the large bed hung in curtains of samite. The white linens looked crisp and untouched, and I grew scared, for I knew what would happen. Mother said it would be over fast, and for a moment, I imagined myself melting into those white linens like sugar into hot milk.

"Good sir," I started. "I do not know how to repay you for rescuing me. My mother bade me—"

"Spare me."

My head jerked up at the sound of your voice. I thought you would sound as solemn as you looked, but there was levity in your tone. I stood there with my hand wrapped around the enchanted drink. You glanced from the cup to me, an amused smile on your lips. I could only stare at you.

"Might as well come in, shut the door, and close your jaw while you're at it," you said.

I snapped my mouth shut, annoyed, and then I did as you asked.

You rose from the chair, not moving toward me or moving back but regarding me with the same amused grin.

"I know what you are, and I know what you're here to do, so let's get on with it, shall we?" You shrugged off your jacket, tugged at the collar of your shirt. You didn't look at me, and I remember how furious that made me. "Do you speak? Well, never mind, probably best if you don't. It's bad enough we have to do this; I don't need to add soothing a virgin's conscience to my list."

By then my shock had faded. I slammed the cup onto the nearest table.

"You don't know me or what I'm here for."

"Sure I do," you said. "It's in my myth marks. You're to be the mother of my son, and after tonight we'll never see each other again. And he'll do great things, and I'll do great things, and all shall be so blessedly . . . great."

I frowned. "And here I thought I would be a fox in the night, stealing your virtue as if it were a cooped chicken."

Your fingers paused at your buttons. You looked at me a little more closely.

"How do you know about the myth marks?" I asked.

Morgan had told me that fate treats men differently. Where Morgan had told me that fate treats men differently. Where women had so many choices, they had only one path. No one read their myth marks, for they had no choice in the matter.

That amused smirk left your face.

"My mother taught me how to read them. She's a sorceress, as well you know. She told me I was destined for legends."

"Is that what you wanted? Or how you thought it would be?"

You looked stunned then, and I wondered if anyone had asked you before. But a moment later you recovered, that smirk reasserting itself.

"I had little choice in the matter," you said casually. "Is this what you thought it would be like?"

"I thought I'd be seducing a knight, not philosophizing with one."

You liked that answer. I think that's the moment you liked me. You raised an eyebrow, walking toward me. Your hand went to my waist and you drew our hips together.

"Surely you can do both?"

Later, much later, we lay beside each other and listened for the sound of dawn's golden blanket hiding the stars from sight. My body felt tender . . . fuller. I dragged my fingers across my belly and wondered at the wisps of life taking root within me. You turned to your side, your rough hand skimming and scratching down my neck and arms.

"Tell me what your marks say."

I told you: I would be adjacent to myth, caught up in its shadow. Free to live without its bright eye turned to me.

"I envy you," you said.

"And your marks?" I asked. "What of them?"

"Glory," you said, simply. "I shall look for the Holy Grail and be permitted a glance but nothing more. But my son—*our* son—will succeed. And I shall fall in love with a woman I cannot have, whose love none shall celebrate until the day I die. That is all the marks say."

I was not in love with you yet, so I did not resent Guinevere's intrusion.

"What does she look like?" I asked.

You looked pained. "She's the most beautiful woman I've ever seen, and I am haunted by the sight of her." Your voice dropped to a whisper. "There are days when I wish I'd never seen her."

You were honest with me from the start, and I liked that. I rose over you, savoring how your gasp of surprise melted into a groan of pleasure. I slid my hands across your eyes, lowering my hips to yours.

"Your wish is granted."

I tried to leave unnoticed in the morning, but you caught me by my wrist and kissed my hand.

"I hope . . . " you started to say, but I did not let you finish.

I wondered whether you regretted our transparency in the night, and I did not wish to know for certain.

"Let us leave it at that," I said. "Let us leave it at hope."

Whatever words you might have uttered, you swallowed them down.

Sometimes I wish I'd let you finish.

Our son smelled of milk and softness. He was shining and seraphic, and the moment I held him, I knew our line had come to an end. I saw the shimmering glyphs of destiny writ upon his brow. Galahad would have neither hearth nor grandchildren nor earthly love to warm his bed. I saw the burden of greatness on him, and I almost wished to take back my choice. But sparing him that burden meant denying his existence.

I was glad it was too late, for I selfishly loved him.

Destiny grew bored of me, and I grew comfortable standing in its cold shadow. I was no longer young, nor passing fair, and the eyes of men turned elsewhere. Unwatched, I began to learn.

I learned the slow language of the herbs in my garden, coaxing their speech into talismans and amulets, medicines that I slipped to the village women. I learned the gruff song of thunderclouds, the untethered gossip of the sea channels that snaked coyly through the kingdom. I learned the dialect of our son's moods—his closed fists of frustration, his heavy-lidded gaze of daydreaming, his wonder-softened smile when he heard tales of your quests.

I did not hide anything from him.

I listened to the winds and to the water, and they told me of your feats and triumphs, your desperate love for Guinevere, and the frantic nights when that love was returned.

And yes . . . yes, I was sometimes envious.

It is not that I have a low opinion of myself, but I confess I never imagined you thought of me.

I remember the day I heard the wind sighing about you. It was a young and gossipy spring wind not fully thawed from winter's grip. It slipped under my scarves and pressed freezing kisses to my neck, delighting in its coldness as it sang: *Lancelot du Lac has lost his head, for his queen has kicked him from her bed, and oh he wanders and oh he is lost and oh he is lucky for such thin frost.*

That was how I found you that day in the garden.

Your beard overgrown and your eyes ringed white like a horse, your clothes shredded or matted to your skin. You could not stop shaking or scratching, hissing at your flesh: "Leave me! Leave me alone! I don't want to see you!"

You did not recognize me as the servants led you to my quarters. You spat in my face when I used my herbs on you. But slowly you came to your senses.

Slowly you allowed Galahad to sit beside you on your sick bed and play with his wooden horses atop your quilts. Slowly you walked in the gardens and kissed our son's head and reached for my hand when no one was looking.

Slowly . . . I loved you.

The legends say we married, but they never spoke of our happiness.

They never spoke of our hours by the fireplace, our eternal disagreement on the choice between blackberry and strawberry pie, how you were miserable at carving toys for Galahad and the delicious joy I took in teasing you for it. Legends do not mention the way you loved to swoop us into a hug and pretend to be a child-eating giant, or how I sneezed after lovemaking, or the nights when I woke to you standing by the window with your sword drawn, whispering to your myth marks: "*Not yet, not yet.*"

But myths are hungry things, and in a few short years, they found you and you had to leave.

I never asked whether you thought of her when you held me. I told myself it was because I was stronger for not knowing, but that's a lie. The myth marks said you were cursed to love someone you couldn't have until the day you died, and that was not me. I belonged to myself, but I was yours, too, and yet my name would never be joined to yours.

When you left, you told me to be happy.

"You'll be glad to be free of me," you said on our last night. "No witches at our door. Or giants kidnapping you. No one to poison your cup."

"Is it strange I'm offended by that?" I asked.

"Yes, wife." You laughed. "It is. Who would *want* that?"

And I made myself laugh even as I wanted to weep for the stupid envy of it all.

CRONE

Though you left, I lived. I raised our child and sent him off to greatness. I took a lover to warm your side of the bed and learned I was passing fair at swimming and weaving. I mourned the loss of quiet things and understood what I had given up in my choice. I did not need to live forever as myth, but I would have liked to be a folktale passed down to grandchildren. Grandmother had a ridiculous temper and hated toads. *Grandmother had strange blood and dark skin and sometimes dreamt of pomegranates. Grandmother was a witch.*

But I was a full tale, complete unto myself for better or for worse.

The years lined my face and stretched my hips, and I reveled in the blessing that I could see such change upon me.

I listened to the wind and learned that you had achieved your quest and lived to be the greatest of Arthur's knights. I heard that you and our son searched for the Holy Grail and found it. I heard that Guinevere blamed herself for the fall of Camelot and renounced her throne. I heard that you followed her into exile.

I thought that would be the end of it, but now I hear the knock on our old door and I go to answer it, and I see you.

We are no longer young, but you still smile like a boy. "They're done with me," you say, and hold out your hand. I do not see the wisp of myth on your skin.

"Let me in, wife."

I can only stare at you. "What about—"

"We are finally free of each other," you say, bowing your head.

But I remember your curse.

"You were to love her until the day you die. If you love her no longer, then you are rather solid for a ghost."

You shake your head, laughing a little, and then you take my hand.

"I was cursed to love a woman I could not have whose love none shall celebrate until the day I die," you say slowly, looking up at me. "I am still quite happily cursed, my love."

We are walking to the edge of your mother's lake. You tell me we can wash ourselves free of destiny's grimy streaks, that we may smear youth over our skin and start anew. We are happy and unfettered, and yet sometimes regret shadows your face.

"They will never know," you say.

But it does not matter. Myths may be hungry things, but they cannot take away what I know.

Once, I tasted snow and softness. Once, I knew the rough poetry of thunderstorms. Once, I ruled a realm entirely of my own making.

Once, I was passing fair and young.

QUINTESSENCE

ANDREW DYKSTAL

Loren's brother-in-law fell sick six weeks after the last rack-and-pinion train departed for the base of the mountain and three weeks after winter closed over the mine like a frozen diamond pane. A layer of cloud hid the world far below, gray and silver in the winter-long night. Thunderheads drifted past, stately as tall ships under starshine, and you could watch them rise and collide and throb with lightning until your eyes froze over. Which took about eight seconds.

And in the stone hollow of a second-shift barracks within the mountain's peak, Loren tried to do what he'd seen the old witch do. Start with the pulse, he thought. That's simple enough.

But when he took hold of Clyde Greer's wrist, the arm shifted with a crackling autumn leaf sound, and Clyde, his brother-in-law, flinched, eliciting a round of soft grinding noises. "It's spreading," Clyde muttered, trying to speak without moving his mouth. "It's growing out from the bones into the muscle tissue. Left leg is the worst."

"Don't talk," Loren said, because that's what the old witch would have said. He peeled back Clyde's eyelids and shined his helmet's gas lamp into each eye, wincing a little when he saw the shatter of light behind the pupil and the slow response of the brown iris. Crystals were forming in the eye jelly. The old witch had had a fancy name for that jelly: vitreous humor. She'd also had a fancy name for the crystallization that was killing Clyde: fatal cascade precipitation. Loren called it crack-up. All the miners did. A name you could say was less frightening.

"Bad luck," Clyde said through stiff lips. He sounded like a novice ventriloquist. "They say it's a one in a thousand chance as long as you take your shots. Just bad luck, Loren. Bad luck."

He'd been saying that for three days, sometimes to his sister, Loren's wife, who was five hundred miles south. A mantra of bad luck; all the worse for being half true. Getting crack-up couldn't be anything but chance. Dying of it was another matter.

The old witch—the *old* old witch—would have fixed him up in a day. It would have taken a massive injection of red, and it would have been expensive, but she'd always been the one to give the Company the rough side of her tongue, usually with a hint that she could give the coin-counters worse if she put her mind to it. "You want to mine Q," she'd say, "you need workers. And you want to keep signing your paperwork, you need your thumbs."

She was the genuine article, the old old witch, all the lifers said—the men who'd spent forty years working this mountaintop and still insisted she'd been an old crone from the day she arrived until the morning two months ago when she was transferred away, and never mind the decades in between.

Loren slouched back into the bedside chair. "We can fix this," he said. "You're going to be all right."

Clyde made a scraping noise deep in this throat. A rivulet of blood dribbled from the corner of his mouth to mat his beard. His next breath had a hard, musical tone. A crystal had broken through his throat and made a whistle of his voice box.

There were no choices left. There'd been no choices since the first hints of pain in Clyde's bones.

"Stay put," Loren said, then flinched back as Clyde's attempt at laughter ejected a fine red mist.

For the third time in as many days, Loren went to see the *new* old witch, and it was only with the utmost of self-restraint that he didn't bring a pickaxe.

* * *

The atlases called this peak Highfall, likely because cartographers have perverse senses of humor. It rose like a shoddy brick thirty-five thousand feet above sea level and more than twenty thousand above the surrounding plateau. Its sisters marching away to north and south were lesser peaks, the tallest half a mile shorter than Highfall. The support camp at Highfall's base serviced all six mountaintop quintessence mines in the chain, its trio of specialized locomotives dropping cogwheels when the tracks grew too steep for mere friction to hold the engines to the rails. But even the cog-driven trains couldn't run in winter, which at this latitude was three months of freezing night.

It was more than the mundane cold, which could kill you in minutes if the thin air didn't asphyxiate you first, and it was more than the wind, which screamed through the night like God's own wolf out to howl down the moon. It was the aether. This high, the aether that flooded the world's nightside from the far depths of space was a hungry, invasive thing. It tore the warmth from anything it touched, anything not shielded by several feet of solid rock or panels of quintessence-treated insulation. There were rumors that even these precautions weren't always enough; that if the aether got your scent, it would bore through anything to find the heat of your blood. There was no surety against it but the light of day or a few thousand feet of good air over your head. Winter at Highfall offered neither.

Which was why there was no climbing or descending Highfall in winter, which was why the rack railway always loaded the mine to the rafters with supplies during the last weeks of autumn, which was why there were crates of medicine that could save Clyde's life in the new old witch's keeping—medicine she was refusing to dispense. Which was why Loren was stalking through the upper reaches of the mine with a slow-growing desire to break her already crooked nose.

The witch lived at the far end of the vault everyone called Main Street, in a tidy series of chambers adjacent to the oldest shafts. Main Street was lit up with gaslights but poorly; a lamppost or artificial stalagmite stood every thirty paces and cast a circle of weak, chilly light.

Lamps cost oxygen. Fuel cost train space and coal. In some regions of the mine, they posed a fire hazard.

But without them, everyone went insane, so the Company groused and grumbled and ate the expense.

Perhaps in a gesture of twisted corporate solidarity, the new old witch kept her chambers even dimmer than Main Street. Her name was Gristle, which suggested either a cartographer's wit or parents who had lost a bet. Then again, the old old witch's name had been Lurga, so perhaps it was just a witchy tradition. She looked, when she opened the door at Loren's knock, like ninety years of old leather topped off with a wig stolen from a tallow maker. Only her eyes were lively: a hard, piercing green.

"Mistress Gristle," Loren said, and he said it respectfully. He liked having two legs, and an irate witch was apt to change that situation.

"Loren McCully," she ground out. Her voice was like broken glass. "Here begging for red again, are you?"

"He's dying," Loren said. "Clyde's dying. He needs the shot. Look, it's what, twenty days' ration? That's inside the margin. We can spare it."

Gristle's jaw worked, warts and all. "How do you know we can spare it?"

"We can always spare it." Desperation was slipping into his tone. Clyde handled the manifests for the supply shipments, and he'd not been shy about sharing that knowledge with Loren, rules be damned. "I can pay. Cut it out of my share, for all I care."

Gristle studied him, and there was something brittle in her eyes that he couldn't read. Frustration? Fear, even? "Go home, Loren," she said. "You're young. Patience takes time to learn. I'm finding alternatives. Trust me. He has a little time yet. In the worst case, I can put him in stasis and buy another few days. People wake up from that almost half the time."

He hesitated, looking for an angle. "I could skip a few doses—a bunch of us would, for Clyde. If twenty of us skip a day—"

"No," she said sharply. "Nobody skips. Red's a better prophylactic than a cure. If people start skipping the injections, we'll have twenty Clydes, and maybe you'll tell me what to do then, too." Her eyes bored into him. "If I hear you've been balking your medicine, Loren McCully, I'll have you tied down and inject you myself." A watch appeared in one liver-spotted hand. "You're a second-shift man? Then you're running late. Go on, now."

For a moment, he wanted to dart past her, seize what he needed, and run. But the impulse faded. Gristle and old Lurga had one quality in common: power. They hummed with it, the same reedy whine you got from standing too close to a Q outcrop. He'd felt it when Lurga sang a man's broken bones back together, and when she'd cleared a rock-fall with a snarl of something that wasn't quite sound. And that power wasn't all benign. There'd been a murder in the mine ten years back, in Loren's first days here as a miner, and when they'd caught the killer, the old witch hadn't waited for the noose. She'd mumbled something, and the man's head had burst.

"The hell with you," he said to Gristle, but he said it quietly, and he left to start his shift.

The preparations were second nature. Helmet, light, treated gloves, surveyors' gear. An injection of red to stave off crack-up, a Locksley pill for extra oxygen, a swallow of Norton's Patent Winterizer for the cold. The last was the worst. It kept you warm, but it made you crave fats. Midway through his shift, Loren would eat a cup of vegetable shortening or lard, and he'd like it. Then, after his shift, he'd remember the feel of it coating his mouth and throat, and he'd like it a hell of a lot less.

Nielsen, the senior engineer and second shift supervisor, moved down the line of miners, checking gear. He was a stern-looking man with severe features and a manner far older than his forty years. "How is Clyde?" he asked quietly when he came to Loren.

"The same. Gristle won't treat him."

Nielsen's mouth tightened, and he nodded. "There are four other cases," he said. An edge crept into his voice. "We *will* figure this out. Everything will be all right."

Loren could almost believe him. There were stories about what Nielsen had been before he studied engineering: a sailor, a politician, a lawman, a thief. They changed every year. The men loved him, and they loved inventing lies about him even more.

But what Nielsen was now was worried. He kept tossing uneasy glances at the cloud chamber set against one wall, a man-high glass case filled with alcohol vapor and meant to measure the threat of crack-up. Tiny trails of condensation flickered through it every few seconds, marking the paths of objects too small for even a microscope to reveal: aethersleet, particles of condensed aether shed by violent events in remote reaches of space, streaming down in a constant barrage throughout the months-long winter night. Now and then, they struck ordinary rock just so and triggered the crystallization reaction that produced quintessence in great jagged seams within the peaks of high mountains. Now and then, they struck human flesh and left a brother-in-law breathing raggedly and trying not to move as his flesh went glass-brittle and lifeless.

As Loren advanced down the newest shaft to set survey reflectors and ensure the shaft was running true, he imagined he could feel that sleet slashing through him. Invisible bullets. Invisible, slow-killing bullets.

There were two firearms in the mine. One was locked in a case in the administrative offices. The other was locked in Nielsen's desk. But that wasn't what would make Nielsen dangerous. The man was smart. He wouldn't brook with theft—not of coin, tools, provisions, or red. Anyone who posed a threat to the well-being of his men would find himself bleeding out or hanged from a handy cross-brace.

Dimly, Loren realized that he was already seeing Nielsen as an adversary.

He spent his shift like a clockwork man, thoughtless of his tasks, hardly even noticing the tooth-rattling buzz of the Q formations as he inspected the survey markers meant to guide the next shaft extension. The shafts were perilously near the surface here. A degree off, and the shaft might break through the mountainside into near vacuum. He ate his lard in silence and cleaned his gloves with detergent. All through those ten hours, he could think only of the blood on Clyde's chin and, in feverish conflation, drops of blood welling in Deirdre's eyes and drawing pink tracks down her cheeks. Spring would come, and he would descend the mountain with death in his mouth. It tasted like rancid fat.

Only one event broke through his anxiety. In the last hour of his shift, an outer seal blew, exposing the mine to the outside world. The overpressure sent a howl of wind down the shaft. There was cold, and there was cold, and the sudden pressure drop could freeze your bits off; or so the lifers said, usually with a few crude gestures and an invitation to see for yourself.

Then the gaslights, starved of oxygen, went out.

Nielsen reacted immediately, shouting for everyone to stop and hold still, dammit.

Against every instinct, against the force of panic, Loren did. He couldn't breathe. His face was going numb. The blackness was absolute, and noises had a strange, thin quality. Muffled curses as someone blundered into a wall. He stood there listening in the dark, and a strange sound drifted down from the outside world, cutting deep.

Then came the ratcheting snarl of freed clockworks, and a spring-run arclight blazed to life. Nielsen held it up and pointed down the tunnel, then raised four fingers. There was no fear in his face, merely irritation. Of course: there was an emergency cache of lights and oxygen four cross-tunnels away. They'd all trained for this. It just took a second or two—sometimes a fatal second or two—for the training to kick in. They withdrew up the shaft in single file, Nielsen at the tail of the line, his free hand on Loren's back, light held high to send their shadows on ahead.

They cleared the first airlock just as darkness began to play around the edges of Loren's vision. At Nielsen's signal, he put his shoulder to the door and shoved, then spun the wheel to lock it. The wind stopped. Safety crews were already coming to meet them, bearing more Locksley pills and Winterizer and emergency oxygen tanks—none of which worked because the cheap rubber masks and hoses had degraded after years of disuse.

So the last hour of the shift was spent grumbling and swearing that the Company was out to kill them all and sell their contracts off at cheaper rates. Loren hardly heard any of it, even when Nielsen threatened bloody revolt against any pencil pusher who'd never set foot above twenty thousand feet. Loren fixated instead on the sound he'd heard the moment the pressure dropped. For a bare second, he'd heard the wind flowing over the breached seal and sounding a perfect musical tone. It touched his memory, harmonizing with the whistle in Clyde's throat.

There was no logic to what came next. He realized that the tone had made up his mind. Powers and Nielsen be damned, he was going to take what he needed from Gristle's cache. The Company might not care, but he still did. He'd lost enough—Deirdre had lost enough.

So he went home to the chambers he shared with Clyde and a dozen other second-shift men, and he made sure Clyde was as comfortable as possible, and then he lay awake, waiting and listening as the lamps went out.

Three hours slid by. Adrenaline sang in his blood and honed his hearing. He imagined he could count the distinct snores. He might even know which ones went with which men; he'd shared quarters with them for long enough, with only occasional breaks to descend the mountain and spend a week or two with his wife Deirdre. The difference made him ache inside. When he was with her, he slept in silence and warmth, her body soft and smooth against him, her breathing a regular sigh over his chest. He always slept well, either because they'd made love or because she'd read to him. He could read but not like she could—not with feeling, like she could get at the life under the words.

Here, it was a ragged chorus of men snoring and farting and reeking of sweat—if it was a good night, only of sweat.

A thin, high sound. Clyde's breathing whistling past the crystals growing in his throat. He had even more formal education than his sister. Hell, he'd landed Loren this job, back when Loren had been a free-climbing prospector with minimal qualifications and a bare handful of years left in his life expectancy. He'd introduced him to Deirdre with an odd, knowing look.

I owe him, Loren thought. I owe him everything.

When he counted thirteen distinct snores, he rose, dressed, and slipped out, carrying his boots and trying not to cringe at the cold eating up through his thick socks into his feet. He brought a few tools tucked into his belt: a lamp, a ghostlight, a probe for locks, a chisel for bigger locks, a crowbar, a rag to deaden the sound of his work. He could not imagine that Gristle slept any way but lightly. Maybe with one of those hard green eyes wide open.

Nobody was on Main Street. Third shift was the worst, the agreed-upon night shift, and the living areas of the mine were deserted. He picked the lock on the old witch's door easily, which was frightening in itself. The simple lock was a sign of perfect confidence. Or that the Company was as cheap about locks as it was about everything else.

He left his boots inside the door and passed through into darkness, feeling his way, reaching carefully with feet and hands. Soft carpeting muffled his footfalls. Gristle's predecessor had let him all the way into the inventory room a few times, even made him a cup of tea there. Lurga had been kindly. Chatty, even, when the mood took her. He remembered the way, but remembering it in fear and the dark was another matter. Every time his foot tapped something, he thought his heart might blow a gasket.

But there were other sounds: the rumble and hiss of the steam engines that ran pumps to kept parts of the mine pressurized. The almost subsonic crunch of the Q grinders that processed the crystal for loading into train cars when spring came. The *plink plink plink* of a distant graywater trickle raising fantastic ice sculptures no one would ever see. The night was not altogether silent. He had a chance.

He slipped through an inner room and immediately kicked something unyielding. At this rate, he'd kick his toes black before he reached the inner room, never mind the noise he'd make. He forced himself to crack the ghostlight, tapping one end to break the glass vial inside and fill the tube with faint blue-white luminescence. It was just enough to keep him from stumbling—and just enough to reveal the silhouette of a head and shoulders less than a yard away. The cry of alarm died in his throat when he saw it was a dummy, like the ones he'd seen in dressmakers' shops down in the warmer world. This one, though, had a reproduction of the witch's face on it, lifelike but lifeless, blank eyeholes mocking him for his panic. A fetish, he supposed, though why she'd want one in her own likeness was beyond him.

"Dammit, Gristle," he breathed. "Just when I thought I couldn't like you less."

He held tight to the ghostlight and made his way to the inventory room. There, he risked lighting his lamp, hooding it to a narrow beam. Crates were stacked on floor-to-ceiling shelves, arranged and labeled with librarian precision. There were cabinets with drawers of fine powders and metal flasks of other chemicals—precursors to various witchy brews, he supposed. The previous Company witch had been open about what she could and couldn't cure, and she'd even shared a few of her methods. Most of them hadn't sounded like magic at all. Then again, she'd once mumbled a man's head into blowing up. She could afford a bit of demystification.

He pried up the top from a crate of red with his crowbar. The nails squeaked, and he went still. No sound followed—no footsteps, no crone's shriek of alarm, no thunderclap inside his own head that left his brains all over the walls. He finished prying, plucked out two glass vials, and tucked them into his pockets. They'd be missed when Gristle opened the crate herself in a month or two, but what could she prove? They might have been omitted from the shipment. And when Clyde recovered, Loren would just claim he'd prayed extra hard. It would be thin, but it would fly. It had to. He couldn't contemplate the alternative.

Now came the hard part: resealing the crate. He lowered the lid, positioned the first nail under his rag, and set to tapping with the flat side of the crowbar. It was slow work, and it sounded like thunder in his ears. Only when he was halfway done did he realize he just might be all right. Gristle didn't sleep with one eye open. She was an old woman. She probably slept like the dead, being halfway there already. He began to relax.

A sharp intake of breath and flood of light from behind snapped his head around. There was Gristle, a small, stooped silhouette in the door, backlit by the lamps in the room beyond. She was drawing breath, preparing a spell—

Panic overrode thought. She'd caught him, she'd caught him, and he'd die now or by the noose, and Clyde was dead too, would go all brittle and die when his lungs couldn't draw breath or when his heart shredded itself on a thousand crystal needles.

He lunged and swung the crowbar overhand. It was a clumsy blow, but the points punched into Gristle's collarbone, and his weight bore her backward through the door, driving her to the ground. Her head cracked hard against the stone. He pulled the crowbar free in a spray of blood that flashed red in the sudden brilliance of the gaslights, blinding after his hour's work in the dark. He raised the crowbar again even though it weighed a thousand pounds and his muscles had gone all liquid, like in those dreams where you had to fight but all the strength had drained out of you, and he had to squint through watering eyes to see—to see—

He stopped. Bright green eyes stared up at him from a young woman's face. She was pretty in a girlish sort of way, with delicate features and long black hair fanned out on the stone floor. Her mouth worked soundlessly, and her eyes darted, frightened. Blood still leapt in spurts from the wound in her neck. She was trying to inhale but couldn't. He'd crushed the wind from her with his tackle. One small, long-fingered hand groped toward his face. He pushed it aside. He had to explain himself. If he could just tell her why—if he could make her understand—

The fear in her face was giving way to something else. Hairs on his neck rose as power gathered.

"I'm sorry," he tried to say.

Sudden pain bit into his chest and rocketed up into his head, but he kept his grip on the crowbar and brought it down one last time, and Gristle lay dead beneath him.

The next hour passed in a strange calm, as though he'd decided the entire affair was a persistent dream. He found rags with which to clean up the blood. He wrapped Gristle in the one ruined carpet, trying not to touch her, flinching every time his hands brushed the thick flannel of her nightgown. Fully lit, the room's function was obvious. Half was a simple laboratory. Half was a dressing room. The mannequin wearing Gristle's false face stood before a three-panel mirror. Stacked cases held cosmetics of all sorts: powders, pastes, fake warts, little clusters of bristles. Pads and brushes and mixing trays. Three pairs of brushy, winglike eyebrows stared accusingly at him from their compartment. When he opened her closet, he found that her coats all had a wood and whalebone apparatus to raise a hump across her shoulders. Gristle hadn't been old and bent; she'd just been short.

He also found a single case of red in her closet, half-empty. The seal on every vial was broken. He didn't know what that meant, but it broke his dreamy calm and set his hands shaking. He couldn't administer the stolen drug now. If Clyde recovered just after Gristle was robbed and murdered, well, there was no story that would convince people to turn a blind eye. And when they found her body, saw what she'd really been . . . .

Would he have felt better about killing an old woman? Yes, he would have, and the thought twisted his guts.

But he had a little hope left. With Gristle gone, the senior-most shift supervisor would take over what parts of her job he could. And that meant Nielsen would be in charge. He'd treat Clyde. He had to, didn't he? He cared.

Just not enough to intercede sooner.

Loren replaced the stolen vials, tacked the crate closed, and stood for a long time in Gristle's dressing room, considering the shapeless roll of carpet.

Nothing but dumb luck preserved him from discovery when he bore the wrapped body down to the inactive shafts. He carried her—it, he told himself, it—to the deepest of the old shafts, the one that ran straight down almost half a mile before corkscrewing off, and tipped the body over the edge. It fell and fell. If it raised a sound when it struck bottom, it was too far away for him to hear. He wanted to say something, one more apology, but he didn't know her name. The realization raised a bark of rotten laughter. Of course Gristle had been an alias. Nobody would name their child Gristle. Just another part of a disguise for a young woman who had to spend years alone in a company of sexually frustrated men and command their respect and obedience.

He ran his gloved hands over his face and jerked them away, suddenly sure that he'd smeared blood all over himself. But when he unhooded his lamp, he saw that his gloves were clean. It didn't matter. Anyone who saw him would know what he'd done. They'd see it in his eyes, in the crook of his hands. He had to leave. Escape. There were handcars in the little roundhouse outside the main mine entrance—there might even be one or two inside the airlock. It was easier to keep them inside than to break the ice off in spring, wasn't it? If he kitted himself out, took a few extra Locksleys, brought an oxygen bottle—

—he'd freeze to death in an hour. It was that three-month winter night, that three-month rush of aetherfall, and it was more than mere cold. The aether *fed*. It would reach through whatever he wore and suck the life from him. Assuming that the winds didn't blow the handcart from the tracks, his brittle corpse would arrive in the support village, where the skeleton crew would have a morbid conversation piece.

There was no escape. Just this cave—the one in the mountain and the darker one behind his eyes. When he crept back to his barracks, stripped, and slid into his cot an arm's length from Clyde, he fought to keep the crunch of that second blow from his mind, along with the vision, just before the stroke fell, of the terror and rage that had twisted the girl's face. An impulse to confess blossomed and died inside him.

"I have to live," he murmured to the unconscious Clyde. Then, soundlessly: if only so I can go down the mountain in spring and tell my wife I let her brother die.

He could already see Deirdre's tears, taste the salt on her cheeks. She was twenty-six, four years younger than he, but she'd already seen more loss than he cared to think about. Dead parents, dead sister, a string of miscarriages that had burned into her in ways he knew he couldn't understand. Grief had twisted inside him at each one. He'd seen that same grief inside her, but also guilt, shame, and maybe feelings that didn't have names. And now her brother was dying. She would forgive him—that was the worst part—and sink a little deeper into the silence that had punctuated their visits more and more over the last few years.

When he went home, he would have his own silence, a dead space around Gristle's final expression and the feel of a crowbar striking bone. The sensation clung to him as consciousness faded, and she was waiting in his dreams, smiling coldly and whispering, her breath hot and close in his ear.

"I hadn't expected this," Nielsen said. He stood in Gristle's dressing room with the lamps turned all the way up. He frowned at Loren. "Though I see the rationale. Do you think all the Company witches do likewise?" He prodded at the false face and gave a low whistle. "What do you suppose she really looked like?"

Loren kept his face neutral. The rumors had reached him with the morning's injection: Gristle was missing, Gristle was dead, Gristle had been found staked up in an old tunnel. The summons had come soon after, and he'd been transfixed with anxiety, sure that he'd left some obvious clue, like a glove with his name sewn into it or a somnambulist's confession painted on a wall in blood. But Nielsen had merely waved him into the witch's quarters where another shift supervisor— Jackson, his name was—and a miner Loren didn't know were peering in perplexity at the trappings of Gristle's hidden life. "No way to know, I guess," Loren said.

Jackson held up a roll of clean white rags. "If these are what I think they are," he said, "she was a lot younger than she made out."

Nielsen averted his eyes.

"Oh, be a man," Jackson said. "Don't you have sisters?"

"Do you think she just . . . left?" Loren asked.

Nielsen shook his head. "All her cold-weather gear is still here. From the dust on the floor, there's a carpet missing. It's roughly the right size for wrapping a body. So either she liked that carpet far too much and thought she could climb down Highfall in winter without so much as a coat, or she's dead." He caught Loren's questioning stare and added, "I did a stint as sheriff in a copper mining town about ten years ago. I knew a little law, I could read and was sober, and that made me the best-qualified soul in a hundred miles. In the matter at hand, I'm given to understand I'm the best we have. So now we have a hundred and forty men who were not in the active mines last night, and the question of who would want our only witch dead."

"She was doing a shit job," Jackson said. "So there's that. Five men down with crack-up, and her sitting on the red. Fair enough, she did good work on the ones that got their hands mangled when that steam drill gutted itself, but who's going to say no when a man's bleeding out right there? I'll say it if nobody else will: this was one frosty bitch, and nobody liked her. The old witch left big shoes." He pointed to where Gristle's boots stood beside the door. "This one had tiny feet."

Loren rubbed at his eyes, trying to find a pattern that would point away from himself. "Is anything missing?" he asked. "If it was about how she was handling the crack-up, somebody might've robbed her for a heavy dose of red." He hesitated, then added, "I was tempted myself. With Clyde and all."

Nielsen gave him a long look. "I'd wondered," he said. "But breaking into a witch's quarters would have been suicide. Correction, breaking into Lurga's quarters would have been suicide. This was done in either folly or desperation. No one here is either of those—not yet. Right. Time to take inventory."

So they did, Loren contriving to inspect the crate he'd already opened. Four hours later, with nothing missing, Nielsen sent them away with instructions to share what they knew and quash any rumors that followed. "We don't know what happened," he said, "but we have all her supplies and some halfway decent medics. We should be fine."

The miner Loren didn't know, a squat, scraggly looking man named Wilson, held up a slim book from the shelf in Gristle's bedroom. "Who gets her stuff?" he asked. "Spare me the righteous looks. You're all thinking it too."

"That's evidence," Nielsen said. Then, without heat: "And you are unseemly."

Wilson snorted. "You picked me."

"I did. Because your supervisor is Shoemaker, who has three men down with crack-up and is growing desperate about meeting his quota. Your task is to watch him."

Wilson sobered. "All right. So. We going to get the red and treat our men, or what?"

Nielsen hesitated. Loren fought the weightless feeling in his stomach, the painful mingling of hope and doubt. "I don't know," Nielsen said at last. "It's possible that our Gristle was callous or outright evil, but I don't see that. It is more likely that she lacked social skills. What if she had a reason for not treating those cases?"

"What if she didn't know what she was doing?" Loren countered.

Nielsen gestured at the storage room around them, his precise, mechanical movements highlighting its organization. "Does this look like it belongs to an incompetent? Now spread the word, go back to work, and for the love of God, keep your eyes open." He drew a deep breath and let it out in a hiss. "I have thinking to do."

Clyde's condition continued to deteriorate. His pulse came faster and weaker. He couldn't speak. The whites of his eyes had gone bloody. Whenever he moved, he gasped, and his face tightened in pain.

And Loren could do nothing but tip water and broth down his throat. Soon he'd have to worry about bedsores, and he hadn't a clue about how to handle those. Rolling Clyde over would tear him up inside, wouldn't it? Moving him enough to get at the bedpans was torture enough.

He lost himself in the immediate practical questions. With Clyde in front of him, he could almost forget what he'd done in trying to save him. Trying, and probably failing, unless Nielsen had a change of heart damn quick.

But after his shift in the mine, when the lamps went out and sleep closed around him like a cyst, there was nothing between him and the memory. He dreamed her face, her weak struggle, her reaching hand. Then pain in his chest and head, and now, in the strange drift of dream country, a brightness that passed between them, joining them in a luminous braid.

He jerked awake to a flash of pain and found himself sitting on cold stone and gripping a utility knife. When he groped at the burning in his left arm, he discovered three parallel cuts like claw marks down his bicep and blood sheeting his arm to the wrist. Then he realized that while his right hand was exploring the cuts, his left had picked the knife back up. He made himself drop it. It clinked on the floor beside a portable gas lamp.

Nobody can see this, he thought. Nobody. I can't explain it.

He looked around for witnesses, suddenly frantic, but he was no longer in his barracks. He sat in a disused shaft beside an airlock. Someone had broken the welds and opened the lock. A narrow exploratory tunnel opened beyond, one just broad enough for a slim man's shoulders. When he raised the lamp, he could make out the clutter of an imperfectly cleared passage—and there, at the far edge, the eerie glint of Q. His teeth ached, and nausea pooled in his guts. The far end of the tunnel had to be fifty feet away. For the Q to feel like this, it had to be a massive seam.

He dropped back behind the shelter of the half-open airlock and waited for the nausea to subside. He was woozy from either blood loss or half-remembered pain. And he was starting to shiver. He'd shed his jacket to get at his arm, and now he was breaking out in goosebumps. If he hadn't woken up, he might have died. Blood loss or hypothermia: dealer's choice.

He groped his way to the infirmary, found it unmanned. Unsurprising. There had been a lot of accidents this winter, mostly problems with the machines. The medics were always out. He stole a roll of bandages and doused the arm in alcohol, gasping at the new shock of pain.

You deserve this. The thought came sudden and sharp-edged.

He did. He deserved worse.

He grabbed enough rags to—he hoped—clean up the blood before he returned to his barracks. A few of the men were awake, whispering together in the dark. "Bad dream," he mumbled.

"Small bladder," somebody replied.

A single weak laugh answered. And no wonder. Their witch was dead. The medics were good, but they weren't Gristle, and everyone knew it.

He fell into his cot and tried to claim a few more hours sleep, first making sure his footlocker was shut and locked. If his guilt wanted to cut him in his sleep, it would have to find his keys first. His arm throbbed with his pulse, the pain somehow soothing, and he slid toward sleep.

It won't matter. The thought was clear against the fog of fading consciousness. *It was all for nothing, Loren McCully. You still don't understand what you've done.*

Funny, he thought as the next dream took him; it sounded like a woman's voice.

Nielsen decided to treat the crack-up cases. Two were worse off even than Clyde. Which made no sense. "We shouldn't have five cases of fatal cascade at all," he said to his impromptu investigators in Gristle's receiving room. "I've been monitoring the cloud chamber. The aether-sleet rates are holding at normal levels. With the red regimen, I would expect a single case every two years. That's what we've seen in the past. That's what we've *always* seen. Five cases in a week means that something has gone wrong."

"Six," Jackson said grimly. "I've got another man down. Can we up the daily dosage?"

Nielsen spread his hands in helplessness. "I'm unsure what side effects that could cause. That's what Gristle was for. I don't even know how red works. We'll have to administer horse-sized shots to save the sick ones. If they pull through without, say, growing an extra head, we can start taking more ourselves. That said, there's only so much margin. We could run out before the trains start running again. If that happens, we die up here." His gaze slid around the room. "Something's wrong," he said again. "Too many crack-ups, and our witch is gone. Dead, in all likelihood."

"Too many equipment failures," Wilson cut in. "You know we had one of the pump engines throw a rod? Haven't seen that in years. Damn near took a man's head off."

This is good, Loren thought. This is what I need. They're looking everywhere else.

You selfish, clueless son of a bitch.

"I heard about that," Nielsen said. He wore a faraway look. "Was it a new rod?"

"Eh, no. New fix, though. New bolts, maybe?"

Nielsen nodded. "Trace the shipment of spare bolts. I want to know when it arrived."

"You thinking something, boss?"

Nielsen knocked the top off a crate and pulled out a vial of red. "I might be. I sincerely hope I'm wrong."

Unsure why, Loren went with Wilson to check the lot and shipping numbers for the replacement bolts. This used to be Clyde's job, he thought. He used to have his own little room off the office, not a spare cot in a barracks full of second-shifters.

"Here we go," Wilson said, holding up a typewritten page defaced with a scrawl of notes. "Came up on the last train. Why'd you suppose the boss cares?"

"Don't know," Loren said. Then his mouth added, "Check what else came up on the last train."

"Sure. We've got rations, a hell of a lot of veggie fat—God, I hate that stuff—the winter stock of red, spare hoses for the oxygen tanks, all the usual shit. Why?"

"The winter stock of red," Loren's mouth said. It seemed to have gotten ahead of his brain.

"Yeah. Want to dose Clyde yourself? You're buddies, yeah?"

He did, even though he couldn't stop thinking about the separate stock of red that Gristle had kept in her closet. He kept on thinking about it even as Nielsen signed out the prodigal injections and as the medic guided him through the first dose. "Two more in the next six hours," the medic said. "It'll work fast. It's supposed to, anyways. I've never seen a case go this far."

Still panicking, still not thinking. It's all right in front of you.

He sat by Clyde's cot that night, waiting for the whistle in his breathing to subside. He kept his boots on and knotted the laces together. There'd be no sleepwalking tonight. He drifted off that way, head drooping down to his chest, fully dressed and wrapped in a blanket on the cold floor. Everything might still be all right. All he had to do was spend his life never telling anyone, never telling Deirdre, what he'd done to buy Clyde's life.

He woke in the middle of the night. He was sitting in an equipment closet, his boots neatly relaced. A cracked ghostlight lay beside him, and a notepad of coarse paper was open on his knee. He trousers had been pushed down to his knees, and his right hand held a knife under his crotch.

A faint sense of exasperation fluttered in his mind before fear took over and shriveled his testicles back from the immediate danger.

His hand dropped the knife, took up a fountain pen, and wrote in a neat, looping script on the notepad:

Do I have your attention?

It wasn't his handwriting, but he recognized it from row after row of neat labels. "Gristle?" he whispered.

The written answer seemed to take forever:

Obviously. I should have killed you.

The full stop was a spreading blot where the pen had stabbed the page. "I'm sorry," he said. He tried to move his right hand, found that he could. "I—"

His hand jerked, resumed writing:

I still could. Stop fighting me. No matter what, you have to sleep sometime. Remember that, Loren McCully.

"What did you do?"

What I had to. I was dying. You were there. I crossed over. It's not a smooth process. I wasn't even sure why they taught us that spell.

More ghost sensations crossed his mind: regret, pain, nostalgia, gratitude. A vague impression of quiet halls and rooms full of books. Stern but not unkind voices.

"You can't kill me," he whispered. "You'd die, too, wouldn't you?"

His hand hesitated over the paper. Then:

I could make you wish you were dead. There are parts of you you'd miss.

He tried, with some success, to pull his pants up left-handed. "I might bleed out."

There are other parts of you I could take away. You expect to see your wife when spring comes. I'll still be here. Think on your sins, Loren.

His breath caught. "You wouldn't."

You killed me.

This time, the words echoed in his head like a fading scream. A flood of fear and anger burst through him—not his, he realized now. Gristle's.

Carefully, and of his own volition, he added an exclamation mark to her last sentence. "Clyde was dying," he said.

I know.

He could hear her voice more clearly now, as though the notepad were merely a synchronizing gear between the two minds caught in his head. She sounded sick and frightened and tired—like a young woman trapped alone in a strange place, not like a witch threatening to castrate him or murder his wife. Guilt blossomed in his mind, followed by pity.

Keep your pity.

He took a deep breath. "I know you're desperate," he said. "But if you threaten Deirdre again, I'll kill myself."

Well, look who's decided there's something he'll die for after all.

Then somehow he was up and striding out of the closet, one hand awkwardly holding his trousers up. He recognized the tunnel at once: two sets of rails ran down its length, and its far end flared into a loading bay. This was the outer edge of the mine, just below the western side of the peak. There was an airlock less than fifty yards away. And Gristle was marching them towards it. He could already imagine the aethersleet flashing invisibly, imperceptibly through him. This near the surface, he had to be getting a higher dosage. And the aether itself would be pouring down outside the airlock doors in a silent roar.

He tried to stop walking, managed to make himself stumble. Gristle released control at once.

I thought so. I'm in here, too, remember? I know you. You don't have the courage.

She was right—almost right. "I'd turn myself in, though. They'd either hang me or lock me up. They'd never let you near Deirdre. Never."

He held up the notepad, waiting. The pen didn't move. A suggestion of doubt from Gristle.

"What's your real name?"

The pen remained motionless, but he heard the name anyway: *Rose.* Then: *Damn, I didn't mean to say that.*

"Rose. What are you going to do? What do you want from me?"

No answer. Her presence faded. His right hand was his own again and shaking like mad. He tore the used page from the notebook and shredded it. Then he went to check Clyde's condition. It was still worsening.

Morning came, and he took the most awkward piss of his life.

I've already seen it all.

"Not helping," he muttered, keeping his voice low and hoping no one else at the urinal trough would notice. "Why isn't Clyde getting better?"

Because the red you injected is saline and dye. The whole winter shipment is. I'd been diluting the regular doses to make the real supply last as long as possible, but a higher incidence of crack-up was inevitable.

"You have the real stuff? Oh. The crate in your closet." He buttoned his fly. "There's enough for—"

There's enough to keep some of you alive all winter. Possibly. Or you can use it all to temporarily cure six men, who will then sicken again and die without daily prophylactic injections. Just like the rest of you. There's a reason I showed you that abandoned exploratory shaft two nights ago. Think about it. A promising vein, abandoned. An increase in illness and accidents, compromising your quotas. I think John has almost figured it out, by the way.

John? he thought. Ah, yes: John Nielsen.

A few faint thoughts that were most assuredly not his own floated to the surface of his mind, all to do with Nielsen, who had strong hands sometimes a bit of shyness in his face, a depth under that stern exterior, and clear blue-gray eyes—

"Stop it," he muttered, louder than he'd meant to. A couple of heads turned toward him, in clear violation of urinary etiquette.

I'm circumstantially celibate, she said, *not dead. Well,* now *I'm dead. A girl can look.*

An upwelling of frustration, of lost possibilities. An anger already fading into deep, deep grief. He wanted to scream, or Rose did. Or maybe the difference between them was starting to break down. That was a disturbing thought, and a true one. He remembered, now, that the spell which had jammed Rose into his head did nothing to preserve the integrity of either mind.

"We don't have much time," he murmured, imagining both the crystallization of his body and the muddling of his mind with Rose's.

No. Not much time at all. It's about time you troubled to read your contract carefully and maybe had a look at the records room. Recall our first excursion together?

A rich vein of Q that someone had hidden and left untouched even as the rest of the mine began to peter out.

"Aw, hell," he said.

The administrative offices were five hundred feet below the barracks and accessible only via an open-cage elevator. They were also deliciously warm. A gas fire burned in a grate, and bearskin rugs covered the floor. Loren wanted nothing more than to strip, don a soft robe, and stretch out on one of those rugs with a stack of those medical journals Rose had been meaning to read for weeks.

He caught himself. Stop it, he thought again.

Mocking, feminine laughter in his head. *I don't see how you're the victim here.*

Nielsen was already sitting in the records room. The administrator, a mousy man named Kurtz, had been displaced from his chair and was slumped against the wall, wearing a broken nose and a stunned expression. "McCully," Nielsen said quietly. "Please shut the door behind you."

"It's the Company," Rose said through Loren's mouth. "If the mine falls short enough of its target yields this year, they have the option to cut all our contracts and renegotiate or hire new crews."

I already knew that, Loren wanted to say, and Nielsen had to know it too. Get on with the rest, he thought.

"If we're all dead or sick, or enough equipment breaks, we'll miss those targets. The question is, why now? I had a look around last night at what are supposed to be dead ends." She paused expectantly.

"We're being lied to," Loren said, taking up the thread. "There's a tunnel, one marked as an exploratory dig that came up dry. Airlock was sealed up. But it didn't come up dry. There's Q there. A lot of it, I'd guess. But someone must have known . . ."

Nielsen nodded, then prodded Kurtz with a foot. "Tell him," he said.

Kurtz cringed, and a fresh drop of blood wobbled from the tip of his nose. "It was just two or three records," he said. "Just the Q concentrations in the new northeast shaft. I only . . . adjusted some of the numbers. It happens all the time. Can't saturate the market, you know? It's standard practice. Then in a short year, prices would jump, and I'd just 'discover' the mistake, and we'd all be better off. See? It's good for everyone."

"And your bosses knew about this?" Loren said.

"Of course. It's standard."

"How much Q?" Loren asked. When Kurtz hesitated, he kicked him under the ribs. "How much?"

Kurtz pulled himself upright. "It's—it might be the largest vein ever discovered. There's no way to be sure. And we were so sure this mine was close to played out, so . . ."

So they gave you all a higher percentage of the revenues than they normally would have. Now that this will be the most lucrative mine in the hemisphere, they have to take it away. They arranged for bad luck with your replacement parts and supplies, including the red. The Company will have already arranged for one of its suppliers to take the blame for the counterfeit treatments. It will be tragic and highlight the unprofitability of the mine. The contract with your replacements will feature much higher flat rates to balance the risk and virtually nil points on revenues—the typical hedge to keep the mine open while they hold out for a price spike. The Company will make a fortune once they re-open that vein. Such a shame we'll all be dead.

Loren realized that he was spilling this analysis in his own words, stumbling whenever Rose added an aside. "And you didn't see this coming," he finished, rounding on Kurtz. "You're up here too, you know. I wonder how many days until you start showing symptoms. The cascade runs faster in rats, I'm told."

"I didn't know," Kurtz said, his eyes wide. "I swear to God, I didn't know."

"I believe you," Nielsen said. His voice was gentle. "But you knew something. So did several others, starting with at least one of the miners who drilled the shaft. Who else saw the original concentration studies?"

Kurtz spilled the names. Loren recognized only two, but Rose knew them all. Seven of the ten had been rotated to other mines before the trains shut down for the winter. Two had suffered accidents. One—a logistician named Clyde Greer—was dying of crack-up five hundred feet above their heads.

It had to be a mistake. Or Kurtz was lying. Or Loren was hallucinating. He'd been hearing voices, after all. "He couldn't have known it would go this far," Loren said. "He couldn't have. He never—" But there was no making an argument based on Clyde's character. Not anymore. And of course they'd have needed someone in the supply office to sign off on suspect parts, someone to make sure no one opened crates and inspected the contents too soon. It was obvious in hindsight. He rubbed at the heat in his eyes.

Still not thinking, I see. Why would Clyde have wanted a handsome payment now, of all times? The memories are here, Loren McCully. Noticed anything different about your Deirdre these last few months?

Loren shut her out. "He wouldn't have stayed if he'd known. Or let me stay. Sabotaged equipment to force a slowdown, all right, maybe, but the counterfeit red—"

All it means is that he's dying in denial.

"Interesting you should mention that again," Nielsen said. "I finished testing a vial an hour ago. You're correct. It's basically salt water. How did you find out?"

Ooh, he's smart. Smarter than you, anyway. I see why Lurga liked him.

"I—figured it out. Clyde's not getting better. None of them are, I'll bet."

Nielsen sighed. "You're right about that, too. Come on. We need to convene the other shift supervisors and the senior men. We have another problem now, too."

"What?"

"Isn't it obvious? Gristle. The Company has a plant here. He killed her before she could realize what was wrong with the red. Perhaps she could have made more, or found a way to keep us alive through the winter." His voice hardened. "That means he knows about the red, and so unless he was on a suicide mission, he has his own supply. After the speech you gave, I'm surprised you didn't figure it out."

Loren wasn't. He felt numb, foggy, caught at the threshold where a good drunk starts to go bad. "I'm . . . not a detective."

No shit. You're on the other side of the law, aren't you? What would happen if we confessed now? Do you think it'd be a clean drop or a slow rope? There's a daguerreotype of me hidden away in my rooms. I could make you tell Nielsen about it, show him who you really killed. Maybe I should. Otherwise some poor scapegoat will take the blame, won't he?

Loren bit his tongue, felt Rose twitch away from the pain. "What about Kurtz?" he asked.

"Leave him. We'll find a solution, or we won't. If we don't, he dies too." Nielsen's eyes slid to Kurtz. "I trust you consider yourself well-incentivized to help?"

But here was a scapegoat, and not an innocent one, not by half. "He could have killed Gristle," Loren said. "He could have a locker *full* of red down in the old shafts and we'd never find it—"

Kurtz sat up straighter. "Now, wait—"

"Look in his eyes," Nielsen said.

Loren looked. Then Rose extended his hand, took Kurtz by the chin, and tilted his face towards the light. Tiny points of light shimmered in his pupils. Crystallization.

Kurtz must have read their expression, because he began to cry.

Nielsen said nothing during the elevator ride back to the living areas. But he did lean against the cage and fold his arms, and his coat shifted to show that he was wearing a revolver.

Sheriff indeed, Rose said. *Hold it together, McCully. I still need your body.*

Loren didn't know what to say to that, so he said nothing at all.

The conference went poorly. There was shouting. There was a fistfight. There was no clear decision, just a circle of accusations and compounding doubts. Loren held his peace throughout, though he had to endure Rose's running commentary in his head. She could be funny in a snide, pitch-black sort of way, and her mental voice had taken on an edge of giddy desperation. She was funny when she borrowed his voice to pitch in to the argument, too, and people were starting to give him odd looks.

The worst problem was the inferred cache of red—not enough to save everyone, but maybe enough to save *someone*. Rose argued Loren's throat hoarse insisting that it probably didn't exist, and even if it did, they'd never find it. Nielsen reinforced her point with absurd reasoning framed in irrefutable gravitas.

But it does exist, Loren thought. The real stuff is crated up in your closet, and you know it. So does Nielsen.

Not enough to matter, and he knows that, too. Imagine three men in a lifeboat, a thousand miles from shore, with no hope of rescue. They have a single ladle of water among them. What is humane?

Find someone to give it to, he answered. Draw lots, or pick the man with a family, or—I don't know.

Tip it over the side. There's a time when letting go of hope together is the best thing you can do.

The thought echoed through his head—their head, he supposed—all through the rest of the debate. I want, he thought, to say you're wrong. I just can't see why.

Me too.

When the fight broke out, he backed Nielsen by pure reflex. So did Rose. He hadn't known how to dislocate a pair of shoulders with a touch and whispered word, but she did, and she took him through the motions in a single violent blur that left Nielsen's attacker screaming on the ground.

I'm getting good at wearing you, she said, and then there was blessed, blessed silence in his head.

I'm lucky I got in that first lick with the crowbar, he thought. Then: No, no I'm not.

Cooler heads eventually prevailed, aided by a dozen or so concussions. Night found Loren by Clyde's cot. Clyde's breathing was uneven, ragged, undercut by dissonant chords. When he tried to call Rose in his mind, she didn't answer.

He bent as though speaking to Clyde. "Rose," he murmured.

What do you want?

"I could ask you the same thing," he muttered. "We'll all be dead in a month. You knew it. Why didn't you tell us? And why are you riding me around like—like—"

A sedan chair. An ugly sedan chair that ought to shave and wipe itself down and that hasn't heard of soap.

"Whatever."

I didn't know what to do. I tested the red, but I was still assessing options.

"You could have told somebody."

And then we'd have had two hundred panicked souls underground. We have that now. How is it working out for you? You'll all kill each other trying to survive. I had to find a source of hope before I told you a word.

"And you didn't, I guess."

Not so much. There should be supplies staged in the support village, but we can't descend the mountain in winter, and even if someone reached the village, there's no way the Company would send a train back. The trains are insulated against aether, insofar as that's possible, but the wind or ice are still likely to derail it.

Despite himself, he smiled. "You're still trying to save us."

Don't ask me why.

But he could feel why. The miners were her responsibility. That had been drilled into her again and again, and she believed it with the certainty of axiomatic faith. It was the same conviction he'd sensed in the old witch, just rougher, rawer, like new wine.

The realization broke over both of them at once.

I was part of their plan. They installed a novice witch because they knew I couldn't handle this crisis. Those motherfuckers.

He had to stifle a laugh. With slow horror, he realized that he rather liked Rose. And why not? She was lively, driven, and she wasn't *really* dead.

You're still a murderer. I haven't forgotten. You want to know what that crowbar felt like?

Remembered agony ripped into his shoulder, and he gasped.

I still haven't decided what to do with you.

"A moot point," he hissed through the pain. "We'll just die together, won't we?"

Probably. The pain faded. *Probably, we will. I'm scared. I shouldn't be. The worst has happened, but I'm still scared.*

Deirdre would have known what to say. Hell, Clyde would have known what to say. Loren just sat there, feeling stupid, then awkwardly wrapped his arms around himself.

Nothing happened. Then Rose's laughter rang through his head, no longer mocking, and he joined in: great, shuddering gales of laughter at the absurdity of the situation and his weak attempt at comfort. Low conversations subsided all around him as men turned to stare at him as though he'd gone mad. Perhaps he had.

The laughter subsided, and when Rose spoke again, she sounded breathless:

I didn't tell anyone because I was scared and didn't know what to do. That was it. I just didn't know what to do.

"I know," he murmured. "Hell, I might even understand."

They sat together in silence. Then Clyde jerked with a sharp crackling noise, like footfalls on snowcrust, and went slack. Blood began to leak from a thousand lacerations where the crystals inside him had punctured his skin in that final convulsion, but it was only a slow ooze. Clyde's heart was no longer beating.

I suppose you never really know someone.

He flinched as though slapped. When he found the words, they spilled out in a torrent: "He wasn't worth what I did to you. He risked us all. He had to know. Dammit, Rose, *he wasn't worth it.*"

You still don't see it—how very like you he was. But it's better not to use terms like worth, I think. Because soon you apply them to everyone, and eventually you examine yourself, and what will you do then?

By the next day, there were seven new cases of crack-up and three of the first round had died. Jackson was among the newly afflicted and didn't stop screaming until the medics doped him.

"We can narrow down our suspect pool," Nielsen said over lunch. Not a slab of fat, thankfully; no one was digging anymore, and that meant no Winterizer. "Third shift was all accounted for on the night Gristle disappeared. That's seventy-one men. We can eliminate anyone showing crack-up symptoms. Much of first shift was awake. If we discount everyone who had at least two steady witnesses to their whereabouts, we can reduce the list of suspects to ninety-two." He pushed a list across the table, then sat back and rubbed at the dark circles under his eyes. "And no, I didn't sleep much last night. I'll need your help with more interviews today."

Loren glanced down the list. "I'm still on here. Why are you trusting me?"

I'm not on the list, Rose said smugly.

"I've met Deirdre," Nielsen said. "You have too much to lose to risk something like this. I could almost see you doing something foolish for Clyde, but for money . . . don't see it, no."

Rose reached out and put a hand on Nielsen's arm. "For what it's worth, you're doing a fine job with the information you have." A moment too late, Loren turned the gesture into a manly slap. "But we need to know more. Shouldn't we concentrate on the crack-up situation?"

Nielsen gave his own arm a puzzled look, then shook himself. "I . . . don't know how to fix that. If our killer has a supply of red, and we find it, it might buy us time."

Time to do what? Rose said bitterly. *I couldn't do anything. It's why they put me here.*

"My God, that's it," Loren said.

"What?"

"They got rid of the old witch—transferred her—and gave us Rose. It was part of the plan. So Lurga must have been able to do something Rose couldn't, something that would have let us survive."

"Rose?"

"Gristle," Loren said hastily. "Gristle. She let her real name slip once. A different name, anyway. You didn't think her parents named her Gristle, did you?"

"I don't know. It did seem to fit."

Jackass. Why are the pretty ones always rude?

"But you're correct," Nielsen went on. "I admit, it's hard to picture her as anything but old and worn down. Those eyes, though . . . her eyes make me wish I'd seen her without the mask."

All right. He gets to live.

"So," Loren said, a bit louder than necessary, "what's the key differentiator between Lurga and Gristle?"

I met Lurga a few times. She was brilliant at the quick-and-dirty physical magics. Give her enough Q and mundane chemicals, and she probably could have blasted a tunnel down to a livable altitude. It might have set off a chain reaction and leveled the mountain, but she might have tried anyway. She always was determined. *Ah, here's a memory of her exploding a head. Yes, she had a well-developed sense of justice. Better than mine, seeing as you're still breathing. But there's no point to asking the question. By definition, I can't do whatever she could have done.*

"I don't know," Nielsen said. "We don't know as much about Gristle—Rose—as we'd thought. Perhaps we don't know as much about Lurga, either. She must have started out the same way: wearing a mask and a wig, almost never coming out, keeping the lights dim. No wonder the lifers claim she was an old lady for forty years. She must have been lonely. It does make me feel better about always imposing on her for coffee or tea. She had real coffee . . ."

"I remember," Loren said, but it was Rose's memory: coffee and cookies with bits of candied ginger, taken in leisure and the bright, stately quiet of the monastery library with its tall windows and warm papery smell. Lurga's voice, rough but kind. A little unpolished but intensely practical advice about how to stay sane when spending a year in crowded isolation. *Find one you don't like,* she'd said, *it'll be a stupid one, and you just tell him that when the air hits forty below, it makes railroad track taste like whiskey. Just have warm water ready to get his tongue off the rail. There's good fun, and there's maiming, and they're the same thing less than half the time.*

He wanted to weep and could not. Rose was holding herself together, and him too. That library was the living world, and it was so far, far away from both of them.

"Are you feeling all right?" Nielsen asked, a little unease creeping into his voice. "Need the medic? You're looking white as the dead."

Anger. He had Rose's anger to back his own. That was easier than sorrow. He'd killed her, and the Company had killed Clyde and put them all in this situation. "Fine. Forget the question."

Nielsen took a wild guess and guessed wrong: "Clyde couldn't have known it would go this far," he said.

"Forget it." Loren turned inward. *Can you still work magic?* he asked. *You popped that man's shoulders right out with it, didn't you?*

I can do some. This is kind of new to me, you might have noticed.

"They still killed Rose," Nielsen said, visibly groping for safer ground. "She was still a threat to them. We should pull her rooms apart and see if there's anything we can use."

Don't you dare.

"It's better than doing nothing," Loren said. He had to fight Rose for control of his legs to follow Nielsen back to Main Street, but he won in the end, and with a minimum of stumbling. She still fired a parting shot before sliding into the back of his mind:

Did you notice he's stopped talking about interviews to narrow down the suspect pool?

Loren cursed violently, cursed again under Nielsen's questioning look, and said, "Stepped funny. Bad ankle."

They had to pass through a milling crowd that wasn't quite a mob, not yet, to reach Rose's rooms. The lamps on Main Street were burning brighter. Someone had decided that dead men didn't need light, so why not enjoy a little more illumination? A few of the miners shouted questions at Nielsen, who fielded or evaded them. "There's a solution," he said with easy confidence. "We haven't died yet. It's what we have in common. We're survivors."

This front crumpled inside the witch's receiving room. "Search," he said shortly. "Find out what she could do and whether there's a way to copy it."

Thus began one of the stranger hours of Loren's life. Rose explained the uses of her various chemical and alchemical compounds, her simple laboratory equipment, her Q-fed instruments and tools. Loren managed to keep any of her monologue from reaching his mouth. Now and then she snarled at him not to touch something, and she lapsed into irate, sullen silence when Nielsen found a leather-bound journal under her bed and read the first few pages. He frowned, flipped to the middle, reddened, and put it away. "Not relevant," he said.

Loren, who had ghostly memories of writing in that journal, didn't press the point. Besides, Rose might have cut his throat or spontaneously combusted with mortification.

"It's almost all medical." Nielsen was holding up a typewritten page. "These spells are strictly biological, even the ones with temporal effects. None of her magics concerned fire, force, telepathy, or transport."

He was almost right. Loren reached out and tapped a line of characters. "This one's different. It's entropic. Think of it as the genus that includes fire magics."

"Correct," Nielsen said. He sounded impressed. "Lurga used to talk my ear off about how laymen always misunderstood the categories."

Then Loren was flat on his back, head ringing, and Nielsen had a knee on his chest. The barrel of the revolver was a black cave blotting out half the world. "What—" he began.

"I know that," Nielsen snapped, "because I spent hours keeping Lurga company. But Loren doesn't know that, on account of him being, and I mean this kindly, not burdened with an overabundance of formal education. 'Entropic?' You might have slipped that one past me, Rose, but you used 'differentiator' earlier, and I'd lay odds Loren would think that's a piece of a steam engine."

"Dammit," Loren said. At least, he was pretty sure he was the one who said it.

"There is another possibility we didn't discuss," Nielsen said. The eye behind the revolver's sights was flat, expressionless. "That our witch was in on this from the beginning. What was the plan, Rose? You would switch bodies repeatedly, keep a healthy one all the way to the end? Play the odds that a few of us would survive the aethersleet unprotected? Not much of a plan."

"I concur," Rose said. "Which is why I didn't make it. This oaf murdered me, trying to save Clyde. Ask him."

Slowly, Nielsen swung the revolver aside and lowered the hammer. "That was my second theory," he said. He settled back on his haunches. "Goddammit, McCully—you're still in there?"

"Yes. You knew?"

"I suspected. Clyde was the only sick man with anything like kin. Usually, it's friends and family who lose perspective in a crisis and do idiot things. Why do you think I involved you in the investigation? I had to keep you close. Either you'd murdered Rose, or someone was going to accuse you of it. Or both. I'm told that sometimes happens. Wilson, too. The man sees himself as the zeitgeist of the mining world. I thought he might have killed Gristle—sorry, Rose—just because of the feeling in the air." He squinted at Loren, fingering the revolver. "But you're not shilling for the Company. That's clear enough."

"No," Rose said, sitting up, "the Company would have picked someone competent."

Nielsen gave them a helpless look.

"It's Rose speaking," she added. "I could do a falsetto if you'd like."

"No. God no. This is strange enough." He laid aside the revolver and put his face in his hands. "McCully, how could you do this?"

"It was an accident."

"Some accident," Rose added, taking their voice up a third. "He just tripped and put his crowbar through my brachial artery, and then, oops, he tripped again and cracked my skull."

Gaping, empty silence. "I'm sorry," Loren said. The words didn't feel real anymore, perhaps because they'd never meant much to begin with.

"Never mind that," Nielsen said. "No one is allowed to collapse. Not now. Vexing as it is, the truth changes little, except that now I know the only genuine red is the few hundred doses in Rose's closet. We still need to decide what to do."

"Simple," Rose said. "We see if Lurga told you anything I don't know. Then we find a way to keep our people alive. That's our job, isn't it?"

Six hours later, they had nothing, and word came that two more men were nearing the terminal stage. "I can try putting them under a stasis spell," Rose said. "It might kill them, or it might preserve them for a few hours."

"Why not just leave them in stasis until spring?" Loren asked.

"Because if the crystallization doesn't kill them, the spell will, in about three days," she snapped. "The human body isn't meant to be suspended out of time like that. The ones that survive more than three days tend to come back insane. If I can do the spell at all. The meat I'm wearing isn't tingling with magical potential."

"Try it anyway," Nielsen said. "Even if it accomplishes nothing else, it will feed more material into the rumor mill. As long as the men are asking questions, they won't be attempting to kill each other for a pittance of red."

"Or," Loren said, "we could tell the truth. There's no Company spy. There was just . . . me. What I did and why. They'll believe it. You know they'll believe it."

Nielsen stared at him for a long moment. Then he gripped Loren's arm and nodded. "Yes," he said. "Yes, we will. But not yet."

"Why not?"

"Because we can't know what they'll do, and I still need Rose. And we might need you, too."

"But we'll tell them?" Suddenly, that seemed important.

"Yes, if we can't save them. Better to go knowing the truth."

Loren let out a long sigh. A pressure in his chest he hadn't noticed eased. "We'll write it all down, then, too. We can leave the whole truth behind. Maybe the right people will find it. It wouldn't feel right, dying without, I don't know, a testimony."

It's a shame you killed me. I'm beginning to think we might have been friends.

We might have to be if we get through this, he thought, trying to keep the idea quiet. Seeing as we're stuck together. Then, absurdly: How the devil do we explain this to Deirdre?

Both men went into stasis, and Rose pronounced them stable.

"How stable?" Nielsen asked.

She waggled a hand. "Not particularly. A blow from, for example, a crowbar would still kill them, but they won't die of disease, anoxia, hypothermia, old age . . . anything that degrades the body on a small scale, if you will. But no, before you ask, you can't put a man in stasis on a handcar and roll it down the mountain. Someone would have to recover him at the other end, and the Company obviously isn't worried about us trying to send messages. Either the support village is deserted, or the only people there are complicit." She bit their lip. "The former, I think. It's simpler. And cheaper."

"You're likely right," Nielsen said slowly. "You can't put yourself in stasis and wake yourself up?"

"Have you ever tried to lick your elbow?"

He paused in mock consideration. "My *own* elbow?"

He's flirting with her, Loren thought, and it's working. Fascinating.

Are you taking notes? You should be. Ten years of marriage, and you still don't know what you're doing.

He felt their cheeks burning.

"What?" Nielsen asked.

"You don't want to know," he said. "Is there a point?"

"There might be. Tell me more about your body-switching spell, Rose."

So she did: "I was dying. The spell carried my mind into Loren's, preserving my memories and personality alongside his. In wounding me, he'd opened a conduit, and there's power in death, or more precisely, in sacrifice—"

"What I need to know," Nielsen said, "is whether you could make the leap several times in a row?"

A pause, a fleeting image as Rose pictured bodies arranged like the rungs of a descending ladder. And Loren felt her comprehension—a sweet, sad thing—spreading like sunrise through them both.

"That can't be the only way," he said. "It can't."

You said you were willing to die to protect Deirdre from me. Will you not die to protect two hundred men from a slow and painful death?

"They're not *mine.*"

No. But they are *mine. If I still had my body, this would have been my sacrifice to make. Now it's yours, too. This is your doing. Accept it.*

Their right hand cupped his cheek. Their other reached out and gripped Nielsen's hand, interlacing their fingers. "It's the best we can do," she said aloud, half to Loren, half in answer to Nielsen's puzzled look.

"What happened to giving up hope together?" Loren asked.

We both know that was bullshit.

He let out a strangled laugh and squeezed Nielsen's hand. Or maybe Rose did. It mattered less, now.

They found eight volunteers, most of them in the earliest stages of crackup. The last was Kurtz, the little administrator, who had not been initially enthusiastic.

"Would you like a chance at redemption?" Rose had asked him.

He'd answered with a look like a frightened deer.

"It's a rare thing," she went on. Their voice took on a strange harmonic, almost musical. "So many need it, so few find it. Your name will be written somewhere, Kurtz. The question is where, and how people will read it."

He'd jerked a nod then. "I'll die?"

"Mostly," Rose said. Then, in a blatant lie: "It doesn't hurt."

Nielsen's insistence on coming was the hardest to accept. He had to do it, he maintained. Otherwise how could he expect it of anyone else? The conversation left a twisting coil of pain in their chest. It was love. Loren recognized it: a younger, sharper iteration of what he felt for Deirdre now that he had to leave her behind.

Iteration, he thought. I'm starting to sound like Rose even on the inside.

Let's get this over with.

But he still stopped halfway to the mine entrance and wrapped his arms around himself; around them. There was no laughter this time. Just quiet.

"I'm so sorry," he murmured.

I know. I feel it. I don't know whether I can forgive you yet.

"You should have given Nielsen your picture."

It would only make things worse.

Nine men, Nielsen included, were bundled tight and stacked like cordwood on the handcar and the small flatbed car trailing behind. Bottles of oxygen and gas heaters were racked within reach of the operator's perch, right next to the handbrake that was the only control they'd need on the descent. The airlock door was still shut, but it shivered and hummed with the force of the wind outside.

Nielsen and Loren had drawn up designs for a crude enclosure to protect the handcar and flatbed from the wind, and they'd covered the finished product in panels of aether insulation. It wouldn't help much, but it was all they had. The trade-off was a higher profile. A strong enough wind would rip the car from the tracks and send it tumbling down the mountain.

One by one, Rose put the men into stasis, then buttoned and tied their masks closed. They wouldn't suffocate, not while their metabolisms were suspended. She was almost as sure that the aether and mundane cold wouldn't affect them. "They're not altogether in the world," she said as Loren buttoned their outermost coat closed and pulled on a final pair of gloves. "They should be fine."

The last word came out muffled as he fixed their own mask in place and then tied a scarf around it.

That was rude.

She was whistling in the dark. Hell, after that episode with the knife at his groin, she'd spent the last couple of days whistling in the dark. She'd whistled right through her own funeral. Graveyard whistling.

That was almost funny. Time to go.

He threw the bolts and starting turning the crank to open the outer airlock door. Air fled with a thinning scream, and their ears popped. A chill began to eat at his bones—not air, but aether. The ordinary cold would start in on him later.

He kept cranking, then climbed aboard the handcar, shut the crude hatch, and set it rolling with a single, laborious cycle of the lever. It rolled onto the tunnel downgrade and began to pick up speed. He clung tight to the handrail and brake, peering out through the eyeslit. Too slow, and they'd run out of bodies before they reached a habitable altitude. Too fast, and they'd fly off the tracks on a switchback.

Then the car broke from the tunnel, and the night winds were upon them.

Screaming eternity followed. There was no room for thought, scarcely room for fear. Time and pain were far away. The car ground to a halt against ice after the first mile, and they had to leave the sheltered cabin to chip the rails clear. Outside, the wind and aetherfall tore into them, flooding their body with a cold mindlessness that persisted even when they resumed the descent. Only Rose's constant, snarling force of will kept Loren anchored, kept him aware of their body, and of when it began to fail. *Now*, she said. *It has to be now. We've made it almost two thousand feet down, I think.*

I'm afraid, he thought back.

I was too.

He pulled the handbrake, and the handcar ground to a stop. He hauled Kurtz from the pile and started oxygen flowing to his mask. He relaxed his mind, and Rose summoned a final burst of will to drag Kurtz up from stasis.

Kurtz sat up, thrashing, grabbing at his face. Loren gripped his wrists until he calmed. Kurtz was trying to shout over the wind outside, but he might as well have been a thousand miles away. So Loren ignored him and pressed the revolver into his hands, hoping the cold hadn't damaged it. Then Rose tapped their chest.

Kurtz's eyes were wide behind his goggles, but he nodded, aimed, and fired.

Pain. Then a rushing sensation, like flying down a tunnel of lights. Rose was taking him along with her, he realized. Had she meant to? Then the weight of unfamiliar flesh closed around him.

They—Kurtz/Rose/Loren—descended another two thousand feet before the false warmth that signaled the final stages of hypothermia began to set in. So they woke the next man in line and gave him the revolver, and again there was a moment of pain, of flight, and it was almost a relief to have that fleeting moment out of the wind, to feel like they were flying and not being torn away.

Seven more times they changed bodies, a growing committee of ghosts. They took Nielsen's last. The outpost was still three thousand feet below, but the wind was weaker here and the aether less deadly. Through the fading wind, they could hear themselves all too clearly, a cacophony of desperation and pride and fear and sadness.

We'll make it, we have to make it—

Can we tell Jane what happened to me and what I did—

At least these knees don't ache, God what a morbid thought—

If that bitch had just asked for help in the first place—

I think I could have loved her—you—in time or another life—

There's a picture I wish I'd shown you—

If I could take so many things back—

The handcar drifted to the end of the line and stopped. They piloted Nielsen's body out and into one of the outbuildings. It was empty. They opened gas valves until they found the right ones and lit the heaters. *The cellars*, Loren thought through the noise. *If there's red, they'll have stowed it down where it stays warmer.*

And we'll need coal and heating oil and a hundred other things. That sounded like Kurtz. *They fill the pipes in the locomotives with oil for the winter so nothing freezes. We'll have to flush it out.*

I can show us how, someone else said. *I used to service those engines. Anybody operated one? No? Well, we'll figure it out.*

They did. It took two days, but they did. And when the train began to climb—slowly, slowly, with the wind ripping and clawing at it—they had four crates of red, all the vials headspaced to allow for freezing. They left their spent bodies outside. The cold would preserve them, for what little it was worth. After two days, even perfectly preserved in the cold, none of them looked like home anymore.

I won't get to go home to Deirdre this spring, what remained of

Loren said. His memories persisted. They just didn't feel like his. He was one of eleven drifting minds, all beginning to blur together.

I can tell her what you did, another part of them said. It felt different than the others—feminine, wry, quiet, a little weary. Rose. *Most of it. I might leave one part out.*

Thank you.

She was pregnant when you last left her, you know, she went on. *Clyde must have known. He thought he was buying you all a new life. He was a fool, but an understandable fool. Also, you are remarkably unobservant.*

She's had five miscarriages.

That doesn't mean she'll have six. Life always has a chance. Sometimes it's a strange chance.

Another ghost cut in. Nielsen. *The strangest. This isn't over. If we bring the red to the mine and see the men through the winter, we'll still have to prove what the Company did. The winners in all this will be the lawyers. As is tradition.*

If and if, the wry part said. Her tone was sour, but they could feel their face trying to smile under the mask. That happened whenever these two ghosts spoke to each other. It was the damnedest thing, but there was a warmth to it. They all held to that warmth.

We'll make it, he (Loren?) said. *It'll be cold, that's all.*

I'd give us one chance in three, the feminine voice said, but it sounded untroubled.

Together, they rose into the howling wind. But the sky above was clear, and the moon hung vast and warm against the night, and they were unafraid.

BRICKOMANCER

TOBIAS BUCKELL

There's a demon-possessed Karen stalking you as you set the waxed canvas ruck down on the sidewalk with a clink. She thinks you're here to tag one of the walls out behind her remodeled brownstone, and you can see the self-righteous anger brewing in her posture: back rigid with indignation, Ray-Bans pushed up over the blonde highlights, and a confused but redolent Maltese pants from the heat of the Manhattan asphalt from its throne inside a chunky Graco stroller.

"I called the police," the woman snaps.

The Maltese growls at you, and one of the yellow bows holding its hair back flops to the side.

Adorable dog.

"What do you have in there?"

You look down at the bag.

"You have spray cans in there?"

Her voice shakes. She's scared. Looks on the edge of tears, and she's pushing them down by shoving the white-hot poker of superiority, nosiness, and entitlement up to buttress the rigid, royalist bearing she projects out onto the world around her.

You look back at the canvas bag full of cheap Krylon cans.

This is going to make painting the anti-summoning symbols onto the corner of Chewie's bodega really fucking hard.

"You're live on video," the woman says. Her head tweaks back and forth to emphasize her words. "This is why property values suffer here. There's no pride of place—"

She has a lot to say, but you tune her out like you do the Mad Russian when he starts wandering up and down the D train. One hundred streets up the line and a thesis on satellites that take control of your minds. Fun stuff the first few weeks that you split rent with five roommates, but after a while it's just the background noise of the commute, like metal-on-metal screeches, the sway of the car, and the tired look on the faces of all the houseworkers and nannies from seventeen different countries on the way back up the island to cook dinner for yet another set of hungry mouths.

You look down at the Birkenstocks you scored off the boutique thrift shop around the corner. All the best stuff in the used stores around this place now. Rich people toss out the best stuff. Nice shoes. You found a Gucci purse there that could hold a can for emergency touch-ups, but the ruck is best for more complex work.

But despite the comfortable shoes, you know if you leg it she's gonna send your video to the local police and they'll come knocking at the already-busted-in door on 205th, take you in, and then Yesse's gonna fucking bail you out and tell you all about how you're disappointing your poor, departed mother, God bless her soul and the Mother Mary—

No.

"It's okay." You fold your arms. "Let's wait for the cops."

It's a gamble. A big fucking gamble. Where, you wonder, is Chewie? Because, you swear to god, you're going to shit on his mother's grave if he doesn't show up soon.

You hear the siren warble around the corner. You feel the pit of your stomach lurch. You're imagining all the brutal shit you've heard, and now in this day, you've seen with everyone else on shaky handheld videos. This Karen might yet be setting up to record the next horrible beatdown.

Or worse.

And if those sigils don't get touched up soon, well, the evil gnawing at the back of this Karen's eyes, that dead look behind the colored contacts, that evil would spread out even farther into the world again.

So in the ruck are a set of spray cans and a book of Enochian summoning scripts that your mother spent half her life reverse engineering from the 1500s occultist John Dee's books of angelic script. You'd spend half the day down at the New York Public Library, the main branch, past the magnificent lions. She'd read and take notes on a battered old Moleskine, while you colored with crayons and watched the tourists noisily clump on past to take photos against the hand-carved, wooden backdrops.

Sometimes an old white man would stop and stare at you both, your skin as dark as the varnished bookshelves holding the weight of human knowledge. Stuff you thought was old and musty at the time. Mom paid them no mind. "Mija, listen, we have work to do, and getting distracted by them is what they want. They can't touch us in here."

At the time you thought she meant tut-tutting racists couldn't touch you all in the library, so you hid in libraries whenever you could, as if a book could hide you away.

Much later, you come to realize she meant the demons had no power there, because the main branch ceilings project nullifying energy that dissipated demonic interventions.

In third grade she got called in because you drew a set of pentagrams and a perfect summoning grid on a poster board for show and tell. When you connected the final Enochian binding call to the fifth cell, the power to the school flickered out.

Just a coincidence, the teacher said. But you couldn't be bringing pentagrams to a Catholic all-girls school. No more. They'd put up with this immigrant stuff enough, and young souls were at risk.

They are at risk, your mother agreed. Very much.

Never mind that Becky had a sleepover two weeks ago where everyone used a Ouija board to find out if the boys over at the Episcopalian school liked any of them.

"I don't want any of this for you, Julia," she whispered to you on the subway home. "You shouldn't have been reading those books."

But they're everywhere in that small apartment. When the power went out because she couldn't afford the electric, the candles sat in little dishes on top of books about the occult, flickering away. They seemed more malevolent and mysterious in that yellow light that could never be pinned down, locked in some back-and-forth eternal struggle with the shadows.

You'd give anything to spend a night again in that old apartment over the widow Lester's creaky old house with no power, the mold crawling back up the wall behind the toilet, the heat baking you so hard the windows warped, and eating baked beans straight out of the scratch and dent can as a curtain of her dark hair fell over whatever occultic book she had ready for the evening.

"I always remember, mama," you whisper whenever you load the spray paint into your scuffed up ruck. "I'm still doing the work."

"You think you're some kinda fucking Banksy?"

The cop is out of his air-conditioned car and already sweating in the heat. The wards are getting battered down, and you can feel an oppressive weight in the air.

This patch of sidewalk behind the bodega and the brownstone is balanced on a knife edge. The people in front of me don't have the tattoos etched in cremated ashes that let them see the tall creature just behind the brick. An armored shell of a demon, a core sigil burning it into being.

It wants souls. It wants to suck the life out our husks.

It wants blood on the street.

You could have run. You could have let it ooze out of the brick and fully possess the people here. But you're betting on Chewie. Because, even though you want to slap the twitch of that woman's lips right off, and you fantasize about taking that cop's hand off his holster to snap it in two, you know it's the energy swirling in the air that has the back of your mouth acidic, your heart hammering, and your vision blurring.

Add more rage into the loop and it'll spin up enough energy to snap the veil between the worlds.

"What the fuck is this?" the cop holds up your notebook, open to a grid diagram.

"Art," you say, voice level. He cuffs you, has you against the car. You shiver with indignation, because none of this should be happening.

He steps forward. That dominating pose, and mirrored sunglasses frame your round, tired face back at you. The fourth-wheel earrings, their pattern just barely able to hold back the demonic energy that spills into the air between you, flash, and twinkle.

Those patterns run all over the island. All over the world. Hundreds of years ago, Masonic planners in shadowy rooms behind taverns met to lay out the city grid using occult patterns to create energies that would hold entire cities in their grip. In ancient times, they burned cities to the ground for practical reasons: to destroy the portals and energies unleashed by their street grids.

Since the time of Sumer and ancient Babylon, whole populations had been held in thrall by the patterns laid into the cornerstones of the first cities. It had never been farming that dragged humanity out of the hunter-gatherer mode, but shamans, their minds grasped by entities far out past the guttering lights of dying stars, who established cities long before farming came.

Why did witches live in forests and holy men in caves outside the chaos of cities? Why did Jesus have to live in the wilderness, or the Buddha seek out a tree far from the teeming masses of his India?

Even white people know that here in New York City, Robert Moses and modern-day city planners lowered bridges so that buses couldn't go certain places in NYC. The cities today haven't changed much about redlining, carving up the land in their patterns, they just feel guilty about it and talk about it a lot now.

Your mother fought a war in the seventies. "See that car," she'd say, and point out a tagged up, omni-colored subway car with almost no silver poking through the bubbled sigils. "Every time it makes a loop around the city, it reestablishes a closed circuit that protects us."

Once you saw the magical shapes, buried in the work of a generation, and you knew that the island was covered in protection.

Now, gentrified block by gentrified block, you had all lost so much of it.

From the finance district out, those people once holding the knowledge, the Romani, the brujas, the old-world witches from Ukraine, the hippy crystal-loving artist grandmothers cooking up a cauldron in the back of a squat in the Garment District . . . all forced out by redevelopment.

"We'll lose the soul of the city again, one day," your mother said.

But not here, mama, you think.

Not entirely yet.

"Oye! What's with the cop?" Chewie shouts from around the corner.

He looks out of breath, his face red, and hovering somewhere between apologetic, which you think is aimed at you, and angry.

The cop sees the anger, and pushes me to the side. He's been buried in his rage, and only just now realizes that more people have spilled out onto the street to stare at the scrum of people.

Phones are out. Even retired old Narovka from across the street has the new phone her grandson gave her in hand, and she's shakily recording everything.

"Chewie! Slow down," you snap. You try to get to him, but also, project calm.

"That's Julia!" someone else says. "Why he got Julia handcuffed?"

The rage has spread. The brick wall pulls at them, like a vortex. And the helplessness, the hurt from past arrests of friends, family, people that look like them, it boils around us.

And the thing on the Other Side wants that. It used the Karen at first. Racism was its favorite fuel, an art perfected in the 1800s by its kind. And the cop has been trained to fear us, to use violence as a tool. He's spent his life being told we're the enemy, that any second things could turn.

You can see his eyes dart about. You can see the far back erosion of soul, a lifetime of drip, drip, drip that left the once innocent boy who may have played with a black friend in kindergarten but is now surrounded by neighbors who say Those Things, and watches a single news channel that preaches from the dark sanctification of Fear, Subjugation, and Order, and he's trapped in a pattern laid out by suburban planners of swirling ticky-tack developments that created who he is now: someone who comes in from outside of this block to patrol and occupy it.

"I told you," you say calmly, like talking to a wild animal. "I have permission. This is the bodega's wall. That's Chewie."

"Don't film!" the cop shouts at someone. "Get back, you're interfering with an arrest."

But they all have the phones out.

And for all that hatred in the air, you can taste love. Community.

Yeah, you know, it's a whole lot of woo-woo.

But if there is hatred, there must be love. And if there is an individual, there has to be the opposite, right? Community?

These are people you've known your whole life. You've pledged to your mother to keep this block safe. To keep the bodega a castle against the unseen forces that want it gone in favor of a chain. A chain grocery store that would take this point on a line, a pattern that stretches over this country, and complete another part of a dangerous grid that would snatch a small piece of a person's soul every time they stepped into its repetitive similarity.

"Please," Chewie begs, taking a deep breath. "I hire her to paint my store's logo up there. She's family. Please."

You hate that we have to beg for dignity, beg to be allowed to do what others never even have to ask for.

But the cop shakes his head, broken from the spell as Chewie gets close to him. Chewie's an empath, a healer. He'll get you the right herbs, the right medicine, or listen to you talk at the end of the day about how bad it was. He'll send you on your way with a lightness in your step and a bag of groceries. You can pet his familiar, the bodega cat, on the way out.

"Okay," the cop says.

"Are you fucking kidding me?" The woman rails at the cop, shouting, almost spitting at him.

"Ma'am—"

"Do your fucking job!"

Her dog barks at him.

People drift away, a few stop to rub your arm, commiserate. The moment has passed. Chewie hugs you, sweat and Axe deodorant choke you for a moment. "It keeps the small demons away," he claims.

Someday, Chewie won't be here. Narovka will pass. You certainly can't afford to live here anymore. *E pluribis unum* used to be a motto for the land. It's not a bad one, and for a moment, here, it was again.

For now.

You get your on-sale Krylon cans back, and re-tag the protective wards on the side of the bodega, and the Karen glares at you in deep hatred from her stoop.

Fuck her, she doesn't know what she's missing. Chewie invites you back into the store, and you all hold an impromptu potluck lunch. Friends and family cluster around, gossip, and hug.

It's not a bad life if you have a community.

You can get through it with a good pattern.

Tomorrow you'll be over in the Flatiron District to fix the tags on a playground at the invitation of Rabbi Hoffman. You have to keep fighting the fight, building alliances, or the darkness would break on through.

But like your mother, and her mother before you, you'll carry on. Every little bit moves the world forward.

THE DEMON SAGE'S DAUGHTER

VARSHA DINESH

In one version of the story, nobody dies, and you get to keep the princess as your maid.

She chafes against this, longing for her silks and jewels. You scoff, tugging her after you, a tangle of jasmine wound around her arms. She's tried to break free many times, plaintively singing to the deer and the birds and the sky for help, but everything in your ashram bows to your father, even the quilt of sky above, and he is the one who bound her. And so, your princess just weeps.

But for all her faults, in that version of the story, the princess at least is a pious girl beloved of the gods. So much so that all her tears turn into sapphires and rubies, collecting in little piles by her feet. And although she protests when you sweep them into the folds of your sari, she knows that you are her mistress, and she cannot stop you from doing what you want.

What you want, in that version of the story, is to take the riches from your princess's tears, buy all the weapons of Patala, and then march into Amaravati, the great celestial city, where you will kill all the gods.

Every single one of the three hundred and thirty million.

And when their slithering godblood runs down the diamond facade of Mount Meru, you will bathe your hair in it, soaking until your scalp is drenched and your sari drips crimson, and then—only then—will your revenge be complete.

In that version of the story.

In another version of the story, which is still not the real story, you are on your knees in your ashram, trying to put your father back together. You have already tried this with frantic hands and magic, with careful hands and needles, with sticky paste from deodar trees and the decanted salts of your own tears and the *drip drip* of your blood churned black with incantation. Now, hours later, you are appealing to his logic: telling him how stupid you are, what an idiot-child, can't even put your father back together.

Your father is saying nothing back at all, having burst open some time ago like ripe fruit.

In the version of the story you choose to be true, you are kneeling in your father's blood, silent. His godly killer has just fled the scene, hoisted onto a heavenly chariot, fading into a distant astral blip in seconds. In his wake, at this scene of crime, there is no revenge, no confrontation, no loud lamentation. Only silence.

Lotuses bloom vividly everywhere a piece of your father has landed. They're beneath your feet, climbing the walls. Great lotus leaves brush your face when you move, enfolding you in shadow over and over. Your princess sits slumped on the floor, blowing her nose into one.

"Did you hear it?" you ask, hushed. "The spell. Do you know it?"

Beneath the mountain of lotus blooms, your princess is naked as the day she was born. There is no blood on her skin, clean and new, but gore drips from her hair and coats her shoulders like a grim cape.

"Answer me."

Your princess's nod is miniscule, just a quick jerk of her head before she resumes staring pallidly at the violence.

"I'll free you."

Your princess's eyes snap wide open.

"I'll free you from your curse, and in return, you'll tell me what you heard. Do we have a deal?"

You wonder what you will do if she says no. If she leaves you alone to deal with the shattered bone and adipose florets and stringy grey matter that is all that is left of your father. But the princess is too crafty to pass up this opportunity.

"You'll free me," she echoes. "No tricks."

"None."

"And after I'm freed?" she asks. "What will you do?"

That is none of her business. You wring your father's blood from your hands. You crush a flower under your foot. You wait until your princess stops waiting for an answer, blood-stained face shuttering over.

When you put your arm out, in partnership, your princess takes it.

There are two threads of stories here woven together into a loose braid, one bloodier than the other. Your princess is the strongest strand in the first thread. Your father is the bloodiest one in the other. Between the two, linking force, are you and Kacha.

Maybe you should have started the story with Kacha.

In a more traditional story, he is the hero after all. Kacha, in his blue silks and gold earrings. Kacha, with his silvertongue. Kacha, who even the goats liked, the traitorous bastards.

Some months ago, when his big celestial retinue arrived, all flappy-winged vimanas and heralds blowing conch-shells, some of your hand-maidens crowded the dance hall. They jostled each other, ankle-bells tinkling, a murmuration of gentle creatures hiding vicious teeth. Each one called out a new, juicy bit of information: *He wears a diamond on his chest, the size of a mango! His body is strong and robust like a peach! Oh, my lady, my lady, his servants carry bowls of fruit, gold-stringed veenas, and such heavenly flowers!*

You tossed your braid over your shoulder. "If he adorns his chest with such sizeable jewels, girls, should we worry if he lacks elsewhere?"

"He's come to study with your father, my lady," Maniprabha said. "What he lacks in physical prowess, he must possess in spirit."

"Spirit," Samyukta laughed. "Are the gods' spirits not destroyed after centuries of losing wars against us? Are they not tired of their little sons dying like pitiful worms on the battlefields? Do they not seek peace by sending their own to study here at the ashram of the demon sage?"

"It's not peace they want," you said. "It's something else."

The girls all exchanged glances at that, swooning with curiosity, but you were the mistress. You decided if you wanted to include them in your secret. You decided if you wanted to leave them hanging, spinning their theories as intricately as they worked the ashram's looms.

"The gods have sent him to sniff out a secret," you said. "He's a spy."

"A spy? A secret? What secret?"

But a queen without secrets is no queen at all, and you only smiled. "Father will need me. I must go now to welcome our new guest."

Outside, in the seething emerald fields of your father's ashram, Kacha stood bent in half, hands clasped, all his attendants singing harmonious praises of your father's might. Your new guest's face was neither stunning nor memorable. His voice, however, boomed in messianic thunder when he spoke: "Oh, Saint of Saints! Most Knowledgeable One in Patala! I thank you for accepting me as your most humble student."

He kneeled, bejeweled forehead pressed to your father's feet. Flowers tumbled from the center of his palms: jasmine and marigold, rose mallow and calotrope, oleander and parijat.

Your father cast a bemused smile. Lightning flickered in his coiled beard. Raw cosmic power thrummed from him in tympanic waves, flattening the grass, buffeting the crown off Kacha's head. "Rise, student," he boomed, motioning you forward. You performed the welcoming rituals: washing Kacha's feet with rose water, smearing sandalwood and turmeric paste on his forehead, garlanding him with marigolds so bright the bees swarmed in droves.

"This is my daughter Devayani," your father said. "It's her job to make sure that your stay with us is most pleasurable."

Most pleasurable! Ha! You knew your father. You knew he expected you to sidle up to Kacha and seduce him, lure his secrets from his mouth, feed him lies and flirtations just like you fed milk and ghee to the snakes in the ashram's groves every morning.

Kacha was already assessing the curve of your mouth, your hip where you had shifted your sari to offer a glimpse of your skin. "Lady Devayani," he murmured. "They whisper rumors in Amaravati that the demon sage's daughter is more beautiful than all of heaven's apsaras. I see now that there was no hyperbole."

"You flatter me, my lord."

"I look forward to studying under your father," Kacha said. "But I fear now, after meeting you, that I will have to work very hard indeed to stay focused."

His shoulders blocked out the sun. The diamond on his chest, set amidst repeating lotus-patterns of embroidery, made you suddenly dizzy. You stumbled, momentarily blinded, dropping your tray of rose and turmeric. He caught you neatly, long fingers folding around your wrist.

"Lady Devayani," he said. "I'm sure you will have much to teach me, as well."

Your fingers rubbed unconsciously where his touch left welts on your wrists, an effect of his godblood. Each one was reddened, raised; alphabets in a harsh language carved into your skin. Your father's future murderer saw them and only smiled: a whetted thing, sharp and profane.

That was the beginning.

This is the circuitous route you take to an ending.

You and your princess leave your dead father in the ashram and descend into the realms of Patala.

This is where the demons live, in their underground cities of gold and gemstone trees. At the gates, your princess pulls weakly against her flower-chains, unwilling to go any further.

"They won't eat you," you say. "There are better things to eat in Patala. The exquisite glair of Naga eggs. Black-skinned fish from the river Hataki. Sweets from the tables of the demon-king Bali, wrapped in sugar-soaked silver. They have no need for bland princess-flesh."

She stares at you, aghast. You wonder how she will tell this story to the future princes lining up for her attention. You: demoness, daughter of the Dark Sage, leading her into the realms of ghosts and goblins. She: victim, hostage, held captive by a beautiful monster.

What a repugnant fable.

Your mouth turns in a curdled grimace. "Stay with me and maybe they won't rip the meat off your bones."

The vimana you summon to travel into the underworld is elegant, with swan wings that ruffle at every breeze and seats of blue and gold. A glittering green snake adorns its side, fat diamonds for eyes.

O Pious Daughter! It hisses when you board. *How is your father?*

Your princess opens her mouth, surely to blab about how your father is currently a formless flesh-splatter, but you hum the opening words of an incantation, the syllables slippery as eels. Your princess clicks her mouth shut, *pop*, hands jumping in surprise to her throat. It is not until you're descending into the first level of Patala that you let her speak again.

"You're not my mistress anymore," she spits. "Don't do that again."

"If the demons know their sage is dead, they will march against the gods. The gods will call the sun and moon to arms, and the earth will be plunged into eons of icy nights and monstrous tides. Do you want that?"

"Don't you? It's *your* father who's dead—"

"Another word and I'll stitch your mouth shut. With iron."

Your princess believes you. She looks out instead, eyes wide, at the winding streets and drinking parlors.

The first city of Patala is resplendently beautiful. The demon-architect Maya's miraculous palaces glisten like beetle carapaces, all stained glass and coruscating light-beams. Canopies of ivory filigree and statues of bronze adorn the wide avenues. A vista of gemstones spills slanted light across an artificial sky, illuminating the city in strange, twinkling light.

Your father always called it excess. When the demons came to him for advice, he told them not to test the gods. Build just enough marvels. Keep your palaces just a bit smaller than theirs. Do not tempt celestial wrath, and maybe the demons could keep their cities, their sorcery, their strange and darkling denizens.

"It's beautiful," your princess says. "I didn't think it would be beautiful."

"Did you think it would all be vermin and filth?"

"No. I've heard the stories . . ."

"Women that lie with any man for a drink. Nagas that live in holes like animals. Are those the stories you've heard?"

In the gem-light, your princess looks like she wants to put her fist through your face. "They won't come back, you know," she says. "Kacha's gone. Your father never loved you. So, you can snap at me all you wish, but they won't come back for you. Nobody wants you."

But this is where she misunderstands you. This is not a story about your father, or Kacha. This is a story about *you*.

You are Devayani, daughter of the demon sage, mistress of his ashram now that he is gone. Your father taught you how to meditate for as long as it took to bottle thunderstorms and weaponize blood. In your grottos of horns and teeth, he instructed you on dance-mantras that brought about droughts or floods. Your feet became a palimpsest of scars, layered and sliced by hours of dancing. Your very bones are carved with treatises on the importance of illusions and hypnosis, the mysteries of augury, the secretive, coded stratagems of celestial warfare.

Kacha and your father are in your past.

Your present is about you.

"Where are we going?" your princess asks.

"To the night markets. To find a locksmith who knows sorcery. Your shackles are demon-made and answer only to the one who put them on you."

"But your father is dead."

"Someone there will know how to free you."

"And after that?"

You turn your head away, pressing your lips together, pretending to feast your eyes on the sights. It doesn't take your princess too long to stop asking.

In any version of your universe, this is heaven's most coveted secret, your father's greatest legacy: he can raise the dead.

After the day's battle climaxed, when the battlefields smoked and dozed uneasy at night, your father would walk through mounds of corpses and broken chariots, chanting the incantations. As he walked, demonic corpse-soldiers rose in his wake, shambling after him into the ashram.

You and your handmaidens would sit at the looms, weaving the soldiers' new skins. The dead could not live in the skin they'd died in; their souls hung out of it, untucked, and they flopped about like fish. When the new skins were finished, you and your father stitched them onto the demons, dusted off their thick clubs, and sent them back to war.

The gods and demons have been at war for centuries. The gods were forever dying, being sucked into the karmic pipeline, cycling through reincarnation like leaves buffeting helplessly in a gale. The demons died and simply came back, as if dying was nothing but a mild inconvenience.

It ruffled some big heavenly feathers. Bruised some tall celestial egos.

You and your father were prepared for spies. Many from heaven's ranks had come here before, pretending to seek tutelage, burrowing instead for information on the resurrection spell. But none were as subtle and determined as Kacha.

He was a good student. He studied deep into the night, poring over palm-leaf texts while your father meditated. He took diligent notes and debated for hours with your father on complex cosmic paradoxes. When he was not taking lessons, Kacha whittled wood into fantastic creatures that followed you around. There was a parrot with a green glass eye, and a rabbit so small it would fit in the cup of your palm. A monkey swung from the folds of your sari, bringing you flowers and oddly patterned stones, writing you messages such as:

Today I watched you dance. I have seen celestial apsaras dance in Indra's palace above Mount Meru. They are not as skilled as you are, Devayani, or: *I wish these treatises on conjuring spirits and calculating cumulative karmic scores was as arresting as your singing, Devayani.*

You pretended to be charmed, blushing whenever he sent you a new message. His overtures of love cloyed in your mouth like oversweet rosejam.

At Kacha's request, you took him on tours of the ashram. You showed him the looms and the dance hall. You let him row the two of you out to the middle of the lotus pond, far enough in dawn's fog that there was nothing in either direction but mist-shrouded blooms.

"This is where apsaras are born," he told you, plucking a plush pink blossom. "In the hearts of flowers, soft as morning dew. Have you seen an apsara?"

You shook your head.

"I'll show you one day," he said. "Oh, Devayani, don't you chafe at being locked up here in your ashram? Such a clever girl should see the world. I could take you."

Kacha came to see you after his lessons, coaxing you to feed the deer with him or augur the shapes of clouds in the sky. He tucked flowers behind your ear and told you stories of Amaravati, his home in the skies. He made you a model of it with clay and silk and precious things, laying out wide boulevards and golden gates, sparkling indoor waterways, food-halls where celestial cooks prepared the loveliest of dishes for the gods' banquets.

"What does an ascetic's daughter know of sweets?" he lamented. "When I take you to Amaravati, I will bring you to the halls and let you have your pick of the sweets. Sugar-wafers drizzled with honey so light it melts on your tongue. Milk and khoya confections with surprise berry hearts. Frosted, sugar-soaked cucumber garnished with candied petals."

You cradled a coy grin at your lips. "You seem to have a sweet tongue, my lord."

Tangerine flowers rinsed through the trees like flotsam. Butterflies spun in spiraling drifts. Kacha's smile sharpened. "Would you like a taste, my lady?"

His touch made you burn and bubble, a beautiful firework held too close to skin. Pain bloomed, white and scalding, and you cried out again and again. Still he, feigning oblivion, pressed his mouth to yours, seeking the heat of your tongue.

He did not taste sweet. He tasted like iron, and salt, and the acid tang of godblood. You clenched your fists tight enough to carve bloody moons into your palms but did not pull away.

This was what your father expected from you, after all.

That you would dance close enough to serpents that they showed you their venom. That you would sit through the heat of a hundred scorpion stings. That you would bathe in godblood, if required, let it slough your skin off, if only it meant you could catch your father his godly spy.

"Oh, Devayani, my love," Kacha cried, when you parted at last. "I fear our happiness will be short-lived. The demons suspect me of being a spy. I fear they are plotting to harm me. I am terrified that if I die, our love will break your heart. How could I bear leaving you? How could my soul rest, knowing you will be pain?"

And here, well-rehearsed, you assured Kacha with syrup-thick words that he need not fear. You would speak to your father on his behalf. You were the demon sage's daughter after all. You promised: your love would always protect him.

The very next day, you found Kacha dead for the first time.

The night markets occupy the riverside of the third level of Patala.

The river here runs aureate, casting a glow over the ghosts and goblins that call the city its home. Boats full of men row across it, blowing long plumes of fire. When the fire fans the surface of the water, it spits and hisses, turning into ropes of gleaming gold which adorn the chests of the vendors at the market.

The market is a dizzying tangle of wares, sourced from all seven of Patala's realms. Foggy glass tanks, teeming with bathypelagic creatures from the primordial ocean of the lowest level. Spines of gods, crackling with power, battle-won and encased in silver by Maya's craftsmen. Fangs of panthers and elephant hair, sold by all manners of strange netherworld folk: mottled-blue vetalas, living upside-down in trees; grey-skinned pisacha, feeding on corpse-flesh; dark-eyed rakshasa, shifting shape into whoever you desire most.

You once purchased your dancing bells from here, from a pisacha woman whose breath was thick with death and sorcery. It is to her you go now, tugging your princess behind you.

She blanches at the sight of the shop. "This doesn't look like the house of a locksmith."

Rows of skulls line the shelves, and bones hang from the rafters, tinkling grotesquely. Vertiginous drifts of corpse-ash execute strange calligraphy in the still air. The pisacha woman shuffles to you, bells decorating the hollows of her desiccated ribcage, jangling with each step she takes.

"Pious Daughter," she rasps, her flickering tongue dusty grey. "You smell of death and blood. What can I do for you?"

Your princess quivers. "No tricks," she whispers. "You promised."

Your promises are not worth much. Still: "My father made these bonds," you tell the pisacha. "Can you break them?"

"Upala can do all sorcery," the pisacha says, glassy eyes focused intently on your princess. "Snip, snip with magic knife. Cuts through even Indra's armor."

While Upala goes to get her magic knife, your princess gives you a suspicious look. "If it's that easy, why couldn't you just do it yourself?"

"I have other business here."

When Upala comes back, you ask the price of her magic knife. Your princess's brows furrow. A piece of bone from your father is still stuck in her hastily washed hair. You think of saying something but then turn away, deciding to let her have the pleasure of discovering this ghoulish accessory all to herself.

In some versions of your story, which you do not *want* to be the story, you are nothing but the querulous daughter of a powerful man, spending your days conversing with twee forest creatures. You learn dance and music, but never the spells and incantations that make them your weapons. Your father never thinks to teach you because what use is teaching a daughter?

In those versions, you are simply a distraction in the tales of conflicts between powerful men. A girl living in the margins of her own story.

Those versions of you are not ambitious. Those versions of you do not go exploring Patala, or demand things from your father. Things like *tell me how to brew elixirs*, or *teach me how to enter another's consciousness*, or *give me the secret of resurrection*.

In every version of you that exists, your father chastises you for demanding the resurrection spell.

He banishes you from his hut when you persist, corralling you to your dance hall for weeks. In your rage, you break every pane of glass adorning the latticed walls. You kick at pots of saffron and turmeric and indigo. You dance in the mess, painting the hall vivid in your anger, casting spells to turn all your handmaidens into brightly dyed rabbits.

Your father lets you.

"The only obstacle to the victory of the gods is the resurrection spell," he tells you while you sulk on the floor, boneless. "It's a secret I must guard closely."

"I'm your daughter," you spit. "Why can't you teach me everything?"

Your father's eyes flash, miniature suns. "You act like a spoiled child, Devayani," he says, dispassionate. "What if I teach you the resurrection spell today and you, fickle as you are, teach it to any simple paramour the gods might send to trick you? What if I teach you my greatest secret and you use it on birds to look mighty in front of your handmaidens?"

In every version of your story, you try to show him that you are more than that. That you have bled and scarred yourself to be worthy of him. You siphon secrets. You feed men sweet poison. You press shlokas into silk and bone and metal, turning them into potent weapons. You are a blade: a bedazzled one, but a blade, nevertheless. You can be equals.

Your father only laughs. Your role is set, he says. You are the demon sage's daughter, using your beauty and middling magic to set snares for his enemies.

But you want to be more than that.

You want to be his heir.

When he hears this, your father laughs for so long and so loud that all of hell and heaven reverberates with the sound. So long and loud that the blades of grass seem to shake with it, trees all joining in, your handmaidens hiding their faces with rabbit-paws while they try not to gloat at your shame.

(Nobody's laughing in the end, when Kacha rips your father apart. But that part comes later.)

This is the story of how you find your princess: After your father laughs at you, you leave the dance hall a mess of pigments and tears.

Your sari is dirty from days of tantrums. Your handmaidens are still rabbits, so you go alone to the river, where you stare loathingly at your reflection for what feels like eons.

When you enter the water, the river swirls about you in icy, varicolored eddies. Red for ambition. Blue for humiliation.

You stay for hours, sobbing, breathing a fortitude prayer.

At dusk, you are disturbed by a fit of laughter.

"Do you think she thinks she can wash away the embarrassment?" a voice whispers. Your spiritual cognition identifies the speakers: the king's daughter, and her favored handmaiden. "Look," the princess continues, and you know she's pressing her feet against your discarded sari. "She's the daughter of the demon sage, yet all she wears are rags."

"She's a demoness," her handmaiden says. "This is what they know, princess. Corpse-ash and charnel-house raiment. Filthy things that smell like death."

"Neither a dutiful daughter nor a talented sage. No wonder her father has been so displeased."

It is frivolously cruel. You think of cursing the princess, something inventive and alienating: all her lovers will turn into frogs, or everything she touches will turn to slimy snails.

The princess is beautiful, after all. Delicate face and dark gaze rimmed with rings of kohl. Her fingers are red from the dye of the henna plant, elegant when she reaches down to pick up your sari.

"Come and get it, hut-dweller," she laughs. "Come out of the water."

It is silly, childish cruelty. But you are a child yourself, hurting because of a father you can never please. And so it is that you clothe yourself in the foam of the river, skimming the crests of small waves to weave yourself a sari. So it is that you rush out of the water, sputtering in your anger. So it is that you fall right into their trap: a muddy hole in the ground.

They must have dug it hours ago.

You twist your ankles, scrape your elbows, lose your illusory river-garb. Naked, wet mud slicks and slithers over you, weighing you down with its stickiness. Something else is in there, foul-smelling, squishing underfoot as you try to stand. You cry out when you see it: fish guts, at least a day old, likely gathered from the palace kitchens. The smell sears your nostrils. You retch, and your tormentors' faces glisten with mirth far above you, bright from the sun.

"There, there," your princess says, satisfied. "Isn't that hole much more befitting for a demoness?"

You ready yourself to curse her, but she surprises you once again. Something small falls onto your lap from the surface. You scramble for it, panic squeezing your throat, and lift up a rabbit.

Its hue is unnaturally pink. Its neck is broken.

The next one is grey, still warm and twitching. As you hold it—*her, her, one of your girls, which one?*—your spine turns to ice. Your tongue goes slack in your mouth. The horror of it mutes you, blinds you, stoppers your blood in your veins.

"Can't bring them back to life?" the princess asks. "Maybe your father will show them mercy?"

Later, burying the small bodies of your handmaidens, you will wonder if the princess had known. If she had understood the weight of her cruelty. If she had even had reason, save that she was a princess of something, and you were the disagreeable daughter of the demon sage.

You will never ask her this. Not when you are finally rescued, and your father—apoplectic at the loss of perfectly good servants—curses your princess to be your handmaiden. Not when you set her to impossible tasks, picking up stray leaves in the garden with her teeth, or polishing the dance hall floor with arms bound behind her back. Not even after your father is dead, and his blood is all over her, and you barter with her for her freedom.

Your princess killed six of your handmaidens that day. You do not know how to weigh cruelties on a grand karmic scale, but you think the balance is still tipped in your favor.

You make one more stop before you leave the night markets.

Your princess, newly freed, continues to trail after you, terrified of goblins and ghosts. Her fingers are laced tightly in yours, the scent of her fear sharp and distinctly peppery.

"What will you do?" she keeps asking. Devayani, whose father is dead. Devayani, whose Kacha has fled. What will you do now?

"You're free," you snap, hiding Upala's knife in the folds of your sari. "What will *you* do?"

"If I go back to my father, he'll just make me marry a prince."

"How terrible for you."

"I don't want to marry a prince," she sneers. "I want to learn the things you know. I always have."

You give her your most contemptuous look. "Is that why you murdered my handmaidens? Because you were *jealous*?"

Your princess's face briefly crumples. "I didn't know," she says. "They were rabbits, how was I supposed to know?"

"As character traits go, a rabbit-killer isn't much better."

"I was angry. All this knowledge you have, all this potential, and you waste it all on Kacha—"

"You said it yourself. He's not coming back."

"True," your princess says, restlessly. "So, what now?"

You settle your face into its grimmest expression. "The demon sage is dead," you drone, bored. "Killed by his own treacherous student. It's time for retribution."

You swivel right, dipping into the dim liquor shop of a Naga distiller. Gold-scales dapple his hood, and a ruby glistens atop it. He is surprised to see you, inquiring in his sibilant tongue as to your father's whereabouts. You wait until after you have made your purchases to tell him: "He's dead."

The Naga's hood rises in shock. His lidless eyes travel over you, trying to discern if you are joking. His coils shift closer.

"He's dead," you repeat. "Tell everyone in Patala. Their demon sage is dead. Killed by the traitorous gods!"

And then you leave, turning around and racing down the market, feet slipping against mottled glass and gleaming stone. Your princess trails behind you, hand in yours, gasping.

"This is why you came!" she pants. "This is what you wanted. For them to know, to panic. This is what you wanted, isn't it?"

274

You hide your smile. As your vimana rises, you can hear the whispers begin, rising to screams by the time you are in the sky.

In the version of the story you tell the demons later, you will give inventory of all the different ways Kacha died in his pursuit of the spell.

The first time you let him go cold, godblood congealing against singed grass, while you tried to understand. He was sprawled just outside the dance hall, a great swathe of his flesh ripped, ribs cracked open, his insides glinting like a ruby geode. The expression on his face was that of a man trying awfully hard to look dignified while something tore him open like an orange peel.

You stood staring, mind racing, silent in the afternoon's blood-rich breeze. The proximity of his body to your favorite haunt meant that he had expected you to find him. But why? Simply because he guessed your love for him would propel you to accelerate his resurrection?

You paced for a bit, shooing away the flies and the birds. It was only after you held his heart in your fist that you made your decision.

You tore at your hair and burned your fingers taking his heart to your father: screaming, wailing, begging until your father cried out that you had become exactly what he predicted: a weak-hearted, foolish girl, giving her heart away to sweet-talking paramours.

"I love Kacha," you wept, disconsolate. "He is no spy, father, only my beloved. And now the demons have killed him for no crime but his love for me!"

You were adept at acting. Your father had demanded you be. Now you were putting on a show, playing a part, and he stormed and blustered at you, betrayed.

"You will not take me as your heir," you spat, your throat raw, eyes stinging. "At least give me my lover."

"Be *quiet*!" roared your father. His lightning whip cracked across your shoulder: searing, splintering your collarbone. "I will raise him from the dead because he is my student. *Only* because of that. End this stupidity, Devayani. He does *not* love you."

While your father resurrected Kacha, stitching him into a skin you had woven so lovingly, you hid behind a wall, craning to listen. But your father did not need words for the spell anymore, only the power of his mind. And so thwarted, you ignored Kacha for two days, sulking in your hut while your shoulder healed.

A little before the second time, Kacha lamented repeatedly that he was afraid the demons would kill him again. You wept into his chest. He sighed: *Oh, Devayani, why does fate test our love so?*

The two of you were lying in a boat, buoyed gently by the waves of the lotus pond. You pretended not to notice a lowly demigod creeping towards you. Sunlight glimmered on the assassin's golden crown, throwing shards of brightness in your eye. Kacha motioned with his fingers, as if telling him to hurry up.

You ignored them, playing the part of an idiot, sighing, and pressing your lips to Kacha's neck. When the hitman struck, arterial godblood splashed all over you. It slithered down your throat, liquefying your lungs. You spat a glob of blood contemplatively, and then collapsed against Kacha. When you woke next, both you and he had new skins, and neither of you were any closer to figuring out the spell.

The third and final time, you followed a secretive Kacha into the forest without his knowledge. There he met with his co-conspirators, other demigods, all dressed unobtrusively in the fashions of demon-folk. "The gods are growing tired of waiting," they said. "How long until you have the spell?"

For all his dying, Kacha had managed to glean only a few words of the incantation. He caught them each time his soul was yanked from the astral plane, an echo of a whisper that was not enough. The gods needed all of it, the whole spell, and they needed it fast.

It was time to do something drastic.

This time, you watched as the gods cut Kacha's throat on his instructions and burned his body. You watched them mix his ashes into a chalice of your father's favorite wine. It flummoxed you, this new trick. How was this different from the other times?

But then, as you paced your dance hall and your princess swept the floor, realization crept up on you. "Come with me," you said, tugging at her chains. "I need you."

You took her to a glade, far from the ashram. She huffed and spat on the floor, demanding to know what you were going to do. Throw her in a hole of fish-guts? Ask her to pluck fruits with her teeth?

"You'll see in a moment," you promised. Then you bit your lip against the unpleasantness, took out a knife, and got to work.

Later, when your father requested his favorite wine, it was you who took it to him.

You, dutiful daughter of sweet comportment, had poured him just the quantity he liked. He, pleased with you for once, downed the first cup in a single swallow.

"I am tired of fighting you, Devayani," he said, deep sigh fluttering his beard. "Must we sulk at each other because of an outsider?"

You kneeled, folding your hands in your lap. "Forgive me, father, but Kacha is not an outsider to me anymore. He has promised to marry me and take me to Amaravati."

Your father's face twisted in ugly displeasure, but he hid it under a smile. You poured him more of the wine. He swilled it and said: "If you want him so much, perhaps I can consult the celestial astrologers. But if you intend to marry, Kacha must leave the ashram this instant. It is not appropriate, the two of you living in close quarters."

You nodded, contrite. You had seen this coming. "You will not regret this, father," you trilled, hands clasped to your chest. "Kacha is *wonderful*."

"If you believe in his intentions, I believe you," your father said, sly. He drained the last of the wine. "Where *is* Kacha? I have not seen him today. We must find him, instruct him to leave."

"I've seen neither Kacha nor the princess all day," you lied, wringing the hem of your sari to appear concerned. "But there were some strangers in the forest today. And a strange smell of fire in the afternoon."

A flickering in the air, like ghosts convening.

Your father's expression began to change. A storm descended upon his face, dark and tempestuous, and he snatched the wineglass off the floor. He peered into it, swirling it this way and that, face twisting in a horrific grimace when he spotted the flecks of ash.

"What is it?" you asked. "What is it, father?"

"Daughter," he said, eyes wide and thunderstruck. "I have been tricked."

Varying expressions of disgust crossed your father's face. Someone, he raged, had *tricked* him. Mixing Kacha's ashes into the wine! Knowingly feeding him his own student! What wicked treachery! If the gods came to know, they would destroy the cities of Patala. They would plunge both sides into a catastrophic war. And how was your father to explain, great sage that he was, that he had not been cognizant of Kacha swimming around in his wine?

You wailed, crumpled on the floor, "Oh, father! Father, what will we do?"

"There is no other way," your father said, through violent retching. "I must resurrect him."

"But he's *within* you! If you resurrect Kacha now, it will kill you! Won't you be ripped open? Torn apart?"

A long, querulous moan escaped your father. He clutched his stomach. "Go, make us both new skins," he said. "I have no choice. I will need to teach the resurrection spell to the part of Kacha within me. Once I resurrect him, he can tear out of me, you can stitch him up, and he will revive me. Kacha knows the situation. He wouldn't want to start another war."

"Or," you ventured, quietly, "you can teach it to me. And I can revive you, father, after you resurrect Kacha."

The simpler solution. The safest, most obvious one. But even then, your father's gaze for you was stinging. "You don't have Kacha's aptitude for spell and sorcery," he scoffed. "You trifle yourself with middling spells and think too highly of your own talents. Your place is at the looms, and later at your husband's side. Understood?"

You forced your lips into a rictus grin. "Yes, father."

"Go now. No time to waste."

You worked the warp and the weft at the looms, possessed by a strange calm. The weave slithered and moved, enlivened by the sorcery of its production, quickly taking shape under your skilled hands. Just as they were done, two skins perfectly woven, you heard your father scream: a wretched sound. It went on—bones cracking like fireworks, spine splitting with a wet crunch—for a long while. Only when it stopped did you move, skins thrown over your shoulder, bare feet crushing the grass beneath your feet as you ran.

The scene in the hut was a nightmare. On the floor lay Kacha: bloody, stirring, watching you with empty eyes. He strained weakly in your direction. You threw the new skin atop him, careless. He keened, tugging uselessly at it, fingers grazing your thigh. You simply stepped past him, towards where your father's blood splattered the hut floor, crying out: "Princess!"

A loop of jasmine, pristine, unspooled from the rapidly blooming lotus-field of your father's ribcage. You took it in your hands and pulled. It took you a few tries before you could see her, head and neck crowning, blind terror in her face as you yanked her free of your father's torso.

You had made two skins, just like your father instructed.

One for Kacha. One for your princess, who you had murdered earlier in the glade, mixing her remains with that of Kacha's in the wine.

As you slipped the skin over her, stitching her up tight, you could hear Kacha slithering about. He shuffled and croaked, half-alive, struggling to slip into the skin. His technique was poor, having never practiced it himself. Did he wonder why you were not weeping at his side? What was he thinking, in his untucked mind, that his eyes were starting to cloud with terror?

You began to scream. Loud, deliberate, renting your throat. The scream ripped itself out of you even as you worked fastidiously at fixing up your princess.

Help, he's killed my father!

Help, the gods have murdered him!

Kacha belly-flopped, new skin fluttering like a half-sloughed snake. Footsteps sounded, running into the hut. You smelled godblood and stayed kneeling, clutching your head in despair, pretending to splutter and choke on your own grief.

Just a poor, helpless woman, bereft of both father and lover.

Behind you, there was gasping and grunting as Kacha's people carried him away. In front of you, your princess panted and mewled, stretching out her new skin, gaping at you with the sick terror of something faced with both its destroyer and creator.

You could hear the gods' chariot outside, wheels aflame, taking to the sky with Kacha still flailing uselessly at the back. When Kacha was nothing but a spark in the sky, you straightened up, taking in the scene.

Your father dead. Kacha indisposed. Your princess the sole, accidental keeper of the resurrection spell's secret.

There was silence now, hazy and friable, broken only by your princess's fitful crying. Into that stillness you spoke, hoarse and hushed, the question that would both begin and end your story: "Did you hear it? The spell. Do you know it?"

And in your princess's affirmation, her awed terror, her perfect new skin and the bloody crown of her head, you glimpsed a strange new future: dark, malleable, free for you to shape.

An hour after you return from Patala, you have at last finished collecting your father's skin, piled neatly what is left of his ribs and hips, and placed fragments of his spine in wraps of golden silk.

Your ashram is starting to fill with scores of demons. There are kings and queens, pisacha and vetala, rakshasa and Naga. There are demonic maidens so fragile they waver in the wind. Their loud lamenting rises like song, thrilling your blood, raising the hair on your skin.

You do not know where your princess is. Her absence makes you strangely lonely, but you have let her go. Her arms are free, and she kept her bargain by teaching you the resurrection spell. This is all she owes you, after you cut her throat to outsmart Kacha. Now, the two of you are even.

Briefly, you wonder what your father will think. That in the end it was not Kacha who betrayed him, but you. You wonder if he will be disappointed. But: *oh father, what did you expect?* He had never seen you for what you really are: a weapon, gluttonous for power.

You will suck the marrow of it, for as long as you please, and the sweetness of it will linger on your tongue far longer than any memory of love.

Upala's knife cuts easily through bone. You put away the last sliver of your father's skull, collecting it in a wide-rimmed container. The lotus blooms have all withered away. Outside, the demons wait: for explanation, lamentation, confrontation. You can taste their hunger for vengeance and blood in the very air.

You have rehearsed the version of the story you will tell them. The one where you screamed, and wept, and fantasized revenge on Amaravati. The one where you promise you will help them annihilate the gods—all three hundred and thirty million—and bathe in their blood at the top of Mount Meru.

There is no version of the story branching from here where the demons do not follow you to the ends of the universe. You are the holder of the resurrection spell, the avenger of your father, the savior of demonkind.

You are no longer the demon sage's daughter. You are the demon sage, herself.

But before you speak to them, you will pour them all liquor. A sip to remember your father, to honor and celebrate his great life.

In each glass, you will place a tiny piece of him, obscuring the taste with the strength of freshly purchased Naga wine. No piece of him will go to waste. You will make sure of it.

In this way, distributed bit by bit amongst the demonic army, you will scatter your father's remains, that he may never be brought back whole.

One last safeguard to make sure that this is the deterministic version of your story: the final draft, the inevitable conclusion.

You drink your cup of wine, forcing it all down in one gulp.

Then you go out to start your war.

GRAY SKIES, RED WINGS, BLUE LIPS, BLACK HEARTS

MERC FENN WOLFMOOR

A girl has lost her soul down deep in the City. It wandered away while she chipped out another grave in the catacomb brickyards. She set down her pickax, wiped grit from her cheek, and noticed how empty her body was. Looked down at her wrist and found it blank.

That's what she tells Redcap Kestrel as she sits cross-legged on the abandoned warehouse floor, well away from the grimy windows. The girl who lost her soul doesn't offer a name. Few people do in the City.

"You want me to find it?" Redcap Kestrel asks. She crouches at a right angle to the girl, not looking her in the face. It's for the girl's sake. No one likes to look at a half-alive thing for too long, lest you find yourself on the wrong side of dead.

"Yeah." The girl swallows. "If I go back to the yards, people are likely to try and take advantage."

Redcap Kestrel understands. The soulless are easy pickings in the City. It's all a matter of gradient. How much are you predator and how much are you preyed upon. It varies day-to-day, like most things in the City.

The girl fidgets, rubbing her wrist where the skin stretches raw and glossy like a burn. She doesn't quite turn her head; her gaze skips and skitters towards Redcap Kestrel, then away, away, away. "How much do you want?"

Rarely has Redcap Kestrel allowed visitors, rarer still does she listen to those who need help. She ticks through the old scraps in her head, remembering how conversations like this go.

"I'll take a promise," Redcap Kestrel says.

The girl's shoulders arch in defense. That's dangerous, offering or asking. Too many ways a bargain can go wrong. Everyone knows that.

"It's this." Redcap Kestrel doesn't have much of a voice to raise. It's all tatters and frayed strings in her throat. "When I get your soul back, promise me you'll wear a sleeve so it doesn't go wandering again."

The girl blinks. A sleeve does about as much good as a wish. And it's hardly a promise worth paying with. "That's it?"

Redcap Kestrel shrugs. "That's all."

The girl hesitates, because nothing in the City is that easy.

"See," Redcap Kestrel says, expending more voice and breath than she's got to spare, "you wouldn't take help for free, and I wouldn't give it. So that's the promise I want."

"That's really all?" the girl whispers.

Another shrug. Redcap Kestrel's arms are taut with muscle and her shoulders are sharp like metal wings. She's a half-alive thing, if one looks at her slantwise. She doesn't wear the guard uniform any longer; all the leather she dons, she tanned it herself. There's plenty of skin if you know where to look in the City.

In the silence bubbling up between her and the girl, Redcap Kestrel sees all the times gone by when she ignored the helpless, when the desperate crawled to her and she stepped on their throats. There's a lot of regret built into a hundred years of being half-alive. She's tired. And this is the first time anyone has been brave enough to ask her for help so directly. The girl knocked so loud on the warehouse door, it was either listen to her story or kill her so she'd quiet up. Redcap Kestrel hadn't been curious in a long while until the girl, and she wasn't yet hungry.

"All right." The girl exhales and blows away the silence and the memories trapped in it. "Deal."

Redcap Kestrel hops to her feet. "Good. Wait here." It's dangerous anywhere else, and she's got nothing worth the price of stealing. Meat and breath and bone are all that's worth anything in the City.

GRAY SKIES, RED WINGS, BLUE LIPS, BLACK HEARTS

Redcap Kestrel lopes to the biggest window, glass tarred black and cracked with many a fist, and slips out into the streets. Her boots are worn thin save for the iron heels, hard enough to bruise a god. Her steps warn away the ones that fall into the predator shade, in that gradient that defines the City.

The thing about souls is that they don't wander off. Not unless a body is so broken-down that there are too many cracks to hold even breath inside. The girl isn't that far gone. She's still strong, still has grit, and still believes in a future.

So something stole her soul. Redcap Kestrel knows where to look for the things that steal and the things that kill. She lived among them for a long stretch during her existence in the City. She's haunted and hunted where the buildings crumble, where the damned weep, where the perpetual twilight hides worse monsters than her. It's like going back to the nightmares grown in a home you don't remember.

Up on the top of the horizon, the lights of the Prosperous Above shine. No one from the City is allowed past the Prosperous Gates. There are only rumors: clean water, food aplenty, fuel, medical care. It's said that behind the Prosperous Gates, the grief-eaters can't find you. A lot is said about the Prosperous Above.

Redcap Kestrel was Prosperous once, long ago, before she ripped the demon from her heart. She doesn't talk about that time. Her hands ache when she looks up every once in a while, and sees the Prosperous lights mocking the deeps of the City.

The light hurts her eyes, so she's stopped lifting her head up too far. There's no reason to look up when you know you'll never fly again.

Redcap Kestrel hasn't been to the Brittle Warrens in a decade. She lost most of her voice and part of her throat last time. This is the mulched, bog-deep heart of the City. There are things that creep under the salted earth; there are things that crawl through the long-dried gutters; and there are things that cry out, and the things that eat the criers.

She's not interested in those things. She's here to visit the most dangerous person she's ever known: Windchime Owl, first and last of their name.

It's not really *fear*, per se. Redcap Kestrel doesn't have much of that left. Really, she's hard pressed to decide if she feels much at all. This job she does for the girl, this is new, so it brings a spark of anticipation. It keeps her from thinking too much for a day, and that's a rare treat for a half-alive thing like her.

The slums are made from dilapidated stone and crusted darkness. The living scuttle close to walls and the dead haunt the narrow streets. The in-betweens are the ones you ought to heed. Redcap Kestrel walks as she always does: head tilted down, arms loose at her sides, her boot heels clicking. She skirts scummy puddles and mite-chewed corpses, steps over potholes lined with old teeth.

"Where you going, birdie?" calls a grief-eater from the broken curb. It's stick-like, hungry: long bony limbs canted at uncomfortable angles, a face that's just a wide, gaping hole rimmed in stretched flesh.

Redcap Kestrel glances at it sidelong. She still has her red cap: her skull shaved and tattooed scarlet with the litany of her oaths to the Gray Prince. She wears a hood sometimes—not now, she lost it somewhere she doesn't remember—but those who've survived long enough in the City recognize her by her gait alone.

"Going down," Redcap Kestrel says.

"I can ease your burdens." The grief-eater coos, extending a hand nicked with desperation bites. "It doesn't hurt. Let me have a taste."

"No," Redcap Kestrel says, because the grief-eaters always lie. She took one of them to her nest shortly after her fall. Asked it to eat away everything that hurt so she'd be numb. Grief-eaters are a misnomer. They only slake their hunger on the things you want to keep.

She let hers suck on her body and soul for days, even knowing what it was doing, until it tried to eat the memory of her oath-siblings from the Gray Prince's guard. Then she killed it.

This grief-eater is too starved to be a threat. It slumps back against a charred brick wall. There's so little in the City to feed anyone any longer.

Redcap Kestrel walks on.

Legend says that the City was built in a crater so wide it could hold an ocean. There are still stretches of empty rock far, far away, some wanderers claim, where the City hasn't bled. Redcap Kestrel doesn't believe those tales. The City is too vast. It'll have touched those crater edges and spilled over and swallowed whatever is beyond. The Prosperous Above is like the City's mirror, or maybe its heaven, just as vast and untouchable as the City.

So down she goes, deeper along broken streets, hopping from stairway to stairway as the City burrows itself forever lower, away from the Prosperous Above's sight. That doesn't mean it's all dark in the Warrens: the light here is soaked with bitterness and spite, a sharp incandescence that will betray you soon as not.

Shadowy things skulk and hiss at her, but they know better than to get too close. She has to eat and she's not particular about where her meals come from. Redcap Kestrel used to bask in the biggest light of all—a sun? a moon? hard to remember after so long—when she flew in the Prosperous Above. Darkness is easy. She knows the way into the pitted core of the Brittle Warrens; the City won't let her forget what hurts most.

And then, sudden like a burst eardrum, she's in front of Windchime Owl's palace. The gates are pieced together from bits of finery: quilt squares and finger bones, gold rings and predator teeth, glass fresco tiles and chunks of tanned hide. Basalt pillars and a center post hold up the weight, and a handful of still-living skins sway and shiver miserably, stretched wide with hooks and cord.

The gate guard, a tremulous shadow stolen from a body once human, bristles at her approach. "Do you have an appointment?"

Redcap Kestrel lifts her chin and tilts her head so the shadow can see her scalp. It flinches away and the gates groan wide.

The maze through the Warrens is nonsensical: mirrors and salt pillars, rusted ore and carved stone, all paths twisting in, out, around. Stairways lead nowhere and pits gape in the walls. She keeps her gaze averted from the darkness, where Windchime Owl's oldest secrets lie. She walks past a trio of lost souls, all scrabbling at a doorway upside down. Her heels click against mercury glass and she doesn't look at the visions the mirrored floor shows. She's not ready to go mad.

At last, at the deepest point in the Warrens, she reaches Windchime Owl.

They sit in a large nest made from fur and silk and lost ideas. They're wide at the shoulder, head crowned with a white mane of hair, their skin bleached from decades of shriveled light. They're every inch as terrible and beautiful as Redcap Kestrel remembers.

Redcap Kestrel inclines her chin, taking a breath.

"You're unexpected," Windchime Owl says, their hands never still as they roll marbles between their palms. "Then again, you've always been bold, Red'kes."

Redcap Kestrel shrugs. "You liked that once, Win'owl."

"So I did."

Redcap Kestrel had a name before she joined the Gray Prince's guard. It's been scrubbed away: excised when she had her scalp tattooed in the red cap of her fledge. All the guard were identified only by their caps. She had a hundred Redcap sisters, and a hundred Bluecap brothers. Windchime Owl had a name, too, but they've never shared it. They were here when the City rose, or so the hauntlings say, and they will be here when the City rots beyond saving.

Windchime Owl seems to be in a good mood, their latest meal still twitching at their feet. "What do you want, Red'kes?"

"Your insight," she says. "A girl lost her soul. I need to find it."

"Why?"

Redcap Kestrel expected this. It's no easier now than when she pondered it on her journey. Windchime Owl hates lies, even the slantwise half-truths and omissions that fuel the world. If Redcap Kestrel is anything but honest, Windchime Owl's wrath will engulf her, and she isn't certain she'd win a second fight. Her throat aches where Win'owl's talons cut her clean to spine.

"I needed help long ago," she says. "I should've asked."

The guard died because of her; all her siblings-in-wing. She lost her pride and her purpose, and she spurned her brother who fought to pull the demon out. Bluecap Shrike defied the Gray Prince, seeing through her, seeing what she had done, and she had refused to let him save her.

Redcap Kestrel spits the last of her words out, ashamed. "But I didn't."

Windchime Owl stretches, their body sinewy and fluid. Once upon an age, they were a Prince—or so the rumors say. A Violet Prince, with Greencaps and Goldcaps flying in formation at their sides. One story claims the Violet Prince forsook their duties and cast down their own legions, seeding the deeps with rage and loss. But it was so long ago, no one really remembers why. There are many stories forgotten in the City.

Windchime Owl hops from their nest and offers a talon-tipped hand to Redcap Kestrel. "Give me a piece of your skin, and I'll look for this lost-soul."

"For your collection?"

Windchime Owl sighs. "To taste. I miss your mouth."

Redcap Kestrel let the grief-eater suck away the affection she'd once had for Windchime Owl. They'd fought—and Win'owl had ripped out her throat—not because she wanted to leave, but because she'd wanted Windchime Owl to come with her. *Let's leave the City*, she said, *let us go Above. We can be Prosperous again. Together we can make the climb.* She was a fool. Windchime Owl kept the laws and held back the deeper things that churned under the Warrens; if they abandoned the City, it would sink forever beyond reach of the Prosperous Above. Win'owl nursed her into something less broken after she tore the demon from her heart, after she fell, and she'd repaid that poorly.

"Well?" Windchime Owl says.

"Agreed." Redcap Kestrel pulls a razor from her boot. She reaches back and cuts a strip of flesh from her skull, around the curve of bone, blood trickles down her nape. The air bites at raw nerves, and it's almost refreshing to feel again. She hands Windchime Owl her dripping skin, the piece where tattoos read: *and in the sky bright-burning.*

Windchime Owl inhales as they take the skin, then they swallow it in a single gulp. Redcap Kestrel feels the damp warmth of their throat, the pressure of muscle constricting and pulling her flesh deeper. She shivers, and so does Windchime Owl, as they both savor that moment of devouring.

Then the stinging pain and wetness on her neck jars Redcap Kestrel and she wipes clean her razor. "Uphold your word."

Windchime Owl's eyes glaze over, a white film on which flickers a thousand microscopic images. They are the City's pulse: nothing happens in these streets, in this air, in light or in shadow, that Wind-chime Owl doesn't know if they choose. They curl their bare toes into the earth and tip their head back, throat an arch of pale scarring.

"Oh," they say after a moment, and there's distinct . . . sadness, a regretful lilt in their tone. "Red'kes, you won't like who took your girl's soul."

"Who?"

"Your brother."

Windchime Owl tells her she can find the thief in the Lovers Quarter. Redcap Kestrel hasn't felt shock in years. That electric moment, that impossible revelation, makes her breath catch.

And then cynicism, the fabric of reality, wraps about her once more. She has no brothers any longer. All her sibling-guards are dead.

Whoever this thief is, she will find it, kill it, and return the girl's soul. Another day will settle into calendar dust and blur into the palette of time. Nothing changes much in the City.

Your brother.

Windchime Owl can't lie, which is why they hate falsehood so fiercely. The words burr under Redcap Kestrel's ear, an itch she can't scratch.

She races back through the Warrens, an urgency she doesn't want to dissect burning her muscles. She must *hurry.* Souls don't keep long when stolen from bodies, and she's moved ponderously, deliberately, until now.

Running hurts and makes her think of the clouds.

She used to fly. As one of the Gray Prince's guard, she had wings of silk and steel and shadow, etched with scarlet spellwork. The magic came from the Gray Prince's blood: it flared brilliantly in the light, full of grandeur when she flew in formation. It skewered her enemies' gaze in battle and her wings pierced the sky like blades.

The Gray Prince was the first to die under her hand when the demon gnawed at her heart, and afterward, she cut off her wings and jumped into the City below. The demon kept her alive. The fall hurt.

She runs faster, now, her boots a staccato heartbeat on the streets.

Her breath rattles in her throat, an enhanced pain that siphons away memories of the sky.

The Lovers Quarter is a killing ground.

Once, the Prosperous Above's light reached deep enough to kindle old spheres, globes of living silk that floated pale and luminescent over the park. Like moth-lures, the spheres promised tranquility and revealed only death. The Prosperous came down on moth-dust kites tethered Above to hunt the bedazzled City denizens, a sport that soon turned rancid. The Prosperous gutted the spheres for the light they didn't need, filled with arrogance as bright as Above.

So the shadow things and the hunter things and the mad things rose up and snipped the kite tethers. Without a way back, the Prosperous were trapped. The City things left the Prosperous' bones stripped and glistening in the streets until all the ground was carpeted in calcium and splinters. The things that lived in the City caged the richest and most delicate trophies in blown glass, and the bones eventually stopped wailing.

Redcap Kestrel reaches the stones rimming the Lovers Quarter like islands from the floor of bones. She crouches, breathing ragged. The Lovers Quarter sank, like everything in the City does, until it is now a steep-walled pit with glass jars hung like lamps about the edges. She sees the thief ambling towards the lowest gouge of the quarter: the murky waters of the underground spring, thick with sulfur and despair.

It's human, skeletal, and wearing the scavenged blue rags of a guard uniform. A Bluecap's threads. That dishonor of her old life sparks her rage like kindling. She lunges across the street, toward the edge. The thief spins around and stares up at her.

Redcap Kestrel stills, cold and motionless as a fresco.

Below in the pit is the demon she ripped from her heart. It's latched onto Bluecap Shrike, clinging to the base of his skull.

Her oath-brother. One of the Gray Prince's Hawks: elite, proud, fearless. All dead now. Except her. She thought she was the last, when she watched Bluecap Shrike fall, broken-winged, into the Deathshead River so long ago.

Windchime Owl never lies.

Shrike was a Redcap, briefly, before he came out as a man. The tattoos on his scalp are more purple than blue, and it didn't matter, for the Bluecaps welcomed him. He was Redcap Kestrel's brother-in-arms, her closest friend, and he was her anchor when she flew too high on arrogance. He had never betrayed the Gray Prince. She hadn't let him save her.

And now he's here, possessed and dying, just as she once was, deep in the City.

He lifts his chin, staring up at her with glassy eyes. The demon's tendrils wrap his throat and dig into his ears. The demon is smarter now: it took his head instead of his heart, where it's harder to wrench loose.

Redcap Kestrel takes a breath, air hissing through her tattered throat. "We're not finished, demon."

She knows this wretched thing. It is jealousy and greed and dissatisfaction. It will never be sated. She let it into her heart when she thought it would please her Gray Prince: she thought it would make her faster, stronger, more brilliant than any of the other guards, and the Gray Prince would look on her with favor.

She knows now that they never saw her, nor any of their guard. All were peripheral to the Gray Prince's own glory. Now she's a half-alive thing, and still has her red cap and disappointment takes a long time to die.

The demon wrenches its teeth from Bluecap Shrike, and her oath-brother collapses. His lips are already tinged drowning-gray. She doesn't let herself flinch.

The demon wriggles. *You came to us.*

"That's right," Redcap Kestrel says, extending her hand and clenching her fist in challenge. "You belong to me."

The demon flies at her, a spill of burned oil, once as addicting as poppy and as beautiful as obsidian and as tempting as forgiveness. It ripples with teeth and hook-tipped legs and it smells of decay. She dives down to meet it in midair. She has no wings, but she's never forgotten how to fall in the City.

The demon's greasy film bites down hard into her shoulder, coiling about her arm and neck. She carries it to the ground, landing hard on her back in the bones. She rolls, crunching brittle, bleached remains. The sound is like her heels: sharp and hard and echoing. The demon's teeth nick her collarbone.

It used to suck at the inside of her neck, sensuous, the stinging pain arousing as promises of glory. *She saw the Gray Prince embrace her, call her their favored, and her wings turned silver at their touch.*

Redcap Kestrel lurches to her feet. She pries one-handed at the demon, her left arm numbed by its venom. The demon grinds through muscle, down into her breast, seeking the heat in her ribs. It is so much smaller than she remembers. When she first found it, when it crawled from the edge of the City into the Prosperous Above, it was mighty as a Prince itself. An eagle made of inverse light. Now it scarce stretches the length of her arms spread wide.

It wants her heart, like it did before. It wants to fill her with its twisted dreams and promises of void. It wants to devour her like it does everything else, pressing visions into her eyes so she won't notice how weak she's become.

She senses where it's been. The demon, riding Bluecap Shrike, has preyed on the weary and made the poor hopeless. She tastes the dozen lives it has sucked dry since she drove it out.

If you had only kept us, there would be no need for such waste, the demon hums. *It is your fault we needed to feed so often. The blood is on your hands.*

She gasps, sinking to one knee. Faces blur like smoke before her, screaming, wailing, pleading, dying. Ten, then twenty, then—then Bluecap Shrike, and after him, more and more and more and more, unless she accepts it back, unless she surrenders.

Together, they will grow strong. Together, she and her demon will feed on Windchime Owl and the haunts and the girls who work the brickyards and the children in the river-reeds, and the people who beg for crumbs and the grief-eaters who crumple in alleyways: all will welcome her devouring, for there is nothing left to live for in the City.

The girl's soul is but a morsel in the demon's belly; it is being digested with tantalizing slowness, and Redcap Kestrel can know that satiating fullness herself.

Let go, you need us, you want us, you are nothing without us. Let us in, and we will let you climb from this tomb, take your place Above!

No one escapes the City.

We can, the demon says.

"I'm too weak," she says. She isn't bound to absolute truth. "Share your feast . . . give me . . . strength . . ."

The demon undulates. It coughs up the girl's soul and Redcap Kestrel catches it, tucks it in her palm.

Then she stops fighting. The demon squirms and digs and she grits her teeth against the pain—so sharp and fresh—as it slithers fully into her body, worming through her meat, and at last: it sinks into her heart. Not just the muscle and fat and veins, but deeper, into her innermost self.

Its glee echoes through her like a cleaving knife, for now it can drain her like it has always wanted, revenge itself on her for disowning it. It will eat her heart and make her watch every delicious, spiteful bite—

Redcap Kestrel laughs. She throws her head back and her splintered laughter bounces from the glass orbs and the shattered bones in the Lovers' Garden.

Inside her, the demon screams in rage.

Her heart is empty, already hollowed out. And now the demon is trapped, nestled in emptiness, where it will wither and starve, and she laughs, she laughs, she laughs.

Her body remembers; her bones and her flesh and her blood all recall how they were sustained on the demon's vast, plentiful bounty. Meat doesn't *forget* in the City.

She's hungry, and with the girl's soul caught safely in her gloved palm, she has nothing else to eat except the squirming, wretched thing inside her heart. The demon shrieks, the demon flails, the demon is being devoured from within one spiteful, delicious bite at a time.

Redcap Kestrel's body contorts as it remembers how to feed. She arches her back, jaw locked. Only the wound in her shoulder offers escape.

The demon, shredded into fragments of what it was, makes one last desperate escape. It is scarce the size of a singular wrist bone. It drills up through its entry passage and writhes like a maggot, one broken hook-leg caught on her collarbone.

She grips the demon's slippery body. Her arm is not so numbed anymore, nurtured by the demon's sustenance. It writhes and thrashes, but she holds tight. She crushes it slow and methodical in her fist. Panicked, it squirts fresh memory at her.

Down deep in the City, a girl lost her soul. It was stolen in the night: cold hands choking her silent, greedy teeth sucking her wrist and yanking out her deepest self. She's ashamed that she didn't fight harder. Didn't leave more than a scrape of nails on the thief's arms. The girl cried. The thief was gone, leaving her gasping and hollowed out. The demon likes shame. So heavy and rancid, dripping thick into the heart, where it rots away the will to live.

Redcap Kestrel remembers shame, oh yes she does, the burning horror of her willing betrayal, the knife she slit the Gray Prince's throat with. Remember how their eyes met hers, so full of hatred? Or the shame as she burned the rookeries and let her brothers and her sisters drift on ash. Oh, that deep and abiding *shame* that curdles her soul, the *shame* that will never let her forget what she has done—

"You're too late for that," Redcap Kestrel tells the demon. "I don't need you any longer."

It squirms, spitting again into her eye.

It can find the others of her rookeries, the lost 'caps scattered through the city! It can—

—die. But not with her.

She lowers it to the ground and crushes it with her heel. Grinds her boot down until there is nothing left of the demon but a smear of discontent. It squeals and the City swallows its final cry. The demon is dead.

She allows herself one shuddering sigh and wipes her face. Her shoulder will heal. She's not as hungry as once she was.

Redcap Kestrel sprints across the pit to where Bluecap Shrike lies prone. He's half-alive, like she always is. His body is more bone strung together with stretched skin and fragile tendons. He's starving and he's alone, but he *lives.*

Redcap Kestrel kneels. She cups the back of his skull in her free palm, supporting his neck. Blood seeps between her fingers.

"Red'kes?"

She nods. "Hey, Bluetop."

"You . . ." He coughs, a rasp-rattle of air in his lungs. "Look good."

Redcap Kestrel can't stop a twitch of a smile. "You don't."

"Harsh as always." His eyes roll back. "Why'd you come?"

She has no satisfactory answer. If she'd known he still lived, would she have sought him out? She's not much for what-ifs or probabilities. So long she's endured, a half-alive thing, day to day, carried along by apathy and stupor in the City.

"There's a girl," Redcap Kestrel says. "Needed someone to help her."

Bluecap Shrike's mouth quirks. He slides one hand atop hers behind his skull. "You would."

"Learned it from you." The wound across her scalp still aches, crusted in scabs. She matches him now. They used to compare scars and he won more often than she. Redcap Kestrel lifts him into her arms. "You never let go."

His head lolls onto her shoulder. "Not 'til you do."

Redcap Kestrel carries her oath-brother through the City, untiring. She ignores the begging of grief-eaters, the threats from those who remember the Gray Prince's guard, the offers to buy what's left of Bluecap Shrike for soup.

She lays him in her nest to sleep.

"Red'kes?"

"Here," she says.

She unfolds her old guard uniform from where it's collected dust, fabric that once wrapped her in glory. It's just a coat now. It'll keep him warm.

The lost girl is still where Redcap Kestrel left her. It's been a long time since someone genuinely surprised her.

"Didn't know where else was safe," the girl mumbles, hunch-shouldered and wary. Under the defensive cowl there's something else Redcap Kestrel hasn't seen in years: possibility.

The girl slept restlessly but safely, she says, and without dreams manifesting. This building is painted thick with Redcap Kestrel's viscera, one brush-full at a time. She's got her own nest and nightmares can't intrude. If you live this long in the City, it's because you learned how to survive.

"Don't lose it again," Redcap Kestrel says, and hands the girl back her soul.

The girl swallows it down and looks at her wrist, which glows again with the faint imprint of life. Her name's embedded in those lines and dots. Redcap Kestrel doesn't read it, though. If the girl wants her to know, the girl will share.

"Here," Redcap Kestrel says, offering the scrap of her jacket hem. Too much effort to sew it back on. And then, because she's still raw, and hasn't let herself scar, she adds, "If you need somewhere to stay, there's room here."

The girl nods. She wraps her wrist, and inhales like she hasn't breathed in days. "Thanks."

Redcap Kestrel shrugs, missing the weight of her wings. She limps to her nest, her heels dulled, and snuggles against her brother.

When Redcap Kestrel wakes again, Bluecap Shrike is drowsing by her side, and the girl hasn't gone. She's leaning on a shovel, her pickax slung over her shoulder. The coat hem is still bound tight about her wrist.

"I'll earn my keep," she says, chin thrust out. "I like it here better than the brickyards. This place could use some renovations."

Redcap Kestrel blinks. Bluetop will need his own nest when he's strong enough, and after that? Perhaps she'll try and think of a future. She could use some help, and the girl is offering.

Hope isn't as rare as it used to be, not even this deep in the City.

DRUNKARD'S WALK

JAMES ENGE

At first the omens were hardly omens: a scratching on a window in the middle of the night; a voice calling in the woods when no one was there; a shadow standing alone in a sunlit field. But then the monsters began to be born: a calf that spoke a few words in a human voice and then died; a foal without legs that crawled on the ground like a worm; a human child without a head whose tender, long-fingered hands reached out to strangle its mother. In the end, the sky began to utter abrupt words of ill-omen; the moons did not rise when they should; there were days when the sun disappeared at noon.

"This is not good!" the wise men of the town declared.

The people grunted, unimpressed. You didn't have to be a wise man to see that!

It was about this time that the crooked man appeared in the woods west of town, an omen of the end—of some kind of end, or so the wise men thought.

Morlock Ambrosius felt the shape of space changing around him, but he was too tired and too irritably sober to make much sense of the feeling. He shifted his heavy pack to rest more comfortably on his uneven shoulders and stepped forward, weaving cautiously through the densely grown, dark tree trunks, stepping carefully across the dark, root-crossed ground. The irregular crunch of his footfalls among leaf-strewn roots was the loudest noise, the only noise in the empty night; even the wind was silent.

At last the trees thinned. A pale path appeared among the lightless roots and he walked out into a clearing. A town was before him.

He strode forward more confidently. His stride did not become much more regular: one of his legs was longer than the other, and he had formed the habit of swinging it to the side, so that his paces were mismatched¾long-short, long-short, long-short.

The buildings on the outskirts of town were unpromising: lightless and boarded up, as if no one lived there. Soon he came to the town square, though, where he saw his first signs of life. On the far side of the square, under a lamp, a boy was rolling a pair of dice out of a cup.

The boy's brownish skin was gray under the lamp's blue light, but it looked bruised and swollen as if from a beating. His eyes were alert and interested as he took note of Morlock, but he said nothing as Morlock approached.

"Good evening," said Morlock as he came up to the boy. He used the language of Old Ontil, which was what most people spoke around this corner of the wide world.

"Evening," the boy replied in the same language, and snapped his mouth shut as if he were afraid to say more.

Morlock himself was a man of few words and he would have passed by without wasting any more of them, but there was something urgent on his mind. "Is there a wineshop or a bar in town?" he asked. "Hope-fully someplace with a room to rent?"

The boy took a surprisingly long time to think this over before he said hesitantly, "I guess Wollickers' place—on the east side of town—it has a room upstairs. But nobody uses it anymore."

"Why not?" Morlock didn't mind the occasional bedbug—any bug that bit him soon regretted it—but he hoped to sleep without anyone trying to slit his throat.

"No one comes to town anymore," the boy said, as if this truth were self-evident.

"Why not?"

The boy shrugged uneasily, opened his mouth, closed it again without speaking. Either he wasn't used to talking much, or he had a thought too difficult to articulate.

"They go to Gennistrag, I guess," the boy finally managed to say. He rattled the dice-cup and threw snake eyes with his sixteen-sided dice.

"What's so great about Gennistrag?" Morlock asked.

The boy chanted in a singsong voice, "They have a market every nine days, and there is an inlet from the sea there where men can fish, and there are vineyards so a man can drink wine instead of beer like a pig or an Anhikh, and there is a Two-Temple of the Masked Powers, so there are many gullible pilgrims who will give you money if you just ask for it and look hungry, and then you can take the money and drink. That's what my father the Turnkey says." He had learned his lesson well, possibly under the threat of force.

"And why have you come to our town?" Turnkey's son asked, after he took a breath. He was obviously hoping he could get Morlock to do some of the work in the conversation.

"It's on the way to Gennistrag," Morlock said. "Thanks, Turnkey's son."

The boy looked away wordlessly. He scooped up the hexadecagonal dice in his cup and rolled them out onto the paving stone, getting snake eyes again. As Morlock walked away he rolled the dice again and again.

Morlock was not a man of much feeling, or so he often told himself. But he felt a strange sympathy for the bruised boy, rolling his dice endlessly, alone in the empty square. That was no kind of life for anyone. But it was not his problem, of course.

In fact, they both had the same problem, but Morlock didn't know it yet.

Morlock strode with his uneven, swinging stride down the town's single street until he came to a two-story building whose weatherworn cuneiform sign proclaimed that it was Wollickers'.

A tall, barrel-shaped woman and a thin, bent man were talking on the stoop in front of the open door. They broke off their conversation to stare at the newcomer.

"This is Wollickers'?" the crooked man asked.

"It is indeed, stranger," said the woman. "Welcome! I am the Wollicker. This here is Turnkey. Mind if we ask your name?"

"Morlock." He eyed the locals closely to see if they recognized his name and was relieved when they appeared not to. He distrusted people who used pseudonyms, but the fame or infamy of his own name had sometimes been a problem to him. "I think I spoke to your son on the edge of town," he said to Turnkey.

Turnkey's face closed like a fist. "Why? What was he doing?"

"I wanted to know where I could find a drink and a room. He told me."

"And what about me? What am I supposed to drink?"

Morlock now knew all he needed to know about Turnkey. He said, "Not my problem. The Wollicker, have I gone wrong? You have no rooms nor drinks here?"

"You have gone exactly right. Come in! Come in! We've not had news of the outside world for some time."

Morlock strode toward Turnkey as if he were an open door and the other stepped, grumbling, out of his way. Morlock heard Turnkey pass through the door behind him, still grumbling.

Wollickers' was like every other wineshop Morlock had ever seen, but emptier than most.

Seven gray-bearded men, wearing gray clothes embroidered with astronomical figures in silver thread, sat at a round table. They turned to stare intently at Morlock. He walked past them and sat on a stool at an empty table. "I'd like a plate of food and something to drink. Wine if you've got it."

Turnkey, standing nearby for some reason, snorted for some reason.

"No wine, I'm afraid," the Wollicker said shamefacedly. "I don't know if you noticed . . . ." She nodded toward a board with some wedge-like writing on it.

It was a kind of menu.

BEER: 1 finger gold.
TRENCH: 3 fingers gold.

Morlock's first casual assessment of the horrible little town was that four gold coins would have bought everything in it, with change left over. But perhaps times were tough locally.

"The trench is some kind of food?" he asked. "Bring me one of those and a couple of beers." Before the Wollicker could even begin to delicately inquire about the color of his money, Morlock shook seventeen gold coins from pockets in his sleeves. "This may cover the rent on the room, too."

The Wollicker's eyes were full of careful respect. "The room you may have for free. No, really—there is no one else staying with us at present."

"Thanks," Morlock said. He glanced around the room. The seven old men and Turnkey were staring at him, open-mouthed. "Perhaps you could serve another beer to each of these wise old gentlemen, and five more to me as the evening wears on."

Now the Wollicker's eyes took on a tolerant look, like someone humoring a lunatic or a drunk, a skill every bartender needs—as Morlock (a drunk) knew full well.

The trench was a wooden trough partly filled with forked red beans fried in fat, with a slab of flatbread on the side. The beans had been dried long before they were cooked, Morlock guessed, and the fat was slightly rancid. The flatbread was stale even as flatbread goes. Morlock was no prissy epicure, to turn up his nose at food not fashioned into high art. He ate the beans, mopped up the grease with the bread and ate that, too, and washed it all down with tepid drafts of the tarry, ill-tasting beer. But he gave up any lingering thoughts he had of staying here after he woke up tomorrow.

Turnkey was whining his way around the table with the seven wise men. They were still nursing the beers Morlock had bought them: a remarkable display of thrift. Turnkey was begging them for a bit of beer; he had a wooden mug in his hand, and he held it out with a keening plea to each of the elders in turn, and each one turned his gray beard away and sipped without answering.

Morlock was the worst drunk in his own (fairly wide) range of acquaintance, but he had never lowered himself so far as to beg in a public room for drink. Not yet, anyway. He watched in fascination as Turnkey completed one circuit and began another. Then he could stand no more.

"The Wollicker!" Morlock called.

"Yes, sir?" The innkeeper appeared at his elbow.

"Don't call me 'sir.' Give that man a mug of beer and mark it against my reckoning."

"But, sir—"

Morlock thought he understood the host's objection. To give a whiny drunk a drink is no way to stop his whining, not in the long term. But Morlock did not choose to argue the matter, and he let the Wollicker know that without speaking a word.

"Very well, sir," the Wollicker said resignedly. "Here, Turnkey, it's your lucky night. This gent is buying you a beer."

Turnkey straightened up with surprise, and his expression was far from pleased. Then a wet thought sank into his thick, dry skull, and he bent his ugly mouth into a snaggle-toothed semblance of a smile. "Thank you very kindly, sir," he called over. "I honor your kindliness, sir."

"Don't call me 'sir,'" Morlock called back. "Don't talk to me at all."

Turnkey's expression unbent into its usual mask of hate. He stumped over to the Wollicker, who was drawing a mug from the dregs of a black-stained barrel.

The seven wise men, seizing their chance to drink without annoyance, drained their cans and licked the foam from their beards with somber satisfaction. They seemed to think that something remarkable had happened, an omen of some kind. The word, afloat in the currents of their soft-voiced conversation, kept reaching Morlock's ears: ". . . omen . . . omen . . . omen . . ."

Turnkey slurped down his mug of beer, threw the empty mug against the wall so hard it broke, and then screamed that they could all fornicate with dead pigs in hell. He turned and stomped out the door still laughing and screaming unlikely sexual prescriptions.

The seven wise men looked at each other somberly and wagged their beards. There was no more talk of omens. They clearly found the prospect of infernal sex with dead pigs depressing.

For that matter, so did Morlock, although his views on the afterlife precluded such dubious entertainments. He called the innkeeper over and said, "The Wollicker: another beer with me, and another round to cheer up the old gentlemen yonder."

"I'm sorry, sir. That was the last of the barrel you bade me serve Turnkey."

"Well, open another barrel. And don't call me 'sir.'"

"There isn't another barrel, sir."

"I said—" Morlock paused to let the dry thought sink into his wet skull. He decided he must have misheard (because the alternative was too horrible). "Did you say, 'There isn't another barrel'?"

"That was the last barrel of beer in my house. And all the wine and whatnot gone long ago."

"Is there another house of entertainment in this town?"

"No, sir. Nor a barrel in anyone's basement, I don't think. Don't know for a fact, but I don't believe there is. I'm sorry, sir. I tried to warn you."

"Don't call me—" But it didn't matter. A town with no drink was no town for Morlock. He would move on down the road tonight, and he would never see the Wollicker or the seven graybeards or Turnkey or any part of this hellhole ever again.

"The Wollicker, farewell," he said. "Gentlemen, good night." He walked out of the door into the darkness and trudged on to the end of town and into the forest beyond. He wove his way cautiously through the densely grown, dark tree trunks, stepping carefully across the dark, root-crossed ground. The woods were strangely silent; he would have expected more night sounds: insects, night-foxes, owls, crow-cats—something. But the irregular crunch of his footfalls among leaf-strewn roots was the loudest noise, the only noise in the empty night; even the wind was silent.

In the end, though, the trees thinned. A pale path appeared among the lightless roots, and he walked out into a clearing. A town was before him.

He walked up the unpleasantly familiar street with an increasing sense of dismay. On the far side of the town square, under a lamp, a boy was rolling a pair of dice out of a cup.

Turnkey's son looked up and nodded in recognition. "Tried to leave? Could've warned you. Can't leave town these days."

"Thanks," Morlock said briefly and walked on to Wollickers'. The Wollicker herself was standing in the door. "I'm sorry, sir. I would have warned you—"

"I understand."

"You do?"

Morlock did. He had studied geometry extensively in his youth, and it was obvious that space hereabouts had been bent back on itself. A cloud of calculations, dense with possible causes and solutions, hung like mist in his eyes and his wet, weary brain. Perhaps tomorrow he could see them more clearly.

"I'll need that room after all. And, mind you, the Wollicker: if you call me 'sir' one more time, I'll toss you off the roof and people will start calling this place Morlock's."

"Yes. Yes, of course, the Morlock."

"Eh." It was not quite the effect he'd desired, but it was a kind of improvement. He waved the Wollicker on and followed her up to the rentable room.

Morlock awoke gradually, with a groggy sense that he had slept too long; his mind felt thick and greasy, like rancid butter. But when he looked out the unshuttered window, he saw it was still dark. Or: dark again? Could he have slept through the daylight?

He ate some flatbread and blockmeat from his pack and drank a little water from the waterstone. Provisions in the town were clearly growing thin; there was no need for him to make them any thinner. Not yet, anyway.

He threw the pack onto his crooked shoulders before he left the room. If he found a way out of town, he'd want to take it without going back for his luggage.

The Wollicker was arguing at the door of the common room with an elderly man and three short, hairy youths, all of whom seemed to think that the morning trench was overpriced. It was not Morlock's problem, so he sidled past and walked out the street door.

The stars overhead formed no constellation that Morlock recognized, from any world he had ever visited. In fact, they formed no constellation at all. After watching them for a few minutes, he saw that they were moving in relation to each other. No pattern was fixed in the sky. Not even the motions of the individual stars were regular; they speeded up and slowed down in a jerky, uneven rhythm.

"Weird," Morlock remarked, with technical precision, and walked down the street.

Turnkey was standing on the steps of a stone building that looked to be the town jail, haranguing a small group of shadowy townfolk.

"We will come to it sooner or later," Turnkey said. "We might as well admit it. And we might as well start with the children. They would be helpless anyway, without their parents to love and care for them. And they will probably cook up better than the old people. We have a duty to survive—a duty to ourselves—a duty even to our children, for who will remember them when we are gone? If—"

Morlock disliked jails, jailors, cannibals, and sanctimony at about the same toxic strength, so he hopped up the stairs and knocked Turnkey down into the muddy street. The shadowy crowd was surrounding him there before Morlock walked away. Turnkey's rhetoric seemed to be taking a different turn, but Morlock paid it no attention.

"You can't come in here!" hissed a voice from a nearby door as he walked past.

Morlock paused to glance about. It was some time before he saw which lightless door was open a crack, with a single eye gleaming wetly in the gap.

"I don't want to," he said. "Unless you have something to drink," he added, with hopeless hope.

The owner of the single eye cackled. "Drink them. Yes, and eat them, too. You'd like that. But my dear ones are safe. You'll never get them now."

Morlock walked away. The cackling continued for a few moments in his wake, and then the door slammed shut.

Morlock felt the edges of panic. There was a knot here he had to untie. But so far all he could find were loose threads.

To die would not be so very terrible, perhaps. But he disliked the thought of dying in this hellhole, icily sober, gnawed in death by some desperate, starving townie.

To die dead drunk, drowned on one's own vomit, and then be tossed into a convenient river or the sea: that was a death to strive for. Or so it seemed to Morlock. Anyway: not now; not here. That was the main thing.

Since he had no other destination, he followed the street until it emptied into the town square. Before he entered it, he heard the familiar rattle of dice on stone. Once in the square, he saw Turnkey's son, still rolling dice, but now in a different doorway.

"What is it that you're doing, anyway?" Morlock called across.

Turnkey's son looked up warily. "I'm watching the thing."

"What thing?"

"The thing that is happening." The boy waved his free hand vaguely. "All around."

"By rolling dice?"

"The numbers are real. Sometimes I think they are the only thing that is real. Soon we all will be dead. But if I understand the thing, at least . . . I want to understand the thing."

Morlock walked across the square. The boy cringed before him in the shadows of the empty doorway. "I'm sorry," he said.

"Don't be sorry," Morlock said. "And don't be afraid. Explain to me about the numbers."

"There is always at least one place in the square where I only throw snake eyes."

"Show me," Morlock directed him. The boy gathered his dice, shook them in his cup, and threw snake eyes.

"Now it is here," Turnkey's son said. "Yesterday it was where you saw me for a long time, and then it changed. I am watching the thing happen."

"So you are." Morlock thought about the business and shook his head. "Something is disrupting probability hereabouts, so that very unlikely events become inevitable."

"Like the drunk on the cliff," the boy said.

"How do you mean?"

"Say that there's a drunkard walking along a cliff. Sooner or later, he'll fall off. But something here is keeping him from falling."

"Eh." Morlock disliked the metaphor for a couple of reasons but could hardly quarrel with it, based on his own experience as a drunk. "It's too bad we don't have records of your findings," he continued. "We might be able to discern a pattern."

The boy's brown face, gray in the uncertain starlight, squinted at him with interest and admiration. Then he picked up his dice, stood, and walked away across the square. He paused at the entry of another building and gestured at Morlock. "Come and see," he said, and disappeared through the dark doorway.

Morlock followed—with reasonable caution. It was unlikely that this was the springing of a trap, but this was a place where unlikely things happened.

There was no trap, though. By the time he got to the building, the boy had lit a lamp within.

The interior of the building was a single room with a curving table at the far end. The rest of the space was open floor.

Open, but not empty. A charcoal outline of the city square and its surrounding buildings had been sketched onto the floor, and on top of this diagram was a set of stones. No: sets of stones—at least five different sets, with different colors of stone in each set.

"These are your observations on different days?" Morlock asked the boy.

The boy shrugged uneasily. "What is a day, anymore? But I try to use a different marker for each time I watch, so that I can spot the pattern of change. But I have not spotted any pattern yet."

It was true that the stones were an image of chaos, but Morlock was impressed by the boy's methodical approach. "So you have been watching for five periods?" he asked.

"No." The boy's face looked rueful. "Many more—I don't know how many. But I was getting nowhere, so I decided to track my observations by time."

Morlock nodded, said nothing, and thought.

"I'm still nowhere, aren't I?" the boy asked.

"Thinking is never a waste of time," Morlock said. "We'll need more dimensions to track the path of the thing, though."

The boy nodded eagerly. "I thought of that. But my observations were always on a flat plane, so . . ."

Silence fell as both their minds moved around the problem.

"The phenomena are in at least five or six dimensions," Morlock said at last. "So I guess."

The boy didn't flinch. "But there is a constant contact with the flat surface of the town square. Does it matter if the event is . . . is . . . what you said?"

"You may be right. The real issue is whether there's a path to the source of the phenomena. If we find that, then we can—"

"—understand it!" the boy said, just as Morlock said, "—destroy it."

It took time. Morlock had to tutor the boy in multidimensional geometry. Then they began to build a four-dimensional model (with motion standing in for time: the boy's inspired suggestion). This required Morlock to teach the boy some simple magics of force weft. He was an apt pupil, but it took time.

What was time, though? Sometimes when they went out to take new observations, the sky was bright. Sometimes there was a sun. Once there was a single moon with a curved shadow slicing its light into a crescent, a lurid and unnatural sight. Sometimes it was dark. Sometimes it was a mixture of these things, and others besides.

But they got hungry, and they got tired. When they were unbearably hungry and thirsty they ate and drank, sparingly, from the supplies in Morlock's backpack. When they were unbearably tired, they slept.

But after five sleeps they had a dynamic fractal image, apparently the intersection of several five-dimensional shapes.

"It's never the same, but each step follows naturally from the other," the boy said excitedly. "It is inevitable, but impossible to predict."

"Not impossible," Morlock disagreed. "But we'll have to chart the improbabilities as we go. Your snake eyes are still the key."

They set up a web of glide wefts to run parallel to the ground and put a slab of wood atop it. The boy rolled his dice on the slab and got sixteen, an eight and an eight.

The boy shook his head. "I think that's a coincidence. We'd have to throw more runs to find if it's significant. Anyway, it's not the pattern we're looking for: We want to go down the snake-eye zone."

Morlock nodded. He hadn't been calling the boy by name. He disliked Turnkey as much as he had grown to like the son, and the boy didn't seem to want to be reminded of his father, either. But it rankled Morlock to associate with someone who had no name.

"You're old enough to have a naming," he said to the boy. "What do you say to Reckoner? You're the best natural mathematician I've ever met."

The boy blushed and looked away. "If you say so."

"Do you say so? It'll be your name."

The boy hesitated, then nodded. "I say so."

"Come along then, Reckoner," Morlock said.

The boy blushed again but didn't look away. He looked right at Morlock with an expression Morlock hadn't seen for quite a while. Admiration was part of it, but it was warmer than mere respect. If Morlock had been compelled to put a name to it, he would have called it love. Not the sticky love of romance, but the love of a student for a teacher, a friend for a friend, a son for a father.

Morlock shrugged, threw the pack across his crooked shoulders, and walked out the door. Reckoner followed him, pushing the slab of wood through the air in front of him.

Their moving map said that the snake-eye zone should be crossing the center of the town square by the time they walked out to it. There was no light from the sky, but the buildings themselves were glowing redly. They could hear shouting on the other side of town but ignored it.

"We should be in the zone," said Reckoner, and threw his dice. "We are."

Morlock had the map in his mind, as far as they had been able to calculate it. He led the way, without speaking, and Reckoner followed with the board, throwing the dice to check their path. When Morlock passed the edge of the square, he went beyond their map but continued walking without pause. It was partly his insight telling him they were still in the zone; it was partly calculation on the fly. There was a rhythm in the changes, not so different from his own irregular stride: long-short, long-short, long-short, over and over again.

He now knew something he hadn't before, and would have shared it with his partner in this adventure, except that he was counting heart-beats and didn't want to lose the rhythm: long-short, long-short, long-short . . . .

One turn took him toward the outbuilding of a farm. He drew his accursed sword Tyrfing and slashed his way through the wall without losing a step. He kicked his way through the far wall beyond without losing the rhythm. The rattle of Reckoner's dice behind him confirmed that he was still in the zone.

"What's that?" called Reckoner after an uncounted series of heart-beats. They were deep in the surrounding woods by then. Morlock didn't answer because he didn't want to lose his calculations, and also because he didn't know.

What it looked like was a gray-green web suspended in the middle of the air. The web was near the ground at one of its fuzzily defined edges, but not resting on the dry forest grass. It didn't seem to be resting on anything. They approached it along a coiling fractal path, slowly but inevitably. It was the center of the improbabilities, the source of them.

The web, Morlock decided, was immaterial—made of tal, the force that bound immaterial mind to mere matter. But it had accumulated a coating of material slime: mold, and moss, and dust, and who-knew-what. He had seen this sort of thing before.

They reached the lower edge of the web. Reckoner's dice fell silent.

"Wait for me here," Morlock said to Reckoner, shouldering off his pack.

"Would rather not," the boy said unsteadily.

Morlock shook his head firmly. "If I become entrapped in whatever this is, you may have to do something about it."

"What?"

"I don't know."

The boy nodded solemnly, accepting the trust.

Morlock stepped into the talic web. The surface was slimily material, but the immaterial tal-force held him aloft. He stepped from juncture to juncture, deeper into the web. It didn't seem to be trapping him, or changing him. But: would he know if it had? He could feel power pulsing through the web in a heartbeat rhythm: long-short, long-short, long-short . . . .

At the center of the web was the naked, gray body of an aged man. He had been clothed at one time: rotten rags of cloth dangled from the web beneath the body.

The body itself had not rotted. It was still alive, in a way. It was woven into the web: strands of bloody light passed out from where the eyes had been, through the earholes and nostrils and mouth, from the anus and the shrivelled remains of what seemed to be the man's penis.

The bloody light faded as it got farther from the body and wove itself into the talic web. But while it was visible it pulsed in a heartbeat rhythm: long-short, long-short, long-short. There was a clot of fiery light in the body's chest, shining through the translucent gray skin, spread from the breastbone to the upper-left quadrant: where the heart would be, if this were still a human being.

Morlock walked cautiously around the thing that had been a man and speculated on what had happened here. Clearly, he had been a magical adept of some kind, and the web distorting this part of space was some kind of magic gone wrong.

An immortality spell? It was possible. The man had been old, and Morlock knew from experience that some elderly folk grow insanely greedy of life as they feel it flickering out inside them.

More likely, though, the adept had wanted control. He wanted absolute godlike control of some space, be it never so small—to be the god of this region, this hellish little village. That was why he had put himself into the circuit of the spell, so that he could directly affect natural forces. Even without ascending to visionary rapture, Morlock could feel the rustle of talic forces about him: strung up into the sky, sunk deep into the ground, stretched out to the horizon, moving, pulling, pushing, turning.

Morlock shook his head. Had the adept never considered that a doorway out is also a doorway in? Or had he just assumed that the energy of his unclothed will would be sufficient to master the elemental forces of nature—the weight of the moons, the speed and light of the sun, the power of the world's winds?

In any case, he had risked it and it had destroyed him. There was no intelligence shaping the adept's ruined face now. His body was simply a focus for forces to mingle and interact, unpredictably, chaotically, according to the rhythm of his beating heart.

There was an obvious solution to this problem: destroy the heart. No doubt it could be dangerous to be at the center of these forces as they were severed, but (unlike some) Morlock had no interest in living forever.

Tyrfing was already in his hand. He stabbed the black-and-white crystalline blade through the adept's burning heart, severing the web of talic forces at its core.

He fell three feet to the ground and sprawled amid a shower of moldy filth.

Morlock was not a cursing man, but this made him grumble a bit. He shook some mold out of his hair and brushed himself off as he got back to his feet. He wiped his sword clean and sheathed it.

Reckoner approached tentatively through the honeycombed piles of mush left behind by the vanished web. He stood beside Morlock and looked solemnly at the dead body of the old adept.

"Is that it?" Reckoner asked. "Who was he?"

Morlock explained his surmises to Reckoner.

The boy nodded. "I don't recognize him."

"He may have been trapped out here in his own web from before you were born," Morlock said, "as the chaotic mingling of forces built up slowly until this region of space became separate from the world. Or maybe he came here from elsewhere and worked in secret, and has been out here only a few nine-days."

"And everything will go back to normal now?" the boy said. "The dice are rolling normally—I checked."

"Things will be different in town." Morlock thought about the last time he had seen the boy's father and said, "You should leave, anyway. Find a lyceum where you can learn more math. There's a fairly good one in Narkunden."

The boy looked sharply at him. "Won't you teach me? You know a lot."

Out of all the things he might have said, Morlock replied, "Others know more."

Reckoner didn't argue the point, though he clearly wasn't done with it. "We should go back to town. At least we should tell the wise men that everything will be all right now. You'll have to explain it: I don't really understand this stuff."

"You go," Morlock said. "I want to make sure the spell is totally destroyed."

Reckoner nodded hesitantly, shrugged, and ran off without saying good-bye. He left his dice and the diceboard behind.

Morlock spent a few moments making sure the space-distorting spell was no longer active, so that the last thing he said to the boy would not actually be a lie. He then shouldered his backpack, turned, and circled eastward around the village, until he found the road to Gennistrag.

As usual, he swung his longer leg to the side, giving his footfalls a slightly irregular thump: long-short, long-short, long-short . . . .

In Gennistrag there was no one who loved him or hated him or knew him at all. There was, however, plenty of wine. That made four good reasons to stay on for a while.

For a while, anyway.

IF THE MARTIANS HAVE MAGIC

P. DJÈLÍ CLARK

"The first Martian War was won not by man, but microbes. The second we fought with Martian weapons that nearly broke the world. The third invasion we stopped by our own hands, using magic."

—WEI-YIN SUN, IMPERIAL HISTORIAN IN THE COURT OF THE EMPRESS DOWAGER, RESTORATION PERIOD.

Marrakesh's streets were a dizzying affair at any time. But at midday they were unbearable, a churning morass that moved to their own rhyme and reason. And though Minette called the city a second home, navigating its roads was a feat of skill, luck and perhaps, she was willing to admit, sheer stupidity. She dodged a rider on a high-wheeled electric velocipede and rounded about a diesel trolley—only to be brought up short by a young woman who stood in the middle of the busy thoroughfare, beseeching a stubborn goat to follow. Yet no matter how hard she pulled the taut leash, it would not move. The girl yelled, then begged. But the goat only bleated its obstinacy, having decided to start its revolution here and now. Minette slowed to watch, momentarily lost in the goat's stubborn cries—and was nearly run over by a rickshaw.

A tall dromedary pulling the two-wheeled hooded vehicle of gilded iron pulled up short, jostling its two occupants. Both gasped, their sculpted eyebrows rising above long overlapping rose-colored veils. But it was the camel that turned an irritated glare Minette's way.

"Mind where you're going!" it brayed, making a gesture with its split upper lip she knew for a curse. Minette frowned at the discourteous display, and with a suck of her teeth shot back a curse in Kreyòl. The camel's eyes widened at the unfamiliar words and it might have said something in return, but she had already moved on.

Of all the creatures gifted sentience with the return of magic, the good God Bondye alone knew why those rude beasts were chosen. But that was the way of magic, unpredictable in its movements, its choices and ceaseless permutations. That's what all of this was about—why she'd canceled morning classes and now rushed to a meeting to which she wasn't invited. Because someone had to speak for the unknowable in magic, the nonlinear, the indefinable.

Someone had to save her Martians.

She stopped out of breath, just across from the Flying Citadel. The stone fortification sat atop a jagged rock that floated like an unmoored mountain peak high in Marrakesh's skyline. Its ivory walls and gold domes looked stolen out of time—or perhaps beyond it—spreading a shadow on the streets below where hawkers sold magic rope and enchanted rugs to gullible tourists along with more useful thaumaturgical devices. A fleet of lavish vehicles were parked nearby: wheeled automobiles driven by golden metal men; air balloons of giant puffer fish that pulled at their anchors; and gilded carriages drawn by fantastic beasts. One of them, a spotted ocelot large as a horse, lapped a blue tongue against its fur and held up a snow-white wing like a canopy beneath Marrakesh's glaring sun. The vehicles bore insignia from over a dozen nations, evidence that the Council was indeed meeting.

Minette swore. Looking around she caught sight of a few taxis, ferrying tourists up to the citadel by way of flying carpets. Absurd. Fortunately, she had other methods. Closing her eyes, she composed a quick prayer.

The loa could be persuaded to answer the call of a Mambo in need—

as drawn up in the new understandings (they bristled at mention of the word *contract*) that now administered interactions with their priests. All part of bringing them more devotees in this modern world, where spirits and gods walked unbidden, ever competing for the attention of mortals. Of course, the loa acted in their peculiar time, and followed their own interests—new understandings or no.

After two attempts, she was set to call again when the image of a man in a broad-brimmed hat flashed across her thoughts. He held a mahogany smoking pipe precariously between pursed lips and his leisurely gait resembled a dance. Legba, the Keeper of Roads, opening the Door. A flaming ram followed. Bade's sign, who she truly wanted. His presence stirred against her with the weight of a feather and the pressure of a mountain all at once. She hashed out a quick agreement—some offerings to perform, a drapo to commission—and was fast swept up in gusts of air. An accompanying rumble of thunder startled those below. Bade's twin, Sobo. The two were inseparable and you didn't get one without the other.

Bade kept to the pact, sending Minette soaring up to the Flying Citadel. Looking down she saw the winged ocelot had paused its cleaning, and now stared up at her with four red sapphire eyes. She shook her head. The powerful and their toys. On a draft of wind accompanied by peals of thunder-like drums she rose higher still, above rounded minarets, to reach the citadel's upper levels.

Her feet struck stone and she stumbled once before breaking into a run along a lengthy parapet, holding the ends of her white dress up so as not to trip. She moved into a passageway, easily slipping through a set of wards meant to deter interlopers. Aziz's work, and predictable as always. Well wasn't he in for a surprise. She stopped at reaching a red door inscribed with repeating calligraphy. Taking a breath to collect herself—it did no good to look hurried—she tightened the white cloth that wrapped her hair, adjusted her spectacles, and (remembering to release the grip on her dress) stepped inside.

The Council on Magical Equilibrium was a rare gathering. And, as it was, featured an impressive who's who, and what's what, from across the world. Some faces Minette recognized. Some she couldn't see, and others she didn't know at all. Each however turned from where they were seated about a curving table to stare at her entrance. Aziz, who sat at its center, broke off his words entirely.

"Minette?" His call came too familiar for colleagues. He must have realized as much because he coughed into a waxed moustache before starting again. "Please excuse the interruption. May I introduce Professor Francis. She teaches here at the Academy and comes to us from Port-au-Prince—"

"Port-au-Prince!" a small slender woman in a crimson gown repeated in a throaty slur. A veil of swirling gray mist obscured her face, all but her eyes—black on black pools, deep as a fathomless sea. "Aziz, you did not tell us the Academy held a Mambo in residence. I see no distinct loa hovering about you. One of the Unbound then?" She craned her neck and inhaled deeply. "Oh! But the magic in you is no less for that." Those black eyes narrowed hungrily, and Minette fought the urge to step back. It was unwise to show weakness to their kind. They remembered that.

"Professor Francis is one of our most *valued* researchers," Aziz interjected, seeming to sense the danger. "She has done wonders with Martian–human interactions. She was the one who first made the—ah—discovery."

Minette raised an eyebrow. Were they so afraid to just come out and say it?

Another woman at the table gave a derisive snort. She looked older than Minette by a decade or more. But the body beneath her burgundy military uniform was solid, and the dark hands folded before her thick and scarred. If the number of medals decorating her breast was anything to go by, she knew how to use those hands too. She pinned Minette with the one eye not covered by a black patch—an owl examining a mouse—and flared her generous nostrils.

"And," Aziz went on, "though the professor is one of our finest faculty, I don't recall her being summoned to this meeting." That last part was said with an unspoken, *and you should leave now.* But Minette hadn't come this far to be scolded. She tried to ignore the gazes of the two women and stepped forward.

"Apologies, Director Aziz. And to this Council," she began, reciting what she'd hastily rehearsed on the run here. "I only learned you were meeting this morning and thought my expertise might be valuable. I'm certain my absence was an oversight." She met Aziz's gaze squarely at that. It was petty of him not to invite her. But rather than taking up the challenge, his eyes creased with concern. That only annoyed her further.

"Well, she certainly is direct," the mist-faced woman slurred. "I for one would like to hear what the Mambo has to share. I say she stays. Any objections?" None around the table gave a reply—though the one-eyed woman shrugged indifferently. Aziz put on a resigned look, beckoning Minette to sit.

"Come, Mambo, whose scent of magic is sweet enough to taste," the mist-faced woman purred. "You may sit near me." She patted an empty chair with a long-fingered hand, pale as alabaster. Those depthless eyes looked even hungrier.

Minette politely declined the offer three times (any less was just inviting trouble) and took a chair several seats down—feeling peculiarly conscious of her smallness between a broad giant in a blue turban and a fiery djinn encased inside a towering body of translucent glass.

"We were discussing," Aziz began anew, "what we are to do with the three entities following the recent revelations."

Minette's heart drummed. There it was. "There's only one," she spoke up. Heads—and other things much like heads—swiveled back to regard her. "You're calling Them three, but there's actually only the One."

Aziz blinked but then nodded at the correction. "Yes, of course. Professor Francis is referring to how the Martians see themselves. Three are required to form their collective consciousness, and then They become One. The professor is one of the few non-Martians to successfully join a triumvirate."

"Join?" It was the one-eyed woman. She now glared incredulous. "So you allow the beasties into your head?"

Minette paused, trying to place that English accent. "They aren't beasts," she replied. "They're sentient beings, like us."

The one-eyed woman's laugh was brusque. "So you say, Professor.

But I've grappled with them face-to-face, not all tame like in your lab." She tapped a finger at her missing eye. "And they're damn beasts if I ever seen one."

Aziz coughed again. "Professor Francis, this is General Koorang. She's here representing the Nations League Defense Forces."

Minette's eyes widened. *The* General Koorang? Who had broken the Martians at Kathmandu? So, that accent was Australian then. No wonder the woman was so hardline.

"In my time in the triumvirate," she tried diplomatically, "I've found Them to be capable of many emotions. They have been kind, even gentle."

General Koorang sputtered. "Kind? Gentle? Is that why they set about invading us *three* times?"

"Not every Martian was a soldier," Minette reminded, speaking as much to the others gathered. "The One I joined with were worker drones. They never even saw fighting. That's why it was so easy for the Central Intellect to abandon Them in the retreat."

"And what did they *work* on?" the general asked, unmoved. "Was it their stalking dreadnoughts? Their infernal weapons what almost blew us to hell? Come visit the Archipelago sometime, Professor, and I'll show you Martian gentleness."

Minette bit her lip to keep from replying. That was unfair. The Archipelago was all that was left of what used to be Australia. The waters of the South Sea were mostly off-limits now: teeming with monsters that wandered in through torn rifts between worlds. That it was humans playing with Martian weapons who had brought on the disaster seemed to matter little to the general.

"Perhaps we should get back to the heart of the matter," Aziz suggested, breaking the tense silence. "We must decide what is to be done with the entities, um, Them, in light of Professor Francis's discovery."

Minette felt a flurry of annoyance. Were they going to dance around this all morning? "By discovery, you mean that Martians can perform magic," she blurted out. Her words sent up murmurs through the Council. Aziz gave her an exasperated look. The general cursed. And the mist-faced woman's eyes creased with a hidden smile.

319

Minette took the moment to press on. "What we should do with them is clear. They are a conscious soul, protected within the Nations League Charter on Magical Practitioners drawn up over a decade ago in 1919. They should be encouraged to develop those talents."

"Outrageous!" General Koorang roared, her face a thunderhead. "The Charter wasn't made to protect bloody Martians!"

"But it does not exclude them," the mist-faced woman interjected. "The Charter was made quite broad in its application—as evidenced by the makeup of this very Council."

"Precisely," Minette said, seizing on the opportunity. "We already accept a diverse world of spirits, gods, and no end of magical beings. The previous head of this Council was a minotaur, and she served with distinction. How is this any different?"

"A point of clarification," a squat shaman at the far end of the table called, raising a hand that rattled with ivory bracelets. "The Charter the professor references was created to protect unique magical abilities in their nascency. Have these Martians exhibited some magical talent indigenous to their . . . kind?"

"Not yet," Minette admitted. "But I believe it's only a matter of time," she followed quickly. "The triumvirate I share, They claim Mars once had magic. But it's been lost, much as humanity lost it once, too concerned with our factories and industry. Through the rituals to the loa, they've shown that they can understand and practice magic—something we once thought impossible. They're on the verge of self-discovery. We should allow them that right."

"Martians don't have any rights as citizens," General Koorang countered. "They're not even from this world. Just because the Academy lets you keep a few as pets, doesn't change the fact that these creatures are prisoners of war."

Minette clenched her fists to keep calm. "We aren't at war, general."

The older woman leaned forward, imposing in her size. "Oh? Did we sign some peace treaty that I'm unaware of? Is there a Martian consulate? A Martian ambassador?"

Minette pressed on, counting in her head to keep calm and trying to forget she was arguing with a living legend. "The Martians invaded three times, precisely three years apart, on the exact same day. The last war was in 1903. It's been more than thirty years, and we've seen no sign of another invasion."

The general smacked the table heavily and Minette was proud that she didn't jump. "Damn right! Because we beat the hell out of them last time! And we did it with magic. That's our greatest defense, the one thing their calculating overgrown minds can't understand. And you just go ahead and give it to them." She shook her head, that single eye glowering. "I expected more, from a Haitian."

Minette felt her face flush at the insult. The houngan Papa Christophe had been the first to use magic in the Third War, halting the Martian dreadnoughts and sending their armies into disarray. The rout at Cap-Haïtien set an example for the world. She was fiercely proud of that fact and didn't need reminding—not like this.

"I didn't give them magic," she said tersely. "They were drawn to the loa and the loa to them. None of us have the right to stop this development." She turned her appeal to the wider Council, moderating her tone. "I'm not just being an idle academic here. I'm not insensitive to all of your concerns. I understand the suffering the Martians caused this world. But I believe there's a practical side to all of this."

The general folded her arms and struck the posture of someone politely suffering a fool, but Minette continued. "The rediscovery of Martian magic could be a new step for all of us. A new magic system built on Martian ingenuity. Think of all the possibilities! The Martians here on Earth could become valued citizens, sharing what they know. If Mars invades again, as the general believes, we would have a valuable Fifth Column ready to come to our defense. What if this curtails their appetite for conquest? What if it helps them find themselves again, the way we have? We should seize this opportunity to integrate them into society, not shun it."

"Or we should be frightened," General Koorang grumbled. She spared a glance for Minette before turning to the Council. "The professor's determined, I'll give her that. But let's say she's right, and there's some old Martian magic waiting to be tapped. What happens when they rediscover it? Can we trust they won't give it up to protect their own kind? The last three invasions decimated the old powers of this world. Europe's a blasted-out hellhole that might never recover. We're barely managing that refugee crisis as it is. I for one have seen enough of Martian *ingenuity*. When the fourth invasion comes—and it *will* come—do we want to look up to see new Martian dreadnoughts powered by magic marching across Cairo, New Èkó, or Delhi?" She let her one eye latch onto every gaze before continuing. "I'm a soldier, not a diplomat. Thinking about peace isn't my job, and I'll admit I'm no good at it. But I know how to keep us safe. First rule of military defense: deny your enemy any chance of mounting a challenge. The professor's admitted these Martians haven't found their lost magic yet. She says we should give them time. Well I say we use that *time* to stop this threat in its tracks. Now—before it goes any further. Because allowing these Martians to have magic is a risk we can't afford."

Minette felt the weight of those words, settling down with the force of a hammer. So, it seemed, did the rest of the Council. Fear, it turned out, was a potent weapon of its own. And General Koorang was as skilled in persuasion as she was on the battlefield. When the motion was made to declare the prospect of Martian magic "a threat to global security and magical equilibrium," not one voice rose in dissent.

The beat of drums guided Minette's movements. About the room, the loa that had been invited into the Hounfour danced along. Others like Papa Loko only sat watching. The First Houngan had been convinced by his wife to accept the Rada rites of this new world. Now he kept strict governance to see they were properly followed. He was especially taken with the Martians.

With their bulbous heads, it was easy to at first mistake them for giant octopuses. But where an octopus was reduced to flimsy sacks of flesh out of water, Martian bodies were quite sturdy. Their skin was pale verging on a dull violet that extended the length of sixteen thick tentacles, the latter of which were remarkably malleable. At the moment, they intertwined like roots to form the semblance of a man beneath each head—with arms, legs, and even a torso.

Two of the triumvirate moved gracefully to the song, swaying in hypnotic undulations. A third used myriad tentacles to beat a steady rhythm on a batterie of conical drums, matching the rattling shells of Minette's asson. On the ground, Papa Damballah's veve lay etched in white. He sat as a white serpent, coiled about his shrine and the feast prepared for him: an egg on a mound of flour, bordered by white candles, white flowers, and white rice. His red eyes watched the writhing limbs of the Martians and swayed with them. A current filled the room, and it felt as if they were no longer within this plane, but some other realm of existence where every star in the cosmos danced.

Then it was done, and she was back in the room at the Academy she'd transformed into her own Hounfour. She let herself fall, weakened after housing the loa. Martian arms caught her, strong but gentle, leading her to sit. They sat in turn about her, keeping their semi-human forms and regarding her with round, silver eyes that never blinked. A tentacle extended to wrap warm and sinuous about her wrist: an invitation to join the triumvirate. Still flush from the loa, she accepted.

"That was . . . nice," came the harmonious voices in her head. They layered each other: the three that were One.

"Wi," she answered back, also in her head. The Martians had mouths, sharp beaks like birds. But their speech was beyond human ears. This was much easier.

"Nou danse kont danse nou," They remarked, switching between English and Kreyòl much as she did. "I am very fond of Papa Damballah."

Minette didn't find that surprising. Damballah was the Great Creator of all life, peace and harmony. He was also the protector of those who were different. It made sense that the Martians would be drawn to him, and he to Them.

"You are quiet," the voices noted. "Sa ou genyen?"

"Mwen regret sa," she apologized. "My mind is elsewhere."

"On your meeting with the Council."

Minette frowned at her lapse, building up her mental guards. In the triumvirate, your mind was an open book if you weren't careful.

"Aziz was there," They said, catching a stray thought. "Was it difficult seeing him again? Much time has passed since the two of you last coupled. But your feelings for him remain disordered. Perhaps the two of you should couple again?"

Minette flushed, absently pulling her dress more tightly about her. An open book indeed. "Non. I won't be coup—intimate, with Aziz again. I explained before, nou te mal. We let things get out of hand." He was married for one. And they'd collected too many gray hairs between them to be getting on like schoolchildren.

"I have made you uncomfortable," They said contritely. "Mwen regret sa. I am not always aware."

"It's not your fault. I just . . ." She sighed. There was no easy way to say this. So instead she let down her guards. Her memories of the past morning flowed to the triumvirate at the speed of thought. The Council meeting. The debate. The final decision. They examined each recollection and in the silence that followed, Minette waited.

"Your Council is frightened," the voices said finally.

"Wi," she replied in frustration. "It's disappointing they give in to their fears."

"Their reasoning is not unsound."

Minette's alarm reflected back to her in six silver eyes. "How can you say that? It's preemptive nonsense. They're punishing you for something you might do—not what you've done. It's wrong!"

There was a pause as three heads cocked as one, considering her statement. "I do not say I welcome their verdict. But the fear is understandable. My people have not been kind to your world. Even you were frightened of my kind once."

Minette's memories intruded without invitation. She had been a girl of thirteen during the Third Martian War. She remembered hiding in the shelters of Gonaïves with Grann Louise, who whispered assurances that Papa Toussaint and Papa Dessalines would not allow the island to be invaded again. She had grown up with all the fears about Martians, until attending university and becoming fascinated with courses on them. She'd jumped at the chance to study with the three housed here at the Academy, even if in faraway Marrakesh. It had taken her a while to see them as more than "specimens," and even longer to see them as less than monsters. But it was difficult to convince others to understand Them as she did.

"You've read my thoughts," she said. "You know what they plan to do."

"Separation," the voices whispered.

The word struck Minette as hard as the first time she'd heard it. General Koorang had called for euthanasia. But the Council balked. What they proposed, however, was little different, and perhaps crueler. Martians abhorred individualism. Separated, They would lose their single consciousness: effectively cease to be. Like cutting a human brain into three separate parts. It was a murder of the soul, if not the flesh.

Her guilt pulsed through the bond. "If I hadn't introduced you to the loa none of this might have happened. Li se fòt mwen."

"Non!" The sharpness of the voices startled her. "This isn't your fault. You have given my time in captivity meaning. I would not undo this, even at the rescue of my life." There was a pause. "I have something to show you. Es'ke ou ta vle promnen?"

Minette frowned at the question. Go for a walk? But she gave a tentative mental nod of acceptance. She barely had time to brace herself before their combined consciousness enveloped her whole. The world broke apart, shattered, then reduced to a pinpoint of light before expanding everywhere at once—taking her with it. When she found her bearings again, she stood on the edge of a calm moss green sea. Strange plants tall as trees rooted in the russet soil, with wide blue petals opened to a sky blanketed by clouds.

"Do you like it?" They asked. The three that were One stood about her, their human forms abandoned, and tentacles gliding freely just atop a field of mustard colored grass. The air here was thick, almost viscous, so that she could feel it hugging her skin. Above them, a flock of feather-less creatures soared on broad flat wings that looked more like flippers.

"Se bèl!" she breathed. "What is this place?"

"Home," They answered, with longing in their voices.

Minette gaped. Mars? But how? They had shown her their world in similar mental visions before, taken her to the sprawling subterranean mechanical cities, to the magma fields beneath the birthing catacombs and to the hanging megaliths that housed the technocratic Central

Intellect. But the surface of that Mars was lifeless, scoured sterile by the relentless march of Martian industry.

"This is how it was before," They explained, hearing her unspoken thoughts. "The memory lay within me, passed on by forebears millions of years dead, for no consciousness truly dies. The loa awakened it again. And awakened this."

There was a wave of tentacles, and from them flowed a ripple through the air.

Minette gasped. They were symbols and patterns of a multihued cascade, with dimensions that defied description. She reached to touch one with a finger, and the sound of hundreds of chimes trembled the world. In a rush, it all vanished and she was back at the Academy.

"Was that . . . ?" She couldn't even finish.

"The magic of my people," They replied.

"You've recovered it?"

"That is difficult to say," They answered. "I have been trying. But it is not easy working with something from which I have been so long separated. It is alien to me and will take time to understand."

Minette sighed wearily. But there was no time. Once the Council moved to separate the Three, the possibility of Martian magic would die before it even had a chance to begin. "Do what you can," she told Them. "And if there's a way I can help, you must let me know." She was set to say more when a tremor shook her. She turned with the triumvirate to look to the door, sharing their preternatural senses.

"Someone has come to see you," They said.

Minette withdrew from the One, returning to her singular consciousness and feeling suddenly very alone—her mind still ringing with what had just been uncovered. She was prepared to tell whoever it was to go away. Between housing the loa and joining the triumvirate, her body was weakened almost to the point of exhaustion. But it was rare they received visitors. Fear lanced through her. Was this the Council? Had they come for her Martians already? Gripped with trepidation, she forced herself up on wobbly legs and made her way from the room through the hallway. Reaching a door, she paused to lean against it for strength before pulling it open to reveal a stone courtyard where the

Martians were allowed access once a day—and found an unexpected sight.

It was the six-wheeled white carriage, pulled by a giant winged ocelot—the very same she had seen beneath the Flying Citadel. The door to the conveyance opened and the haughty beast turned to regard her with four sets of expectant sapphire eyes. Hesitant, Minette stepped forward and climbed inside. Naturally, the carriage was larger within than without, revealing a room lit by flickering tallow candles. At the far end of a long black lacquered dining table sat a familiar figure in a high backed red chair.

"Greetings, Mambo," the mist-faced woman slurred. "Please, you will sit?"

Minette remained standing. Such offers had to be thought through.

"You may put away any fears, Mambo. True enough, your delectable magic is like sugar to me. It is why I have placed such distance between us—to avoid temptation."

Minette weighed that. She could walk out now. But curiosity gnawed. What was a councilmember doing here? "I accept that and no more," she said sitting.

"And no more," the small woman agreed.

"Your visit is unexpected."

"Of course. That is why it is a *secret* visit." She placed a shushing finger to the place where her lips might have been. "I have come to save your Martians."

Minette sat stunned. "But you voted with the others."

The woman waved dismissively. "That cause was lost before it began, Mambo. General Koorang will have her way. But perhaps you can have yours. My sisters would like to take in you and your Martians. We would offer them sanctuary, away from the prying eyes of the Nations League."

For a moment, Minette only stared. Sanctuary? "Where?" she finally managed.

The woman wagged a scolding finger. "A secret, scrumptious scented Mambo, would be less so if I told you. But I am willing to provide passage to this place."

A hundred hopes flared in Minette before she smothered them with doubt, remembering who (and what) this creature was. "Why? Why do you care about Them?"

"Why, for the magic," the mist-faced woman admitted openly. "My sisters and I make no pretenses to our desires. We devour magic, savor its many essences. The possibility of Martian magic is most appealing! So exotic and untried. How we would like to taste it!"

Minette grimaced. There was always a price. "So you just want to eat them—drain them of magic."

The woman sighed. "Our kind are too maligned in your fairytales, Mambo. Contrary to those stories, we are not like the boy with the goose and the eggs of gold. We would not deplete something so precious as to not see its like again. Think of this as an exchange. We offer sanctuary. In turn, we take only small bits at a time—as one would any delicacy."

Minette's stomach turned. Bon mache koute chè, she thought darkly. Like soucouyant she'd known back home, these vampiresses couldn't be trusted. That was certain. But a secret place, where her Martians could be together, and They could explore their newfound magic. That couldn't be dismissed out of hand. Her mind worked anxiously. There had to be a way. She had negotiated agreements with loa and demigods. She could handle this.

"You will promise by heart, head, and soul that no lasting harm will come to either myself or the Martians in your care," she stated. "We will hash out a binding compact with a fair exchange between us and your sisters, where any offer of their magic is willingly given. Any breach of our agreement and I will have each of your names."

Those black eyes above the misty veil narrowed to slits, and Minette thought she heard a low hiss. A minor gale picked up, bending the flames on the candles. To demand the names of their kind was as good as asking them to offer up their cold barren souls. The mention alone was offensive. Minette held fast, however, a few choice charms at the ready in case she needed to make a hasty exit. But the gale fast subsided and the woman slurred pleasantly, if also a bit tight: "Heart, head, and soul. Or our names be given." Her eyes creased into a smile. And Minette had the distinct feeling that beneath that misty veil awaited a mouth of grinning fangs. "Now, crafty little Mambo, let us see to that agreement."

It was two days later that Minette walked Marrakesh's night market. The Souq was held beneath a full moon and spread out between alleyways and courtyards covered by colorful tents. Hawkers competed for customers, crying out their wares. Behind her followed three figures, two men and one woman. Some might have noted their odd gait: a glide just above the stone streets more than a walk. But in a city brimming with magic this was hardly worth a second glance. Not that a third or fourth glance would be able to penetrate the glamour now enveloping the three Martians.

They seemed to relish their freedom, casting human eyes in every direction. At the moment, they were taken by a guild of harpy artists whose talons inked henna that bled and slithered across the skin. Under other circumstance Minette might have been sympathetic to their gawping. But as it was, she simply wanted them to move faster.

The mist-faced woman had offered passage and sanctuary, but escaping the university was left to her. There was a dirigible waiting at the dockyards waiting to ferry them off. Minette just had to get them there. So far, that had been a success. Concocting a medsin that left the guards who watched over the Martians standing in an awake-sleeping state was simple. Now they only needed to reach their destination before the ruse was discovered.

As the four stepped from beneath a canopy, the dockyards became visible. And Minette dared to believe they just might make it. Until someone called her name.

"Minette?"

She went still as stone, heart pounding at the familiar voice. Turning, she found herself looking at Aziz. He was striding towards her hurriedly, four Academy guards at his heels. Beside him was another recognizable figure. She cursed. General Koorang.

Panic blossomed in Minette. She thought to shout for her charges to run. She would somehow allow their escape. But as she saw the rifles in the hands of the guards, she faltered. The second the Martians ran they would be cut down. Uncertain of her next move, she resolved to stand her ground as the group reached them.

"Didn't I tell you?" General Koorang declared boldly. "Didn't I say she'd try something like this? Your professor's spent too much time in her Martian's heads. Can't find her way out again. Good thing we had them watched."

Minette glared at Aziz. "You had me watched?"

"And for good reason it seems," he retorted. "Do you know how much trouble you're in?" He ran a hand over his mouth, the way he did when thinking hard, then leaned in close. "We can still fix this. We can say the Martians coerced you, did something to your head. Just get them to return. I'll talk to the general. Maybe your post can be salvaged—"

"I wasn't coerced," she said tightly. The nerve of him to think she was simply the dupe of someone else's machinations. He damn well knew her better than that. "I planned this, Aziz." The disappointment on his face only made her want to punch it.

"Enough for me," the general rumbled. She looked over the Martians still cloaked in their glamour. "Arrest her. Then take these creatures back to their cages. If they give trouble, use whatever force is necessary."

The four guards advanced. Minette glanced back to the dirigible meant for them, wanting to scream in exasperation at the nearness of freedom. So close! So infuriatingly close! Something slender and warm curled about her hand. She turned to one of the Martians, the unspoken request writ plain on that human mask. She consented, joining the triumvirate. The sound of drums flowed through their bond, the rattle of an asson, falling white petals, and the call to the loa of the batterie.

"Open the Door for me," the voices came.

"There's no time for this!" Minette said.

"Open the Door," the voices asked again.

She shook her head. "Now? I don't understand!"

"You asked how you could help. I think I know. The magic. I have been trying to make it work as a Martian. But I'm not a Martian anymore, am I? My magic was born of two worlds. It is that two-ness, I must embrace. Open the Door. Be our Mambo. And I will show you."

Minette looked into those unblinking human eyes, that seemed to plead, and did as they asked. Her spirit moved in time to the music. And though she had no tobacco or fine things to give the doorman, she sang:

Papa Legba ouvre baye pou mwen, Ago eh!

Papa Legba Ouvre baye pou mwen,

Ouvre baye pou mwen, Papa

Pou mwen passe, Le'm tounnen map remesi Lwa yo!

Papa Legba came as called. There was a look in his eyes beneath that wide-brimmed hat that Minette had never seen before. He thumbed his pipe and instead of going his usual way, settled down to watch. In the bond, a mix of Kreyòl and Martian tongues sent a current flowing through Minette. One that she'd only recently felt before. Martian magic, both alien and exhilarating. It blended with the song, played along with the batterie and asson, merging her voice and spirit with the three Martians until all became One.

On the ground a symbol appeared all around them, drawn in ghostly white. Damballah's veve: serpents winding along a pole. The flows of Martian magic superimposed themselves upon it, creating multiple dimensions that folded and bent one on the other, calling on the loa who was their protector.

Papa Damballah appeared. But not like Minette had ever seen.

This Damballah was a being made up of tentacles of light, intertwined to form the body of a great white serpent. And she suddenly understood what she was seeing. The loa met the needs of their children. Papa Damballah had left Africa's shores and changed in the bowels of slave ships. He changed under the harsh toil of sugar and coffee plantations. And when his children wielded machetes and fire to win freedom, he changed then too. Now to protect his newest children, born of two worlds, he changed once again.

Minette opened up to the loa and Martian magic coursed through her, erupting from her fingertips. The guards, General Koorang, and Aziz drew back, as the great tentacles of Papa Damballah grew up from her, rising above the market tents as a towering white serpent: a leviathan that burned bright against the night. For a moment brief as a heartbeat—or as long as the burning heart of a star—it seemed to

Minette she saw through the loa's eyes. The cosmos danced about her. It trembled and heaved and moved.

And then Damballah was gone.

Minette staggered, so weakened she almost fell.

Once again Martian hands caught her, lifted her, supporting their Mambo. She caught a glimpse of Legba and her thoughts reached out to him. Had she seen another face of Papa Damballah? Or was this the birth of a loa? Something old, yet new and different? But the Keeper of Roads didn't answer. He only smiled—as if to a child asking at the color of the sky. With a flick to the brim of his hat, he vanished.

Minette returned fully to the world to find Aziz staring. His face was rapt, gazing over both her and the Martians—and every now and again glancing skyward. He had seen Damballah. She looked about. All through the Souq, tongues had quieted as eyes watched both she and the Martians—gaping at the phantom glow in the night sky left in the loa's wake. They had all seen.

"Nice show you've put on," General Koorang growled. "Doesn't change anything." Her voice was brusque as usual. But something of it was less sure than before. Oh, she'd seen too. But this woman was too tough—too stubborn—to be quelled by even a passing god.

"Actually, this does change things." Minette turned in surprise to see it was Aziz. His voice tremored but he turned to address the general. "The Martians have shown that they can create their own magic. You saw it. Felt it. Everyone did." He gestured to the gathered crowd. "That at the least allows them protection under the Nations League Charter."

General Koorang's jaw went tight. To his credit, Aziz didn't back down—though Minette was certain the woman could go through him if need be. The guards at her side looked on, nervous and uncertain. Finally, something about the woman eased: an owl deciding perhaps there were too many mice to snare at once. She spared a withering glare for Aziz before eyeing Minette. "Do what you want with your Martians professor, for now. Just you remember though, laws can be changed." Then turning on her heels she stalked off, shouldering her way through the crowd.

"She's right," Aziz said, releasing a relieved breath. "Things could be different by morning. The world will be different by morning." He nodded towards the waiting dirigible. "Wherever you were going, you should get there. At least until we can sort all this out." There was a pause. "I should have backed you."

"Yes," she told him "You should have." And then, "Thank you." She thought she even meant it.

Not waiting for things to get awkward, she allowed herself to be helped by the Martians to the dirigible. Once inside, she slumped into a seat just as the craft lurched off the ground and watched their slow ascent into Marrakesh's night and down to where Aziz still stood. He grew smaller as the pulled away, melding into the city. Turning, she looked to the Martians that sat nearby. No longer wrapped in the glamour, they regarded their mambo with silver eyes. Expectant eyes. There was more to show her.

When a tentacle extended in invitation, she gladly, eagerly, accepted.

And the Four became One.

A MINNOW, OR PERHAPS
A COLOSSAL SQUID

CARLOS HERNANDEZ AND *C. S. E. COONEY*

From the Monograph Sirenas of Garganta *by Ven. Damiana Cardosa
y Fuentes, Doctora de Filosofia Naturál*

*T*hey are gigantic. We could not see sirenas because they are
gigantic!

Too long have our imaginations been limited by sea shanties that
portrayed sirenas as lusty, acid-tongued wenches who (how?) learned to
speak flawless Mariposan while underwater; or else sly anthropovores
whose songs make thralls of concupiscent mariners; or any other myth
that characterizes them as anything resembling us.

They are not like us. So that I, Ven. Damiana Cardosa y Fuentes, do
not die in vain, understand this: they are not human. They are as different from humans as the butterfly is from the fly.

The eternal challenge of humanity can be summed up thusly: you
are a small animal of little stature; you are mortal; you are scared. Think
bigger. Die young if you must, for even if you live to be a hundred years
old, you will die young. Think bigger.

But enough poesy. Let us turn to natural philosophy.

* * *

Estrella Santaez y Perreta was the "empress" of el Estanque. Estrella always liked to imagine herself empress of something, and she would work with whatever was in front of her. When she was younger and far more imperious, her gifts had brought her to the attention of the royal executioner, who in time had offered her this apprenticeship. One day, Estrella herself would be royal executioner.

But for now, she was merely el Estanque's empress—which on most days amounted to being royal aquarium cleaner. She looked after the morosely pop-eyed fish who used to be debtors, cleaned their tanks, changed their water, and shook earthworms and shrimp meal over their pools at dawn and at twilight.

"El Estanque" was just how it was commonly known—the name mothers used to frighten fractious children: "Behave, diablito, or I'll pitch you into el Estanque!"; leg-breakers to warn delinquent gamblers: "It's either your kneecaps or a stint at el Estanque!"; or words of warning whispered in the dimly lit Mariposan lupanars: "Not that one, love; his one true mistress is el Estanque, who eats every coin he makes." The proper name of el Estanque, the one by which every prodigal noble of the court of Reina Ténebra knew and feared it, was el Acuario Real para los Deudores y Pobres de la Isla de las Mariposas. It was engraved right there on the marble facade. It would be one of the last things you read with human eyes if you were drowning in debt and unable to pay your way back to breathable air.

When Estrella first came to apprentice under the executioner, she was surprised to be given as her first duty charge over el Estanque. She thought she would be learning how to transform murderers into birds—like a proper executioner—not debtors into fish.

But, as her mentor told her, "Well, your grace, even an executioner has to start somewhere."

"Your grace" was what was what the executioner had called her ever since the day they met—Estrella at age six, the executioner who knew how old? It was both a tease and an honorific. The executioner was comfortable expressing herself in contradictions.

But it was not as if Estrella did not enjoy learning a lot about fish. And rarework. And how to turn people into fish.

The most popular fish, naturally, was cod, because everybody knew what that was. If you didn't have a better thought in your head, you became a cod. But the wise and studied conspired to become convict cichlids, as these fish were hardy and long-lived. Their lifespans ranged from eight to ten years; if you couldn't clear your debts in a decade, well, you were never going to clear them, were you?

Some nobles thought the cichlid beneath them, however. They tried to bribe the pretty, young guardiana del Acuario Real to give them a shape more robust and alarming, like that of the gurry shark or the bowhead whale or the bigmouth buffalo. Estrella never accepted their bribes. Instead, she talked her tongue to chalk attempting to explain the numinous nature of rarework. Pescafication was a compromise between herself, the debtor, and los Matadores, who watch from beyond the sky and decide who lives and who dies and what shape they must take meantime. But try sometime to tell a rich person that money will not solve their problems if you want to waste your life.

There were many other kinds of fish in el Estanque, as many and various as there were ways to go into debt! There were goldfish, koi, clown loaches, and pacus, not to mention quahog clams, crabs and lobsters, octopuses of every size, and alligator gar as long as your nieta.[*]

There were two kinds of pools in el Estanque: salt water and fresh water. Both were crowded to such a degree that Estrella always found many fish—too many fish—floating at the surface when she unlocked the doors each morning.

Those were the worst moments of her apprenticeship. Her dread began before she even mounted the steps of el Estanque every morning, for she could feel within her the emptiness of the prisoners who had died overnight. Her rarework created a bond between herself and those she transformed that was only severed when they became human

---

[*] Ven. Aurelia Tierradulce y Matos, famous for her extravagance, became an entire coral reef. So robust a reef, in fact, that when she was returned to her human form a mere four months later (her debt having been paid by a windfall from a dying uncle) much of the coral remained. It was transported to the beaches near the Palacio de las Sombras where it could flourish.

again or when they were no longer anything. But nothingness, though substanceless, is not weightless. Not when that nothingness was once a living soul.

"It does not seem like justice, tía," Estrella told the executioner, who was not her tía, but who was everyone's tía. She had that sort of face. "Did not Reina Ténebra build her aquarium to improve the plight of debtors?"

"Fewer die now than did," replied the executioner. "And their lives are much gentler. Surely you learned in school of the squalor and misery of the debtors' prisons of yore?"

"The squalor of the past does not excuse the iniquities of the present."

The executioner conceded the point with a nod. "If you think el Estanque is an unjust holding cell for debtors, your grace," said the executioner, "how will you feel when your apprenticeship is done, and I hand you over my keys to the Henhouse, and your job becomes the care and maintenance of the avified?"

The Henhouse, like el Estanque, was the vulgar word for Her Majesty's Aviary of Murderers, where resided all the most dangerous criminals of la Isla de las Mariposas, whom the executioner had changed, via her unparalleled rarework, into birds. The condemned were given the option to take their chances as a bird out in the wild, but everyone knew that birds in the wild had a much higher chance of dying, or of forgetting too much of their human selves before they could rejoin Mariposan society as repentant, model citizens. Most, therefore, laid their nests in the Henhouse.

Plenty died there as well, of course. But more survived their stints in the Henhouse than had ever survived the gallows or the chopping block. Because, really, who survives a chopping block?

"Ah!" Estrella scolded, shaking her finger at the executioner. "I know that when you start asking me questions, tía, it means you are done answering my own!"

"When we are exploring questions of philosophy," replied the executioner, genuinely surprised, "I believe that your grace has as many valid answers as do I. Have we not conversed thusly all our lives?"

They had, and Estrella laughed in apology for her teasing.

She then begged leave of the executioner to go away and dress for the party she was attending that night. The executioner, feigning indignation, asked who would be feeding the fish whilst Estrella danced with courtiers and delighted in genteel persiflage?

"Why, I will, of course," Estrella replied. "Afterwards."

She attended her party, only for an hour or so. But in that hour, she shone brighter than even her namesake. She danced every dance, drank the dry, sparkling wine her host pressed on her, and flirted her fan and fishtailed her train at every eligible courtier with a swagger and a jaunty grin. From the center of her circle of sycophants, even Reina Ténebra raised a glass to her.

But Estrella left the party early and went, still dressed in her glittering gown, to pace beside the ceramic pools of el Estanque, dreamily scattering fishfood. The night guard was surprised to see her; this was not her usual shift. But Estrella was Guardiana en Jefe of el Estanque, and if she chose to spend her nights here rather than in the arms of a lover, who would gainsay her?

She stayed until dawn, absorbed in her charges. Patiently she separated the fighting fish by rearranging their potted plants, driftwood, and rocks to confuse their territory. She checked the pale, listless fish for tail rot or dropsy, and whenever she found signs of infection, she quarantined the sick in large glass bowls, which she left in the office of the chief veterinarian, who would diagnose and medicate them properly in the morning.

Sometimes, rage surged in her like waves crashing against the malecón. Maybe el Estanque was a better prison that the cruel prisons of the past; that did not make it good. Or just. Or desirable. Tonight, like so many nights before, she felt a nigh-irresistible urge to turn all the fish back into humans and end this inhumane practice herself.

But she never did.

CARLOS HERNANDEZ and C. S. E. COONEY

* * *

From the Monograph Sirenas of Garganta *by Ven. Damiana Cardosa
y Fuentes, Doctora de Filosofía Naturál*

I base the following description of that animal known popularly as
"sirena" and called by philosophers "las ahogaderas"[†] on four different
specimens that I recovered during a voyage, which I myself financed, to
the eternal maelstrom Garganta. I spent my family's fortune in the name
of discovery, and I have succeeded. If we are a society that values truth
and knowledge, then my endeavors will be seen as valuable.

And if not, not. I will give you in these pages everything that I
have learned. It is for you decide what price this knowledge merits. If it
merits nothing in your seeming, turn me into a minnow in el Estanque
where we Mariposans, in our wisdom and mercy, deposit our debtors. A
minnow, if you will: I pray to be eaten quickly, since there is zed chance
I will ever have the funds to spring myself out of that algae-choked hell:
not without intervention from la reina herself, and we all know how
likely that is.

No matter. My only regret is that I have never encountered a living
sirena, now that I know what to look for. Add it to the list of indignities
that are the contents of my life.

But come, enough self-pity. Let us turn to natural philosophy.

Estrella always anticipated Debtor's Day with both dread and excitement. Today would be more merciful than most: she had three debtors
to release, and only one to imprison!

There in la reina's throne room, before the mighty Trono Sapiente
itself, two of the three potential parolees (a flirtatious koi with beautifully brocaded scales in metallic gold and silver, and a feisty fighting
betta with a fierce bite and fins so flowy they resembled Rojas lace)
were swimming in their separate crystal bowls. The third parolee was

---

† Or "the women who drown [humans]." At this point in history, there are exactly zed verified cases of
humans who have been drowned by sirenas. Let this serve as proof that natural philosophy needs to engage
in a great deal of self-examination before it can claim it has freed itself from the prejudices it has inherited
from society at large.

a handsomely spotted horn shark so large that Estrella had to conscript two of her crew to wheel its glass tank into the palacio.

The courtiers who loitered in the throne room gasped and tittered behind lace fans at one another, each outdoing the other with their histrionic horror. A shark was still a novelty to any Mariposan who did not live and die by the whim of the sea.

The three parolees, as you might have guessed, were themselves all courtiers. Commoners rarely found means to pay off their debts, and when it happened, the event was surrounded by no pomp. But the courtiers—ah! They were given mantles of velvet from Reina Ténebra's own hands, and a kiss of welcome on each cheek, a third upon their forehead. Often, there was a ball held in their honor that night—should, that is, their families be able to afford such a festivity.

Many borrowed heavily in order that they should.

Today, Estrella was most nervous about the debtor she was to imprison. She was a great admirer of Ven. Damiana Cardosa y Fuentes. She'd read every monograph on the *Sirenas of Garganta* that the doctora had penned, had saved all the illustrated broadsides detailing "Damiana's Adventures at Sea"—often in song or verse. The discoveries she'd made at the edge of the whirlpool, the recovery of those colossal cadavers, and the public autopsies she'd performed in the old coliseum, which she'd mortgaged her family's ancestral home to turn into a medical theatre: there was no one in the world like Dra. Cardosa y Fuentes.

Once, Estrella had attended a lecture Ven. Damiana gave at the Royal University. The executioner, who knew the infamous natural philosopher more than just casually, had cadged Estrella an invitation to a private dinner held afterwards at an exclusive restaurant. (The executioner was a master of giving Estrella inimitable, priceless gifts.)

Estrella had been too intimidated to say much that night, and could barely eat anything, but she'd listened to Ven. Damiana hold forth ever more eloquently as the fine wine flowed. The others in attendance, courtiers to a one, lost interest long before Estrella did. Before the evening was over, she found herself the sole audience of this fascinating, formidable woman, who looked right into her eyes without ever seeming to blink or breathe, and spoke to her about sirenas—myth, history, fact, wonder.

And now, here was Ven. Damiana Cardosa y Fuentes, a debtor by any definition, who had declared in her latest article, which had been circulating like wildfire at court, that she wanted Estrella to turn her into a minnow.

A minnow!

Estrella didn't know if she could manage it. She could not *imagine* Ven. Damiana as a minnow. In no world could this wild-haired woman, with her tall boots and patched trousers, her strident, raspy voice that overrode all other sounds, her spectacles that seemed to reflect blue-violet fires—like the ghostly corposants that cling to the masts of ships in peril—be reconceptualized as a bait fish. Estrella just could not do it. Not even the Matadores, she was convinced, could do it.

But when Estrella murmured her concerns to the executioner that morning before they each took their places to the right and left of el Trono Sapiente, the executioner merely returned her a strained little smile.

"Rarework," she replied, "rarely goes awry. It may not go as anyone expects, but it will not play a fair worker foul. Try not to fall prey to your anxieties. Remember your forms and rituals. Be respectful, be precise, and—if at all possible—be impartial."

"But you are never impartial!" Estrella cried.

The executioner shrugged. "I am your cautionary tale."

On cue, Reina Ténebra's herald of arms announced the official commencement of Debtor's Day. All the courtiers assembled shook out their hems, and repositioned their feet, and contorted their postures into attitudes of attentiveness and expectancy. La reina herself mounted the steps of the dais and settled onto el Trono Sapiente.

"Presenting la Guardiana en Jefe del Acuario Real!" shouted the herald of arms.

Now Estrella stepped down from the dais, removed her outer robe to stand in a short tunic of byssus which served as her ceremonial swimwear, and made her courtesy to the court. Clearing her throat, she pronounced:

"I, Ven. Estrella Santaez y Perreta, stand before el Trono Sapiente and before all of you who are gathered here, to perform la reina's justice."

Silence filled every throat in the room.

A MINNOW, OR PERHAPS A COLOSSAL SQUID

From the Monograph Sirenas of Garganta *by Ven. Damiana Cardosa
y Fuentes, Doctora de Filosofia Naturál*

But first, my indulgent reader, a word on how terrible we are at knowledge.

What a mess our language is! How orotund and phatic, brimming with folderol, convoluted and locution-laden. It is a wonder anyone can become literate at all! If we were wise, we would create a single language so perfect that we would never need turn to a separate language for mathematics, philology, alchemy, or rarework. Instead, we insist on dividing knowledge into false categories, thereby assuring ourselves gaps in our knowledge of nature and supernature.

It is almost as if we are insisting on remaining ignorant.

To the future natural philosophers who will find my feeble attempts at a taxonomy laughable, I say this: swallow your laughter and shit it out later, when you're alone on the pot and it will do no one harm. For I, too, as a young philosopher, spent a great deal of time chortling at the mistaken notions of my forebears. I wondered how they, presumably among the finest thinkers of their respective generations, could have been so wrong.

The answer, of course, is that it is easy to see the answer when you have already been given the answer.

But enough epistemology. Let us arrive, finally, at the meat course of this dinner. What follows is the most complete and rigorous taxonomy of sirenas ever written on the planet Gloriana.

Estrella's rarework went off without a hitch.

Well, except that Ven. Zaira lost her grip on Estrella's hand as she was being helped from the shark tank and fell back in and floundered for a while.

And Ven. Vega almost bit a chunk out of Estrella as she was being un-bettaed back to her human form, but remembered herself just in time and apologized most humbly and profusely.

Ven. Oriol, upon being relieved of his koi-ness, fainted coyly. His grateful husband clasped him close to his breast and revived him with kisses in no time at all—to the great entertainment of all gathered.

But the real entertainment was yet to come, when Ven. Damiana Cardosa y Fuentes was to be brought before el Trono Sapiente. Only after the puddles were mopped away, the crystal bowls and shark tank cleared, and Estrella toweled off, newly composed for this next, much harder piece of rarework, did the guards bring their newest prisoner into the throne room.

She was already talking. Ven. Damiana did not have to be dragged; she marched forward, gesticulating so hugely that the guards surrounding la reina kept stiffening like hunting cats with every sweep of her arm. But for all she noticed them, they might have been flower arrangements at a banquet.

"This is your last chance, Patricia Viviana. You still have it within your power to forgive my debt and fund my next expedition. Do so, and your name will be illuminated in all the history books as the most rational monarch that our benighted Isla de las Mariposas has ever known. *Yours* shall be the eponym for the Ténebran College of Marine Biology that I shall found upon my deathbed."

Reina Ténebra rolled her eyes. "Dami," she returned, in a voice so fond it was querulous, "you will never found a college, or even so much as a country school. You have thrown your house out the window, and then thrown the window after it. The money that we have already lent you—a great deal of it, in good faith, with promises of tremendous return—we will never see again. True, you have made some discoveries that might yet benefit Mariposas. Even now, if you agree to indenture yourself to our great fisheries in order that you might work off your debt in honor, we would consider commuting your—"

"Don't bother," said Ven. Damiana, not horrified or furious, just contemptuous. "I have no interest in murdering whales for their grasa. Besides, who's to say that once you've hunted them to extinction, you won't go after my sirenas?"

Reina Ténebra retorted, "Why should we hunt sirenas—which would require an outlay of considerable resources, nay, an entire renovation of the industry!—when we have no proof that they possess assets of any value?" She leaned forward on her throne. "Unless . . . did you, perhaps, find evidence of their potential usefulness in one of your precious carcasses? Something, perhaps, that you concealed from publication?"

From the Monograph Sirenas of Garganta *by Ven. Damiana Cardosa y Fuentes, Doctora de Filosofía Naturál*

As I have stated, sirenas are gigantic. But what an incomplete conveyance of meaning "gigantic" provides you, estimable reader! Should I rather say "ciclópeo," or perhaps "descomunal"? Would "monumental" better render the breathtaking, expectation-destroying enormity of our sirenas? Perhaps "ingente"? "Inconmensurable"?

You are free to choose any word you wish when you write your own etiology. The only word I forbid, now and forever, is "monstruoso." Only fear of the unknown would compel a philosopher to call them monsters. And fear is the opposite of natural philosophy.

The four sirenas I recovered measured in length as follows: 41.246m, 41.471m, 44.028m, and 49.533m. The span of their two superior arms, which resemble human arms in proportion to the rest of the body, measured from the tip of the longest of their five fingers (that is to say, the index finger) of each hand, for each specimen and in the same order as given above, are as follows: 31.202m, 30.97m, 32.055m, and 36.624m.

The span of the two inferior arms, which connect at the midpoint of the sirena's torso,[‡] range in the four specimens as follows: 24.339m, 24.567m, 25.097m, and 29.428m. Given the strong musculature, the suppleness of the tendons, and signs of wear at the elbow and inferior shoulder joints, there is every reason to believe that the inferior arms are not vestigial, but are actively used by sirenas in their daily lives, though their exact functions I must leave to future philosophers.

Their tails formed more than half the length of their bodies: 20.724m, 21.221m, 23.793m, and 25.588m. Each ends in a horizontal fluke resembling in size and proportion that of the spermaceti whale,

---

[‡] The inferior hands are webbed, four-fingered, and, unlike the superior hands, lack opposable thumbs. They thus resemble the frog's manus.

complete with medial notch. Also similarly to whales, their tails are controlled by powerful epaxial and hypaxial muscles.§

The diameter at the shoulders for each of my four specimens run as follows: 4.701m, 4.684m, 5m exactly, and 6.11m. At their hips, I measured each at 4.963m, 5.177m, 5.385m, and 7.427m in diameter.

Since I am uncertain as to how public this account may spread, I will for the moment withhold the measurements of the chest and each of my specimens' six dugs. I do not wish to be accused of indecency, despite the fact that there is nothing at all indecent about studying the anatomy of an animal.

I will, however, for the sake of improving society, risk censure by saying this: the sirena possesses a cloaca, from which, it is clear from my dissections, it defecates, urinates, has sexual intercourse, and lays eggs that are larger than any human has ever been. There is no way imaginable for a sirena and a human to fornicate, unless, perhaps, the sirena decided to use an entire human's body as a dildonic appliance. There can be little doubt such activity would leave the human drowned and shattered.

Right-reasoning people of the world should take this as evidence abundant that sirenas and humans have never been, and will never be, amorously acquainted, despite the centuries of sailors' thwarted fantasies that litter our songs and myths.

In fact, my examinations have revealed the tantalizing possibility that sirenas may be a parthenogenic species, self-fertilizing, spermatozoon-free, endlessly motherful and forevermore fatherless. If this is the case, then, with philosophical certainly, I can state that the very last thing a sirena would want in its life—her life—is a pathetically small human seaman.

In reply to Reina Ténebra, Ven. Damiana sucked in such a breath that Estrella thought she was hoping to inflate herself till she loomed over el

---

§ Though I dare not speculate as to what the top speed of sirenas might be without beholding them in the wild, the fact that they prey upon the fastest alpha predators in the ocean, along with the fact that there is little likelihood they have much ability to camouflage themselves, makes the prospect that they can outpace some of the fastest predators in the sea a viable one.

Trono Sapiente. With face empurpled and spectacles ablaze, her strident voice reaching glass-cutting pitch, she declared:

"If you're thinking of going after them, I say to you, Patricia Viviana, it'd be wiser for you to cast your bullion into the whirlpool and your liver after it than to hunt sirenas in the deep. The only place we've found hard evidence of them—and of these specimens, only their dead—is in orbit around the Garganta, which chews up our whaling ships like birria and doesn't bother to spit them out again.

"They're drawn there in death; they don't *live* there. They don't construct castles at the bottom of the whirlpool, and build gardens of seashells, and wear gowns of pearl and pirate treasure, and gossip about the size of each other's dugs. They aren't *like* us. *Their* brains are seven times the size of ours, and like us they possess opposable thumbs— on their upper arms at least. Sirenas might very well use *tools*. Implements. *Weapons*. How might they defend themselves from danger? Imagine a sentient creature, empress of all ocean predators, imagine what she might do to one of your whaling ships once she puzzles out what, exactly, has been depleting her food supply? You think to hunt *them*?

"Try it," she dared them all, a martial gleam in her eye, "Try it, and la Isla de las Mariposas will find itself at war with a superior species— embraced by the powerful arms of the apex constrictor—*squeezed* dry!"

By now her raspy voice had dropped in pitch and timbre, not in exhaustion, but in enthusiasm. It reached from the elaborately painted tiles on the floor to the patterned cedar of the recessed ceiling to the entire court. Everyone in Estrella's range of vision leaned in to hear her, practically salivating: at the scandal, at the downfall of one of la reina's favorites, at the intoxicating vista of strange thoughts and new ideas that Ven. Damiana was presenting them. Estrella, too, felt her heart racing, her ears growing ears, her eyes growing eyes, the meat of her brain trying to trying understand what seven times itself might mean for its own understanding.

And what (Estrella thought wildly, suddenly) if sirenas are *rare-workers* too? What then, tía?

The doctora waved a hand, dismissing her dudgeon as if it were no more bothersome than smoke from a cheroot. "Ah! But I doubt such magnificent creatures would trouble themselves to eradicate a few diminutive, landlubbing, air-wheezing, island-hugging apes who wrongly think themselves the center of the universe. They have remained hidden up to now, after all. You will never find them. And moreover, you should pray that you don't."

"Well, then Dami," said Reina Ténebra into the throat-clearing silence, "if that is your final word on the subject?"

Every prisoner was entitled to their últimas palabras. Estrella was shocked to note that they had arrived at that part of the Debtor's Day ceremony already. Look, there was the executioner, waggling her eyebrows to indicate that it was, indeed, Estrella's turn to speak!

She swallowed and took one step closer to Ven. Damiana.

"Ven. Damiana, as prisoner indebted to Reina Ténebra, until such time as Casa Cardosa y Fuentes can make up your debt in bullion, labor, or a gift of like or equal value to Mariposan society, you are sentenced to pescafication in such form as you and I will shortly agree upon in raretime. Before we enter raretime, I must ask you: do you wish to serve your term in el Acuario Real or in the wilds of el océano Vino Blanco? Either way, you and I shall be bonded by my rarework and by the grace of los Matadores. If you choose the wild, know this: wherever you go in all the great world of Gloriana, I shall by our rarebond receive communications as to your location and well-being, and, at the time your term is up, if indeed there comes such a time, I shall be able to summon you home."

Ven. Damiana was smiling at her now, paying Estrella her full attention. "I recognize you, niña. You're the executioner's prodigy, aren't you? We ate dinner together at la Baraca. You were a marvelous conversationalist." She winked. "I'd like to be dumped in the bay behind el Estanque, thanks," she said in answer to Estrella's question.

She gave another wave of the hand, this time as if knocking down a house of cards. "And I've changed my mind about the whole minnow thing. Do you think you can make me a squid?"

A MINNOW, OR PERHAPS A COLOSSAL SQUID

From the Monograph Sirenas of Garganta *by Ven. Damiana Cardosa y Fuentes, Doctora de Filosofía Naturál*

The logical portion of my mind tells me to request to be turned into a minnow, so that I can die quickly and be rid of all of this unhelpful knowing that I carry around in my skull. But what, instead, if I could die as a meal for a sirena? I would like that, if somehow it could be arranged.

The sirena is omnivorous, as the variety of their cementum-covered teeth and the contents of their stomachs revealed during my dissections. Though I cannot generalize from only four specimens, the sirenas I investigated seemed in life to be partial to sharks, toothed whales, and colossal squid, since their digestive tracts and multiple stomachs were a treasure trove of teeth and beaks. They might, in their biomes, serve as a check to the outsized growth of top predators.

How exactly the sirenas kill these animals must remain a mystery until we acquire empirical evidence. Were I to conjecture, I would hypothesize that sirenas use their four arms to constrict their prey to death. Ram ventilators such as sharks would be immobilized and would immediately find it difficult to breathe, whales would have their lungs emptied and would soon drown, and colossal squid—well, sirenas probably need not waste time depriving a colossal squid of air. They probably just rend it to pieces, and then eat it up as daintily as we enjoy tripe soup.

I make this last conjecture unfancifully: those whales who, like the sirena, dine upon squid have sucker-scars all over their dermises, acquired during the great battles they must have fought with those monsters to earn their dinner. The four sirenas I dissected had no such scars on their bodies. The early evidence indicates that they can dismantle a kraken like a child pulling legs off a beetle.

Yes, perhaps I will ask the guardiana to turn me into a colossal squid and throw me into the sea. Then, I could range the abyssal depths until I found a hungry sirena. I would dance in front of her, cavorting and tumbling and seductively squirting ink. In that way, she would know me to be her meetest meat. She would grab my arms and pull my massive head free of them. Then, as I watched, she would eat my arms like a child eating licorice, twist by twist. I would be in shock and bleeding out, so perhaps I would not be aware when, saving the best for last, the sirena would eat my head and make me nothing.

But perhaps I would. I think I would like to behold my entrance into erasure.

The rest of the court, Estrella knew, were gathered on the southeast loggia of the Palacio de las Sombras, watching her rarework from its sheltered splendor while dining al fresco on delicacies of both surf and turf caught or slaughtered that morning. El Acuario Real flanked the palacio on the west, with the airy Aviary of Murderers soaring several stories high on the east, all part of the campus that included administrative buildings, courthouses, a planetarium, the natural philosophers' cabinet of curiosities, and a few of the oldest colleges of the Royal University, all lining the sea cliffs of los Centinelas.

But for the moment, at least, Estrella and Ven. Damiana were alone on the malecón, the paving stones of the breakwater wet beneath their bare feet. Rarework needed no incantation or grand gesture. The executioner sometimes prayed before she transformed a murderer into a bird. Estrella, rather, looked deeply into the eyes of her prisoner, and fixed them fast in her memory as the humans they were—flawed, desperate, frightened, *specific*. She gave them the gift of her fullest attention, her entire capacity for thought and feeling, an acknowledgement of their humanity. She doubted, in these moments, everything. And it was in that moment of doubt, in the locking of eyes, and the knowledge of her own and her prisoner's beautiful humanity, that she invoked her rarework.

But in that moment, the rarework wasn't hers alone. It was theirs. It was the rareworker's idea of justice, and the prisoner's idea of their transformed self, and whatever inscrutable logic the Matadores applied to these matters. Estrella's mouth would fill with the taste of brine, and her eyes spill over with tears, and then everything would go a clear and pale gold, like the world was being washed in wine.

She, in her swimming tunic, and Ven. Damiana, naked,[¶] made their way down the slippery stone steps of the malecón. Together, they stepped into the gray-green waves of el océano Vino Blanco, until they stood in water up to their thighs. They held hands. Ven. Damiana's hand was colder than the water. She was trembling.

When Estrella saw Ven. Damiana's chin lift, she lifted hers as well, determined to be as brave. Their eyes met.

On the loggia of the Palacio de las Sombras, the court of Reina Ténebra marveled once again at this work, which was, in truth, so exceedingly rare.

Letter from Estrella Santaez y Perreta to the Society of Natural Philosophers, Year 34 of the Tenure of Reina Ténebra, in the Month of Cielo Desierto, Day 17.

To the Most Esteemed Members of La Reina's Society of Natural Philosophers,

It is my melancholy honor to present to you this description of a sea creature that heretofore has not been identified nor described in the annals of Glorianan science. The name I have given this fish carries with it the imprimatur of Reina Ténebra herself and may not be changed, save by royal fiat. What follows below is a description of this new fish which I have called the "chupasirena."

One of the peculiarities of rarework of which you may not be aware is that, at the moment of transformation, the rareworker is accosted by an onslaught of visions pertaining to the transformed. Those visions range from history to prophecy and reveal to me what fate awaits the transformed. When I search my inner life, I can feel every person whom I have transformed, individually and distinctly. I know whether they are well or sick, hungry or sated, frightened or calm. I also know if their minds are irretrievable, or whether they might still be returned to human form with their memories and personalities reasonably intact.

[¶] Her choice. Of course she was naked.

CARLOS HERNANDEZ and C. S. E. COONEY

In the pescafication of Ven. Damiana Cardosa y Fuentes into her chupasirena form I experienced (and continue to experience) the clearest line of communication I have ever known between myself and one of the transformed. I am regularly receiving dispatches from her now—images, sounds, physical feelings—from the lightless depths where now she flourishes. Such an ongoing, powerful, and limpid link between minds is unprecedented in rarework to my knowledge, and to the knowledge of my mentor. I consider it nothing less than a miracle, a gift from los Matadores.

It is from this connection that I am able to give you the account of the heretofore unidentified fish, namely, the chupasirena, that follows.

For clarity's sake, let us say the chupasirena greatly resembles the famous and well-documented remora. It, like the remora, is a symbiote; the chupasirena has formed a mutually beneficial relationship with a powerful creature of the sea. The remora has its famous friend, the shark, and the chupasirena has its sirena.

Once Ven. Damiana was pescafied, I fainted, and my vision joined Ven. Damiana's in an act that can be called nothing less than clairvoyance. We traveled through an ink-thick darkness that was—please note this, philosophers—no impediment to the self-illuminating eyes of the chupasirena. The ocean makes for such a strange, slow medium!

Deeper and deeper we swam, Ven. Damiana assured of her destination as if she were a native of the ocean. I realized suddenly how little time we on land spend looking up. Underwater, however, a predator can attack you from any of 1080°. How two-dimensional my life on land felt, and how wide my vista underwater!

During a vision, time speeds up during periods of uninterest and slows down at moments of importance—the opposite of how time normally works for us here on land.

I cannot say how long we swam or how deep we dove. At some point, I simultaneously registered that in the black zones to which we descended, the pressure would squeeze a human body to death, and that the chupasirena finds that pressure quite pleasant and comforting. It is built for the deep.

Time slowed again when the chupasirena arrived at her destination. Her destination was a harmony of sirenas.

This harmony consisted of at least seven sirenas, who, despite their massive forms, cavorted with one another with all the obvious and contagious joy of porpoises. They moved so quickly, in fact, and were of such an immensity that I found it difficult to count them. My view was also impeded by the fact that Ven. Damiana was following her new instincts as a chupasirena and, well, began chupando the nearest sirena.

That is to say, she shot over to the nearest sirena and began chewing on some sort of tubæform ectoparasite that had attached itself to the sirena's lower back. The parasite—an eyeless, mouth-and-sack nightmare—had affixed itself just above the seam where mammalian-seeming flesh turned into piscine-seeming scales.

After Ven. Damiana had finished her meal,[**] not a mark was left on the sirena's skin where once the parasite had fed off her.[††] I am recalled to a childhood experience where I yanked a leech off my leg, instead of letting my parents remove it with art and delicacy, and the scar left behind remains there to this day. Clearly, the sirena and the chupasirena have come to an agreement: "You may eat of the bounty of parasites on my body," says the sirena to the chupasirena, "and I, in turn, will not make a meal of you."

But here my clairvoyance began to fade. While my mind retreated from hers, I saw, swarming around the sirenas, a large school of chupasirenas. They zipped about, circling and tumbling as much as the sirenas themselves—and, I came to realize, with the sirenas. I wonder now if the typical chupasirena is an exceptionally intelligent fish, one that perhaps the sirenas have domesticated and bred for its usefulness, as we have dogs. Indeed, the chupasirena reminds me strongly of the dog, for its frolicsome nature and its desire to please its master. This I felt from within Ven. Damiana herself, who, in my last memory of her, was charging gleefully into the school of chupasirenas and playing

---

[**] It is my pleasure to inform you that either my clairvoyance did not also impart a transmission of the gustatory sense, or the chupasirena does not possess it, for I tasted nothing of that ghastly meal.

[††] I have adopted the convention in Ven. Damiana's late writings to refer to sirenas as "she/her," with the understanding that you, as natural philosophers, may in due time find a more appropriate referent for this species, which, as you know from Ven. Damiana's writings, may be sexually monomorphic.

CARLOS HERNANDEZ and C. S. E. COONEY

among the harmony of sirenas. It was as if she had always been a part of their community.

Her feeling of happiness was so complete in that moment that it has no equal in the human mind.

Ven. Damiana's felicity is our loss. She will never, ever, ever, come back to us, no matter how I call her. Humanity will never again benefit from her numberless gifts, save through the messages she deigns to transmit to me, for as long as they last.

But know, natural philosophers, that I will dutifully relay to you everything that Ven. Damiana teaches me about sirenas, chupasirenas, and life under the sea. Even now, I must write to you a second letter regarding the means by which sirenas use the scalding ejecta of fumaroles to bathe themselves and their beloved chupasirenas!

Until then, please know that I remain the obedient servant of los Matadores, la reina, my mentor, and you, friends and colleagues. My greatest desire is to witness a growing alignment of science and rarework until that momentous day when our two disciplines will become one.

With all Gratitude and Respect,

Ven. Estrella Santaez y Perreta

Guardiana en Jefe del Acuario Real para los Deudores y Pobres de la Isla de las Mariposas

THE FOX'S DAUGHTER

RICHARD PARKS

W hen the messenger arrived at my Kamakura estate, I knew he wasn't human, and that meant trouble. I read the letter three times, as if repetition would lead to better understanding. Foolish of me, as Lady Kuzunoha's direct nature would not allow for misinterpretation:

"I have been summoned to serve as Guardian of the Inari Shrine. This will require my absence from Shinoda Forest for half a year, possibly longer. As you may not be aware, I have a daughter now, Kimiko. This is a dangerous time for one of her age, and to leave her with neither protection nor guidance for so long is out of the question. I regret I must presume upon our old friendship to ask if you would be willing to assume that role until my return . . . "

There was more, but this was the core of it. "I didn't know Lady Kuzunoha had a daughter."

My wife, as was her habit, took the news with serenity. "Foxes like to keep their secrets," Tagako-hime said.

I frowned. "You knew Lady Kuzunoha was a fox?"

My lady did me the courtesy of not laughing. "Foxes are the traditional messengers and guardians of Inari. In addition, I've known Lady Kuzunoha almost as long as you have. When I served at the Ise Shrine she was a frequent visitor. As with Master Kenji, she is very pious . . . in her own way."

My day had started well enough. Warm enough for a fall morning, the momiji leaves were starting to show their red and yellow autumn colors. And yet again I was being reminded of all the things I did not know, either about people or the world itself. It was at once exciting and frightening. The first because understanding I still had much to learn reminded me that my life's journey was nowhere near complete. The latter because I well knew the dangers of ignorance.

"Lady Kuzunoha is a fox, and thus so is Kimiko," I said. "If we take her in, there are risks involved, and I have you and our daughters and my son to consider. What must I do?" I immediately felt foolish as Tagako-hime deftly clarified the situation.

"Beloved, your son is away, as he often is lately, and I will see to our daughters. Lady Kuzunoha considers you her friend, a word I know she does not use lightly. A friend has asked for your help. You will do what you know is right."

The messenger was waiting. I went to my studio to compose my reply.

Kenji, to my annoyance, found the entire situation rather amusing when we spoke that afternoon at his temple. In his role as abbot, he considered this "counselling" me. I found that annoying as well. "You've often complained of boredom in your new status as a provincial daimyo, Yamada-sama. I think perhaps those days of tedium may be at an end."

"I fail to see the humor in this," I said.

"Then, with all due deference, you're not trying. Clearly this is some aspect of your karma manifesting itself. That it would do so in the form of a young fox vixen I find intriguing, to say the least."

"I am not responsible for the way your mind turns, Kenji-san. I am, however, responsible for the safety of the people on my estates, as well as that of Kimiko-chan when she is under my care. I trust you do understand my concerns?"

"For my own part she has nothing to fear, and thus neither have you. Lady Kuzunoha is a dangerous creature, but there's no harm in her save for those who seek to do harm to *her* or those she cares for. I suspect we will find Kimiko the same."

"Lady Kuzunoha hinted that Kimiko's age may be an issue. By which I understand she is now a nogitsune, a wild, uncultured fox. If true it's not a shortcoming on Kimiko's part, but rather a matter of age and experience. That could complicate matters."

Kenji looked thoughtful. "I daresay. We both know the nature of Lady Kuzunoha's home, which is as dangerous as she is and rough and wild besides . . . did it never occur to you that Kimiko's mother may have a dual purpose, the second of which is to expose the girl to gentler influences than those present in Shinoda Forest?"

"Gentler? Kenji-san, are you not acquainted with my daughters at all?"

Kenji grinned. "Now you're trying. Still, if it will allay your concerns, I will make it a point to be present when the girl arrives. If there's any hint of malice or evil intent, I should be able to sense it."

"With all due respect to Lady Kuzunoha, I would appreciate your assistance."

Couriers brought word on the third day after my discussion with Abbot Kenji. Kimiko would be arriving at my estate the following afternoon. Tagako-hime had of course already arranged for an appropriate room, or at least one appropriate for a human girl, with clothes chest, writing desk, plus assorted other items of a more feminine nature that I barely understood. My own preparations consisted of sending for Kenji at his temple. By the next day we were as prepared as one could be, not really knowing what to expect.

Kimiko arrived early that afternoon, in an ox-drawn carriage suitable for a young lady of high birth. It was all illusion, of course. The attendants and guards and the ox were all foxes, though of course they appeared perfectly human save for the ox. It was only my trained senses that let me discern their true nature, betrayed in the sudden appearance of a paw where a hand should be, quickly hidden up a sleeve. That, and the fact I expected nothing else. The cart itself was nothing but shaped mist and foxfire. Even so, the illusion was quite powerful. I had no doubt that anyone else—aside from a trained priest like Kenji—seeing the carriage and escort passing by would be absolutely convinced of its reality.

"Well done, indeed," Kenji whispered, echoing my own thought.

When Kimiko descended from the carriage, it was quite a different matter. As Lady Kuzunoha herself had once explained to me, her human form was real, not illusion, but rather a sort of mask concealing her true nature. When Kimiko politely kneeled before us, I did see a human girl of about sixteen with long black hair down her back tied with a red silk ribbon, and no fox at all. Tagako-hime took the girl's hands and raised her up, and it was only then I got a good look at Kimiko's face.

So much like her mother.

"You are welcome here," I said, and Kimiko blushed.

"My mother thanks you for your kindness. I will try not to be a burden to you," she said.

I was full of questions, which of course Tagako-hime suspected as she used this chance to spirit Kimiko away with my daughters Kaoru, Rie, and Raishi close behind. I heard excited chatter and some giggling before they disappeared into the house.

"Well?" I asked Kenji.

"No ill intent, yet . . . interesting," was all he said at first.

"I trust you have more of an impression than that."

He grinned. "Oh, several. What's interesting is, whoever her father may have been, he was no fox. The girl is at least partly human, I'm sure of it, only . . ."

"Only you would expect her to be at least half human, and she isn't?"

He frowned. "Yes, how did you . . . oh. Then you think you know who the father is. So do I."

"Unless we're both badly mistaken, it's Lord Yasuna."

Lady Kuzunoha had been Lord Yasuna's wife before her true nature had been revealed, forcing their separation. Yet Lord Yasuna himself was half-fox, a fact I was certain he remained ignorant of to this day. It was now clear they had been together on at least one more occasion since their separation, and the result was now becoming acquainted with my wife and daughters.

"Whether that was wise on either of their parts is their business, not mine," I said. "Yet the consequences still reach me."

"Quite a lovely consequence. She's as beautiful as her mother," Kenji said. "In her human form."

"I hope you're simply pointing out the obvious, you old letch," I said.

He just sighed. "Time has since taken what my priestly training could not. One of my many failures, Lord Yamada."

Despite our new addition, all was peaceful for the first several days. Tagako-hime especially, I noticed, seemed as taken with the girl as my daughters were. As they were far better suited to the task, I was more than happy to leave the matter of "gentling" Kuzunoha's daughter in their capable hands. It was not as if I had nothing else to do, with overseeing the training of our mounted archers in my son's absence and settling the endless disputes among the villages in my domain.

Unfortunately, Kimiko-chan had other plans. About two weeks after Kimiko's arrival, Tagako-hime came to me.

"There's something I think you should know," she said. "A few days ago Kimiko came to me and said she needed to get outside for a while. I thought at first she simply wanted to spend time in the garden. No. She meant as a fox."

I took a moment to reflect. "Well, I suppose it's natural that she might find her human form . . . constricting."

"I considered that as well. She did ask, and as there are no hunters on our estate I didn't see the harm. Now she says she feels more comfortable in the abandoned temple. She wants to stay there for the time being."

There had been a temple on the estate long before I acquired it, but that temple had fallen into ruin. Kenji's temple was built on a more fortunate site, or at least we hoped this was the case.

Perfectly suitable den for a wild fox, I thought. *Arguably less so for a young woman, even one almost but not entirely fox.*

"What do our daughters think of all this?"

"As for Rie, Kaoru, and Raishi, they think it's a marvelous idea. I had to dissuade them from joining her."

I was not at all surprised. "That is out of the question. As for Kimiko, I want to refuse, yet I am unsure if that is the proper course. As a fox, Kimiko knows her business better than I do, and nowhere in Lady Kuzunoha's letter did she ask me to train her daughter to be human."

"She is a fox," Tagako-hime said firmly. "As she is part human, I hope we can have some influence still, but nothing will or should change her true nature. Perhaps allowing her to make her own decisions—and her own mistakes—is a reasonable course."

It was still against my better judgment, but I saw nothing but unreasonable alternatives. "So be it."

Two weeks later I received word of an outbreak of a strange plague in four of the villages in my jurisdiction. Kenji took it upon himself to visit them all. While he had always been pious, in his fashion, his selfless dedication to the people under his care would have been remarkable a few short years prior. Now, I was not surprised in the least. Responsibility changes a person, as I knew as well as anyone.

Upon his return, Kenji sent me a message requesting a meeting. He asked me to come to his temple, and I tried not to read anything ominous in the fact.

While my escort waited outside, I found Kenji in the temple lecture hall, alone, looking over a map spread out on small table.

"Lord Yamada, thank you for coming. While I believe the sickness did not follow me, for your family's sake I thought it might be safer to meet here. Feel free to keep your distance if you think it best."

"Is the disease so virulent?" I asked.

"Buddha be praised, no one has died yet," he said, "but that's only a matter of time if we do not eliminate the cause. I have seldom seen worse, yet at the same time I sensed nothing at any of the villages. A god of pestilence, a vengeful spirit, or even some variety of curse would have shown some sign of its presence."

That was strange indeed. While Kenji had no small ability as a healer, his true talent was in perceiving, identifying, and eliminating the causes of disease and other misfortunes. It did speak well of him that he volunteered his services in this matter, but in truth there was no one else as qualified. If he sensed nothing, then a resolution might prove more difficult than I had imagined.

Nor, considering Kenji's information, did we have the luxury of time.

"While I take you at your word that this pestilence, whatever it is, has not followed you, as a precaution I will send word to Tagako-hime that I will be away until this matter is concluded."

"She will not be pleased," Kenji said.

"No, but she and my daughters will be safe, which is more important. For now, show me what you're looking at."

"Here you can see the borders of your estates clearly marked. And here," he said, pointing to four black pebbles arranged in a rough square, "are the positions of the four stricken villages. I was trying to see if there was anything connecting the outbreaks. Routes of travel, that sort of thing."

"And?"

Kenji sighed. "And nothing. Of course there is trade and travel—and bickering—among them, but that's true of every village in your jurisdiction and beyond, including those communities which have been spared. So far the contagion is confined to these four, with no apparent cause."

"While it is fortunate it hasn't spread, the fact that it hasn't is very strange . . . . Oh."

I saw it then. Something Kenji, surprisingly, had overlooked.

"The old temple," I said. "Kimiko has taken up residence there."

He took another look at the map, and then shook his head. "I must be getting blind as well as old. It's in the center, isn't it? Almost equally distant from all four."

"No doubt why it was built there in the first place. A strategic placement, if not a fortunate one."

"Likely something aside from Kimiko-chan has taken up residence in the ruins. Something malevolent," Kenji said. "I should have burned the place to the ground."

At that moment I agreed with him, and I strongly hoped that the malevolence in residence Kenji suspected was not Kimiko herself, a possibility Kenji had tactfully omitted. Still, I had no choice but to consider the possibility.

"What shall we do?" Kenji asked.

"What we must," I said. "If we leave now, we can reach the old temple before nightfall."

Closely followed by the two Yamada clan archers who made up my escort, Kenji and I set a brisk pace to the ruined temple. It was a long path which gave us time to talk. This was not always a situation to be desired.

"Lord Yamada, why does Kimiko live out here? Even if you didn't feel comfortable letting Lady Kuzunoha's daughter into your house, surely you could provide better accommodations?"

"My comfort had nothing to do with it. Kimiko lives here because it is where she feels comfortable. As I said before, Kimiko is a nogitsune, a wild fox. The least experienced and cultured, but also the lowest rank in the fox hierarchy."

Kenji frowned. "As I understand the matter, Lady Kuzunoha is a zenko, which is a very high rank indeed among foxes. So why isn't her daughter of higher rank?"

"I do not pretend to understand everything, but I do know fox hierarchy doesn't work that way. Her birth matters little to anyone aside from Lady Kuzunoha herself. It is only with time and wisdom acquired that Kimiko will advance in rank . . . if she survives. Simply being young and ignorant is a difficult and dangerous time for someone like Kimiko-chan, as Kuzunoha-sama hinted."

"In that way humans and foxes are not so different. Lord Yamada, what will we do if Kimiko is the source of the contagion?"

I had been asking myself the same question since I looked at Kenji's map. If Kimiko was at fault and the act was malicious, would I, in order to protect the villagers under my care, be forced to deal with her and thus make a mortal enemy of someone as powerful as Lady Kuzunoha? Someone I still considered a friend? I wasn't as sure of the answer as I wanted to be, but I still had a faint hope, and I clung to it tightly.

"I have met the girl. While it is certainly within her power as a nogitsune to spread illness, I don't believe she would do such a thing, even as a trick," I said.

Kenji looked grim. "I hope, for her sake, you are right, Yamada-sama. But we must make certain."

The old temple came into sight. It was an eerie, shadowed place, even in daylight. The upswept corners of the roof always left the interior in shadow despite the missing roof tiles and the sagging lintel. I sent one archer to guard the rear of the building while the other kept close to us.

"Kimiko-chan? I need to speak with you."

She emerged onto the veranda almost immediately. She was in her human form as a winsome young girl, but I knew that was mostly to humor us. She kneeled. "To what do I owe the honor of this visit?" she asked formally.

I nodded at Kenji, who asked, "Kimiko-chan, several families near here have fallen ill. Do you know anything about it?"

While Kimiko, like any fox or indeed anyone, was capable of lying, it sounded like truth when she replied, "While I understand why you might think so, I do not. I've been here all the time, playing with my new doggy."

The hair on the back of my neck prickled. "A dog? Where did you find a dog?"

She smiled. "He found me. Apparently we were sharing the temple."

"Please show us."

Kimiko led us inside, toward the rear of the main hall where the cobwebs were thickest. "He stays here most of the time."

Something moved in the shadows. "Kenji—"

"I think I know," he said. There was a paper ward in his hand. We both saw what looked like a bundle of hair in the corner. It was definitely not a dog.

I pointed. "Kimiko-chan, *that thing* is a keukegen. It is a pestilent spirit that spreads disease and bad luck."

She looked surprised. "Really? My mother has mentioned them but I'd never seen one. I thought he smelled funny for a dog."

The creature growled much like a dog and gathered itself as if to spring. Kenji had apparently anticipated this and leaped forward with startling agility for his age and slapped the ward onto what appeared to be no more than a mass of hair.

The creature yowled, but the ward held it firmly in place as Kenji began the rite of exorcism and my archer kept a keen eye on it, bow drawn. I noted a single tear on Kimiko's otherwise stoic face, and I kept a close watch on her but she did not interfere.

When the rite was concluded, Kimiko-chan bowed again. "I have learned something today. I apologize for whatever trouble my ignorance may have caused."

"It wasn't your fault," I said. "But if any more creatures aside from yourself take up residence here, I would appreciate you letting us know."

When all was done, Kenji and I were back on the same path.

"Do you think she'll ever learn better?" he asked.

"Likely," I said. "She has time. The real question is, will we?"

It was just over a month following the incident at the old temple when my fellow vassal and neighbor, Lord Daiki, came to see me in person quite unexpectedly, and he was not in the best humor. I listened to everything he had to say and took a deep breath.

"I've heard your accusation, Lord Daiki. What I haven't heard is evidence."

Everything I said was accurate but perhaps not as diplomatic as it should have been, given his agitated condition. Lord Daiki was a hot-tempered blowhard of a type I knew well. Despite my personal opinion of the man, it was in our mutual interest to maintain good relations. Our overlord, Minamoto no Yoshiie, insisted upon it.

"Lord Yamada, my men followed the creature to your western barrier, where it disappeared; it must have entered your lands from there. What more evidence do you need?"

Actually, if I didn't already suspect the answer, I would have required a great deal more. As it was, I felt a surge of melancholy, fondly if fool-ishly remembering my time as the impoverished heir to a disgraced clan, with no responsibilities other than the temporary sort. Those days were long gone, and a feud with my neighbor certainly wouldn't bring them back, nor did I wish for either event except in moments of weakness.

"Lord Daiki, please understand—I consider a threat to you and your own the same as a threat to myself. If there is such a beast hiding on my estates, you may be assured I *will* find it. However, since your son was involved, I must ask if he had any explanation for what occurred? Did he see this thing you mentioned?"

For the first time Lord Daiki looked more uncomfortable than simply belligerent. "I *think* so, but I'm afraid Hideo made little sense. He kept calling it a 'she.' Such as 'Where is she?' and 'Where did she go?'"

I felt a chill. "What did your men see?" I asked.

"It was too dark to be sure, but it was nothing human. A wild beast of some sort, as I said, and right on my son's veranda."

"That is a serious matter. Rest assured I will take whatever action is necessary to protect us both."

Immediately after Lord Daiki's departure, I sent a message to Kenji with specific instructions, after which he was to meet me at the ruined temple we both knew well. The sun had not quite set when I arrived with my inevitable escort. Kenji appeared soon after.

"Well?" I asked.

"I sent my two best acolytes. They'll be finished before nightfall. Now then, what's all this about?"

"You'll see." I approached the ruins, with Kenji close behind. "Come out, Kimiko-chan. I know you're in there."

First there was only a pair of bright amber-yellow eyes visible, then a young fox vixen crept cautiously into view, a fox with two tails. I wasn't totally surprised at the number of tails. After all, she was Lady Kuzunoha's daughter, but this was the first time I had ever seen Kimiko in her true form. In another moment it wasn't a fox but a very pretty girl kneeling before us. I sighed. *So much like her mother.*

"You visited Lord Daiki's son last night, didn't you?"

"Yes, Lord Yamada," she said. "But—"

At least she didn't bother to deny it. "No excuses. I promised your mother I'd shelter you on the condition you stay out of trouble. How is *this* 'staying out of trouble'?"

She glanced down. "I honestly didn't see any harm. I saw him once when I was out hunting. He seemed lonely. I understood, since I'd lost my doggie."

I shuddered. "Let's not revisit that incident. I understand if you were feeling lonely, but I'd hoped for better judgment. So. Are you in love with Hideo? Tell the truth or I'll have Kenji-san compel it from you."

She looked down. "He was fun, and I liked him, but no. In truth I was bored."

That was a relief. Love always complicated things. Kimiko's mother and I, separately, had both learned that lesson.

"Kenji-san has placed spirit wards at Hideo's home. If you go there again, he will not see a beguiling girl. He will see a fox. With two tails. Do you understand?"

"Perfectly," she said.

Still a hint of defiance, despite everything. As expected. After all, she was Lady Kuzunoha's daughter. I had the answer to that, too.

"Kimiko-chan, don't force me to write your mother."

She lowered her gaze. "It seems I must apologize again, and I do. You may not believe this, Yamada-sama, but I really am trying."

Late fall turned to winter. I went on several occasions to the old temple during the harsher months to assure myself that Kimiko's den there was as comfortable as possible and that she wanted for nothing. As she still refused to move back to the main house, there was little else I could do. Fortunately there were no more incidents, or at least nothing to cause me concern.

That, in its own contrary way, caused me a great deal of concern. All winter I felt as if I was simply waiting for Kimiko to appear, smiling, in the center of some new complication, likely something terrible, something that I would not be able to fix with a simple exorcism or conceal with one of Kenji's inexhaustible supply of wards. Yet winter proceeded inevitably to spring in relative peace as the snow melted away.

The sakura were now in blossom. Tagako-hime invited Kimiko to our traditional flower-viewing party, the annual hanami, and she agreed to come.

I knew Kimiko was humoring us by accepting. On the other

hand, she knew she was still on shaky ground after the incidents with Lord Daiki's son and the plague monster, so her acceptance could be seen as more diplomatic than heartfelt. Still, I was more grateful for it than I cared to admit.

If any of these considerations weighed on Tagako-hime's mind, she didn't show it. She efficiently ordered and oversaw preparations as if nothing at all was unusual. I was just hoping for a quiet afternoon. I did not think I would get it.

We had three very fine cherry trees in full bloom; it was a sunny, warm spring day. Conditions could not have been more perfect, a situation which made me all the more uneasy.

Kenji arrived first, dressed in clean robes with his head freshly shaven. Tagako-hime brought out our daughters, Rie, Kaoru, and Raishi, dressed in their spring kimonos, perfectly groomed and on their best behavior. Kimiko arrived soon after, looking hesitant, but Tagako-hime and my daughters greeted her warmly and we took our places beneath the blossoming sakura.

"They're very lovely," Kimiko said, and that was all anyone said for a while.

Most eyes were on the pink sakura, but I simply couldn't concentrate. I was on edge, though there seemed no reason to be. Kimiko sat demurely between Tagako-hime and my daughters, and occasionally Tagako-hime or one of the girls would lean over and whisper to Kimiko, who more than once had to cover a giggle with her fan. Everyone seemed in good spirits, and I had to admit that even Kimiko's kimono was perfectly appropriate for the season. It reminded me of one I had seen before, and she was every bit the image of a proper young lady.

I'm missing something. What is it?

I glanced at Kenji, but he was no help. A servant finally brought saké and tea to mark the end of the hanami as the afternoon faded. Kimiko took her leave soon after . . . and nothing happened.

Later, when we were alone, Tagako-hime touched my shoulder. "Anata, you look puzzled. Is something troubling you?"

"Kimiko behaved herself. Nothing untoward happened, or has happened since the snows."

"And this surprises you?"

"Well . . . yes. She is a nogitsune, after all," I said.

"Whatever else she may be, she is also a young woman. She's been through a great deal."

"That is certainly true, though I don't believe either of us know the whole story."

Tagako-hime smiled then. "Oh, some of us may know more than others. By the way, I think Kimiko-chan will be ready to abandon her den and come back to us before long. Perhaps only as a courtesy, but still for the best."

It was only then that I remembered where I had seen Kimiko's kimono before. It was one our eldest, Rie, had worn the year before.

"You've been to see Kimiko, haven't you?"

"Several times," she said. "As have you. We did promise to look after the child, and I and your daughters were merely doing our part."

"But—" I started to protest when Tagako-hime pressed a finger to my lips.

"There are many things you know, Beloved," she said. "And there are some things which I know. One of them is simply this—not everything in the world is a puzzle to be neatly solved. Some require listening, forbearance, and patience."

I looked at her. "You've been counselling Kimiko all this time, haven't you? Something I should have been doing."

My wife demurred. "Counselling implies talking, and I doubt she was ready for that. Mostly I listened and set an example. You helped keep her out of trouble in your own way."

I could only marvel. "Listening, forbearance, and patience? I imagine I am also one who requires the services of all three."

She just smiled again. "Kimiko was right—the sakura were especially lovely this year, don't you think?"

As was often the case where Takago-hime was concerned, I could but agree.

THREE TALES FROM THE BLUE LIBRARY

SOFIA SAMATAR

THE CHILDREN OF PARADISE

They were a pair of fools, husband and wife, and none of their labors prospered. Their mint grew ragged, their chives sprouted thorns, and their child swelled and shrank with the weather. Nobody knew what this child's sickness was. In winter he filled up with poisonous gas, his limbs grew too stiff to move, and his parents had to drag him about in a wagon. In summer he withered and red streaks appeared on his skin. His desperate parents devoted their every instant to keeping him alive. They tried hot baths, ice baths, sunshine, darkness, vegetables, sweetbreads, gruels, exercise, study, rest, affection, beatings, purgings, and prayer. Their child possessed none of the patience of dying children in popular novels. "I hate you," he told them daily, "you fucking losers." At last his mother collected the dregs of the family silver, packed it in the pig's bladder that served as her purse, and went to visit the Good Friar Tello.

The Good Friar Tello had been defrocked for practicing black magic, but he still wore his brown robe and hempen belt. He lived in the great pine forest, in a crumbling, deserted abbey, with the grateful animals he had saved from death. An angel of stone wept over the door. When the woman knocked, a milk-white goat came to usher her in. Friar Tello was smoking a pipe, his feet resting on a docile boar. He asked the woman if she knew the Well of the Whores. "Of course," she said. This well stood at the edge of town; no one drank from it, for in the old days whores had been drowned there. "You must drop one gold piece into this well every Sunday for seven years," the friar murmured sleepily, as a barn owl gently fanned his tonsured head, "and at the end of them your child will be cured." The woman burst into tears. "Where am I to get gold?" she sobbed. "Get it you must," said the friar, with neither cruelty nor pity, "and you must leave off all attempts to cure your child. You must not even speak to him. Nothing matters now but the pieces of gold. Through the well, they will be transported to the Children of Paradise, who are the smallest and most powerful of the angels. They are so pure they feed on gold, so transparent that even God has forgotten them. After seven years, they will reward you."

The woman went home and told her husband, who wept so hard it frightened her. The two fools began their seven-year quest for gold. They sold all they had. They danced in the streets for coins. They abased themselves before priests and princes. They carried heavy loads, they chopped wood, they reaped, they winnowed. Throughout all this time, they could scarcely care for their child, who looked after himself like a half-grown bear cub. Miraculously, the two fools managed to earn one gold piece a week. Every Sunday the woman took a coin to the Well of the Whores, and as she threw it in, a white bird flew down and seized the gold in its beak. At first she screamed and chased the bird, attempting to get her coin back, but it always flew off, and after some time she began to comfort herself, reasoning that the Children of Paradise, the smallest and purest of angels, could hardly dwell at the bottom of a dark well. "The white bird must be taking the coins to Paradise," she thought. Perhaps this was true. The bird always flew toward the highest peaks of the mountains. However, some say that the beautiful bird, which was in fact a barn owl, was simply taking the coins to Friar Tello.

In any case, after seven years, the child of the two fools turned into a handsome prince. What joy! This fine creature was their first and only success. Now the old man, his father (for the two fools have grown quite elderly), sits in the café and tells his story for the price of a pint of beer. Sometimes, after an especially lively evening, he can be seen outside the palace where Friar Tello has taken up residence, scraping his feet on the pavement and singing pathetically one of the tunes he used to warble for money during the seven years. Sometimes the Good Friar Tello, who now sports a black satin cape, opens the balcony doors, revealing a pink corner of his illumined parlor, and throws down a copper coin. As for the mother of the handsome prince, she lives winter days, an entire lifetime of winter. It's as if her whole life is ice, as if she's trapped in the seven-year winter during which she used to climb the deadly, avalanche-haunted mountains, where she'd squat in the snow and dig for the frozen bulbs of the herb called Reticence, which can be boiled to make a powerful aphrodisiac. The ladies of the town would pay her well for this precious herb. I can see the snow high up, she says, and the snow below. Up high is the realm of Paradise; below, it's the world of men. Sometimes I recall that there was something I meant to do with my life, but I can't remember it now, and anyway, I no longer have the strength. I am following the tracks of the Children of Paradise. They hold skiing parties up here, and because they are children, they lose their little gloves, ski poles, and scarves. But what blindness, and what numbness! I can hardly see their tracks in the snow, and when I pick up their tiny ski poles, they feel like icicles. I will dig a hole for myself. I will be the herb called Reticence. When boiled with the angels' tears, I will create love. After all, it's preferable to looking down. I can't bear how high I've climbed! Tell me: Who are they? Who are the Children of Paradise?

THE LITTLE CHILD WITH THE UNFORTUNATE CONDITION

She was a little child with an unfortunate condition. She had acquired it, perhaps, on a family vacation, though no one was sure; she might have been served a piece of poisoned meat at the hotel restaurant or gotten stung by a strange animal in the woods. The important thing, her mother always said, was not where the unfortunate condition had come from, but how the child could live with it most easily, especially since a number of doctors and specialists had confirmed that it could never be cured, but was rather like something bonded to the child's genes. It was the child's father who lay awake at night, gazing at the curtains that enfolded a fatty, yellow, gelatinous moon, and castigating himself for his bad decisions—for everyone knows it's dangerous to take your child on foreign holidays. In the dark, he could hear the weeds in the yard growing right up to the windowsill. He could hear, sometimes, an owl cry among the cedars. And he could hear the child singing, because one of the many symptoms of her unfortunate condition was insomnia.

Happily, the mother possessed a less brooding, more practical nature. She was the one who made the orthodontist appointments. She taught the child to put in the daytime retainer, a discreet, ivory-colored appliance, and helped her attach the massive nighttime retainer with its absorbent pads, steel rods, and straps like a piece of medieval armor. In the nighttime retainer, the child looked sweet, peeking over the apparatus with her soft, dark eyes. The mother kissed her on the top of her head. As the sun sank, the child was seized by an exultant mood, and jumped up and down on the bed while the mother read her a story.

"She is a perfectly contented child," the mother declared to anyone who would listen. "She has a beautiful disposition." There was no reason the child could not lead an exemplary life. She had excellent grades and played the violin. She even had friends, despite her bulbous sunglasses and the nylon garments that covered her down to the ground. Of course, there had been difficulties. Children are naturally cruel, and at first no one wanted to sit by the weird little girl whose gloves were infused with zinc oxide. But her teacher—a brilliant, compassionate, generous teacher, to whom the mother was forever grateful—managed to turn the unhappy situation into a learning opportunity, showing the class a video about people with a range of unlucky conditions, which captured the children's sympathy. Moreover, some of these people had become CEOs or television personalities. It was entirely possible, the teacher lectured, that the little child with the unfortunate condition might, like these luminaries, contain some invisible gift that would benefit her society. The children looked at their classmate with new interest. Despite the lethargy typical of her during the school day, especially when it was almost time for her pill (a nasty, dirt-brown pill, the others had whispered before their conversion, like a scab), the power of their youthful imaginations transformed her into a latent employee of the month. After this, many friendly little colleagues came to visit her house. The child's mother, glowing with enthusiasm, would serve them raspberry popsicles, reserving for the child a special popsicle, prepared according to her restricted diet, which was of a darker color.

A condition is not the end of the world. It's all a matter of management. Eventually, even the child's father was won over to this rational view. His nights of wakefulness ceased, and he was rarely troubled by skeletal trees or baleful clouds the color of human liver. As for the mother, she was an inspiration, everyone said. How cheerfully she had accepted her fate! Only those who had known her from her youth perceived how her face, despite its good nature, was slowly collapsing, undermined by fear. It was as if the bones of her jaw were being ground away by an endless dread, and by the effort of telling herself there was nothing to be afraid of, for after all, plenty of people have sensitivities to certain foods, even just the odor of those foods can be enough to bring on an attack, and plenty of people have strong feelings, inexplicable dislikes and phobias that require attention, for example a horror of spiders, and with a little caution it's possible to avoid ever seeing a spider or, as it might be, a certain four-legged, spidery symbol. All of this was quite manageable. But what the mother really feared, with a terror she buried beneath concerns about allergies, diet, and periodontal health, what she feared with that ruinous panic that was destroying her body from the inside, was that one day her precautions would no longer be necessary. One day—one night—the child with the unfortunate condition would look out the window and see her reflection for the first time. She would see, in the darkness, a figure, or perhaps a group of figures, possessed of an anemic, bone-chilling beauty. Suddenly, as these figures gestured and tapped on the windowpane, the child would realize that she did not, in fact, suffer from any kind of misfortune, and that rather than struggling to overcome her deficiencies in the hope of one day becoming useful to her society, she might, with the flick of a window latch, cast off an order that had never suited her and take her place in the sisterhood of the damned. "How hard I've worked," the little child would exclaim, "and all for nothing!" She would open the window. Her lovely sisters would slip inside, chuckling softly, and with a few twists of their clever fingers remove the hateful retainer so that the child could feel her whole, triumphant mouth. Oh, how good it feels to flex one's jaws! How nice to clasp hands, to belong! The child would lead her new friends down the hall, where, with a jubilant clamor that resembled the shrieking of owls, they would all fall upon her parents and eat them up.

THE LITTLE DAY-MOTHER

The little day-mother carried daylight and no one knew.

She trotted around the town with it. When she passed the iced fish in the grocery store, everything pinkened. Children riding electric scooters on the opposite side of the street glittered like dew as the day-mother neared the door of the church.

She liked the big church, which she entered like a tiny singing lamp. As she stepped quietly into the sanctuary, a baby squirming in the first row saw the stained-glass angels stir their wings and lean toward one another, smiling.

One morning the day-mother realized she would have to find a new house. Every night her legs were growing a little shorter. She could no longer climb the stairs. She could not trot very far. For some time, her toes had not reached the gas pedal of the car moldering in the drive.

She thought of going to live in the Gray Hotel with the other old people. But then she would not be able to walk to town. How could she live so far away from the grocery store, the church, and the public library, whose glassy dome was covered with fine blue ivy?

She began to search for a little house in town—one with no stairs.

Also it had to be cheap, for the day-mother was not rich. A fox in a white cravat, who did not understand why the lobby had brightened so, laughed at her from behind his desk at the Urban Spring Apartments.

The landlady on Main Street, a great green macaw, had no prejudices against old women. She simply could not abide their smell.

The kindly badger on High Street did not wish to rent to someone who might set the place on fire in a moment of abstraction, or simply fall down dead.

The little day-mother trotted back and forth, carrying the daylight, through which bright snowflakes had begun to fall.

One day she did, in fact, leave the stove on. So people were right about her! But nothing happened; only the house was a little warmer. Worse was the day she knelt as usual to wash the kitchen floor and wondered if she would ever be able to get up again.

She thought of buying an electric cart in which she could ride to town. But these were expensive. In order to purchase one, she would have to sell her house. How could she sell her house when she had nowhere else to live? Would she ever sell it? Nobody was interested in buying her old car, though she had gone to the office of the local paper to advertise it months ago, dispersing a silver light among the bulletin boards. Moreover, she had once seen an old man fall over on one of those carts! The pavements of the town were very uneven. No, feet were better—her own minute, trusty feet, which had supported her so cheerfully all her life.

She walked downtown, carrying the string bag for her groceries. Blue light bathed the marble owls on the courthouse steps. No one could pinpoint the source of this light. They simply felt that things were brighter. A young girl shoveling snow in front of her father's restaurant began to whistle.

One afternoon the fox with the white cravat was returning from lunch when he saw a bundle of gray-haired rags lying in the snow. It was the little day-mother! The fox dialed 911 on his cell phone in an icy gloom that, even for winter, seemed extraordinarily deep. Only the day-mother's body showed up softly in that darkness, with a light that, had the fox only known, he could have enjoyed every day.

He glanced about him, whimpering faintly. Sirens wailed in the distance.

Then the Wolf of Night came and swallowed up the earth.

"But," argued Little Dimple, *whose grandmother told this story, "the day-mother would have died anyway! She was very old."*

Of course. Our subject here is not eternity. It is daylight.

"Clink! Clink!" cried the broken teapot from its grave among the marigolds.

BREATH OF THE DRAGON KING

ALLISON KING

There were three tragedies in Drea King's life, all of which occurred before it even began. The first was that her parents, like many other parents, tried to birth her in the year of the dragon. Not only was the dragon the most powerful persona, but it was the year 1988, and eight was a lucky number, so everybody knew the Dragons of '88 would be special. Especially the first ones, the ones born right on New Year's Day. But that New Year's Eve, Drea's mother, in a moment of weakness, had eaten a carrot. Drea was born shortly after, not a dragon, not even a tiger or a horse, but a rabbit.

The second great tragedy was that she had been born a girl. Maybe some people wanted a dragoness, but certainly nobody wanted a rabbit-ess.

Still, her parents were creative and sly (both snakes) and so they told nobody about Drea's birth until the next day, the first day of the New Year. They declared her the first Dragon of '88, and in honor of that, she would be named Dragon King. It is written clearly on her birth certificate in proud bold letters, followed by a smudged date—a straight-backed seven forced into a bent eight. And so we've come to the third great tragedy of Drea's life, which was that her full name was the same as that of the restaurant next door, which served greasy pork topped with wisps of broccoli.

Drea hung out with the other Dragons of '88, as she was expected to. Her parents taught her to lie and misdirect, to convince the other kids that not only was she one of them, but she was their leader. Her parents knew she had to be the first one to achieve her breath of fire, so she was signed up for sleight-of-hand classes, weekend classes all about deceiving and convincing. And she was good at it—her flourishes precise, her memory impeccable, her palming quick and clean. Rabbits are quick, she reasoned, or maybe it was that rabbits and magic have always been associated via top hat.

In any case, the first time she showed off her breath of fire she was thirteen years old and waiting for the bus after school. The Dragons of '88 crowded around her while the other students, as usual, ignored them. She tossed up three colored scarves, then four, then five, juggled them easily, then clicked her tongue. She tasted the bitter fuel and spat it out while waving a match in front of her face. Then she palmed the match. The scarves, pre-laced with fuel, caught fire so a circle of heat framed her. When they fell to the ground, she stomped the fire out amidst cheers from the Dragons. She was immediately sent to the principal's office. He understood nothing of dragons or personas. He was probably a rat.

The other kids stopped teasing her for her restaurant name. Whenever one got too close, she would inhale sharply. They scrambled.

Still, it was strange to be the first with the breath of fire. Age fourteen, fifteen—none of the other Dragons of '88—the real ones—had it.

"It is something about this country," was the rumor that circulated among the parents. "It does not have the power of the old one."

Her parents continued to push her.

"You are the first of the Dragons of '88," they reminded her, a lie they did not even remember as a lie anymore. "You must forge the way for them."

She perfected her breath of fire. She ran to improve her lung capacity—she became captain of the varsity track team. She learned to mix steam into her breath—she excelled at chem lab. She built small steam-powered animals made of popsicle sticks and paper clips. They ran around her when she breathed into them, little rabbits who hopped with lives of their own and won her every science fair.

Teach us, teach us, the Dragons of '88 begged, desperate to have their own breaths of fire, something that would make their difference worth it.

But they were the real ones—she was the fake. They were scared, she realized, to be separated from their old country and to be freaks in their new one. Many of them leaned into it—marked their skin in scales of green, wore jackets with wings printed across their backs. She wanted to help, but she did not know how to breathe wind beneath their wings.

With steady breaths, she began to forge new materials together. She replaced the popsicle stick and paper clips of her rabbits with bits of metal, melted together at careful angles. She gave her rabbits wings and breathed into them, watching them fly around her room.

When nobody else achieved their breath of fire, she turned to the budding internet. She found nothing about Dragons of '88 or breaths of fire, as if it were something that only existed in their small town. She confronted her parents, who slithered and shrank until they shed their second skin, revealing the truth.

"Just something to motivate you all," they explained, "and to unite you. An agreement between parents—for kids to succeed and feel belonging. Drea, our little Dragon King, do you see how mighty you've become?"

She lay down and sighed, one long, warm, breath.

At night, she toured the neighborhood, staring up at each of her fellow dragons' windows. She held up her latest creation—a rabbit, given scales to defend itself, wings to fly, and a stomach of fire to keep it warm and loved. She whispered into each rabbit—*you are here, you are real, and you belong.* She watched her breath propel their little wings into the sky. Each rabbit landed on the window of a dragon in a strange land, twitching its nose at them, reminding them of how far they had already come.

THE PIPER

KAREN JOY FOWLER

I saw the king only once. I was a young boy and he was a young king, only two years into his reign. A courtier came through our village to let us know the royal entourage would be passing and we crowded the road to see them. I remember his horse even better than I remember him. It was black, its tail and mane braided with red and gold, a wild sort of horse that kicked and danced. The queen's carriage followed and we could see the tips of her fingers holding the carriage curtain back just enough for her to look out without us looking in. It was only two weeks later that we heard the bells announcing the birth of the princess, so I wonder now if that was even her.

The king smiled at us and waved. He reached into his purse, but the disk he took out wasn't a coin, just a miniature of his own face on one side and his symbol, the red dragon, on the other. He threw this to Emmalina, a girl around my age, who'd caught her bright hair up in a red scarf for the occasion. Emmalina was as practical as she was pretty. She traded it at the next market for two hair ribbons and a currant bun.

The whole thing was over in a blink and yet how much conversation it provided over the years that followed! First off, everyone said how handsome the king was and then even how beautiful the queen, which puzzled me to hear since we hadn't seen her and we had seen him. My

mother said that since half the day had already been spent on amuse-
ments, the rest might as well follow, so my friend Henry and I took our
fishing poles down to Green River to harry the brown trout.

"Did you think the king was handsome?" I asked Henry. We were
lying on our backs on the bank, hands behind our heads, looking up
into a net of tree branches, our poles propped on the ground beside us
where we could grab them quickly if they bent. The sun was out and the
water whispering past. For some reason, it seemed important to me just
then that Henry agree with me about the king, that he had a scrawny
moustache and a scrawnier neck and no chin at all.

"The way I figure it," Henry said, "the king must always be handsome, it goes with being king. Kings are just given things the rest of us
have to earn." Henry had those big sorts of thoughts. He was always
badgering travelers for news of the great world. He knew the names of
several other countries and also the names of their kings. He used to
stop in the middle of whatever we were doing—hauling water, milking
cows, slipping fish heads into Emmalina's basket so the cats would
follow her home—to wonder if across the sea there mightn't be two
boys doing the exact same thing at the exact same time. And in some
farther country, where they didn't even look like us, another two boys.
It distressed Henry to think of all the places he was never going to see.

My mother always said that there were cats that wandered and cats
that curled in front of the fire—the yowling cats and the purring cats—
and Henry was the first kind of cat and I was the second. It was better to
be me, Mother said. To be content with what you had was the greatest
gift God could bestow on a mortal man.

Someone claimed to have heard the queen say to her ladies that we
were a dear, sleepy village. This wasn't reported at the time, only later,
and the overhearing wasn't even possible what with the noise of the
horses and the carriage and the crowd, but soon it was a settled fact—
the queen had called us dear and sleepy. This, too, was puzzling to me
as we worked hard, and I didn't suppose we slept more than anyone else.

Henry spent the next few days thinking up other things that went
with being king. One he particularly envied. "A king has a story. He
knows he'll be remembered," Henry said.

"Everyone has a story," I told him.

"If that's what you think."

That's what I think. So this story is mine. It may be that you've heard a different version. That one's mine as well.

It was a good place to live, our village—rich soil, the fast-flowing river to turn our mills and water our crops, the winters not so harsh as those up north and the growing season long. The great forest gray and the Fishtail Mountains blue in the distance. We were a small village—not a soul I didn't know by name except for the travelers and even some of those names I'd come to know.

We were well aware of our good fortune, as there were still two people—ancient Estie Moortin and even older Hannah Wright—who remembered the plague years. These were women with stories for sure. After the sickness came, there weren't enough people to till the fields and you just might survive the buboes only to starve the following winter, old Estie said. All the babies and all the old people and a good number in between had died.

But that was then. Now we were small, but prosperous. My own prospects were good. My father was a baker and my mother known for the crusts of her pies. The king came riding through; the seasons spun on their wheel. I was sixteen, seventeen, eighteen. My parents expected me to marry Emmalina. She was the prettiest of the girls, good-hearted and smart. I liked her and I knew she liked me. But I planned to marry Anna Moortin, though I'd not yet told anyone.

Anna was born with one short leg so she walked with an awkward roll and hitch. Her spine was a snake that curved more with every passing year. But she was easy to talk to and I'd begun waiting for her at the well, carrying her buckets home since her limping sloshed the water so much she'd lose half of it.

I'd decided to marry her partly because I liked her company, but mostly because no one else would ask her, and so, whatever kind of husband I'd be, her life would be the better for it, while Emmalina's could only be the worse. Still I put off asking, because the person I really wanted to be with was Henry.

I had none of this settled when the king went to war. We felt it first in the taxes he levied to pay for his ships and horses and swords. Suddenly we were not so prosperous as we had been. But travelers told us of rumors that a foreign country had seized lands across the sea, lands long considered ours, and they were coming now for the homeland itself, so it was a matter of our own protection. Life went on, only with less, and a persistent fear that we might one day wake to foreign soldiers in the village square.

Instead, the soldiers who came were our own. They were boys from other villages and they looked just like us. They wore no uniforms and the weapons they carried were all things you would find on a farm—axes, scythes, and knives. Some few were barefoot.

The day was dry but cold, with a wind from the north. The captain who led them wore fur robes and tall boots and rode a bay horse. He called on the men of our village, anyone not too young and not too old, to join him. The king needed fit men, he said. And brave. "Your king needs the bravest and strongest among you. Stand forth for your king! For your country! For your village! For your family! If you won't fight to keep them, these things you love will surely fail and fall." As he spoke, one by one, our men came as if called, in from the fields, the smithy, the mill, and the school.

Henry was the first to volunteer and he was cheered and kissed and cheered again. Thomas Watts was next. Then Frederick Hayes. I was the fourth. Soon enough, every man who could fight had promised to do so. At first, I volunteered only because Henry had. But the captain talked on, evoking so movingly all that I loved and wished safe and unchanged, and by the time I gave my name I was wild to go.

My parents weren't there to see this. I thought of returning home for the axe, but if I took it, how would the wood be cut, the ovens kept working? In truth, I was afraid to say goodbye. So they only learned I was going when they saw me marching away. My mother's face then was a terrible thing. She hadn't expected this of her purring cat.

I left home weaponless, but we were only twenty minutes into our first day's march when my stout and aging father rushed up, so red and breathless I was afraid he'd faint. He said nothing to me, but gave me a sack containing a tin plate, a sharp knife, his own good bread, and my mother's shepherd pie. Lastly, he pressed our only axe into my arms. And then he stood and watched me leave for the second time that day.

It took us twelve days to walk to the sea. Sometimes I walked with Henry, but sometimes I didn't. Our numbers grew with every village until we were so many, I was carried along like a stick in a current. Already we moved over the ground like conquerors.

It seems to me now that I spent those days in a sort of fog that only occasionally cleared. I know that we were fed by villages along the way and where there were no villages we scavenged or went hungry. I know that my feet blistered at the heels and the weight of the axe was a permanent stab in the back of my shoulder. I know that the sole of my right shoe came loose on the third day and flapped when I stepped, and that a good night was one spent in a barn and a bad one was on the forest floor among the tree roots.

But every time I started minding, the captain came through our lines on his horse and any flagging resolve vanished as he spoke. He praised us as brave lads, the bravest he'd ever seen. How grateful our king would be, how we would be toasted in the highest halls, march in parades in the capitol. When he wasn't praising our sacrifice, he was castigating our enemy. He spoke of appalling cruelties. The enemy was torching mills and executing farmers in order to starve people into submission. The enemy was seizing the children of those who resisted and cutting off their hands. The enemy was stringing up priests in the bell towers to serve as clappers in the bells. The enemy was planting graves.

All these same things would happen to us and ours if the enemy were allowed to land. "The only way to stop their treacherous invasion," the captain said, "is to cross the sea first, take the fight to their own homes. Strike with such ferocity that their children and their children's children will never dare threaten us again.

"I believe in you," the captain said. "I know you'll do what's needed. You are king's men, each and every one of you."

* * *

The terrain was changing underneath our feet, less forest, less brush, less up and more down. "One more day," the captain told us, "and then to the ships." But that afternoon, a terrible storm came in from the sea. Lightning snapped in great white sheets across the sky, thunder cracked directly over our heads, and rain poured down through the cracks.

In among the sparse trees, the water pounded us unimpeded. Rain dripped from my hair to my neck and down my back; there wasn't an inch of me that wasn't wet. My broken shoe filled with mud.

So the captain sent us out to look for shelter and Henry and I found the entrance to an abandoned mine. It was a small entrance, choked now with rocks, and it could only be entered on all fours, but once inside, it widened into a sizable room, with a tunnel at the back that turned into another tunnel and turned again. Henry entered first and I followed, while others crowded in behind. After a few turns, we were past all light, but we kept walking, pushed from the back as more and more soldiers crawled inside.

I felt my way forward, along walls that vanished into openings, over ground strewn with stones that shifted beneath my feet. Sometimes the ceiling dipped and I struck my head, moving forward in absolute darkness until finally the pushing from behind stopped. I sat on the floor in my sodden clothes and shivered. "Are you here, Henry?" I asked.

"Yes." He was beside me. Walking in the dark was the bravest thing I'd ever done, but now I did something even braver. "Give me your hand," I said, "so I know that you're here." And Henry's fingers brushed my knee. I took them in my own and I didn't let go. I leaned against him. I put my head on his shoulder. Eventually I was warm enough to sleep.

I woke to Henry shaking me. He needed to go off some distance, take care of what needed taking care of, but he was afraid of getting lost in the dark. We went together on rising ground, counting our steps, thinking to go just far enough and not too far, but then the walls of the mine came slowly into focus and around another turn, we found another entrance. Night had come, but the rain was gone. The moon was so round and bright that the light was dazzling. We didn't go back, but slept on the farthest edge of dry ground, moonlight pouring down.

In the morning, we could see everything around us. I rose and stretched. "Look," I said. I pointed. In the wall we'd slept against there was a shallow dent that looked like an enormous eye, a shallow bulge like a skull around it. A closer look showed other bits, a section of spine, a rib, and another rib. The skeleton of some great beast was embedded in the rock. I touched it with my fingers and felt the mystery of it.

"A dragon," Henry said, awe in his voice. "The king's dragon."

We stood together, staring. "Henry," I said. "Do you think somewhere across the sea, in another country where they don't even look like us, two boys are finding exactly the same thing?" But Henry had gone while I was still speaking, back through the dark, fetching those soldiers closest, leading them on to see it for themselves.

Word of the bones reached the captain. He gathered us in the morning sunlight, in a world washed clean and new. "We will surely win," he said. "God has blessed us with a sign." We raised our weapons and cheered him.

By afternoon, we were on a cliff overlooking the ocean. The waves were all chop and chaos, but out at the horizon, at the very edge of sight, the sea was still as a mirror. I'd never seen so far nor imagined water and a world so big. I could taste salt in the air. "Henry," I said, but Henry was already gone, down the trail to the beach, a trail so narrow, we could only take it one at a time.

I could see the ships with their red sails below me. There was the captain, a tiny figure leading his horse across the sand. There were the first of our soldiers following him.

I heard the sound of waves. I heard the cries of seagulls. I heard the song of a different bird, clear and sweet behind me. I could no longer hear the captain's voice and in that absence, suddenly, I saw his omen quite differently. That dragon, if it were a dragon, was long dead. And I thought again of those boys in all those other places, those boys who were doing whatever Henry and I did.

I couldn't help the ones like Henry. But I knew I didn't want to send the ones like me to war. It didn't feel like a decision. It didn't feel like a betrayal. It felt like waking up.

385

The bird I was hearing was a thrush. It was a ghost bird—I couldn't find it with my eyes. But I could hear it, and I knew its song, a song I'd first heard in my cradle. I knew that no thrush belonged at the seashore. I thought I could follow that song all the way home.

So, at the last moment, I stepped back from the cliff and the war and the captain. I stepped back from Henry, or maybe he stepped back from me; this is just as true.

Eight years have passed since these things happened and I've stopped thinking I might see him or any of the others again. Still I can't stop myself imagining it. How I'll bring him inside, call for my children. This is my dear friend, Henry, I'll say. He has a story to tell us.

But on the day I saw him last, I was the one in need of a story. I would have to explain to the village why I was back and everyone else gone, and it couldn't be a story that made me a coward, a deserter, and a man who didn't love his king. I wasn't yet sure how this story would go, but I wasn't really worried about that. I had twelve whole days to work it out and I could already see its bones.

A SPELL FOR FOOLISH HEARTS

ISABEL YAP

The Rulebook for Witches had over three hundred entries, but Aunt Gemma stressed only three:

1. Tend to your jar of blackberries.
2. Beware men's hearts; never let them be your master.
3. The shape of things can be deceptive.

She'd copied them by hand on card stock, drawn a row of hearts and stars as a border, then tucked it into the front cover of the Rulebook, which she sent Patrick for his eleventh birthday. He read it all the way through twice, wondering if he should tell Mom and Dad. It was weird, the wondering. Why shouldn't he tell them? Aunt Gemma never said it was a secret, and it didn't seem prohibited per witch laws because he carried the book around in plain sight.

Once, over breakfast, Mom asked him, "What are you reading?" He answered: "The Rulebook for Witches." She smiled fondly, because her son was a bookworm and she probably thought this was a new wizarding school series.

Gradually Patrick understood, without wanting to, that he was afraid of telling them because they'd either not believe it, or it would upset them. There would be something inherently *wrong* in the revelation that Patrick was a witch. Both those reactions would hurt, because he *was* a witch. He'd been doing spells for years, he just didn't know they were spells until Aunt Gemma sent him the book. Magic thrummed in his veins, sparking off him in small gestures: in the words he'd mutter under his breath, in the look he'd give a wailing toddler in the food court—*don't do that*—so that they'd snap their mouths shut and stare at him, affronted. He already knew that few people could do magic, but it didn't make you all-powerful. It was rare, but only in the sense that being really good at instruments or sports was rare. It could be used or not, and you could develop it or not. It could be noticed or ignored.

The longing to tell his parents swelled. He felt as if there was a jar of water balanced on his head, whenever they were around. The worst was the hope: that Mom might say, "Oh, don't worry, I'm that way too," carelessly waving a hand to revive the dead herbs by the kitchen sink. Or Dad might admit that he wasn't afraid of cats, he just didn't like hearing their thoughts.

When he finally told them, Mom cried: quiet tears, running down her cheeks, the lack of drama highlighting how *truly* sad it made her. Dad turned away and muttered something under his breath.

"Are you sure?" Mom asked. Patrick nodded.

"I should've known," Mom sniffled. "It runs in my side of the family. Mother had it, and so did Gemma, but I thought it might be thinned out between me and your dad. *Dammit*, Gemma should have *asked* me first."

"One of my cousins has it too," Dad said sheepishly. Mom said, "Alan!"

They started arguing, while Patrick sat on his hands and marveled at his shame. He should've kept his mouth shut. At least he wasn't crying.

Mom blew her nose and said, "No it's not something he can go to a doctor for—"

"It's not a big deal," Patrick blurted. He felt awful.

His parents looked at him.

"I mean, no one really needs to know, and I'm not—I've never like, shown it off. Most people don't notice magic, unless they're looking. It'll be fine."

"You mean you won't," Mom paused, considering her words. "You won't be a witch?"

"I," Patrick said, faltering. That seemed impossible to answer. "I'll, uh. Try."

That conversation was sixteen years ago, though some mornings, halfway through coffee number one, Patrick recalled it with crystal precision. He wondered what he could have said instead. *Yes* would be wrong; *no* was inaccurate. Eleven-year-old Patrick had done his best. There weren't massive consequences, either. Sometimes you needed to get the bad feelings out of your system, cry and argue, and plod on.

They rarely spoke of his witchcraft after that. Patrick continued to work minor spells because he couldn't *not*, but being a witch didn't spell his doom. He didn't run away from home, quit school, or launch a drug cartel like maybe his parents feared. He went to college and got his degree (in physics, on a whim, with a minor in design). Patrick felt he was doing a decent job of adulting. He had work as a UX/UI/Marketing Designer at a "fast growing, VC-backed start-up," and an apartment in San Francisco (tiny, out in the Richmond, but it was all he needed). He knew where to get quarters for laundry. He paid off his credit card every month. His only witchy activity was the part-time work at the Mission Spell Shop, just off Valencia Street, mostly because Myrtle was a sweetheart who let him tinker with ingredients. They donated some of their proceeds to a nearby shelter program, which served both magical and non-magical folks alike. It was nice to stay tangentially connected to the Bay Area magic scene, even if most people were hobbyists like him. Rent was too high, magic too impractical; there were much more lucrative ways to spend one's time.

The Rulebook he kept on his nightstand, the notecard on his refrigerator. Sometimes he wondered if maybe he'd taken those rules too seriously. Number one he'd followed faithfully, after Mother gave him his blackberry jar ("I have no idea what it's for, but I kept it anyway, upon Grandma's orders, so you might as well have it"). He didn't exactly *tend* it. He just wiped dust off the lid every few months. Number three seemed fairly obvious, less a witch rule than common sense, though he suspected it might hold some deeper meaning about fae or humanesque glamours.

Number two he'd never had experience with, because he'd never been in a relationship.

Patrick didn't know how to be in one. He wasn't *dissatisfied* with being single—most days he didn't even think of it. Now that he was on the other side of twenty-five, it seemed unlikely to change, unless he had one of those movielike encounters in an airport or a party (he didn't go to parties). He'd been on a dating app for all of three days before deciding it was too stressful and deleting his account.

He wasn't sure how to feel about being single. He wasn't sure he *felt* much about it. It was sad in this remote way, like an acquaintance's tragedy. He could empathize with it . . . to a degree. On the other hand, he was certain that he'd saved himself a lot of personal drama by never falling for anyone. He didn't even know how to fall for someone. The concept was mysterious. Did you *choose* to be attracted? Did you pluck someone from your environment and decide to attach feelings to them? If all of media was to be believed, he was highly unusual in this regard, but it didn't exactly bother him. He'd never even had a real crush—besides Ben Whishaw, he was really into Ben Whishaw. But Ben Whishaw was a celebrity and taken, so.

Sometimes Kat, who ran Product Marketing at his start-up, tried to cure his remarkable lack of dating by inviting him to go dancing in the Castro. Kat was very concerned for Patrick's happiness, which was sometimes exhausting, but he liked Kat a lot so he didn't mind. He thought life would probably be a lot easier if he and Kat could be a couple. Kat was sweet and took excellent care of him, and they could have had a very happy life together. Only he wasn't into women, and she wasn't into long-term relationships. Kat was the only person at work who knew about the witch thing *and* the gay thing, and Patrick intended to keep it that way.

Monday. There was a boy with hair made of starlight in the elevator. He blinked luminous gray eyes at Patrick as he stepped inside, and parted bow-shaped lips to say, "Thank god! I was starting to think I'd have to take the stairs the whole way."

Patrick was halfway through a Starbucks white chocolate mocha, which he only indulged in on days that started out not-good. His hair was not-good that morning, his face was not-good. He had mystery sniffles, and he'd overslept. He flinched, but it was only a *mental* flinch—a jolt of feeling that ran through him, so unexpected he barely had the composure to say "Er, hi." He blinked. The boy's hair wasn't starlight, just a bleached platinum that really *shouldn't* have worked. He wore a stud earring and a dangling earring in one lobe like a K-pop star, a dark blue button-down under a tailored jacket with elbow patches, and new-looking Cole Haans. "What floor?" he asked.

"Sixth. I didn't realize the elevator needed a card reader. I'm surprised no one else came in! Is everyone here fit enough to take the stairs?"

"It's health awareness month," Patrick said, and tapped his card on the reader. "It's also a little . . . early, for most people." Only weirdoes like Patrick came in at 8:30.

When Patrick didn't press any other button, Starboy said, "Well, seems like we're headed to the same place!"

"Marquet?" Their core product was a platform for quantifying the impact of various Marketing activities across the funnel; one of the cofounders had thought the name incredibly clever. Most employees disagreed but were resigned.

"Yeah!" Starboy says. "I start today. Product team. I'm Karl." He stuck his hand out, and Patrick shook it.

"Karl, like the fog?"

"What?"

Awkward. The elevator doors slid open. "Oh. It's a Twitter account. Karl-the-Fog. Haha."

"*Ohhh.* Yeah, it's Karl with a K."

"I'm Patrick," he said, trying not to feel like an idiot. "I'm on the Design Team. Um. I would take you to HR, but I'm not sure she's in yet. Do you, uh, want some coffee?"

"Coffee would be great."

They walked into the kitchen, where Melody was starting to unpack the weekly Costco delivery. "Hey! Another newbie today? You guys are *multiplying*!" As she and Karl started chatting, Patrick busied himself making coffee for the earlybirds. He pictured his blackberry jar to calm down. He felt ridiculous. Starboy—Karl—was not even his type. That *hair*, for one thing. Patrick had never known what a crush was like, and if this was it, it was a bad idea. He was a firm believer in keeping work and personal life separate. That shit was messy, and if there was one thing Patrick did not like, it was messy shit. Plus he didn't really believe in things like attraction at first sight, even if those *were* awfully nice Cole Haans.

Karl was good at his job: efficient and communicative, confident but not controlling. The first product Karl and Patrick collaborated on was a long-awaited v2 feature release spurred by vicious Tweets from angry users (#marquit). Patrick initially felt sorry for Karl; he'd been given a shitty project, shipping something that already fostered negative sentiment. But Karl had risen to the task admirably, translating all that user fury into clear pain points that Patrick could actually design solutions for. They'd sat in a brainstorming session together for half a day, and at the end of it they had three options to show the rest of the team. Patrick had actually been excited to get back to his desk and prototype. It was the good kind of start-up rush. Talking to Karl, picking his brain, felt easy.

Karl was also super friendly. By the end of week one everyone knew his name, which was rare given how many newbies started each week. He and Kat got along amazingly; they quickly established weekly lunch dates, which made Patrick slightly jealous (of who, he wasn't sure). Kat, being Kat, looped Patrick in, so he found himself spending a lot more time with Karl than expected. Before he knew it his Slack convo with Karl was a minefield of GIFs, they regularly ate lunch together, and he'd spent more than a couple nights in a stupor, lamenting the unfortunate problem of crushing on a coworker.

It *sucked*.

Denying the crush had worked for all of two-and-a-half weeks, but eventually Patrick admitted defeat. He mused on this while making bacon pasta for dinner. He was cat-sitting Miranda for Aunt Gemma;

she blinked at him owlishly from the counter, judging his agony. He did not want to like Karl. He was not prepared for this stupid crush. Why should he have a crush at all? And on *Karl*? He didn't even know Karl.

Well. He knew some things. Karl was a Bay Area native, and most of his family was still here. He'd gone to school at Berkeley, studied economics with a minor in art history. He was bad at sports but liked long walks ("And hiking . . . but I know literally everyone likes hiking. I'm not, like, the best hiker. I just like trees. Haha."). He claimed to enjoy karaoke and museums, and once he'd brought in a Tupperware full of white chocolate chip and macadamia cookies that he'd baked from scratch. Before Marquet he'd worked at another start-up which had tanked after its series A; before *that* he'd been at Apple. It was unclear how old he was, and he didn't have LinkedIn.

Patrick also knew that Karl moved like water, like he was possessed by some internal rhythm. He crossed the room in liquid strides and teleported from either end of the whiteboard when Patrick wasn't paying attention—which, in this situation, was almost never. Perhaps he'd been a dancer in undergrad. Also, apparently Karl didn't bleach his hair. It was that color naturally. "Some genetic mutation!" Karl said, laughingly, and Patrick had thought *what, for hotness?*

Patrick was constantly hunting for clues about whether Karl liked men. Had he ever mentioned an ex-girlfriend? Ex-boyfriend? Had he ever mentioned a type? Patrick did not know how to broach queerness without bringing it up himself, hence: never.

Anyway, nothing was going to happen. They did not hang outside of work. "I can be his friend," Patrick said aloud. He flapped a hand at Miranda, vaguely worried that her hair would get in the pasta. "He's a great work-friend, a great colleague. We probably wouldn't enjoy weekends together anyway." He set the timer one minute less than the package stated and stirred sauce in an adjacent pot. "I don't even know if he likes boys. He probably doesn't. And yes, he's really nice to me, but he's also nice to everyone. That's just how he is."

That morning Karl had randomly brought him a white chocolate mocha, with matching milky smile. "This is for turning those mocks around so quickly," he'd said.

Patrick didn't think he'd been particularly efficient. He tried not to read into it. "Thanks, dude, but now I owe you one!"

Karl said "Okay, you can get the next one," and walked off to get his requisite granola from the pantry.

That smile though. What was it about that smile?

He missed his timer. The noodles weren't firm. Miranda meowed thoughtfully at him as he slurped dinner and resolved to get through this.

"Are you coming to Pride?" Kat asked the next day, which meant: *You are coming to Pride.*

Patrick hrr-rr-rrmed. "I work Saturdays, remember? We're having a June sale. Lots of people expected that day."

"Dude, that works *perfectly*. We can hit you up and then head to Dolores Park for the rest of the afternoon!"

"I don't know . . ."

"Come on, man! Karl's going, and he's new."

Why was Kat mentioning Karl? Had Patrick been obvious? "He's not new anymore," Patrick said carelessly. "And I dunno about Pride. You know I'm not out."

"That doesn't matter," Kat said. "Everyone goes to Pride. It's full of straight people. You've been living here, what, two years? And you haven't been to Pride yet? You can't be native SF until you've been to Pride!" She noticed his extreme discomfort and softened her cajoling. Kat, Product Marketer Extraordinaire. "Okay. At least try to join us for an hour or two?"

"Okay. Fine. Only for you."

"Yesssss. I love you." She got on tiptoe and kissed his forehead. "Don't come to the shop," Patrick said warningly. "I'll find you at the park."

Contrary to expectations, Kat did not come to the shop with the twelve-strong contingent of Marqueters. Patrick was relieved. Kat was very spur-of-the-moment and could easily forget, or pretend to.

Myrtle had urged Patrick to partake in the festivities that morning, but he assured her that he was happy to hang around 'til the afternoon. They'd done pretty well that day: regulars coming in to pick up their herbs and tinctures and pills, and some new visitors as well, curious and buzzing from the day's festivities, browsing light spells on the shelves. The shop offered more intricate, specialized potions, but those you never saw out in the open. San Francisco laws were fairly lenient on magic, but it still wasn't something you blatantly advertised.

To non-magical people the place would just seem like an eclectic collection of knickknacks, liquors, and herbal supplements. Their magical clientele was diverse, though it had diminished somewhat in recent years as the shapeshifters and sorcerers moved to the Pacific Northwest, or Denver, or Pittsburgh, escaping explosive rent prices and the devouring maw of the tech industry. Myrtle often sighed about losing some of her favorite customers: the Daly City diwata who was a nurse at UCSF and moved back to Manila to look after her ailing mom; a sylph that had had a falling-out with the local mist elementals and decided to try her luck being an artist in Seattle. Patrick always hoped to see a mythic creature come through, but they'd gotten so good at blending in with humans, he could almost never tell.

"It's hot," Patrick said, because it was, and like everyone else in this city he became sluggish and confused in anything but perfect sweater weather.

"I want an ice cream," Myrtle replied, idly petting Josiah, the shop cat. Josiah, unlike Miranda, actually allowed himself to be petted. Myrtle's gray hair was in an intricate bun-braid that morning. She was a friend of Aunt Gemma's, a long-time Berkeley resident, and utterly cool. Unlike Patrick, she seemed completely at peace with her witch identity.

"Go and get an ice cream, it's slowed down," Patrick said.

"You want an ice cream?"

"Nah."

"I'm gonna get an ice cream."

Patrick waved her off, then assumed her place next to Josiah. He was noodling on a new brew which was supposed to provide better outcomes to Tinder dates. It was powdered, meant to be something you could mix into any beverage. It wasn't a commission, exactly; more of a suggestion from numerous regulars, bemoaning the shitty app-driven dating scene. If you liked the person, this would speed up their reciprocation. ("It's a love potion," Myrtle drawled. Patrick thought about it, then said: "Kinda, yeah.") He'd managed to make something that actually quickened attraction and improved flirting—*in theory*, as it was something he still needed to test with willing subjects—but it always took too long. It wouldn't work at all on a first date. Right now the best he'd gotten it down to was a few weeks. Which wasn't what people were looking for. He threw in another handful of dried rosemary and wondered what it was missing. Or maybe he'd put in too much of something? Vanilla? Dried tears?

After ten minutes of silence, the bell tinkled, and Karl stepped inside.

He was wearing one of the garish rainbow tank tops that Kat had screen printed for everyone. Pink plastic shades from a competitor, gleaned from their last trade show, were propped on his head. His smile was bright as the rare sun over San Francisco; those gray eyes bleached all shadows from the room. "Hey, Patrick!" he said.

"Hey," Patrick answered. His heart skipped fluttering and went straight to jumping jacks. Did Myrtle go to Bi-Rite? Why'd she have to go to Bi-Rite? The line always took forever. "What . . . are you doing here?"

"Picking you up! You weren't answering your texts, so Kat sent me on a mission."

"Sorry. I was, um, preoccupied. I was meaning to go, in a bit."

"S'all good." Karl languished by the counter, where Patrick was aware that his Fail Tinder Brew was still cooling off. Patrick had only ever read the word *rakish* in books, but Karl right then was the very definition of it, despite the rainbow tank. "You seem troubled. Am I not allowed in here?"

"It's fine," Patrick said. "I just . . . I like to keep this separate from work." He waved a vague hand. Maybe Karl did magic too? Maybe that explained the hair? And the pheromones?

"I won't tell," Karl said, hand over heart. "What exactly are you selling anyway?"

Okay. Either he wasn't a witch or wizard, or he was pretending not to be. Patrick skritched Josiah behind the ears; Josiah looked at Karl with interest. "Unique brews," Pat said, because he didn't like to lie. "We get IPAs and lagers from special suppliers, mostly West Coast, but a few from Hawaii and the Midwest, too. And uh. Some kombuchas, and teas and stuff."

"Anything you'd recommend?"

Were they flirting? Patrick had no idea how flirting went. "What do you like?"

"You."

Patrick gaped. Karl slapped his shoulder, one easy motion, and snickered.

"Just kidding." Patrick tried not to feel too hurt. "I'm not picky. Hmm. Give me your favorite tea."

"*My* favorite?" He paused. "I like white teas. Gentle stuff."

"Works great." Karl reached out tentatively to Josiah, and beamed when the cat nuzzled his hand.

Patrick fought blushing with everything, which was a doomed move from the beginning. He fished under the countertop for something normal, and gratefully found a packet of White Needle. It had been taped, which meant some of it had been used, but that was fine. "Here. Free of charge. Also, it really does taste better when you brew it four minutes exactly."

"Thanks, dude." He was starting to sound a little like Kat. He took the packet, stuck it into his shorts, and paused expectantly. "You're really not ditching?"

"And risk Kat's wrath? No, of course I'll go. I'm just waiting for"— the bell tinkled, and Myrtle stepped in, licking a double ice cream cone and eyeing them . . . Patrick didn't want to use the word *suggestively*, but it seemed most apt—"my colleague to come back."

"I'm back," she said, waggling her eyebrows. Every woman in Patrick's life was trying to set him up. Life was grim. "And you are?"

"Karl. One of Patrick's colleagues from his . . . day job." The smile went lopsided, stupidly endearing.

"Nice. I'm Myrtle. From Patrick's side hustle. You come to finally take him to prom? It's happening out there."

"You know I don't like things that are *happening*," Patrick mumbled, while Myrtle stepped behind the counter and nudged him.

Imperiously, she said: "Go forth, you young'uns."

Patrick sighed and put on his rainbow tank over his shirt—he wanted to show solidarity. If he was going anyway, might as well be shameless like the rest of them. Myrtle gestured at the pot he'd been boiling the FTB in, asking *does this work?* Patrick shook his head. "I'll wrap it up next weekend," he said.

"Thanks for the tea," Karl called out as they left.

Pride was . . . Pride-ish. There were a lot of people milling about Dolores, fastidiously Instagramming. The cluster of Marqueters cheered as Karl appeared, Patrick in tow. Kat had stripped off her rainbow tank and was wearing an American flag bikini. Everyone was eating tortilla chips dunked in Papa Lote salsa; someone had brought a Bluetooth speaker and was playing a 90s mix with generous amounts of Britney. A Coors Light found its way into Patrick's hand.

This was the first time, he realized, that he was hanging out with Karl outside of work. And it was . . . fine. Whatever. It wasn't anything special. Karl was the same: easy and smiley, spouting puns, tenderly shooing away a cluster of drunk girls who had started to twerk aggressively beside them. He was the first to offer everyone alcohol, though he didn't push if refused. He was full of small, affectionate gestures—like that shoulder-slap back in the shop—touching an elbow here, the small of someone's back there. Karl was a flirt. A massive one. No one was exempted from his winking, his casual familiarity.

One other reason why it wouldn't work. Perhaps now Patrick could convince himself.

After Pride weekend, the crush went away. It was glorious. Q3 started up, and everyone started scrambling to hit their year-end goals. The v2 feature release went so smoothly that Karl got tapped to redesign their entire web platform, setting him up for a long customer discovery project with Kat. Patrick was in the middle of creating new iconography for their marketing materials, and after that he had to update the main corp site (a priority, per the second annual board meeting), which kept him from most new product development. All this meant a good month of nearly no interaction with Karl. When they did cross paths, it was brief and collegial. Sometimes Patrick looked at Karl and thought, with a relish, *he isn't even that cute!* Then Karl would catch him looking and grin, which would ruin things slightly. But not too much. Patrick had broken the crush's stronghold.

Besides, his thoughts were occupied with magic. The Tinder Brew was taking longer than expected, a worthy challenge that excited him about witchcraft in a way he'd missed. The problem was emotions and their volatility. You could temporarily tweak human chemistry all kinds of ways with the right proportions of salt, crushed seashells, and essence of spring, but one couldn't totally control it. You could just make enough suggestions that it bent to your will.

"Maybe it doesn't work because it shouldn't be made," Myrtle suggested. He'd been calculating chemical compositions for an hour, and she was bored.

"It's not forbidden, because it's temporary," he answered. It was frustrating that it wasn't even good enough to test yet. "It's a little attraction spell, old as time. The final version is supposed to only work if they're also curious, anyway."

Patrick, with his Level 0 Romance Experience, had no business making what was ostensibly a love potion. But he liked challenges. He was precise and creative, and often bored. It was Aunt Gemma who gave him the missing element he needed. She'd swooped into the city one afternoon, back from exotic travels, and dragged him out for dim sum. Patrick could not reject dim sum. And he loved Aunt Gemma; she was one of the reasons why he'd moved to San Francisco in the first place. Of course, as luck would have it, once he arrived in the city Aunt Gemma got a promotion and started consulting abroad for half the year. That was how he ended up with Miranda. She'd offered him her apartment, too, a really nice place in Pacific Heights. It was stupid to decline, but somehow it mattered that he get his own place.

"Witches must have their own sanctuaries," Aunt Gemma acknowledged. "Number forty-six. You still have the rulebook, Pat?"

"Of course."

They were having wine in her place, post Yank Sing. Aunt Gemma was always concerned with his progress in the craft, even if she knew he spent most of his time being a designer. She cheered him on, told him he had talent, introduced him to Myrtle so he wouldn't stop working at it. If not for her he would've probably quit magic long before.

She'd brought some mooncakes and shrimp-flavored Pringles from a visit to Taipei, several herbs that he couldn't identify on sight, and half a dozen new volumes for her book collection. Aunt Gemma had an impressive library; it was always a pleasure to inspect her shelves and see what had changed. *Magical Creatures of Northern California* cut an imposing figure next to Mary Canary's *Homemade Kitchen Spells*; there was a four-volume set on *Discerning the Fog (Strategies, Tactics, Symbols,* and *Befriending Elementals)* squished between *Romancing the Rogue* and Strunk's *Elements of Style.*

Patrick flipped through one of her new editions: a photo book of Hong Kong in the 80s, filled with neon lights and some incredibly stylish people that he assumed were actual elves and not merely cosplayers. Aunt Gemma was stroking Miranda idly (Miranda made it very clear she knew who her master was), sipping a glass of Prosecco. "What are you up to these days?"

"Something I call a Tinder Brew." He explained the objective and the problem he was facing: how could one shift attraction from a slow burn, built over repeated dates, to something instant, a spark that caught fire upon ingestion?

"That's a terrible name," Aunt Gemma laughed, then: "You shouldn't be using rosemary. You have to go harder. Snake oil."

"*Aunt Gemma.*"

"Yeah, kidding. No, you could use this," she swirled her drink and lifted an eyebrow. "Right?"

Patrick blinked. "That's genius."

"Well," Aunt Gemma said modestly, and raised her glass.

The Working Tinder Brew, dubbed "Pucker-Up Powder" thanks to Myrtle's dry humor, was a hit with city spell-dabblers. Myrtle took him out for tacos. Patrick's next product was innocuous hexes to discourage pesky suitors, but he was taking that challenge easy, still basking in getting the last spell so right. By the time August rolled around and he was pulled into Karl's redesign, Patrick was confident about his new-found nonchalance against Unfortunate Office Crushes.

He walked into a meeting with a mug of meh afternoon coffee in hand. Karl was at the whiteboard, jotting down bullet points under the header *Beta Issues*. "Hey!" he turned and beamed at Patrick. "I missed you! I feel like we haven't talked in weeks. Like, not since Pride."

Patrick smiled back, utterly disarmed. "Yeah, it's been busy. But we're here now, right? Solving problems together?"

"Totally," Karl said. "And there are lots of problems. The survey results from yesterday's mocks are in . . . and they're pretty brutal. But you know I'm not the best at mocks. You're gonna have to save me."

He smiled sheepishly. Patrick had the presence of mind to think *oh no*. God, his hair was still that color.

And it still looked good.

That meeting proceeded in a perfectly normal fashion, as did the next ones. The following sprints were loaded with long evenings, but Patrick didn't mind. He and Karl made a good team. He was still attracted to Karl, but not in the *alert-alert-danger* way he'd felt when they first met. It was mellow now, and most days bordered on a fuzzy happiness. This was what some people called a happy crush, the internet told him. As long as it didn't evolve into anything else, Patrick was content with it.

Until that Tuesday when Karl asked him to dinner.

Patrick tried to play it cool. "Yeah, to talk about the upcoming sprint, right?"

"No," Karl said, his gray eyes all weirdly soft. *Sweater-weather-like.* Patrick hated that there was now apparently a bad teenage poet living in his brain whenever Karl was around. "I just want to have dinner with you." He paused, then scratched his arm, a throwaway gesture that was out of character. "But we can talk about work. Or whatever you want."

"Okay," Patrick said. He debated freaking out to Kat, or Googling "what is a date?" before deciding he needed to handle this on his own.

At 6:30 Karl stopped by his desk, easy as anything, and they went off to dinner. Neither of them had preferences, so they ended up in a Thai place not far from Union Square. Patrick ordered a green curry and Karl got cashew chicken, and they split a tom yum soup. Along the way they'd discussed the current project, naturally, and also the latest episode of *Black Mirror*. Patrick relaxed, because it wasn't that different from lunch after all. They could have good conversations like this. As friends.

"So tell me more about the day job," Karl said. "The real one." He winked, which was illegal.

"The shop in the mission?"

"Yeah. With the hip lady. Why a liquor store on weekends? You . . . don't strike me as someone who drinks much." They'd been to company happy hours together before; he knew Patrick wasn't big on alcohol.

Patrick was possessed with an irrational burst of honesty. "It's actually a magic shop," he said. "We make minor potions and spells. Nothing people would really notice, nothing that's too influential, mostly impermanent . . . but we do come up with some pretty cool things."

"Really?" Karl's eyes were bright. "You can actually do magic?"

"Sure." He sounded like he was bluffing. He was surprised Karl kept playing along. Maybe he'd misread Karl's magical ability after all? Why was it so hard to tell this stuff?

"Woahhhh. You're a *wizard*, then."

"I'm a witch, actually," Patrick said, and was heartily relieved when the waiter came by with their soup.

Karl laughed, but it wasn't a mean laugh. It was a laugh of delight. "That's *awesome*." He ladled out some soup for himself and for Patrick, and added, "Well, you can't say that and not show me something. Or is that against the rules?"

"Not really," Patrick said. He was in deep already. Might as well keep going. "Okay. Watch." He held one hand over the soup in its boiling tureen, breathed in, and concentrated. It went from bright red to deep purple, to grassy green, to milk white, before turning red again.

Karl watched, open-mouthed. "Woah!" he said. "That's amazing!"

Patrick shouldn't have felt so pleased—color-changing was *nothing*, a very basic glamour—but he didn't get to show his magic often, and the look in Karl's eyes made him really . . . proud of himself. He wondered how different things would be, if not for that conversation years ago. What if, instead of always hesitating, he'd maybe practiced magic more openly? He took his hand away and picked up his spoon, embarrassed by how pleased he felt. "I've always kinda done it, but I only found out when I was eleven. My aunt encouraged it and stuff."

"Eleven! That's pretty young." Karl started spooning soup into his mouth. "So why be a designer at all? I mean, it's great working with you, but this is so much cooler."

This, at least, was easy to answer. "I really like designing. I like start-ups. I wouldn't enjoy magic so much if I was stressed about making money with it. I enjoy it as kind of a . . . design puzzle, actually."

"That makes sense," Karl said. The waiter swept by with their mains. Patrick didn't really want this conversation to center too much on him; he was still surprised it had turned out easy like this.

"And you? Why Product?"

"I guess I like solving problems too. And making things from the ground up. Things that are mine. Plus I love being able to work with all different kinds of people, you know? People are fascinating." He talked about getting lucky in an internship mix-up—how he'd originally gone in for a role in Operations and ended up in Product. This led to a discussion about terrible undergrad internships, which somehow evolved into general memories of undergrad.

Patrick talked about New York, the newfangled magic of living in a big city, how that and the career options had made San Francisco a no-brainer. "It's such a cliché," he said. "But I really did love it. I mean, my family's all mostly in this coast, so I knew I wanted to move back West. But I couldn't imagine going back to Fresno."

"It's cool that you moved away, though. Sometimes I wish I had done college outside of the Bay Area," Karl said. "Gone somewhere different for a while. I'm too rooted here."

"Why not go now?" Patrick asked. "You're still young."

Karl shrugged. "I can't leave this place. The hills, the weather."

"Sure."

"The job options, too."

"Good point."

"Let's just say that San Francisco and I are inextricably linked." Karl chewed the single piece of broccoli on his plate and considered the flower-shaped carrot slice that went with it. "So you gotta indulge me: why a witch, not a wizard?"

"Well," Patrick said. "*Let's just say* that's not something you get to choose."

Karl smirked and nodded. "Magic makes its own rules, I guess."

Outside the restaurant, Karl asked him if he wanted a drink. Patrick umm'ed and said he had to feed his cat. Drinks felt like pushing it. He'd survived dinner—really it had been a *nice* dinner—but he needed to decompress, debrief this step by step in his head.

Karl nodded, an aw-shucks smile on his face.

Patrick inclined his head towards Market Street. "I take the bus," he said.

"See you tomorrow?"

"Sure. Thanks for having dinner with me."

He'd already turned away when Patrick said, "Um, Karl." He turned back. "What's up?"

"It's . . . it's not exactly a secret, but um. No one really knows at work. Besides Kat."

"I got you," Karl said, and waved. Patrick knew he meant it, too. Truthfully, it wasn't the hair or the dimples, or the elbow patch jackets. It was his kindness, his way of somehow always understanding, that kept making this so hard.

He and Karl started going out for dinner regularly: pizza in North Beach, Korean food in the Richmond, ramen by Market Street. They talked about the latest updates in self-driving cars; how you got better at magic ("It's like learning an instrument or a foreign language: feeling silly, guessing, getting it wrong . . ."); Patrick's younger sister Ann who was in her sophomore year of college, taking up biology, debating whether to become a veterinarian or a doctor; Karl's multitude of cousins scattered around the West Coast, from Seattle to Orange County; whether

Marquet was growing too quickly and needed to slow down; what were some good ways of improving visual design skills; how insufferable yet lovable San Francisco was.

The dinners were only *sometimes* agony, and only because it was getting very difficult for Patrick not to wonder what they meant. It didn't help that their project meant endless meetings together, and that they were always *on the same page*.

"You can't mind-read, can you?" Karl asked once, jokingly. If only.

When Karl invited him to a non-mutual friend's birthday one Saturday evening, Patrick hesitated only briefly. A friend's birthday seemed like a very platonic setting, and Kat would probably be there. The address was in Nob Hill; the fog curled around Patrick as he climbed up the streets, huffing, grateful for the chill so that he wouldn't start sweating. He gave Karl a call when he was by the door, and Karl came down to pick him up.

He opened the door, smiling widely. "You came!"

"Why wouldn't I?"

"I dunno. Shyness?"

"I'm not *that* shy," Patrick said, and wondered what else Karl thought of him, and how accurate it was. "Besides, my current spell involves how to avoid people at parties, so I can use this as research." *And I like spending time with you*, he didn't add. He took off his jacket as Karl led him indoors. "Where's Kat?"

"Oh, she can't come."

"Oh, really?" Patrick should've checked with her first. Now that he was here there was no way he could bail.

"Too hungover," Patrick said. "She was out dancing 'til two." The background music had increased during their progression down the hallway; they emerged into a giant-for-SF-standards living room that was full of stylish people holding wine glasses and paper plates filled with cheese nibbles. Karl felt strangely undone by this scene. He'd done SF house parties before, in the Marina and the Mission; he knew how to hang. But he didn't know anyone here, and they all seemed to know Karl. They even had that same strange glossy sheen to them that Karl did, a sort of high-fidelity attractiveness that made Patrick feel very . . .

ordinary. And out of place. He hadn't exactly been conscious of it 'til this moment.

"Here, give me your jacket. Do you want something to drink?"

"Oh. Uh, sparkling water, if there is."

"Karl! Who's your friend?" A girl in a dark denim jumper was sitting on a loveseat, waving her rosé.

"His name's Patrick!" Karl said. Turning to Patrick, he said, "That's Sal. Let me grab your drink."

The *why-don't-you-go-say-hi* was implicit, but Patrick felt like a boneless, compliant creature by this point. He wandered over to Sal, who had extremely circular glasses and a classy bob. "Yo," she said. "Welcome!"

"Thanks. H-happy birthday?"

"Aww, thank you! So glad you could come! This is Dara, and Arnie. Come sit." Two people sitting on the floor waved up at Patrick. He sat next to them, trying to relax.

"You work with Karl?" the girl named Dara asked.

"Yeah."

"What's that like?"

"He's great," Patrick said reflexively.

"I mean, I don't know anyone who doesn't like Karl," Arnie said. "*Seriously.* I get to say that because I'm his cousin." Patrick had noticed the gray eyes, the sharp jawline. Arnie's hair was also that paler-than-pale blond, reinforcing Karl's claim that the color was natural. She had a frail, ethereal beauty that looked like it could fit in a high fashion ad.

Patrick wasn't sure how to direct the conversation. "I mean, he's really good at his job. And sweet. And I guess kinda mysterious?"

"He *is* sweet, isn't he?" Dara said. "About the only people who'd disagree are his exes. Remember that girl Lauren? She was the worst."

"Ah," Patrick said. He fought the instinct to touch his chest, surprised at how badly it hurt. Wasn't this what he wanted from the beginning? Some reason to stop obsessing over Karl. Some form of closure. *Of course* it wouldn't be that easy, that the first person he ever liked would reciprocate. *Of course* Karl was into girls. Maybe he even had a crush on Kat. They were always doing one-on-ones, whispering and snickering at each other.

"Are you guys gossiping about me? Don't scare off my friend." Karl appeared, La Croix in hand. Patrick sincerely regretted not asking for a glass of wine instead.

"We were about to stir up the legend of Lauren."

Karl slapped his forehead. "Please, no. Anything else. My love life is tragic, full of terrible women. Sal, didn't you just come back from Tokyo?"

"Oh my *god*," Sal said, and launched into a story about taking the wrong bullet train and ending up in Kyushu. Patrick tried to follow, but it was surprisingly difficult. Of course Karl being fashionable didn't mean he was queer; of course Karl saw him as a cool coworker. Patrick wanted to leave but felt he couldn't. He wasn't sure if he was supposed to be having fun. He wasn't sure why Karl invited him over. Various people would stop by and Patrick was introduced to them, but he didn't know what for. The next hour he spent in that room felt like agony, and when it was sufficiently late enough that people felt like heading out to a bar to drink more, Patrick didn't say anything; he just left. Everyone else was too wrapped up in themselves to notice.

Beware of men's hearts, and never let them be your master. He turned this over in his mind the whole walk home. For some reason, this whole time, he'd never thought that passage would mean his *own* heart.

"Something's messed you up," Myrtle said. Since he last saw her she'd chopped her hair extra short. She was constantly messing it up, unable to get used to it. Tonight she was hunched over, darning a protection spell into a child's sweater—a birthday gift for a friend's nephew.

"What do you mean?"

"Pat, you look *woebegone*."

Patrick looked at his blurry reflection on the countertop. He looked the same. She was trying to wrangle a confession out of him. That was such an Aunt Gemma move. He sometimes wondered if they were dating. "I'm fine," he said. "Just . . . stressful stuff at work. Lots of late nights. We're having a major product launch soon."

Myrtle murmured, unconvinced.

"Josiah," he told the cat, who was watching the street outside with lazy interest, "Tell your mom to stop bullying me." Josiah flicked his tail.

"I just worry about you, kid."

Patrick grinned down at his diagrams. "You don't need to." People were always worrying about him, and it made him feel sheepish, eleven again and not standing his ground like he should have.

Myrtle, did you ever not want to be a witch? How do you deal with a broken heart, when nothing's even happened?

He dusted away the chalk on his fingertips. "What does the jar of blackberries mean?"

Myrtle hmm'ed. "You're supposed to mush it into jam and feed it to people you want to keep by your side. I tried it once with an ex-girlfriend. She was *not* into it."

Patrick stared. Myrtle burst out laughing. "Kidding! Hell if I know. I don't think it really means anything. It's superstition. We love superstition."

"But superstition *means* something to us."

Myrtle shrugged, shook out the sweater to see how it looked. "Rules are easy. Living despite them, that's the hard part."

There was a Starbucks cup on his desk. *Hang in there.* Karl's all-caps handwriting.

Patrick was suddenly angry. At himself, mostly, for not getting his feelings under control. But also at Karl, for messing with him like this when he—when—this had to stop. He picked up the cup and veered for Karl's desk, where Karl was bouncing on his heels, bopping along to something on Spotify. Patrick wasn't sure what to say, but it was hugely important that he deal with this *right* now. He waved a hand in front of Karl's face.

Karl pulled down his headphones. "Morning!"

"What's this for?" A measured tone, that hopefully communicated: *stop doing this to me, I'm dying.* There was the teenage poet again. Yuck.

"Umm," Karl said. "It's a stressful week? With the launch? I like you?"

"*Stop saying that,*" Patrick said, the measured tone slipping away. "You, you just—I'm sorry. I don't want you to keep doing nice things for me." He sounded like an idiot. He was an idiot. Myrtle was right—he was messed up—and he braced himself, waiting for Karl to say *Jeez, dude, it's just a coffee!*

Instead, Karl said, very gently: "Want to go to a conference room?"

The sting of tears. Patrick fought them with every ounce of self-preservation he still had—he always cried too easily. (He could hold it in when it mattered. He had done that, sixteen years ago, in a conversation about who he was.)

All the conference rooms were empty. They entered one where the whiteboard still held their diagrams from the day before, last-minute tweaks after their testing party brought to light two conflicting user flows. Karl eased the door shut and stood in front of it, leaning his arms on a chair, watching Patrick's face.

"What's wrong?"

Patrick gathered into himself, let out a shaky breath. This was a completely ridiculous time to be having a meltdown over a crush. If he had more experience with this stuff, he wouldn't be such a wreck. But this was first-time everything, his heart was on fire, and the boy across from him always made him smile and had no idea *how much that hurt.* There was nothing he could say that would make sense. "I'm sorry," he said. "I don't know what's gotten into me."

Karl drummed his fingers on the top of the chair. "Maybe I should apologize," he said.

This was so unexpected that Patrick looked up.

"It's the flirting, isn't it?" Karl asked. He sounded sorry.

Yes would be wrong; *no* was inaccurate. Patrick pressed his lips together.

"I didn't know the right method," Karl said. "I'm a Product Manager, right? I had to do my research, but also work with assumptions. Test a hypothesis."

"What the fuck are you *talking* about?"

"I was trying to figure out if you liked me."

Patrick went red. In the glass pane behind Karl's shoulder he saw Kat reach her desk and wave at them. It was perfectly ordinary for a PM and a Designer to have a last-minute meeting the day of a massive product launch; that meeting just didn't normally involve gay feelings. "That's not funny," he said.

"What? Why are you mad?"

"Because, I—" *don't want to hope*, Patrick thought; maybe that was the start and end of it. "It's not a joke."

"I'm not joking."

"You—you like guys, or something?"

"Maybe." Karl smiled, not his usual beam of unshakeable goodwill, but something more tender and—tentative, almost. "Or the more accurate way to phrase it is . . . that kind of stuff doesn't really matter to me, given what I am."

Patrick started to laugh. "Oh my god, what's happening?" he said aloud.

"I'm saying I like you," Karl said, reaching out a hand—Patrick caught it. Wondered if this wasn't a dream—something he'd concocted for himself, a draught he inhaled so that this would happen, too good to be true. Karl squeezed his hand. "I've been telling you that for *weeks*. That's okay, isn't it?"

"It's . . . okay," Patrick said, and forgot to wonder if anyone could see when Karl raised his knuckles to his lips and kissed them reverently.

"It's going to be stand-up soon," Karl said. He let go of Patrick's hand. "We can talk about this more later." He seemed sunny, radiant, and as the clock inexorably ticked to 9:15 and others started to file into the office, he did not stop smiling. Patrick was sure he had the dopiest expression on, but right now, that didn't really matter.

It was easy, Patrick realized, in a way he didn't expect it to be. It wasn't even that different from being friends: the same dinners, the same heart-fluttering spasms, how every time he glanced at Karl he thought, *Shit, he's cute*. Except there was this separate awareness in his head—even if they'd never quite said it—they were *dating*, he was dating a guy. It was like the songs, being in love—because that's what this was, right? Now that he wasn't fighting it every minute, now that he was letting himself be okay with the feeling: sunshine on a cloudy day, hooked on a feeling. You really got me; you make my dreams come true. They didn't act differently at work, either, so no one could tell. Which was fine. Neither of them felt like being the topic of office gossip, and they collaborated so closely that it was better if no one else knew.

Kat, of course, was in on it. Patrick half-expected her to say, "Fucking finally!"—but she actually laughed in surprise, and said, "Oh my god I had *no idea congratulations you two* but oh my god really?! Oh my god!" She dropped the taco she'd been holding, and they had a good laugh while mopping away salsa. "Come to think of it," she said to Karl, "you are somehow the perfect definition of bisexual."

Surprisingly, Patrick's heart still hurt sometimes. The ghost of rule number two, looming. How fragile things seemed. How he was still hiding, in a way. The happiness melted everything, made the edges fuzzy, but there were still times when Patrick was sure he was going to mess this up because of how badly he wanted it. How ashamed he was, of that wanting.

The first time Karl asked if he could come over Patrick had said "Sure." Internally he'd been nervous, totally unsure of what was about to happen. They walked back from ramen at Japantown, discussing the latest trivia night at the office that had ended with Marlene from Marketing crying drunkenly about not knowing The Rock's real name. Patrick's mind was only half on the conversation.

"It's messy, sorry," Patrick warned, as he turned his key in the lock. He'd been practicing pentagrams that week, things to conjure a little spring for winter. "I don't usually have visitors."

"I don't mind," Karl said. He inspected the diagrams on Patrick's table. "Are these spells to summon a sexy boyfriend?"

"Ha-ha." Patrick cleared a stack of books off a chair and pushed his papers out of the way, while Karl migrated to his bookcase. Patrick realized his jar of blackberries was sitting in plain view but decided not to worry about it.

"You want something to drink?"

"White tea?"

Patrick snorted and flipped his kettle on.

Miranda poked her head out from the bedroom, eyeing the inter-loper.

"Aw, she's such a cutie." Karl squatted down and reached out his arms to her. She turned her head aside, unimpressed, and sauntered over to Patrick to rub against his leg instead.

"She plays hard to get."

"Like you?"

"Don't know what you mean," Patrick said, but he bit his lip to keep from smiling. Karl had wandered over to the refrigerator and was now looking at the pictures Patrick had tacked up: of his family, random wedding invites, Aunt Gemma's note.

"Interesting list. What does *the shape of things can be deceptive* mean?"

"That's a secret." Patrick envied Karl his mysteriousness, a little; sometimes he wanted to do the same, be even *slightly* alluring. He handed his boyfriend a mug.

"I mean, it doesn't sound too secretive. It just sounds like good life advice." Karl took a sip, standing close. He had long eyelashes—sooty, Patrick thought, that was the book-word for it—and his hair had grown out from when they first met. Now he had bangs that kept falling into his eyes. He was wearing a green sweater, and there was a ball of fuzz on his right shoulder. Patrick didn't know why he was noting all of these things, except this felt like an important moment. Worth turning into a memory. Patrick brought his mug up to shield his face, acknowledged he was freaked out. Excited. But freaked out.

Karl put his mug down on the counter. "Why are you so cute?"

"Stop it. You're the worst."

"No, I'm serious." He crept closer, and because he was a gigantic flirting *idiot* he completely ignored the fact that Patrick was holding a steaming mug of hot tea and just *leaned in*, went for a—kiss—this was Patrick's first ever kiss—Karl wouldn't know that, but maybe he'd guess it—and Patrick's hand jerked, spilling tea, even as his body relaxed. The tea fell harmlessly onto the carpet. Miranda hissed like she was going *oh-please*. It was . . . really *interesting*, a kiss was, sort of mushy and Karl's mouth was soft, a kind of dissolving into nothingness, the taste of tea and dinner beneath it, and Patrick was lightheaded with this sensation, suddenly present with himself—not forwards or backwards, not thinking too hard—alive here with someone's mouth against his. Why did Karl taste like rain?

They broke apart, and he put the mug on the counter. Bit his lip, for a different reason this time. Watched Karl's eyes flicker with interest.

I can do that to someone? Holy shit.

Karl waited. This time, Patrick was the one who reached out, cradling his head—and—was it always this impossible not to close your eyes? The kiss went on forever, even through Miranda skritch-skritching somewhere in the background (*my pentagrams*, Patrick worried faintly), and then Karl slid a hand up the back of his shirt, palmed his ribs. He made some unfortunate sound into Karl's mouth, and Karl pulled away.

"Sorry," they said at the same time.

Karl kept his hand where it was, warm against his side.

"It's not that I don't like it," Patrick said. "I just, uhhh. I've never. Been intimate." He'd never even made out with someone, but the words *make out* were too embarrassing to say aloud. Even the word *intimate* made him feel ridiculous. He should have just admitted he was a virgin. For a long time Patrick had wondered if he might be ace; he'd guessed he wasn't, and recent feelings had made him *sure* he wasn't, but this was all still very new to him.

"We don't have to do anything you don't want to," Karl said. Then, since he had no shame whatsoever: "Should I take my hand away?"

Well, if it was going to be like that, he could play too. Patrick looped his arms over Karl's shoulders and looked him in his absurdly hot, thundercloud eyes. "Leave it."

He told Karl the story one November evening, rain falling steadily outside and someone in the floor above them playing Spanish guitar. How he'd come out four years ago, shortly after moving to San Francisco, back in his old apartment that he split with four other people in the Mission. He had a charm for courage tied around his wrist while he called his mom and wondered when his heart had been replaced with a jackhammer. It was cowardly, to come out over the phone. Cowardly and still more frightening than anything.

There was a long pause while she digested what he had to say.

You don't have a boyfriend, Mom said. *Do you?*

No.

You're not dating someone?

No.

So how do you know?

Patrick had pressed his head against the wall. What use was a stupid courage spell for? Why did he always feel like he had to *say what he was,* when it hurt the people he cared about?

I just—I know, I'm sure. I've known for a couple of years now.

But how *do you know?* Emphasis on *how,* like that was the part of her question he was struggling with.

Patrick had stared at Miranda, who was more at home in this city and in her skin than he'd probably ever be. Cats were not sages and they were not guides, she wasn't even Aunt Gemma's familiar per se, but maybe if he stared at her long enough she'd deign to give him an answer. Miranda stared back. Nothing happened. He soldiered on.

I find boys cute.

That's not the same thing. I think some girls are cute.

I would only like to date boys. By then Patrick felt remote and help-less. He thought of adding, *I would only like to kiss boys, and fuck boys, and be fucked by boys, and it has taken me forever to reach this conclusion, and for the longest time I thought saying this didn't matter, and a part of me still thinks maybe it doesn't. But a larger part of me has just gotten tired of hiding this, and not flinching away at every mention of it, and pretending that I'm not what I am. I've come here. This far. This far and I am still turned away, at this gate, this shore, I cannot cross, Mom, I've gotten this far, and you still can't see me. I have carried myself here and I am at your feet.*

Is this related to the witch thing? That was Dad, suddenly—Dad who'd been listening this whole time, as Patrick had been expecting. Dad who only knew what he knew: that his son was a witch and now gay. Dad whom he loved, who loved him back, who could not know how much those words hurt. Being a witch didn't make him gay and being gay didn't make him a witch. Patrick was just Patrick; being Patrick was hard.

No, it's not related to being a witch at all.

They were all quiet for a while.

Mom had sighed. *We love you so much,* she said. *We worry about you. We don't . . . want things to be hard for you.*

I know, Mom. Dad. He wiped his tears away, didn't inhale deeply like he was longing to, so that it wasn't obvious he'd been crying.

We want you to be happy.

Okay.

Okay.

He was tearing up again, recounting the exchange. He swallowed and said, "We've never really talked about it since, even when I go back home. I mean . . . I don't really want to talk about it either. I don't know what they think."

Karl's head was on his lap and he'd closed his eyes during the story, making soft noises to show he was listening. Now he opened his eyes. Patrick couldn't look at him, suddenly; he gazed outside, but there wasn't much to see. Fog pressed against the windows, like a stray seeking shelter. Karl reached up and touched his cheek, gently. "Does it matter what they think?"

"It does to me."

"Sorry. What I meant was, does it matter . . . if you all love each other?"

Patrick bent down and kissed his boyfriend's forehead. Karl's skin was always cool, always tasted faintly of rain. "Yeah. But knowing that makes it matter a little less."

Halloween started off innocently enough. It was on a Friday that year, one of those unexpectedly warm fall days, the sun beaming down, bouncing off all the glass windows in SoMa. Patrick counted six Where's Waldos on his commute. That had been his default costume (having obtained the requisite striped sweater the previous year), but Kat had been insistent about going as the Bananas in Pajamas this year. ("Fine. As long as I get to be B2.") Karl's costume was a secret.

By lunchtime almost everyone was only pretending to work. It was too nice outside. Most people went for the food trucks then lounged in South Park for way too long. Marquet had closed a Series B in the last week and everyone was in high spirits, and the evening's party was hopefully going to reflect a wee bit of that cash in the bank. At 4:00 p.m. Melody started walking around with a jug full of beer, and people began queuing for the bathroom. Karl got his turn at last, and emerged wearing a T-shirt, beanie, and jeans—all bright red.

"Ooo, let me guess!" Kat clapped her hands together. "Sexy Santa? A drop of blood? Wait! A . . .period?"

"I'm the Golden Gate Bridge," Karl said.

Kat leaned towards Patrick. "Your boyfriend is an idiot."

"He's not the one dressed as a banana," Patrick replied.

Angeli, the newest Android engineer, cracked ice for old-fashioneds in the kitchen. Richard the CTO appeared from behind his desk dressed as a piece of salmon sushi, and was swarmed by people wanting to take selfies. Melody dimmed the lights and put on a playlist that predictably started with Michael Jackson's *Thriller*. Random friendly relations poured in from the stairwell and the elevator, and soon the room was full of people drinking and talking and not-exactly-dancing, green lights strung up on the ceiling, the fog machine making everyone alienlike. Two girls that Patrick didn't recognize were dressed as sexy witches: black miniskirt-eyeliner-lipstick. They came up to Patrick to ask him where the bathroom was, and he wondered if either of them could actually work any magic. At some point Jeremy from Finance made a passable DJ airhorn imitation, and an image of Vodka Ice was projected on the wall. Everyone had to proceed to the cauldron in the kitchen, fish out a bottle, get on one knee and down it. Around this time Kat shoved Patrick and Karl out of the office and told them to get in the Lyft waiting outside, because it was time to hit the city.

Patrick was still lucid. He remembered most of the first club: some of Kat's friends from her first start-up were there, and half the Sales team appeared shortly after they arrived. There was a lot of standing in a circle and pumping knees. He'd discarded his banana hat-thing at the bar; now he just looked like a dude in striped pajamas. He remembered most of the second club too: a Jack Sparrow with the most endearing Australian accent bought them shots of whiskey, gratis; Kat had kissed his fake beard. Karl lost his beanie somewhere on the dance floor, maybe because some girl dressed as a cop had come by and pulled it off to rake her fingers through his hair—Patrick had witnessed this stumbling back from the bathroom. He was too far away to do anything about it. A Luke Skywalker suddenly blocked Patrick's path, laughed in a way that showed all his teeth and tried to give Patrick a hug. He seemed to have four thousand arms. Patrick allowed himself to be hugged, laughed back, felt his stomach lurch. Luke Skywalker kissed him on the mouth. Patrick stepped backwards, into a grinding couple; he edged away from them, helter-skelter, and suddenly Karl's fingers were around his wrist like a vice, dragging him through the crowd towards the door.

"Ouch," he'd said, expecting Karl to stop. He didn't. "That hurts."

Karl tugged him through the door, didn't listen when Patrick said he needed to let Kat know they were leaving. "I'll text her," Karl said, and waved at the Uber making a U-turn for them. "Come on, get in."

"Are you angry?"

Patrick had seen Karl angry exactly twice—once when they'd pushed an update without properly QA'ing it and the support team got flooded with venomous calls and chats (he'd subsequently had a very loud meeting with the Product Lead for approving the decision); and another time when someone had yelled "GET A ROOM" and a slur at them, while they were crossing the street together, holding hands. His eyes weren't the gentle gray of mist anymore; they were deep storm clouds, roiling around a single point of fury. Something in them shook Patrick, fought through the haze of alcohol and the threat of nausea so that he was really *looking* at Karl. Rain broke out, slammed against the car's windshield. Karl only let go of Patrick's wrist once they were pulling away from the neon lights of the Castro, passing a troupe of angels and devils clustered on the street corner.

Patrick pressed his hands to his face, though whether that was to hold something in or blot something out, he wasn't sure. He heard Karl sigh next to him.

When the Uber finally stopped, it wasn't at his apartment like he was expecting. He didn't have time to ask any questions before Karl got out of the car, and he had to follow. Karl was at the gate, already putting his key in. He turned and looked at Patrick, still with that stormy look. Patrick went up the steps and followed him inside, suddenly uncertain. Two flights of stairs. Another key, a deadbolt, and they were inside Karl's flat, which was somehow colder than the hallway or even the night outside. It occurred to Patrick that some part of him hadn't believed Karl *lived* anywhere, that his existence didn't appear to involve anything so ordinary as an apartment, even if that was absurd. Karl flicked on a light, revealing the meticulously clean room. Patrick had taken barely two steps inside when Karl embraced him from behind, pressed his lips to Patrick's neck and kissed him beneath his striped pajama collar. Patrick tingled all over.

He turned and touched Karl's face. "You're drunk," he said. "Stop."

"I don't want to." He kissed Patrick again, almost lunging, full of want. His arms wrapped around Patrick's back, pressing him in. Patrick was surprised by the force, how it made his stomach jump, an aching tenderness in his lower belly, but—no. Not like this. Resisting the urge to kiss him back, Patrick placed his hands on Karl's temple and pulled him away, gave him what was hopefully a stern look. Did the thing he used to do to noisy kids in food courts: *stop that*. The rain outside was so loud it seemed to be in the room with them. Patrick had to strain to get his magic to work. *Stop it.*

After a moment where it seemed like nothing was happening, the storm clouds left Karl's eyes. He blinked, dazed. Then he pressed his face into Patrick's collarbone. "Oh my god, I'm sorry," he murmured. "I don't know what got into me."

"It's okay." He wanted to be reassuring, but he *was* a little worried. He patted Karl's back. "Let me get you a glass of water."

Karl was reluctant to let go. He disappeared into the bathroom; Patrick heard water splashing. He entered the kitchen, trying to ignore a spike of disappointment. On the counter he noticed the bag of White Needle he'd given Karl, way back during Pride weekend, and an infuser next to it. It would probably wake him up, get him back to normal. He rummaged in the drawers for a teaspoon, then opened the bag.

His heart dropped.

That did not smell like white tea. It smelled, instead, like rosemary and vanilla, like dried tears. A spell that didn't work, or worked too slowly. A slow-burn desire that peaked only months after ingested.

In moments of extreme panic, Patrick typically acted with supreme rationality. He took the bag. He fished his phone out of his breast pocket, thanked god he still had battery left, and called a Lyft. He said nothing to Karl, who was still in the bathroom, and left the apartment. He stood on the street outside, getting drenched in the rain, trying not to think, trying not to feel. He failed miserably.

Myrtle was surprised that he hadn't known that she'd been storing the early brews in old tea canisters.

"I always save the earlier batches," she said. "You never know when they'll come in handy. Something wrong?"

"No."

"Oh boy."

"Don't ask." Patrick blinked rapidly when she put a hand on his shoulder and was grateful she didn't press.

hey
I'm sorry about yesterday :(God I was such a dick
I'm sorry
Can I come over?
3 Missed Calls from Karl *:cloud-emoji:*
I understand if you're mad
2 Missed Calls from Karl *:cloud-emoji:*
I love you
See you tomorrow

Had he ever said *I love you* to Karl?

Karl always said *I love you* to him.

He turned that over in his head. He'd always *meant* to, in his embraces, his glances, his heart emojis. But it didn't seem like he'd ever said it aloud. The words were too raw, too trusting. Maybe he'd been waiting for a way to make sure.

It was weird. And sad. That whole weekend Patrick made up dialogues in his head about how this was going to go. He forget them all when he walked into the office on Monday. Karl was waiting for him. Of course. He'd been ignoring Karl's texts and calls all weekend. The office was deserted at 8:30; he should have arranged to come in with Kat that morning, so that he could pretend everything was cool and nothing hurt. But they were in a professional environment, and they were both professionals, and he was going to see this conversation through to the bloody end.

"I'm sorry," Karl said. They were back in the room where this had all started, just a few weeks ago. "I was a little drunk, yes, but it was the sight of that Jedi dude kissing you that made me—I lost it. I totally lost it. I know I act calm all the time but I'm really not, Patrick, you make me so . . ." He exhaled. "I won't make excuses. But I really am sorry, and I get why you're ignoring me but it's driving me crazy. Can we start over? Can I fix this?"

"Stop apologizing," Patrick said. He was going to have to do it after all, break his own heart by breaking Karl's, so that this would be over more quickly. After all, it was his potion. He knew how it worked. He knew it would be wearing off any day now, and Karl's sensibilities would shift and all that ache would be gone, whisked away from his being. The feelings hadn't really been there to begin with. His memories would be vague, the details filed off. Patrick was the only one who'd have to carry the broken pieces.

Which was great. He could bear it. He had lots of practice with pretending.

He looked at his first-ever crush and only-ever boyfriend and reconciled that sometimes things were too good to be true.

"This was a mistake," Patrick said, carefully. "It's . . . it wasn't real,

Karl. I'm sorry. We can't," he waved a hand, then forced himself to say it. "We can't keep dating. I really like you, but I want to . . ." Say it. *Say it.* "Just go back to how we were, you know. I want you to keep being my partner, my PM, my friend." He managed a smile, tried not to register the way Karl's face was spanning an entire history of pain—*it's the potion working, it's doing its job; he's supposed to desire me. He can't help it.* Time to bring it home. "Can we do that?"

Karl squeezed his eyes shut. For a moment Patrick thought he was going to cry. But when he opened them again his eyes were clear. "I don't want to," he said. "But if it's what you want."

"It's what I want."

"Can I hug you as a friend, then?" Karl said. "It'll make me feel better."

"You really are the worst," Patrick said, but he opened up his arms anyway. Karl pressed his nose to Patrick's shoulder and breathed in deeply. Patrick nearly lost it, all the tears he'd been holding back that weekend suddenly welling up, up, up, it had been *so good* even if it had all been fake. He swallowed, gave Karl a firm squeeze, then pushed him away. At least this way they could keep working together. "It'll make sense in a few days," he said, smiling. "You'll see. It won't hurt at all."

This was easy, too, but in a different way—*acting* was easy, because that's what it felt like. They didn't need to be any different. They moved and talked and worked the same, they still had lunch together, still talked about the merits of their new design software and which emo bands they liked in high school, but that was all surface stuff. Everything beneath that was different. They could still work together, but in the silences of a meeting—brief encounters in the kitchen, packing up for home—tension stretched between them, so delicate a drawn breath could explode it.

Maybe the weirdest thing was how Karl dropped the flirtations almost entirely, just a stray gesture here and there: touching his arm when he was making a point over a mock-up or picking stray cat hair off his shoulder. Karl always started when he did those things, as if he was surfacing from a dream. Then they would both look away.

Kat noticed, of course. Patrick didn't tell her about the potion, because the spell was wearing off now and any mention of it might have repercussions. He told her, instead, that he'd known from the beginning it wasn't going to work, and he figured it was better to call it quits early. Kat's forehead went all creased. "You were both hella wasted on Halloween," she said. "Whatever happened, I'm sure it was just . . . you know. A thing."

"No, Kat, it's not one of those things. It's really . . . it's me."

"I could've guessed that," Kat shot back, surprising Patrick with her anger. "You're always fencing yourself off, Pat. You were happy! *He* was happy. I don't get it."

"I wasn't expecting you to," Patrick said. She gave him a dark look and left. He watched her go, weary. He and Kat had fought before; he'd bribe her back with gelato the next day.

Things did, eventually, normalize. Karl went from slightly droopy to bright and sunny again, his smile radiant as ever. Patrick was surprised at how the memory of having that smile directed at him made him lonely. The loneliness was new. It was like their being together had made a space inside him that hadn't been there before, and he'd expanded to contain it, and now he was empty. What happened felt like a dream. A temporary moment of grace: someone else's story. Something to treasure and hold close. The first crush that had come, years and years after it seemed *normal* to get one. It was a lesson, he decided. Someday he'd look back on it and the hurt would be gone, too: his broken heart an artifact to inspect.

That didn't need to be magic; time was magic in its own way. At least they were still friends.

Patrick got a rental car and drove back to Fresno for Thanksgiving. Aunt Gemma joined him. She'd come from Asia on consecutive flights, and by all rights should have been groggy and grumpy. But she was effusive as ever, sharing all her travel adventures during the long drive. Once they arrived she bustled over the turkey Dad was painstakingly trying to roast, and cheerfully whipped up her signature blackberry tart. Ann had flown in from the East Coast and spent most of her break napping, though occasionally she wandered into Patrick's room to tell him about the latest drama at school. Ann had no magic, like Mom, but she didn't mind. She was a peaceful kid, extremely bright, and probably going to med school after all. Do actual healing, instead of the sometimes-fixers that Patrick brewed. It was interesting, how they lived such separate lives most of the year but could pick up where they left off the few times they were together. She lurked now in his room, like they did years ago, before they both left.

"Are you working on a new spell?"

Patrick was at his desk, fishing out notes from high school. "Yeah," he said.

"What for?"

"Mending a broken heart."

"Really?"

"No, not really. That's the kind of thing spells can only gloss over, not fix." He leaned back in his chair, stretched. "Or maybe I'm just not a good enough witch."

"Aunt Gemma's always going on about how great you are."

"She just dotes on me," he said. "Because we're the same."

Ann shrugged. "I'll always be grateful for when you mended Mr. Puttyface without any thread." Her purple rabbit doll, ages ago, when she'd torn off one arm in a rage. "So what are you actually working on?"

"Something to keep the cold away in winter. I had a prototype and it didn't work."

"Few prototypes work," Ann said sagely, then lay on his bed to finish her paperback. "Though I do hope that by 'winter' you don't mean San Francisco getting marginally colder in January. I could *really* use something that works in Syracuse."

"Yeah, yeah."

She turned a few pages. "So, uh. Did your heart get broken?"

"Sort of."

Ann gave him one of her owlish looks but kept reading.

Patrick found the journal he'd been looking for. Flipping through it, he remembered what it was like *not* to feel this way—constantly thinking of someone else, wanting to be wanted. He'd wondered, on and off for several years, what was wrong with him; why he didn't get crushes like everyone else. Turned out he was just as fallible as the rest of them. He nearly missed this old version of himself: not-caring, pre-Karl. He read the journal until Mom called them down for dinner.

"How's work?" Mom asked, while they sat munching turkey and Brussels sprouts.

Patrick talked about their platform redesign launch, which had been a success in that *very few clients had complained*. Kat had been publicly recognized at All-Hands for her good work with messaging, and she'd named all the team members. It had been a warm and fuzzy moment. He mentioned Karl, but only in passing: a part of that project, nothing else. Aunt Gemma engaged them all with tales of getting stranded in the Singapore airport ("10/10, would recommend"). Patrick wasn't sure if she'd sensed his gloom, or simply wanted to talk.

After the meal he helped with the washing-up, then lay down on the couch and drowsed. He opened up Facebook to greet his friends a Happy Thanksgiving, and of course the first post he saw was from Karl: a picture of the Golden Gate Bridge, wreathed in mist, no filter. He'd put a heart emoji and a turkey emoji as his status update. That was it.

Patrick rolled over and wondered how long he was going to keep feeling sad. Aunt Gemma sat next to him on the couch, a decaf coffee in hand, and sipped primly. "Pat," she said. "You got a second?"

"I've got the whole evening, ma'am."

"When I gave you that rulebook for your eleventh birthday, how did you feel?"

He sat up, straightening. He hadn't been expecting that question at all. "I felt . . . grateful?"

She looked at him.

"I felt *seen*," he said. "Like someone had given me permission to say yes to something I'd known all along."

"Did it make you a better witch?"

He scrunched his face. "I don't know that it did, it was just . . . comforting. To know that you were, that I could be, a witch."

"Do you *like* being a witch?"

"Yes." He answered quietly, because he was in his own house, still carrying shards from a conversation that should have bled out of him long ago. Yes was still a betrayal of something, though he knew by now he'd never been wrong about it. He said *yes* under his breath, but he said it with conviction, because it was true.

"That makes me happy," Aunt Gemma said. "I always worried that you did it only for me."

"For you?" Patrick laughed. "But you were never around!"

"I *know*. I mean, your mom's never forgiven me. And I always had to prod."

"No, I like magic for myself," Patrick said.

"It is magic, witchcraft, isn't it? I feel really lucky to have it."

"Sometimes. When it isn't blowing up in your face."

Aunt Gemma narrowed her eyes, then took a nonchalant sip, looking coy.

"Everything works out in the end," she said. "And if it doesn't, you can always blame the cats. Or the weather."

Patrick returned to work steeling himself against the onslaught of feelings he fully expected to have. Sure, they'd been "acting normal" for weeks, but every time he thought about Karl—every time they made eye contact, even every time it *rained*—his chest went tight, like some freaking romance novel heroine. Visiting home had been great, but he knew that a few days eating leftover stuffing and thumbing through old journals was still probably not enough armor against that platinum hair, those eyes that struck him like sunlight through the mist.

Except Karl wasn't at his desk that day. It was only after an hour of meetings that Patrick got to his inbox and saw Karl's email about feeling sick and working from home.

He was out for the next three days. He still replied to email, but it was hours late, which meant he was in a bad way. The front-end team had made a functional prototype of Patrick's mock-up that Karl needed to give the go-ahead on, before the back-end team could start creating new endpoints. Patrick had sent Karl a tentative ping on Slack, but besides the perpetual *out sick* status emoji he'd gotten nothing. So it was that he found himself outside Karl's apartment at 7:00 p.m. that Friday, holding a tub of chicken noodle soup and feeling simultaneously anxious, embarrassed, and irritated at himself.

Kat should have brought it. He was being a dope. On his third try someone finally answered. "Yes?"

"It's Patrick," he said.

"Oh!" Coughing, laced with intercom crackle. "One sec."

He heard the door buzz open, and pushed his way through, up two flights of stairs, 'til he was standing at the door. There was a beat when he considered leaving the soup on the welcome mat and running away, then the door swung open and Karl peered out. He looked . . . not great. His face was flushed under pale, sick-looking skin; his hair was matted to his face with sweat. It looked washed-out, the cloudy color depressing rather than appealing.

"Hey," he croaked. "Sorry, I would invite you in, but I've caught the plague."

"It's okay," Patrick said. "I, um. I brought you soup."

"Magic soup?"

"Maybe a little." He grinned in spite of himself and held it out. Karl took it. "Did you, um. Did you have a good Thanksgiving?"

Karl shrugged. "It was okay, until I started semi-dying, I guess."

"What caused it?"

"Heartsickness." He smiled, displaying an amazing ability to remain cheeky. Patrick sighed.

"Just promise me you'll get better. The front-end guys don't know what to do without you. Actually no one does."

"I'm sure they'll manage," Karl said. "*Some* people can." Before Patrick could open his mouth to reply, he added, "Sorry! Sorry. I'm just spaced out from being sick. Patrick, you're a hero. I will take this soup religiously until I am all better. Thank you. I really appreciate it."

"It's not a big deal," Patrick said. If Karl was comfortable flirting with him again that meant the potion had finally expired; it was totally gone from his system. They could go back to being normal again. "Take it easy, okay?"

He stepped back from the door and waved. Karl waved back. For a moment it seemed like he might say something else, but the moment passed, and he shut the door. Patrick walked back down the steps, tongue pressed to the roof of his mouth, and wondered where to go from here. He felt free, and somehow trapped with it.

Karl got better and showed up the next Monday. He stopped by Patrick's desk that day. "That soup was magic!" He clapped a hand on Patrick's shoulder, then didn't talk to him for the rest of the week, except once to ask if he'd filed that JIRA ticket, post-standup.

One random Thursday Patrick had a sudden desire to walk through the Embarcadero on his way home. There were runners everywhere, and pigeons. He couldn't taste the water in the air so much as feel it. The wind blew dramatically so that his scarf flapped; SoMa debris skidded every which way. There was a flock of birds wheeling overhead, V-shapes turning and turning in ever smaller circles, mesmerizing against the pink-streaked sky of San Francisco in early December.

Patrick sat on a concrete block facing the water. He watched two dudes walk past, smiling; one of them leaned in for a quick kiss. Their laughter seemed to ring as they stepped away, but maybe that was just Patrick being melodramatic.

Maybe it was okay to let himself be melodramatic sometimes. Maybe it was okay to remember the way Karl had made him feel: like sunlight, like things were going to work out. That it was all right to be himself. That no matter what was exploding at Marquet that week, no matter how angry the clients were about the latest release, they'd figure out some way to make things right, with a bit of creativity and enough coffee. Sometimes it was about Karl's smile, his stupid hair, how soft it was threaded through Patrick's fingers when he finally allowed himself to touch it, during that second kiss. How Karl, who always seemed to be dissolving and turning up everywhere, had been firm against Patrick whenever they embraced: something that would never leave.

When did the city become so infused with the memory of one boy? When did every speck of mist and every step on the gray streets become some echo of him?

A bird landed next to Patrick, shifting its his head inquiringly. He flapped a hand at it, but it didn't leave. Soon there was a whole crowd of tiny brown birds milling around him. "Can't I have a broken heart in peace?" he sighed. To his surprise, un-summoned, a gust of wind rucked up and sent the birds wheeling over the Bay Bridge.

In the nearby dog park, a French bulldog and a Corgi erupted in barks.

He stood and walked to the banister, leaning to stare at the shiny rocks and churning water below.

"I should have said it at least once," he said. "Because I really did."

He arranged his scarf again, because the wind had died down. Fog filled the road. He seemed to be alone with it, the air thick with mist. It hung around him like an embrace as he walked the length of the road, turned into Market Street, and took the bus home.

The next weekend was SantaCon. Patrick almost forgot, except he'd set a doctor's appointment by Union Square and had to walk past a distressing number of buff Santas and sexy elves. If Kat had been in town she'd have obviously set up a SantaCon brunch for everyone, but she was in Chicago for her grandma's birthday. Which was great, because after all this time Patrick still had trouble saying no to her.

After his check-up Patrick bought a cup of Peet's Coffee, then walked to Union Square and squatted on one of the steps by a heart sculpture to spectate. A crowd of merry Santas passed by and waved at him.

One of them had gray eyes, over his thick fluffy beard and oversized Santa suit.

Patrick turned his head away and decided it was time for him to be getting home. Too late. By the time he'd stood and tipped back the last dregs of latte into his throat, the gray-eyed Santa had broken off from his group and was striding towards him, faster than the wind. Patrick scurried into the middle of Union Square, trying to lose the Santa in the throngs of people messing about and posing under the giant Christmas tree. By then there was no point denying it: he was running away.

"Patrick!"

Nope. He broke into a full-on run, down 4th Street, looking for some place to take a breather, some place to hide—there was nowhere to hide. He made it as far as Yerba Buena Gardens before Santa reached him and touched his shoulder gently. He would have kept running anyway, if not for the fence of fog around them, blotting out the garden, enveloping them in silence.

He turned.

"I knew it. You're still avoiding me."

Karl had unhooked the fake beard from his ears and taken off the Santa hat. He raked his hair back, pushed those floppy pale bangs out of the way, but he wasn't actually sweating. He looked, as always, immaculate. Patrick felt his chest rise and fall, cursed himself for his breathlessness. Even in a stupid Santa suit Karl was still everything he wanted.

"You freaked me out, that's all."

"I always seem to be doing that." His expression was pained.

"I know you don't mean it." Patrick was too tired to feel embarrassed; he simply felt defeated.

"Hey," Karl said, stepping close. "Can we talk about this?"

"There's nothing to talk about." He said it quietly, a last-ditch attempt at saving himself before he got too honest. He always got too honest. What did it matter anyway, that he broke his own heart further? It was smashed into pieces by now, impossible to glue back together.

"I won't let you run away from this." Somehow the mist around them congealed, 'til they were standing in a white fence, the air solid around them. *Magic*, Patrick thought. He wondered if Aunt Gemma or Myrtle was giggling somewhere, conjuring this. Or was it his own subconscious, tweaking the weather to force this conversation?

Karl reached out and touched his cheek, and Patrick didn't flinch away. He kept his eyes open, felt them sting with sudden tears. He remembered this touch. Like song lyrics, falling rain, Karl's skin always so cool whenever it made contact with his.

"Why are you running away?"

"Because it's not real."

"What about this isn't real?" He reached out his other hand, and gently cupped Patrick's face.

"What you felt—what you feel. It was a potion, the White

Needle tea, it was an accident." This far into speaking, Patrick felt he could finally look at Karl, and not wither into nothing. "You were drinking a love potion that whole time and it was made to be a slow-burn and you don't really like me, you only think you do. You were under a spell."

Karl blinked. He blinked again.

"You gave me a *love potion*?" He squeezed his palms, squishing Patrick's cheeks.

Patrick yelped. It wasn't painful; just shocking. "It wasn't on purpose!"

"Oh my god." Karl took his hands away, pressed them to his face. It took a second for Patrick to realize that Karl wasn't angry, he was laughing. Laughing so hard he actually doubled over. "Oh my god, you— is that why you broke up with me after Halloween?" He made a sound that sounded suspiciously like "Arrrrgghhhh" when Patrick nodded gravely in reply. But Karl was still laughing, and Patrick was too confused to be embarrassed or angry, though he did feel a pang of dismay that he was being serious, and here was Karl, losing his shit. After a moment in which he actually wiped *tears* away, Karl said, "I'm immune to potions."

"You're what?"

"I'm an elemental." He was almost apologetic. It was Patrick's turn to blink.

Karl grinned in frustration, which shouldn't have been so endearing. "I'm *of the fog*"—he waved a hand—"and I'm *immune* to human spells."

Patrick understood all in a rush. The curtain of air fencing them in, the way the fog had crept over him like a blanket so often. Karl's beautiful *eyes*. Old magic, older than witchcraft, entire books on Aunt Gemma's shelf about them, but none he'd ever gone through with any diligence because—he didn't think he'd fall in love with one. Or that they'd be so capable at project management.

"Then—"

"Yeah," Karl said, and without pretense moved like water through the space between them, right up to Patrick so that their faces were barely apart. "Some of it *was* acting, some of it was . . . trying to do this, the way humans do. But it was true. That was all me. *God*, I thought

430

you knew—I thought that's why you showed me your magic—I mean when we first met you immediately said *the fog*. I should've guessed you'd assume something completely different!"

Here was the blushing, arriving far too late, because Patrick was an idiot.

"Then . . ."

"*Yes*, what do you want me to say? I've said it before, I'll say it again: I love you." He wrapped his arms around Patrick, and all the tension left his body, so that he felt he was drifting on air, or nothingness. "My witch boy, witch love. You *did* cast a spell on me," Karl murmured, while Patrick pressed his cheek to Karl's chest, eyes filling with tears, and breathed in. The smell of rain on concrete, condensation, the air after a storm. "You just didn't know it."

Aunt Gemma was behind the counter, enjoying tea with Myrtle, when Patrick came in. They both grinned fiendishly at him; their smiles widened when Karl came in half a beat later. Patrick tried to ignore this.

Karl said "Hi." Then, "So, uh, do I have to impress you ladies? I humbly ask for your blessing to date this precious boy."

"We can't give blessings away! We're witches, not fairy godmothers. Besides, our spells don't work on you." Aunt Gemma extended Karl a cup of tea, which he took.

"Wait. Did you *know* this whole time?" Patrick's jaw dropped open.

Aunt Gemma shrugged. "Just because your boyfriend's the fog, doesn't mean he'll never break your heart."

"Patrick's already broken *mine*," Karl said. "Multiple times."

"Smart boy," Myrtle said. Josiah meowed. It sounded like a giggle.

One weekend in February they walked down the Marina pier, talking in the salt air and circling seagulls, hand in hand. They stopped at the Wave Organ, leaning into the pipes to listen, but only one of them made any sound: a faint humming, like a moan at the end of a long tunnel. It was cold and silly to be walking here in winter, even if San Francisco could make any month seem like winter, because its chilly wind was always more apparent than its sunshine.

Karl sat down first, facing the Golden Gate Bridge. It was completely visible that day.

"Are you that happy, because we're on a date?" Patrick asked.

"Maybe. Why, am I not allowed to be?"

After taking a panoramic photo, because the view was just too good, Patrick sat down next to him, pulling his beanie lower over his head. Karl leaned his head on Patrick's shoulder. Anyone walking that way would see them from a long way off, but Patrick didn't mind.

He reached up and ran a hand through Karl's hair.

"I'm still new to all of this," he said slowly. "And sometimes I'll still freak out. Just so you know."

"I know." Karl held his hand, pressed a kiss to his knuckles. He really liked doing that. "*I* still wonder sometimes if you'll ever like me as much as I like you."

Patrick touched his lips to Karl's, briefly. It seemed the best response.

Karl sighed. "I guess I'm down for this. Whatever happens. I'm down."

Because this made Patrick too happy, and he didn't know what to do with his happiness, he stuck his free hand into the pocket of Karl's coat. "My hands are cold."

Karl laughed. "I'll allow it."

ABOUT THE AUTHORS

MARIKA BAILEY is an Afro-Caribbean author, designer, and illustrator. Her fiction has appeared in *FIYAH, Fantasy, Apparitions Lit, Beneath Ceaseless Skies*, and *Strange Horizons*. She graduated from Yale University with a degree in Fine Arts. It's just as much a surprise to her as it is to her (large) West Indian family that she's managed to make a career out of words and pictures.

ELIZABETH BEAR is the Hugo, Sturgeon, Locus, and Astounding award-winning author of dozens of novels; over a hundred short stories; and a number of essays, nonfiction, and opinion pieces for markets as diverse as *Popular Mechanics* and *The Washington Post*. She lives in the Pioneer Valley of Massachusetts with her spouse, writer Scott Lynch.

Born in the Caribbean, **TOBIAS S. BUCKELL** is a *New York Times* bestselling and World Fantasy award-winning author. His novels and almost one hundred stories have been translated into nineteen different languages. He has been nominated for the Hugo Award, Nebula Award, World Fantasy Award, and Astounding Award for Best New Science Fiction Author. He currently lives in Bluffton, Ohio with his wife and two daughters, where he teaches Creative Writing at Bluffton University.

ROSHANI CHOKSHI is the award-winning author of the *New York Times* bestselling series *The Star-Touched Queen, The Gilded Wolves,* and *Aru Shah and The End of Time,* which *Time Magazine* named one of the Top 100 Fantasy Books of All Time. Her novels have been translated into more than two dozen languages and often draw upon world mythology and folklore. Chokshi is a member of the National Leadership Board for the Michael C. Carlos Museum and lives in Georgia with her husband and their cat whose diabolical plans must regularly be thwarted.

PHENDERSON DJÈLÍ CLARK is the author of the novel *A Master of Djinn,* and the award-winning and Hugo, Nebula, and Sturgeon nominated author of the novellas *Ring Shout, The Black God's Drums,* and *The Haunting of Tram Car 015.* His short stories have appeared in venues such as *Tor.com, Heroic Fantasy Quarterly, Beneath Ceaseless Skies,* and in anthologies including, *Griots* and *Hidden Youth.* He is a founding member of *FIYAH Literary Magazine.* Clark resides in a small Edwardian castle in New England with his wife and daughters.

C. S. E. COONEY is the World Fantasy Award-winning author of *Bone Swans: Stories.* She has narrated over a hundred audiobooks, released three albums as the singer/songwriter Brimstone Rhine, and her short plays have been performed in Chicago, St. Louis, Phoenix, New York City, and Taipei. Her novel *The Twice-Drowned Saint* can be found in the anthology *The Sinister Quartet,* and *Saint Death's Daughter* was published earlier this year. Other work includes novella *Desdemona and the Deep,* and a poetry collection: *How to Flirt in Faerieland and Other Wild Rhymes,* which features her Rhysling Award-winning "The Sea King's Second Bride." Her short fiction and poetry can be found in anthologies including *Dragons, Mad Hatters and March Hares,* and elsewhere.

VARSHA DINESH is a writer and marketing professional from myth-haunted Kerala in Southern India. She is a member of the Clarion West plague-class of 2020, now 2022. Her work has previously appeared in

Strange Horizons and *Podcastle*. She is an avid enthusiast of folklore, theater, and K-pop.

ANDREW DYKSTAL lives in Arlington, Virginia, where he writes across all manner of speculative genres. In 2003, long before the associated meme, he took an arrow to the knee, which was about as much fun as it sounds. His fiction has appeared in *Daily Science Fiction* and *Beneath Ceaseless Skies*, and his novelette "Thanatos Drive" won the 35th Writers of the Future contest.

JAMES ENGE teaches Latin and mythology at a medium-sized public university in northwest Ohio where he lives with his wife and two crime-fighting, emotionally fragile dogs. His first novel, *Blood of Ambrose*, was shortlisted for the World Fantasy Award and its French translation for the Prix Imaginales. He has also written the novels *This Crooked Way*, *The Wolf Age*, and a trilogy, A Tournament of Shadows, consisting of *A Guile of Dragons*, *Wrath-Bearing Tree*, and *The Wide World's End*. His short fiction has appeared in *Black Gate, Tales from the Magician's Skull, The Magazine of Fantasy & Science Fiction*, and elsewhere.

In 2020, **KAREN JOY FOWLER** won the World Fantasy Award for Lifetime Achievement. She is the *New York Times* bestselling author of six novels and three short story collections. Her novel, *The Jane Austen Book Club* was a *New York Times* Notable Book. Fowler's previous novel, *Sister Noon*, was a finalist for the 2001 PEN/Faulkner Award. Her debut novel, *Sarah Canary*, won the Commonwealth medal for best first novel by a Californian, was listed for the *Irish Times* International Fiction Prize as well as the Bay Area Book Reviewers Prize, and was a *New York Times* Notable Book. Fowler's short story collections *Black Glass* and *What I Didn't See* both won World Fantasy Awards. Her novel *We Are All Completely Beside Ourselves*, won the 2014 PEN/Faulkner Award for fiction and was short-listed for the 2014 Man Booker Prize. Her latest novel, *Booth*, was published earlier this year. Fowler and her husband, who have two grown children and seven grandchildren, live in Santa Cruz, California.

ABOUT THE AUTHORS

CARLOS HERNANDEZ is the author of the Pura Belpré Award-winning *Sal and Gabi Break the Universe*, as well as its sequel, *Sal and Gabi Fix the Universe* and the short story collection *The Assimilated Cuban's Guide to Quantum Santeria*. He is also a CUNY associate professor of English at BMCC and the Graduate Center, as well as a game writer and designer.

KATHLEEN JENNINGS' Australian Gothic debut novella *Flyaway* was published in 2020. Her writing has received a British Fantasy Award, two Ditmars, and been shortlisted for the Eugie Foster Memorial Award and for several Aurealis Awards. As an illustrator, Jennings has won one World Fantasy Award (and been nominated three other times) and has been shortlisted for the Hugo and the Locus awards. She has also received the E. G. Harvey Award for Australian SF Art and several Ditmar Awards for professional and fan art.

ALLISON KING is an Asian American writer and software engineer. "Breath of a Dragon King" was her first professional fiction sale.

PH LEE lives on top of an old walnut tree, past a thicket of roses, down a dead-end street at the edge of town. Their work has appeared in many venues including *Clarkesworld*, *Lightspeed*, and *Uncanny*. From time to time, they microwave and eat a frozen burrito at two in the morning, for no reason other than that they want to.

YUKIMI OGAWA lives in a city that lies along the western edge of Tokyo where she writes in English but never speaks the language. Her stories have appeared in *The Magazine of Fantasy and Science Fiction*, *Strange Horizons*, *Clarkesworld*, *The Apex World Book of SF*, and elsewhere.

TOBI OGUNDIRAN is a writer of Yoruba extraction. Nominated for the British Science Fiction Association, Shirley Jackson, and Nommo awards, his dark and fantastical tales have appeared in *Lightspeed*, *Podcastle*, *The Dark*, *Beneath Ceaseless Skies*, *FIYAH*, *Lightspeed*, and *Tor.com* among others. In his day job, he works as a medical doctor in Nigeria.

RICHARD PARKS is an ex-pat Southerner now living in central New York state with his wife and one grumpy cat. He is the author of the Yamada Monogatari series and The Laws of Power series. In addition to appearances in several Best of the Year anthologies, he has been a finalist for both the World Fantasy Award and the Mythopoeic Fantasy Award for Adult Literature.

KAREN RUSSELL won the 2012 and the 2018 National Magazine Award for fiction, and her first novel, *Swamplandia!*, was a finalist for the Pulitzer Prize, winner of the New York Public Library Young Lions Award, and one of the *New York Times* Ten Best Books of 2011. She has received a MacArthur Fellowship and a Guggenheim award and is a former fellow of the NYPL Cullman Center and the American Academy in Berlin. Born and raised in Miami, Florida, she now lives in Portland, Oregon with her husband, son, and daughter.

SOFIA SAMATAR is the author of four books, most recently *Monster Portraits,* a genre-bending collaboration with her brother, the artist Del Samatar. Her first novel, *A Stranger in Olondria,* won the 2014 William L. Crawford Award, the British Fantasy Award, and the World Fantasy Award for Best Novel, and was included in *Time Magazine*'s list of the 100 Best Fantasy Books of All Time. She also received the 2014 Astounding Award for Best New Writer. Her second novel, *The Winged Histories,* completes the Olondria duology, and her short story collection, *Tender,* includes the Hugo and Nebula finalist "Selkie Stories Are for Losers" and other tales. Sofia lives in Virginia and teaches African literature, Arabic literature, and speculative fiction at James Madison University. Her memoir *The White Mosque,* an exploration of family, faith, and border crossing, is forthcoming in October 2022.

CATHERYNNE M. VALENTE is the *New York Times* bestselling author of over two dozen works of fiction and poetry, including *Palimpsest,* the Orphan's Tales series, *Deathless, Radiance,* and the crowdfunded phenomenon *The Girl Who Circumnavigated Fairyland in a Ship of Her Own Making* (and the four books that followed it). She is the winner of the Andre Norton, Tiptree, Sturgeon, Eugie Foster Memorial, Mythopoeic, Rhysling, Lambda, Locus, and Hugo awards, as well as the Prix Imaginales. Valente has also been a finalist for the Nebula and World Fantasy awards. She lives on an island off the coast of Maine with a small but growing menagerie of beasts, some of which are human.

Two-time Nebula winner FRAN WILDE writes science fiction and fantasy for adults and kids, with seven books, so far, that embrace worlds unique (*Updraft*, *The Gemworld*) and portal (*Riverland*, *The Ship of Stolen Words*), plus numerous short stories appearing in *Asimov's*, *Tor.com*, *Beneath Ceaseless Skies*, *Shimmer*, *Nature*, *Uncanny*, and multiple Year's Best anthologies. She has been a finalist for the Nebula, Hugo, and World Fantasy awards, and won the 2018 Eugie Foster Memorial Award. Wilde directs the Genre Fiction MFA concentration at Western Colorado University and writes nonfiction for NPR, the *Washington Post*, and the *New York Times*.

MERC FENN WOLFMOOR is a queer non-binary writer who likes dinosaurs, robots, monsters, and cookies. Their fiction has appeared in *Lightspeed*, *Uncanny*, *Fireside*, *Lightspeed*, *Nightmare*, and elsewhere. Merc's story "This Is Not a Wardrobe Door" was a 2016 Nebula Award finalist and translated into Chinese and Portuguese. Their debut short story collection, *So You Want to be a Robot*, was published in 2017.

ISABEL YAP writes fiction and poetry, works in the tech industry, and drinks tea. Born and raised in Manila, she has spent the past decade living and working in the US. She holds a BS in marketing from Santa Clara University and an MBA from Harvard Business School. In 2013 she attended the Clarion Writers Workshop, and since 2016 has volunteered for the Clarion Foundation. Her work has appeared in venues including *Tor.com*, *Lightspeed*, and *Strange Horizons*. Her debut short story collection, *Never Have I Ever*, was published in 2021.

E. LILY YU is the author of *On Fragile Waves*, published in 2021, and the librettist of *Between Stars*, with composer Steven K. Tran, for the Seattle Opera's 2021 Jane Lang Creation Lab. She received the Artist Trust LaSalle Storyteller Award in 2017 and the Astounding Award for Best New Writer in 2012. More than thirty of her stories have appeared in venues from *McSweeney's* to *Tor.com*, as well as twelve best-of-the-year anthologies, and have been finalists for the Hugo, Nebula, Locus, Sturgeon, and World Fantasy awards.

ACKNOWLEDGMENTS

All stories are reprinted with the permission of the authors.

Special thanks to Rene Sears, Jennifer Do, and Jarred Weisfeld of Pyr and Start. Thanks to all the original editors of these stories. Especially those of you who went the extra mile to get me copies and/or helped me track down authors: Scott H. Andrews (*Beneath Ceaseless Skies*), Bradford Morrow (*Conjunctions:76*), Christie Yant and Arley Sorg (*Fantasy*), DeVaun Sanders (*Fiyah*), John Joseph Adams (*Lightspeed*), Sheree Renée Thomas (*The Magazine of Fantasy and Science Fiction*), Julia Rios (*Mermaids Monthly*), all the senior editors at *Strange Horizons*, Swapna Krishna and Jenn Northington (*Sword Stone Table: Old Legends, New Voices*), Ellen Datlow (*Tor.com*), Jonathan Strahan (*Tor.com*), Lynne M. Thomas and Michael Damian Thomas (*Uncanny*), Gavin Grant and Kelly Link (*Lady Churchill's Rosebud Wristlet*).

"The White Road; Or How a Crow Carried Death Over a River" © 2021 Marika Bailey. First Publication: *Fiyah #18*.

"The Red Mother" © 2021 Elizabeth Bear. First Publication: *Tor.com*, 23 June 2021.

"Brickomancer" © 2021 Tobias Buckell. First Publication: *Shoggoths in Traffic and Other Stories* (Fairwood Press).

"Passing Fair and Young" © 2021 Roshani Chokshi. First Publication: *Sword Stone Table: Old Legends, New Voices*, eds. S. Krishna & J. Northington.

"If the Martians Have Magic" © 2021 P. Djèlí Clark. First Publication: *Uncanny* #42.

"The Demon Sage's Daughter" © 2021 Varsha Dinesh. First Publication: *Strange Horizons*, 8 February 2021.

"Quintessence" © 2021 Andrew Dykstal. First Publication: *Beneath Ceaseless Skies* #324.

"Drunkard's Walk" © 2021 James Enge. First Publication: *The Magazine of Fantasy & Science Fiction*, May-June 2021.

"The Piper" © 2021 Karen Joy Fowler. First Publication: *The Magazine of Fantasy & Science Fiction*, January-February 2021.

"A Minnow, or Perhaps a Colossal Squid" © 2021 Carlos Hernandez and C. S. E. Cooney. First publication: *Mermaids Monthly*, April 2021.

"Gisla and the Three Favors" © 2021 Kathleen Jennings. First publication: *Lady Churchill's Rosebud Wristlet* #43.

"Breath of the Dragon King" © 2021 Allison King. First publication: *Fantasy* #72.

"Frost's Boy" © 2021 PH Lee. First publication: *Lightspeed* #128.

"Her Garden the Size of Her Palm" © 2021 Yukimi Ogawa. First publication: *The Magazine of Fantasy & Science Fiction*, July-August 2021.

"The Tale of Jaja and Canti" © 2021 Tobi Ogundiran. First publication: *Lightspeed* #135.

"The Fox's Daughter" © 2021 Richard Parks. First publication: *Beneath Ceaseless Skies* #344.

"The Cloud Lake Unicorn" © 2021 Karen Russell. First publication: *Conjunctions: 76*.

"Three Tales from the Blue Library" © 2021 Sofia Samatar. First publication: *Conjunctions:76*.

ACKNOWLEDGMENTS

"L'Esprit de Escalier" © 2021 Catherynne Valente. First publication: *Tor.com*, 25 August 2021.

"Unseelie Bros, Ltd." © 2021 Fran Wilde. First publication: *Uncanny #40*.

"Gray Skies, Red Wings, Blue Lips, Black Hearts" © 2021 Merc Fenn Wolfmoor. First publication: *Apex #121*.

"A Spell for Foolish Hearts" © 2021 Isabel Yap. First publication: *Never Have I Ever*.

"Small Monsters" © 2021 E. Lily Yu. First publication: *Tor.com*, 20 October 2021.

ABOUT THE EDITOR

Paula Guran is an editor and reviewer. In an earlier life she produced the weekly email newsletter *DarkEcho* (winning two Stokers, an IHG Award, and a World Fantasy Award nomination), edited *Horror Garage* magazine (earning another IHG and a second World Fantasy nomination), and has contributed reviews, interviews, and articles to numerous professional publications. She's been reviewing for *Locus: The Magazine of The Science Fiction & Fantasy Field* on a regular basis for the last six years.

This is the fiftieth anthology Guran has edited. She's also edited scores of novels and some collections. After more than a dozen years of full-time editing, she is now freelancing. She also now has a day job that has nothing to do with books.

Guran has five fabulous grandchildren she would be happy to tell you about.

She lives in Akron, Ohio, with her faithful cat Nala.